THE HIGHEST FRONTIER

BY JOAN SLONCZEWSKI FROM TOM DOHERTY ASSOCIATES

The Children Star
Brain Plague
A Door into Ocean
The Highest Frontier

JOAN SLONCZEWSKI

THE HIGHEST FRONTIER

A TOM DOHERTY ASSOCIATES BOOK NEW YORK

TOR®

THE HIGHEST FRONTIER

Copyright © 2011 by Joan Slonczewski

All rights reserved.

Edited by David G. Hartwell

A Tor Book
Published by Tom Doherty Associates, LLC
175 Fifth Avenue
New York, NY 10010

www.tor-forge.com

Tor® is a registered trademark of Tom Doherty Associates, LLC.

Library of Congress Cataloging-in-Publication Data

Slonczewski, Joan.
    The highest frontier / Joan Slonczewski.—1st ed.
      p. cm.
    "A Tom Doherty Associates book."
    ISBN 978-0-7653-3741-2
    I. Title.
  PS3569.L65H54 2011
  813'.54—dc22

                           2011018959

Printed in the United States of America

P1

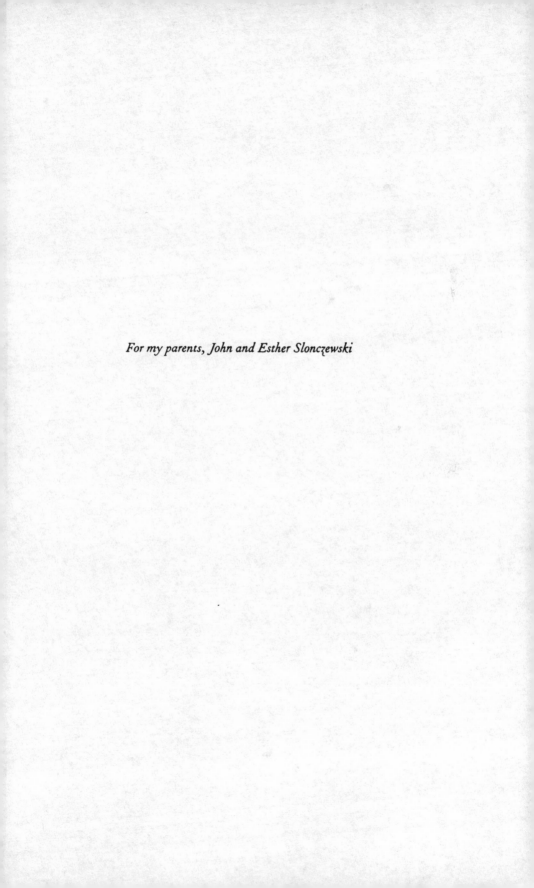

For my parents, John and Esther Slonczewski

THE HIGHEST FRONTIER

1

The space lift rose from the Pacific, climbing the cords of anthrax bacteria. Anthrax would have blackened the blood, before the bacteria were tamed to lift freight into orbit. Now anthrax brought tourists up to spacehab Frontera, ready to hit the off-world slots. And it brought students to Frontera College, safe above their disaster-challenged planet.

Frontera College was tomorrow's destination for Jennifer Ramos Kennedy. The day before lift-off, Jenny was trimming her orchids in the greenhouse atop her home in Somers, New York. Shears hovered at a fading purple vanda as Jenny's brain streamed the blades to snip the stem, just above the node where the orchid would bloom. Outside the window, a laser sliced that afternoon's growth of kudzu. Three-lobed leaves showered down through the vines, revealing the yellow snake-like swathe of an ultraphyte.

"*¡Oye!*" Ultraphytes from off-world had killed three thousand people when they first crept ashore from Great Salt Lake. They'd since spread across the country, to Somers and beyond. The one outside now twined around a kudzu vine, absorbing ultraviolet from the August sun. A squirrel scampered up to the off-world invader, attracted by the eyespot of one of the ultraphyte's thirteen yellow cells. Cells the size of an apple; a microbe you didn't need a microscope to see. But biting one was not a good idea.

Jenny blinked open a window in her toybox, a cube of light that hovered just before her eyes. The toybox windows flashed everything from the president's latest poll to Somers High's last slanball score. The window she blinked was her mother's. It streamed her brain's request into Toynet, then out to her mother, wherever she was just then. The window flashed away precious seconds while the ultraphyte began to slink off through the vines.

At last her mother appeared in the toybox window. "Jenny, *hijita*, did you upload your room? *Un momento*, I've got an investor." Soledad Kennedy, of the Cuban Kennedys, her hair swept up in a fashionable smartcomb. Her Wall Street office overlooked the Hudson seawall.

"Mama, there's an ultra outside. Could I—"

"Call Homeworld Security. Make sure Clive covers you." Clive Rusanov was the ToyNews anchor. Soledad's hovering face shifted, attending her investor. "Yes, *hombre*, anthrax futures are just the thing."

"Homeworld Security? *¡Vaya!*" What a mess, when she should be packing for college. If only she could catch the ultraphyte and keep it in the cellar for experiments, like last time, when she'd found one in the kitchen huddled on a saltshaker. Ultraviolet photosynthesis—a new source of energy. Jenny's science fair project had won her a trip to Washington and a scholarship that she'd donated to the runner-up. But since then, security had tightened in the War on Ultra. Table salt was now a controlled substance. Frontera College would never let her keep a cyanide-emitting invader up there in the spacehab.

When she looked again out the window, the ultra was gone. It couldn't have crept far, but she no longer saw it in the mass of leaves below. If only Jordi were here—Jordi Ramos Kennedy, her twin brother cultured from their grandfather, President Joseph Ramos. The storied "President Joe" who'd launched the drive for Jupiter. Jordi would have been out the window by now, scaling the vines after the ultra. But of course Jordi would never be here again.

Below the rooftop greenhouse, the undulating sea of kudzu bathed all of Somers, from her home on the hill down to the Elephant Hotel and for miles around, all the way to the Hudson. In her toybox, three windows opened, bright cubes of light calling toypoint receivers outside the house. Each window combed the kudzu for the vanished creature.

Another blink, and there was her father, from the second-floor toyroom where he ran the North American branch of Toynet. George Ramos, the president's son, with his usual brush-cut hair and his white shirt with two neckties: red dots on blue, and red squares.

"Dad? Can you help me find the ultraphyte?"

The letters scrolled: "**How long?**" Her father could talk but preferred text. Hard to believe he'd grown up playing coin tricks beneath his dad's desk in the Oval Office.

"**Four point three minutes.**" Her brainstream converted to text. Everyone could stream some text, but children who started young trained their brains to stream fast. Jenny had gotten an early start, by her father's side.

"**How fast?**" texted George.

"**It creeps a meter in about five seconds, then turns.**"

"**Assuming random walk, most probable distance: ten point two meters.**"

"Thanks, Dad." She imagined the entire North American Toynet slowed by a nanosecond while George Ramos looked away.

"Jenny, why must you leave home?" Blue text meant her father was sad. "You could attend MIT or Oxford right here."

"Dad . . ."

"We could add on to the house, just like Iroquoia." The Iroquois had been his passion since childhood, when he'd created the Iroquoia toyworld. The toyworld was so authentic, upstate Mohawks had adopted him as *Dahdio-gwat-hah*, Spreader of Data. "The Haudenosaunee would build a longhouse for twenty families. They would extend it with fresh-cut saplings, covered with elm bark. . . ."

Jenny had seen an elm tree once in the Botanical Garden, a crown of serrated teardrop leaves; it looked naked without kudzu. She scanned three toybox windows out to a ten-meter radius around the original site. As her three views wove in amid the kudzu, one caught a glint of yellow. All three windows zoomed down on the creature, so close she could make out the eyespots on its apple-sized cells.

A trained first responder, Jenny blinked her EMS button, the familiar snake wrapped around a staff. "Ultra sighted." Her toybox filled with blinking windows.

Sprinting downstairs two at a time, she blinked ahead at the door to open, then burst outside. The heat smothered her, and the sun sparkled up from her nose ring. She brushed her long dark hair out of her eyes, already damp from sweat. Cicadas hummed above the fashionably kudzu-graced mansion, red brick like the Somers Elephant Hotel. Overhead whined a Manhattan commuter, less frequent than they were before the methane quake. A drone hovered watchfully above the Ramos Kennedy home, and a pair of white-faced DIRGs moved out from the back. Direct Intervention Robotic Guardians, the DIRGs had always looked out for her and Jordi, now for her alone. Once a DIRG had caught a paparazzo none too gently and cracked his rib. Soledad had arranged a quiet settlement, and the paps backed off.

"Back indoors," warned the DIRG. "Indoors till all clear."

On the ground, Jenny spotted the fallen squirrel. It must have succumbed to the ultra's puff of cyanide. The latest in a long stream of victims, ever since Ultra Day, when the seed had sprouted in Great Salt Lake and the first ultras came ashore, their cyanide asphyxiating people and animals. Jenny checked the cross at her neck for her tube of anticyanide. The cross slipped through the sweat on her palms. She began to climb the fuzzy leaves, wincing as her arm was sore from a twist during slanball practice. A Cuban tree frog leapt out; if the ultra hadn't got the squirrel, the frog probably would have. And a python would get the frog. That was the Somers food chain.

Her windows again converged on the ultra's new position. The yellow swathe had narrowed and stretched, now almost two meters. She blinked to broadcast the coordinates.

"Back indoors." From behind, a firm robotic hand gripped her shoulder.

"¡Vaya! Get off me!"

The DIRG lifted her by the chest like a two-year-old and set her down at the door. Safe on her feet, Jenny blinked her disabler, and the DIRG froze. Qué lata, these DIRGs. There would be no more DIRGs at Frontera—a huge battle with her mother, but for once Jenny prevailed. After all, what was the spacehab if not one giant security drone suspended in space, pristine, free of so much as a mosquito.

From the east sailed six Homeworld Security drones. The drones hummed in the distance, then suddenly grew loud. Shafts of fire bore down upon the hapless ultra, right where Jenny had just climbed. Flames erupted, and the air turned acrid. Kudzu leaves flew in all directions as the flames spread. A good thing the home was brick. Jenny's view through her toybox windows got scrambled, enough to make her sick. But one window just caught a small blob of ultraphyte, five cells worth, that had pinched off and moved out on its own, much faster than the original colony; a typical stress response. The drones did not seem to notice, all chasing the larger portion.

While the other DIRG hosed down the burning tree, Jenny debated with herself whether to inform Homeworld about the escaped ultra. She shrugged. If six Homeworld Security drones couldn't spot a five-celled ultra . . . The last time, she'd trapped it in a tank in the cellar. The captive ultra had huddled in the cellar, while her respirometer measured the gases it breathed. When the UV came on, the ultra made oxygen, just like a plant.

The ToyNews window opened. There stood Clive Rusanov. "Jenny Ramos Kennedy, like other heroic members of her family, strikes another blow for Earth against the alien cyanide-breathing invader."

"Stress response," corrected Jenny. Ultraphytes didn't breathe cyanide; they released it briefly under stress, like a clover leaf. "Nunca lo corrijas," never correct him, her mother always warned; "it makes you sound too smart."

The ToyNews anchor patted down his slick dark hair, style twenty-three, first one side, then the other. He faced her level, his height and those of his interviewees all set the same; otherwise, she would have looked down at him from her presidential six feet two. "Always saving lives." As a first responder, on other calls she'd treated shock and diagnosed a fractured tibia. "Rescuing the planet. Your last day on Earth."

Jenny smiled, and her eyes reflexively closed. *"Ojos abiertos,"* she recalled; her eyes flew open. "Not my last, I hope." An inane start. She found her press prompt, the words already scrolling across her toybox: *It's an honor to do my small part . . .* " 'It's an honor to do my small part . . . for the global War on Ultra.' "

"ToyNews—From our box to yours." They were going live. The anchor put his hands at his sides and leveled his chin. "Clive Rusanov, here in Somers, New York, with an exclusive report from presidential granddaughter Jenny Ramos Kennedy." And great-granddaughter of another, Jenny added to herself.

Clive hovered in the toybox, his view spliced next to hers, as if he were there on the spot with her instead of across the country in his L.A. studio. Jenny's tall elfin form was the very image of her culture source, her mother's grandmother, President Rosa Schwarz. In all, three presidents and four senators in her family tree. Only her eyes were her own, her own eyes dark and furtive as an ancient Arawak in the caverns of Cuba, her mother's home state. At Jenny's right ToyNews spliced a view of the downtown Somers elephant, Old Bet, atop her wrought-iron pedestal: the town's famous statue of the first circus elephant in America. The little elephant perched high above, like a Manhattanite trying to escape the flood.

"Ms. Ramos, in the spirit of her presidential clone source, does her part to rid the Earth of our planet's most toxic invader." Actually, President Schwarz had banned carbon emissions and built the first spacehab. "Ms. Ramos, do you believe we've turned the corner in the War on Ultra?"

The press prompt scrolled: *As you know, Clive, my family . . .*

"As you know . . ." Whispering would not do. Her stomach knotted, but she tried again. "As you know, Clive . . . my family has a long tradition of leadership protecting Earth's precious global environment."

The pollmeter, collecting brainstream from all the millions of listeners, rose a few tenths of a unit. People wanted to help the environment.

"And so . . . I will do any small part I can to help, like anyone in Somers would do." Her eyes lost track of the prompt, and her long lashes fluttered. Jenny was no Rosa; a gene missed in the embryo made her freeze in public. "Public mutism," on chromosome 18. The settlement had doubled her trust fund.

Clive's immaculately combed head nodded knowingly. "Your last day on Earth, before heading up to college at the Firmament." "Firmament" was the Centrist word for the sphere of the biblical heavens that centered on Earth. Centrists now held the Senate and the White House.

"College in orbit," Jenny corrected. Of course Clive knew better, but he always gave equal time. "In orbit around Earth, third from Sol, Orion Arm, Milky Way."

The pollmeter dipped precipitously. Clive smiled with a knowing nod. "The brightest star of two presidential clans." Actually, three. "And here for comment is New York assemblyman Ned Tran."

There stood Jenny's suited neighbor, his height, like Clive's, stretched to equal hers. Ned Tran had led the fight to make public schools teach that Earth went around the Sun. "Thanks, Jenny," the assemblyman was saying, "for your contribution to Somers ultraphyte eradication." Jenny had run Tran's Unity campaign against the Centrists, had tied hundreds of purple balloons, had sent thousands of Toynet thank-yous. He'd won by four votes.

"Those ultras," Tran went on, "destroyed our ozone and poisoned half our country. . . ." Actually, the seed from outer space had taken advantage of Earth's own ozone loss to sprout on this planet and drink the UV, but *nunca lo corrijas*. "But thanks to the efforts of citizens like you, Jenny, this little Somers corner of the Milky Way is ninety percent ultra-free. Another victory in the War on Ultra. Another great reason to reside in Somers, convenient to the Big Apple yet a tidy distance from the next methane quake." And, he might have added, still far from the parched Death Belt that stretched from Nevada to Tennessee.

The assemblyman faded out, presumably drawing less stream from the pollmeter than the Ramos Kennedy star. "Jenny," observed Clive, "your family has made more than its share of sacrifices for the public good." Old Bet now appeared, spliced next to the crowned head of La Liberté, whose feet had emerged just last spring thanks to new pumps at the seawall. Open water— the sight always hit Jenny in the gut. "Your late brother saved how many lives when the seawall broke? How does it feel, going off to college without him?"

Jordi Ramos Kennedy, the cultured likeness of his presidential grand-father, Joe Ramos, beneath whose desk George had played. His speeches already drawing crowds, Jordi was addressing a Unity rally in Battery Park when the methane quake hit. Ocean warming and deep-sea mining had de-stabilized the vast methane ice deposits on the sea floor. The crowd had ten minutes to empty the park and get upstairs before the waves breached the seawall and filled Manhattan like a bowl. Jordi had slipped the DIRGs and run along the beach, calling out, until he was swept out to sea.

Her eyes found the prompt again. Emphasize the consonants, her mother always said. Jenny expelled each word. "I . . . am . . . proud to remember, Clive, that Jordi left his estate to the Manhattan restoration fund."

The pollmeter rose cheerfully. Everyone liked a hero. Jordi, who'd lost his life saving others. And Jenny, the twin who lived.

Abruptly she pulled the diad off her forehead. Lights vanished and silence fell, while the diad lay buried in her clenched fist, its brainstream cut off. No more polls, EMS calls, or notes from her ten thousand playmates. Only the August sun shone, and cicadas keened in the kudzu jungle. Enough of Clive; he'd got what he needed, and he'd edit it to make the family look good. Jenny sprinted back into the house, dodging stray kudzu vines.

She passed the kitchen, where the salt was now kept in a locked safe; one shaker held enough of the limiting nutrient to grow a thirteen-cell ultra to twenty-nine. Then she mounted the stairs, step by step, each step a singular event in the silent world. She looked once more around the Lincoln Bedroom furniture she'd uploaded to college: her portrait of Rosa above the desk, her favorite cups and balls trick, her science fair prizes, and Jordi's slanball trophies. In the spacehab, all her things would print out in amyloid, a bacterial protein that self-assembled any form. Amyloid desk, amyloid trophies, amyloid snacks for her fridge.

Live organisms would not yet print out; nothing more complex than a flu virus. But three of her orchids would join her on the space lift, up the anthrax to Frontera: her prize-winning Blood Star, the sweet-smelling vanilla, and the giant vanda with its plate-sized purple blooms. Frontera, the first college on the high frontier, with its own Olympic slanball court in micrograv. Frontera College might outlast life on Earth, with Earth's methane quakes, death belts, and invading ultraphytes.

2

Early Sunday morning, Jenny rose in the lift climbing the anthrax bacteria from Earth to orbit. The bacteria with their nanotube cell walls had first been engineered at Fort Dietrich to test defenses against weapons-grade anthrax. Now the anthrax grew kilometers long out in space. Self-healing cables were just the thing to hoist freight up through Kessler debris, for growing cells soon replaced those severed. Jenny's mother had managed the Anthradyne IPO, the first anthrax farm in outer space.

From the deck, Jenny stared down through the star-studded dark. Below lay the Pacific like a scoop of blueberry ice cream, the Galapagos sticking out. To the east, on the Americas, black solarplate marked the growing death belts of the Southwest and the Amazon. Where nothing could grow, build solarplate to power cities and spacehabs. But the solarplate absorbed light that would have been reflected, emitting heat, and accelerating the Death Belt's creep.

Above, around the cords of anthrax, dots of light exploded as Homeworld Security lased bits of Kessler rubble, fragments of old spacecraft that had multiplied over the past century. Out of the dark grew a bright solid object, a cylinder with rounded ends like a medicine capsule: the spacehab Frontera. The capsule gleamed purple, its outer layer full of microbes that turned sunlight into power. A bright flash where something hit and vaporized. At the capsule's midline gleamed an eagle feather, like the feather on her tax window. Every toybox was full of tax windows; some people played half their paycheck, the legal limit. But the more adventurous played off-world, where anything goes. Frontera's feather marked the Shawnee casino that had financed the spacehab for the state of Ohio. Frontera was Ohio's high frontier.

Jenny clutched her pot of Blood Star, *Cattleya stellarubra*, each flower a crimson trumpet with five white petals. She'd named it for Cuba's state flag. The petals pressed against the isolation bag, required till the plant passed quarantine. After that, the Life professor had promised, Jenny could keep the plants in her room. Frowning, Jenny held the bag up for a closer look. The bag brushed her face, swollen by micrograv, while her hair floated up around her ears. She chewed her lip pensively, a habit she had planned to quit back in Somers High. But now high school was thirty thousand klicks below, and college lay straight ahead, within that microbial capsule.

"Docking in twenty minutes." The diad was snug on her forehead, feeding her brainstream. "Please return to your seat."

Jenny turned her head, and her hair swung around her face. She pressed the orchid to her chest, where the smartgrip held it fast. One handgrip to the next, she floated back down the rabbit hole, the Frontera capsule floating ahead in her toybox. Along either side sat the passengers: new students playing a Phaistos disk, while their anxious parents finished their breakfast; colonial farmers a head shorter than she, their arms strapped with power bands to harvest their body motion; and taxplayers in head feathers glowing red, green, and blue, ready to hit the slots at the Mound. You could tell who was new to micrograv, those who flailed their limbs and spun around helplessly, then reached for their sick bags. Jenny had years of practice from slanball. Slanball in micrograv; the top high schools and colleges sent teams to practice in spacehabs, like the New York–based Towers. Only Frontera College had its own slanball court, with a spectacular view, a full kilometer "down" all around.

"ToyNews—From our box to yours." Her toybox opened a window at upper right. ToyNews was set to her profile: The national and state races, the Antarctic war, ultraphytes, orchids, and any mention of the so-called "firmament." No ads, just the unseen sensors that tapped your response.

The anchor appeared with his broad smile and hairstyle sixteen: emerging tragedy. This time, Jenny was just a listener. "Breaking news: A Formula One crew on their way to the Lunar Circuit has crashed." A sickening view, as the ship exploded into blackness.

"Kessler debris," explained a spokesman with a French accent. "A piece of an old transport shuttle." Homeworld Security swept the skies for such fragments, like the chunk that had aborted the Jupiter launch. Even so, chunks fell to Earth daily.

Clive nodded. "According to NASA, the doomed ship crashed into the Firmament."

"Tonterías." Firmament, indeed. Jenny brainstreamed her protest, knowing her slanball training focused ten times the intensity of the average listener. She'd add a good dose to the pollmeter. Then she squeezed her eyes shut until the box vanished. Her hand let go of the rails and her body hung by itself.

"Are you okay, Jenny?" her mental aide whispered in her head.

Jenny's eyes flew open. "Okay."

A disembodied face loomed before her, the image of Marilyn Monroe. The mental had only virtual existence on Toynet, a team of physicians to keep the Ramos Kennedy girl sane. The Monroe's pink lips pouted. "Are you sure, Jenny?"

"*Seguro.*"

The Monroe-faced mental must have detected her plunging neurotransmitters. The last thing she needed was for it to alert her mother and make a scene. She slapped an R-patch behind her neck to send stabilizers into her brain. "Just answering my playmates." A couple thousand unanswered notes had accumulated. "**¡*Hola*, Jenny! How's outer space?**" Tusker-12, her best friend from Somers High; Jenny blinked back a quick "**Earth in space looks *chulo*.**" Around her head, all the passengers' feet hung upward from below, and the ceiling lights shone up beneath her rotating feet. A trail of water led to some newbie's open drink.

"*Chulo,*" echoed her friend from Somers High. "**Wherever you go, you'll always be a Tusker.**" The Tuskers, their old slanball team.

"Are you quite sure?" The mental always thought she'd start cutting herself again.

"I'm fine." As fine as she could be, going to college without Jordi. "Go away." To right herself, Jenny stretched her legs and arms till her hand caught a grip. She snapped herself around, then glided forward past the heads of floating hair, back toward her own seat. A glowing scarlet feather floated, until the taxplayer's brainstream retrieved it. The Shawnee Mound Casino and Worship Center still financed the spacehab and a good part of the college, as well as the Ohio Statehouse and the IRS. President Ramos had founded the taxplayer system.

At last she saw coming up the two heads she knew best: her mother's smartcomb, and her father's brush cut. Holding hands; it was cute to have parents who still did that. Above her parents' seats were tucked the other two bagged orchids, filling the bulk of her ten-kilo allowance. Jenny eased herself past her father into her own seat, affectionately patting down his two floating ties, red dots and red squares.

Her mother nodded to an unseen client. "*Sí,*" Soledad whispered to her toybox. "I know you could use an angel right now." She brushed Jenny's hair and inserted a smartcomb. "But an angel expects forty percent return with a three-year exit. And you tell me your Death Belt reclamation scheme will break even in forty years?" Soledad shook her head. "You don't get it: Space is the only place left to build. Almost there," she told Jenny. "Imagine. Don't chew your lip, *hijita*. *No te preocupes*—everything will be fine."

"Yes, Mama, everything will be fine." Jenny gripped the orchid pot in her lap until her knuckles ached.

"Even the greenhouse."

"I'm not worried, Mama." Jenny turned her orchid around, making sure it was not crushed in the bag. She hoped the gas exchange was working. "You're sure about the greenhouse?" The dean of students had promised.

"With sprinklers and barometric control. Right above your room." Soledad Kennedy always made sure. "And your new *compañera de casa* is a person of quality."

"*Sí*, Mama, my housemate is fine." Her parents would have paid for a single unit, with her own kitchen and private pool. Needing a housemate was so uncool, like your parents had produced children at random instead of culturing twins. But the mental said she needed a companion. *Qué lata* having a mental in your toybox. Anyway, Jenny's *compañera* looked sweet; she'd posted her violin recital and her Hun School slanball team.

"Don't spend all your time in the laboratory." Her mother patted her knee. "Get out to know people—you represent our family." Two presidential families, and Jenny could barely talk. Her mother raised a finger. "Be gracious, remember, even to the uncultured."

"*Sí, claro*." At Somers High she knew kids born of random sperm and egg. No nose ring, crooked teeth, they'd be blind by age thirty. No twins, the smart family choice for a mother on the go.

"Church every Sunday—*no te olvides*." Today, of course, they'd attended service via Toynet.

"I'll see Father Clare." The college chaplain, Clarence Flynn, was an old family friend, someone she could speak to without freezing up.

"And community service."

"I'll join EMS." First responder; the one kind of publicity she was good at.

"And visit the Mound every quarter."

Jenny sighed. President Ramos had made the tax system voluntary, but her mother insisted on her playing the "recommended" stake. A Ramos had to play in public, not at the toybox feather like most people. "If I could just blink a fee."

"You need to be seen, *hijita*. You know what they'll say—'the Ramos Kennedys don't play taxes.'" She tugged Jenny's blouse straight. "Be nice to your aunts when they call." California governor Meg Akeda and her twin Elsa were actually Soledad's cousins, all granddaughters of President Schwarz. But Meg and El were Centrists; they'd gone gold, Firmament and all. Childless, they treated Jenny like their own niece. "And remember, green jello for Utah." Florida oranges, Wisconsin cheddar, Cuban *plátanos*, always something for a swing state. "At the debate, *recuerdas?*"

The First Lady debate was that evening. Soledad had arranged it through ToyDebate, of which she was the Unity cochair. The first and most important, the First Lady debate drew excitement during the post-primary lull. The least predictable, it could well seal the fate of the campaign. And this election could seal the fate of Earth: Would Earth's final melt be curbed, or not?

"At the break, Clive will do your first-day-at-college. Remember— Anna needs our help." Anna Carrillo, the governor of Utah, was the Unity candidate for president. Soledad's ambivalent tone signaled that Carrillo's rise to power had come out of nowhere, no family pedigree, but there she was, the Unity choice. It was hard enough holding Unity's old two wings together. And Unity agreed on this: Halt solar on Earth, and build in space.

"*Sí, Mama*, I'll remember." Jenny had her toybox ready, wherever she found herself that evening at seven.

"**Look, Jenny.**" Across her toybox sailed red letters from her father, by her side. Red meant something interesting. "**11A, 11B.**"

Jenny twisted her head back just far enough to glimpse row eleven. "**Rick Tsien**" and "**Reese Tsien**" flashed the windows in her toybox. Cute *chico* and *chica*, they were cultured "Paul Newman," the trademark nose and dimpled chin. Half the twins Jenny's year were Newman, with variations; these two had black hair and green eyes. The *chico* wore double-X earrings and a beaded headband, while the *chica* had a heart-shaped diad. Both wore gene-health nose rings. Jenny blinked their windows, and their images leapt out in jerseys, scoring at slanball. New students together, like she and Jordi would have been. Her mouth twitched with the ghost of a smile. "**Yes, Dad, twins.**" She patted her father's knee.

"**Illyrian twins.**" Unlike Jordi and Jenny, these twins looked alike. The pair was identical, except for a male gene on one X; the economical way to culture twins. George loved anything near-identical. His wrist wore two watches, Earth time and Lunar. His fingers flexed together as if playing cat's cradle, actually still managing Toynet thirty thousand kilometers away.

"**Hi there, Jenny.**" Toytext from Rick Tsien, the cute slanball twin in eleven-A. "**Can I help you set up your room?**"

His sister Reese turned with a Newman smile. "**Jenny, how** *chulo*—**our mom knows your aunt, the governor.**" The California governor was Jenny's Aunt Meg, with her infamous twin Aunt El. Strangers always found some connection. "**The Begonia Garden Club—did you get** *your* **invite?**" Frontera's social clubs were banned from rushing before the start of class, but the Begonia Club had been sending Jenny flowers for the past month.

Jenny's eyes fluttered shut, then opened. "**I raise orchids. Do you like chemistry?**" The line effectively screened her ten thousand would-be playmates.

In her toybox the purple capsule loomed large, and a long cone of shuttle lines stretched to the lift. The capsule looked oddly out of place, like Old Bet atop her pedestal. A new window opened, the Frontera College crest in purple and gold: the Ohio River crossed by a colonial ax, with the ancient Greek motto *Sophias philai paromen*, "Friends of wisdom, we are here." Above the motto, a little boy rode a rocking horse. The boy would be Gil Wickett, whose Toynet fortune had founded the college.

The crest dissolved to the motherly smiling face of the dean of students, Nora Kwon. "Jenny," said Dean Kwon, "we have important news for you." Kwon had a take-charge voice, like the Somers High slanball coach. But what news could be too important to await her arrival? "You have a new housemate."

A new *compañera*? Whatever became of the Hun School *chica*? She must have got off the wait list to Williams.

"I'm delighted to introduce your housemate, Mary Dyer, of Long Beach. . . ." Long Beach, where Rosa Schwarz had grown up watching the ocean's liquid jaws chewing ever higher up the shore until it swallowed half of downtown L.A.

In the box appeared Mary Dyer, a *chica* of average height and medium brown hair. A Newman chin, otherwise nothing special. But the ring in Mary's left nostril meant her genes were cultured. Her eyes and nose fit just right, though her broad jaw gave her a boyish look. Her tan looked as if she'd spent time at the beach, but not too much. Her face shone with skinglow, stylish but not ostentatious, and she held a water bottle. Not too plump and not too thin, wearing a tie-dyed shift, not too long and not too short.

Soledad leaned over, and Jenny blinked to share her toybox. "Nora," her mother asked, "which school is Mary from? What family?"

"Her home slid down Ocean View five years ago. Her family didn't make it out." The dean added in a whisper, "They left her a fortune in pearls."

"Ah, I see."

"Mary was a late applicant," Dean Kwon added. "Jenny, FERPA rules mandate privacy, but Mary asks me to share with you two things: That she is a highly creative and imaginative young lady; and that she has a mild condition in the autism spectrum."

"Sure, Dean Kwon. I understand." An Aspie, Mary was socially challenged, like Jenny's father.

Soledad nodded knowingly. "Mary must have exceptional talents."

The dean's eyes grinned. "Soli, I knew you'd understand. Jenny, we're honored to have you at Frontera; let us know of anything we can do. Your mother knows you're in the best hands." Soledad served on Frontera's Board of Trustees. The president was her friend from college.

"**Be sure to take your HIV.**" More text from her father, blue because he was going to miss her.

"**Yes, Dad, I will.**" HIV was "human improvement vector," the original AIDS virus tamed to guard her health. Back in Somers, HIV made her genes fight cancer and cataracts. At Frontera, it would tune her cochlea for the space-hab rotation.

"**And return to Iroquoia.**" His beloved toyworld, which he'd built in childhood and run ever since.

Jenny patted his arm. "**Of course, Dad, we'll meet in the longhouse.**" Family and coworkers often played along with him.

A sudden tug as the anthrax engaged. War whoops broke out from the feathered taxplayers. The spacehab's centrifugal "gravity" seeped in like the descent of a Ferris wheel. Students and taxplayers unsteadily extracted themselves from their seats; those who hadn't yet used their sickness bag now did, souring the air. Jenny held Blood Star tight and whispered the Lord's Prayer. Her parents reached for the remaining orchids. Jenny looked ahead for Jordi, who always led the way.

She froze; it was months since she'd done that. Perhaps she needed the mental after all.

3

The terminal opened into a windowless gray hall. The air smelled stuffy as if underground. It was buried within the hull of the spacehab, enclosed by the outer layer of sun-soaking purple microbes that made amyloid and hydrogen fuel. "Above," from the gravitational viewpoint, lay the interior where people farmed, studied, and played their taxes. A sign, QUARANTINE, was flanked by two DIRGs in coonskin caps. "Daniel Boone" frontier DIRGs. *Qué lata*; Frontera was supposed to be free of DIRGs. Hopefully after quarantine that would be the last of them. Ahead, someone's father tripped and fell, and his ten-kilo box split open strewing R-patches, a shaving kit, and a toydog that turned on and sniffed around expectantly. Jenny took a deep breath and lifted one foot, then the other, as she always did arriving at Towers for slanball; the local "grav" was never quite Earth standard.

The passengers spread out among three lines. The first line was mostly colonists a head shorter than she, their arms and legs ringed by power bands to glean energy from taking a step or raising an arm. Colonists headed for Mount Gilead; their line faced the poster of a cross, proclaiming TO THE FIRMAMENT—AND BEYOND. In the next line over, taxplayers were already blinking bets ahead to the Mound. Their poster showed Lady Godiva riding nude to save the poor folk their taxes.

Jenny joined students and parents in the third line, FRONTERA COLLEGE PREORIENTATION. A faded poster proclaimed the college's tenth anniversary campaign. Students didn't wear power bands; their power came from the college, unrationed. In her toybox a form opened, ten pages of waivers in fine print, the undersigned to acknowledge the experimental nature of the space habitat; that space debris puncture, solar flare blackouts, fire and asphyxiation, substratum overflow, food and water shortages, cosmic ray exposure, animal attacks, and infections of Ebola, hepatitis Q, and brucellosis were all potential mishaps of college life on the high frontier.

"Quarantine." The flat voice emanated from a coon-capped DIRG. The DIRG pointed to her orchids. A cart wheeled over. Jenny bit her lip as the three bagged plants disappeared inside.

The DIRG pointed right to the next line. "Bodyscan."

As Jenny moved on with her parents for their bodyscans, Dean Kwon reappeared in her toybox. "How's it going, Jenny? I know preorientation is *un lío,* but you'll get through."

Soledad nodded. "No problem." The dean must have connected her too.

Jenny caught her breath. "They took my orchids."

Dean Kwon nodded. "Don't you worry, Jenny, Professor Abaynesh will get them back to you next week."

Abaynesh was the botanist who had promised Jenny a greenhouse and a spot in her lab. But a week? Jenny felt lost without her orchids. She blinked at her toybox to call the professor, but got no response.

"This is how we keep the hab clean," explained the dean. "No kudzu, no dengue fever, no mosquitoes."

Mosquitoes she could do without, Jenny agreed, though she'd miss the kudzu back home.

"ToyNews Ohio." In her toybox a new window had appeared, upper right from the dean's. Ohio news, for Frontera's legal home state. "President Bud Guzmán visits Columbus, and tells members of a returning reserve unit, 'You're doing a heck of a job defending Antarctica.' Cincinnati relocates another twenty thousand families to the northeast, well outside the Death Belt. Don't miss Canton's Olde Tyme Python Festival and church supper, all the python you can eat."

Dean Kwon appeared in her window. "Read the FERPA rules and discuss with your parents." FERPA, the Family Education Rights and Privacy Act, forbade a college to disclose student information to anyone other than the student—even grades to a parent—unless the student blinked permission. Kwon gave a cheerful wave. "I'll see you up here soon, with all the frogs at Wickett Hall."

"Hop, Jenny, hop." Her father grinned slightly.

Jenny smiled indulgently at her dad's joke, and wondered why new students were "frogs."

"Those monster frogs in our trees," recalled her mother, "they eat squirrels. We had them too in Havana."

A long stairway "rose" inward through the substratum, toward the spacehab interior. A bright hole opened, pale green. A fresh breeze lifted Jenny's hair, with a scent of pines. At last she emerged, blinking in the light. Pine trees appeared at regular intervals, individual spikes with space in between; naked without their blanket of kudzu. The naked pines curved up, around, and above, like pegs on the inside of a giant carpet roll. Songbirds warbled, just like a toyworld. Jenny looked for a cage, but the birds just perched out there in the tree, ready to fly away. Their wings flashed yellow, red, and black, like buttons in her toybox.

"Look, Mama! What a colorful bird."

Soledad nodded. "*Recuerdas*, George, when there were birds?" She caught her husband's arm. "When Jenny was little she would point to them in the tree. Her first word, 'bird.'"

Jenny blinked her taxonomy button. "*Carduelis tristis*, **goldfinch**," returned the Toynet database. In the neighboring tree sang a different bird, bright red as a light on a slot machine. "*Cardinalis cardinalis*, **Northern Cardinal**." One flew overhead; she flinched, thinking it might poop on her.

A closer look down the "carpet roll," along Buckeye Trail, revealed geometric shapes of farm tracts, fading out two kilometers "south" to end at a ring of blue. The blue ring was the Ohio River, an endless loop of water that ultimately sank "down" into the shell to feed the light-eating microbes. The loop surrounded a "solar," a disk that shone too bright to watch. The light cast long Scandinavian shadows. But shadows also went the other way, cast by another solar "north." Twin shadows.

Into the Ohio River, upside down, flowed the Scioto Creek, its water aflame with light reflected from the solar. Craning her neck, Jenny traced the creek upstream, back "north" overhead. Impossible, her mind said—that water had to rain "down." But the stream flowed on amongst the green and brown arcs of upside-down farm and forest. A cluster of little tiles and streets; that would be the village of Mount Gilead, population 986, named for Ohio's old colonial town. Colonists tilled their pristine farmlands, free of mosquitoes and ultraphytes.

Farther north, near the end of the capsule, rose the Mound. The Mound was a raised green hill imitating an ancient burial mound, actually the Shawnee Mound Casino and Worship Center, with the taxplayers inside and the powwow ground on top. Beyond the Mound, a racetrack ringed the cap. At the north end, where the creek waters welled up, shone the north solar. Around the solar, jagged hills lifted angular chocolate slopes, pointing inward like teeth into a mouth.

"Frogs over here." Dean Kwon stood at the entrance to Wickett Hall, named for Frontera's founder, Toynet executive Guillermo Wickett. Amyloid marble gleamed white, with four classic columns and a clock tower. A keystone topped every window, each showing one of Gil Wickett's favorite toys.

A rocking horse rocked back and forth, the animated amyloid flexing in and out around the sculpted shape. A box popped open and the "jack" sprang out. A mallet pounded pegs into a board, then the board flipped over. A shovel dug into a sand pile, then poured it into a pail. A wagon filled with alphabet blocks, then spilled them. Above them all, the cornice puckered out forming an antique toy locomotive with its cowcatcher and smokestack. Train cars followed all along the cornice till the caboose disappeared.

"Woo-woo!" cried someone's younger brother, jumping up and down. Jenny smiled, recalling her own favorite toy, the cups and balls trick.

Past Wickett Hall strolled nose-ringed students with stylish little "moon-hole" cutouts in the cheeks of their pants, and shoelaces trailing behind their feet. Amyloid toydogs wagged their tails, and anxious parents strained their glowing faces, as students met their upperclass advisors in purple Frontera T-shirts.

A high-pitched shriek, like a donkey. Startled, Jenny turned, and looked down. A tiny elephant, about waist high, extended its trunk to beg.

"¡Oye!" The mini elephant was no bigger than Old Bet. Island evolution would shrink any animals that were larger than a rabbit, so Frontera's habitat engineer stocked miniatures. The wrinkled little trunk and wide ear flaps looked classic, though the tail was bushy like a donkey's. The little gray creature panted and waved its tusks, then two companions trotted over. "*Elephas minimus*, mini-elephant." One extended a trunk to brush Jenny's leg.

Soledad frowned. "*Animales,*" she whispered meaningfully. "Avoid them. *¿Entiendes?*"

Jenny rolled her eyes. "*Sí, Mama.*"

"Don't feed the elephants!" called Dean Kwon. "In fact, don't touch them for *any* reason. Those little tusks can be deadly." Kwon stared hard, as if there were a lot more left unsaid. "No organic pets, no unapproved produce, and *no* projectiles. All frogs turn in your FERPA forms and take your blood test, over here at the alphabet-blocks door."

Easing her cramped neck, Jenny got in line for the blood sampler to stamp her arm. Besides mosquitoes and ultraphytes, Frontera kept its habitat free of most diseases. Years had passed since her dengue fever, and now the HIV cleaned her blood, but still her pulse raced. What if she carried some hidden plague?

"Remember," warned Dean Kwon, "you'll retake the test every time you return to campus."

Soledad whispered in her ear, "Don't count on it. The *chicos* all carry hepa Q."

"Mama, not now."

"And *los animales* carry—"

"And your Toynet account," Dean Kwon added. "Remember to set the filter against flu and Ebola." Infectious viruses could print out with uploaded baggage.

"Twenty-four, twenty-five, twenty-six." George Ramos anxiously counted aloud the students trudging down Buckeye Trail.

Jenny put her arm through her father's elbow. "How fast do you suppose the hab rotates?"

George looked up. **"Toss your ball."**

Jenny took out her slanball. Precisely nine centimeters, crossed with red lines, the slanball was a regulation brainstream sensor. In the naked oak above her head, a cardinal sang "What-cheer, what-cheer." Taking a breath, she launched the ball straight "up." The ball curved, then shot out east, grazing the top of the oak. Jenny's scalp twitched. "That's the direction we're rotating from. No, I mean toward."

"One hundred meters per second," her father estimated. **"Rotation speed at one g."**

Jenny focused on the ball to draw it back. The ball came brushing through the leaves, then fell to the ground as the local grav overcame her brainstream. She wondered, "Where's the slanball cage?"

"Overhead." An upperclass *chico* stood by rather stiffly, with a very serious air. His window in Jenny's toybox said, **"Rafael Marcaydo Acuña, from Mexico City. Politics major. Owl Advisor."** Rafael's nose ring confirmed his superior genetic health, and his double-X earring meant restored-X chromosome. His purple T-shirt showed the golden boy on the rocking horse, crossed by the colonial ax, and the Greek words *Sophias philai paromen*. "Friends of wisdom"; would she find them, Jenny wondered. Rafael put his heels together and bowed stiffly. "Welcome to Frontera, Jennifer Ramos Kennedy. I'm your 'owl.' Owls assist new students."

Jenny took a breath and nodded. She flexed her hands uncomfortably, wishing she had her orchid. When meeting someone new, it was easier at first talking to the plant.

"Los Marcaydo," observed her mother. "Marcaydo Windfarms." After solarplate, windfarms powered much of the Americas.

Rafael nodded again. "If you please, the slanball cage floats straight over-head."

Jenny looked up. Across the hab lay a zipper track of homes—that was Mount Gilead. Rooftops of little square houses, like lollipops at the end of driveways. A church with its spire pointed down toward the college, its roof proclaiming in block letters, LEVITICUS 18:23.

She focused closer, halfway. The slanball cage sprang into view: a gleam-ing cylindrical net of anthrax along the axis of the hab. Within the cage, at near-zero g, floated student players with their purple slancaps. They propelled themselves from the cage toward the slanball, aiming to get close enough to slan it toward the goal. Only the goalie was allowed to catch it in his hands. **"The Great Bears cage,"** Jenny texted her Somers friend, Tusker-12. **"What do you think?"**

"¡*Fantástico!* **Imagine if the Tuskers had a cage like that."**

Two windows appeared: Yola and Kendall Kearns-Clark, cocaptains of the Great Bears. Ken and Yola had helped Coach Porat recruit her at Somers High. Their purple jerseys had the Great Bear constellation, pointing toward the pole star. Ken's window showed their residence below, a crenellated for-tress they called "Castle Cockaigne." Yola's showed the drawbridge down, with two knights in chain mail riding out. The twins floated in the cage, eye-lids swollen, wisps of hair streaming out beneath their slancaps.

"Hey, Jenny, that was a great assist, your last game." Yola jittered a ball before her, her brainstream invisibly moving it side-to-side. Her space-black Aymara braids floated up in a V. Kendall's hair floated free; he was cultured Inuit with a round nose and level eyes. Their Quaker parents had picked their two favorite ethnics. "Ready for practice?"

Jenny nodded. "When do I start?"

"Right away."

The slanball flew off to Ken, who had snatched it invisibly from his sister. He jittered it before his chest. "You start tomorrow. Frogs must pick their courses first."

With no outward move, Yola snatched the ball back. "Professors rule," she agreed. "But get here the minute your courses come through." Yola's major was Life Science, which Jenny planned to follow.

"'Who yields to time, finds time on his side.'" Ken majored in Religion. "But don't be a moment late."

Yola pointed her finger. "We'll need you, to help us beat Whit." Whitcomb

College, Centrist affiliated, was Frontera's big rival. "See you." The cocaptains winked out.

Rafael nodded courteously. "Your brother was magnificent on the court. . . . My deepest sympathy."

Jenny studied her shoes. Jordi had been the Somers captain, and their record scorer. She had boosted his shots with her own brainstream, to make sure. No one ever caught on.

"Students live south of Wickett. This way." Rafael beckoned down the trail, his long shoelaces trailing stylishly behind.

"Jenny," her father mailed. "You'll watch your shoes, won't you?"

No one Jenny's age would be caught dead with tied laces. But trailing laces upset her dad. She never wore moonholes, either; they upset her mother.

She and her parents followed "owl" Rafael down the trail. The trail led "south" between rows of kudzu-less trees, trim as a grove in Iroquoia. Their shapely green crowns left no place an ultra could hide. Birds trilled, and insects popped up disconcertingly like spam in a toybox: dragonflies, a ladybird beetle, a butterfly. Flowers bloomed wild, broad purple petals with party-hat centers. *"Echinacea purpurea,"* texted her taxa window. "Coneflowers." Above, along the spacehab axis, grew a long row of clouds like deer tails strung together. The cloud-tails sailed north, on a breeze that blew steadily from the south. A heli sailed lazily in the micrograv, not needing lift until it had to land.

"ToyNews—From our box to yours." The national news again. "Clive Rusanov, here in Salt Lake, with a troubling turn in the War on Ultra. In Great Salt Lake, the ultraphytes take a new form." The Great Salt Lake was where the salt-loving ultraphytes had first sprouted, first as single floating cells the size of an ostrich egg, then as elongated streamers, and then the crawlers that invaded dry land, their cyanide emissions killing a thousand people. Now the ultraphyte rose in towers like Mordor from the slick jaundiced biofilm that stretched for kilometers across the lake. "New ultraphytes broke off and turned green, like plants. The new plantlike form will be even more challenging to root out than the old. . . ."

Whatever could make the ultraphyte change its form; what internal signal, and why?

"Here for comment is Utah Governor Carrillo. Governor, do you think we are losing the War on Ultra? How does this affect your chances for the presidency?"

A statehouse veteran, the silver-haired Governor Anna Carrillo smiled and nodded to show everything was under control. "As you know, Clive, in Utah we spend more per capita on ultraphyte research and containment than any other state. Our state is the pioneer in the War on Ultra." The Unity governor had doubled Utah's economy, building its vast flock of flying windmills, and she'd done her best to contain ultra when the mysterious life-form first appeared. Dugway Proving Ground ran a huge alien invasion program. Still, this latest news did Carrillo no good.

"And how's Glynnis holding up? All set for tonight?" The First Lady debate, when Glynnis Carrillo faced Guzmán's wife Betsy. And Clive would want Jenny's interview at the break.

"Jenny," Rafael called back, "you're in Fairfield East, no? A stylish address. This way, past the seniors." A Victorian mansion with a steep roof and gables. A Frank Lloyd Wright–style ranch, with cantilevered deck. Castle Cockaigne, complete with keep, outer wall with four towers, and a moat all around; that's where Ken and Yola lived. Rafael walked on ahead.

"Why 'frogs'?" The lack of eye contact helped Jenny get out her first words.

"First-year students are 'frogs.' Fresh out of water, just gaining your legs." Rafael turned to her, a superior twist to his lip. "Don't miss the Frogs Chorus, this evening at eight. All frogs gather south down Buckeye Trail, at the Ohio River."

The east side led between two rows of miniature New England–style houses. A pink one with a white porch and a garden of fluorescent orange flowers. "*Cosmos sulphureus,* **orange cosmos.**" The next house was split down the middle, half cream, half mauve. Several maintenance workers in power bands stood outside brainstreaming the amyloid to push out a dormer window. Next door stood a square ranch, stucco-like finish, with open windows and a couch on the lawn. Out front sat a crimson race car, low-slung chassis with outsized wheels and a prominent steam vent from hydrogen fuel. The car was emblazoned RED BULL MOTOR CLUB.

"*Chusma,*" muttered Rafael. Then he straightened, as if recollecting himself. "A real community, that's Frontera: 'Home without Mosquitoes.'"

Jenny remembered dengue fever, back in middle school. Her eyes had ached, her joints ached, her tongue burned till she wanted to die.

"And secure." Rafael spread his arms. "Where could a thief hide?"

If she could see homes up there in Mount Gilead, they could probably read her chemistry notes.

"A future doctor," Rafael observed from her toybox. "Excellent. We need more doctors in government." He nodded smartly. "A tip: Avoid Abaynesh. All the premeds drop her Life class, and take toyHarvard." Professor Sharon Abaynesh was the botanist who'd promised Jenny a job in her lab, and took her orchids. Rafael looked up and leaned toward Jenny confidentially. "Another tip," he whispered. "For politics, take Hamilton. He's magnificent." He pointed across the street. "There's your home."

Across the street stood a peach-colored amyloid cottage with a clear dome on the roof, the promised greenhouse. Nearby in a tree a cardinal tweeted as if impressed.

Soledad paused before the gracefully shaped tree, with its curious multi-pointed leaves. "Maple," she sighed.

"Acer saccharum, **sugar maple."**

The cottage was surrounded by a well-mown lawn, although one spot looked dug up by some kind of animal. Furrows in the mud suggested long claws.

"A bear tried to dig a den," explained Rafael. "Just a teddy bear," he reassured her. "Maintenance will fill it in. A tip: Mothballs discourage bears."

A lizard scampered up the wood-textured shakes, whipping its blue tail. *"Eumeces fasciatus,* **five-lined skink."** At Jenny's gaze, the door slowly opened.

Inside the cottage, a sitting room with a wide picture window looked out upon pines. The printer was still forming cushions for the couch, out of amyloid pumped up from the microbes. Barely noticing, Jenny ran upstairs. The dome-shaped greenhouse was there, the sprinkler system, the level trays, the drains. All set, except for her plants. What if that Professor Abaynesh didn't know how to care for them? Orchids were tricky.

"Jenny?" called her mother from the living room, to be shared with her *compañera.* "Remember to print out breakfast, every day."

"Sí, Mama." Jenny went back down to the living room. At the window, she froze. "Look out there—a deer, and there's another. So tiny, with their cream puff tails." The deer were minis, of course, like most of Frontera's other fauna, about the size of terriers.

Soledad frowned. "They carry brucellosis." President Ramos had died of brucellosis. Jenny and her brother had never been allowed pets of any kind.

As Jenny came downstairs, Rafael was telling her father, "Let's check out the toyroom." He tapped a door; it slid into the wall, revealing a toyroom. "You'll spend lots of time here."

The toyroom looked standard, eight plain gray walls and a floor that was solid for now. Jenny stretched her arms to touch both sides.

At her touch, the room filled with sunlight. The walls vanished, and blue "firmament" of a sky rose all around, above an island ringed by a beach. A sultry voice called, "Hey, *chico*, where've you been?" The beach divided in eight pielike sections. Each pie section presented a different reclining swimsuit-clad *chica*. Two of the *chicas* were felines with a cat face, claws, and a long twisting tail. A third had a long elephant trunk.

Jenny stretched her arms; one hand touched, then the other, too wide for comfort, she thought. The beach vanished, and the gray walls returned.

Rafael's face had darkened. "My deepest apologies. The teddies should have cleared the previous user."

"System clear," called her father in a level voice. "Code oh-six-oh-oh-four-two-seven." The room filled with white noise.

"Not to worry," assured Rafael, "Toy Land will send a teddy out to restart." Rafael looked aside, his eyes defocused as if checking a call. "If you'll excuse me, my next frog just arrived. Permit me however to request the honor of your presence . . ." In her toybox appeared an engraved invitation to Monte Carlo Night, a black-tie formal at the Ferrari motor club. "After the first week of class. An evening of elegance," he emphasized. "I will see you shortly at the powwow." As Rafael left, an actual frog appeared, a tiny brown thing that sprang across his trailing shoelace. It was nothing like those monster frogs that gobbled squirrels in Somers. "*Pseudacris crucifer,* **spring peeper.**" The peeper leapt again and vanished in a bush.

In the bedroom, Soledad already had Jenny's one little bag open, setting Great-Grandma Rosa's picture on the amyloid desk printed out next to her Lincoln bed. "Mama," Jenny insisted, "you don't have to do all this."

"Why not? It's my last chance." Her back was toward Jenny, her black hair hiding her face. Mama would soon be gone, Jenny realized—ten thousand kilometers away. Her stomach tightened. She could never think of things to say at a time like this.

"Remember," Soledad warned, "your aunts will call." Soledad's cousins, the Centrist governor and her twin, were genuinely fond of Jenny, but they always managed to call her at the most embarrassing moment.

"Hello?" From outside called the voice of a child. "**Layla Vimukta, South Andaman, Toynet Specialist.**" The girl outside looked about age six, with long black braids, holding a Phaistos disk. She pressed a button in the spiral; the Phaistos lit up "WINNER!" and set a new pattern. "Someone called in a toyroom?"

Jenny nodded. "We did."

The teddy strode inside, her back pocket sporting a jump rope. At the door to the toyroom, the teddy paused. "Commence testing power-up, oh-oh-six-seven-nine."

A crosshatch wove across the eight walls, stretching and squeezing enough to make you sick. "New client entry; restart Toynet four-point-two," added the teddy. No visible response. "Eight-fold splice call." Several incantations later, the room came alive. Eight different wedge-views faced each other, like slices of world pie: a library, a beach, a tree house.

"Good afternoon," spoke the melodious generic voice of the toyroom. "Welcome to Toynet, the universal networld service founded by Gil Wickett. Please select your homeworld. You may pick one of our eight default worlds, or custom order. Be advised, however, that custom orders may not splice correctly with all locations."

"*Bien.*" Soledad offered the teddy a lollipop.

The girl's face lit up. "Thank you oh so very much."

George asked, "Have you tried Toynet Five?" His voice was measured, without inflection. "T-five splices better."

"We've got T-five in testing." The teddy licked her sweet. "Remember to set your ghost protection." Popping the sweet in her mouth, the teddy headed outside, braids dancing, then skipped her rope down the street.

The default world categories appeared: "Beach Caribbean," eight different islands; "Famous Streets," from Fifth Avenue to Champs Elysées; "Lost Atlantis," eight different coastal landmarks, from Long Beach to the Florida Keys, submerged among the fish. "Tree House" looked *chulo*: eight different tree houses, in different forest settings from Canada spruce to Costa Rican rain forest. Jenny picked the house that stood tallest, upon a slender pine nearly bare of leaves, even taller than Old Bet on her pedestal. From inside the cozy cabin, windows looked out upon the canopy below.

"School in a tree house." Jenny smiled. Here she could visit Jordi. At home, someone might always walk in, but here, she could door-chain through to meet Jordi's sim, and no one would know. The mental forbade her, but she got to him in her toybox when she could get away with it. This toyroom would be even better.

A wall of the tree house melted and shimmered, revealing a laboratory full of plants. The laboratory spliced seamlessly with the tree house, as if it were just extending the room. Beyond the plants sat a desk, above which loomed a gigantic model of DNA. A woman in soil-stained jeans looked up from one of the flats and turned around: Sharon Abaynesh, professor of science. Her jeans had a flap torn down at the knee, and she wore a tight Italian sweater. Her black hair was twisted up into arches. "I'm glad I caught you before the powwow. You can see your orchids."

The Blood Star cattleya, the sweet-smelling vanilla with its unassuming green petals, and the giant vanda with its plate-sized purple flowers. Orchids were epiphytes, their roots growing on air and mist. A few leaves drooped but the water bulbs beneath each flower stood full. An automatic mister sprayed the vanda.

"Thanks so much," exclaimed Jenny. "Are you sure they're okay?"

"I scanned them all. You've kept them virus-free; quite a trick, that. You can have them back tomorrow."

"¡Guao! Thanks so much, Professor."

The professor gestured toward a flat of what looked like weeds with little lollipop leaves. "You wanted research. You can work on *Arabidopsis sapiens*."

From a cluster of leaves thrust a stalk with an odd white inflorescence like a pair of ears pressed together. Jenny blinked her taxa button, but no response. Not a well-known breed.

"Your experiment will test—"

At an angle, another door opened; the view jiggled sickeningly for two seconds before it spliced. Dean Kwon had donned a black robe over her purple T-shirt. "All students, parents, and owls," she called, "report to the Mound for Opening Powwow. Owls, line up your students on Buckeye Trail facing south. . . ."

Soledad nodded with a knowing smile. "We don't want to miss Dylan's entrance." Dylan Chase, who Jenny knew as "Uncle Dylan," was president of Frontera College. President Chase would welcome the students and their parents. And then the parents would leave. For just a moment Jenny felt a chill.

In the plant lab, Professor Abaynesh picked up her black gown. "Powwows, enough already," she muttered. "Always interrupting research. See you at the Mound." She looked around. "Where is it?"

A stalk of the mouse-eared plant shivered, and the pressed ears parted wide, revealing a coiled tendril. The tendril extended toward the wall, where a mortarboard hung from a peg.

Abaynesh took the mortarboard. "Thanks, Ari," she told the plant. The lab vanished into the tree house wall. Jenny stared after her.

"Let's not be late." As Soledad headed out, she paused by the other bedroom door. "Is your *compañera* here?"

Jenny knocked on the door. No answer. No sign of Mary Dyer in the tie-dyed dress. "We'll try again later."

"Your father and I will have to catch the lift right after the powwow." Soledad frowned, disappointed to miss her daughter's *compañera*.

"**Look here.**" Her father was waiting outside. "**Come look.**" From outside, he was staring into Mary's bedroom window.

Embarrassed, Jenny nonetheless peeked through the window. The bedroom had no luggage, but there stood an enormous aquarium. The aquarium was full of water with a bit of sand at the bottom and a light bank overhead, but as yet no sign of live occupants.

"She keeps fish." Jenny smiled. "I'll bet the coonskin DIRGs quarantined them."

A low rumbling began. The sound vibrated in the ground beneath Jenny's feet, so low in pitch that she could barely hear. The sound grew; the beating of drums. The drumming filled the spacehab in all directions.

In her toybox Dean Kwon opened a window with a blinking map. "All frogs head north to the Mound. Line up at the powwow ground."

4

Jenny and her parents strolled north up Buckeye Trail amid the naked trees, toward the deepening roar of the drums. Behind them the south solar had dimmed, while ahead the north solar brightened, casting long pencil shadows south. The space between trees burst with color, blue heather and yellow coneflowers. Now that she'd seen one peeper, she saw them all over, tiny frogs leaping out of a bush and getting squashed underfoot. From the woods a mini-deer bounded out across Buckeye Trail. There followed a mini-elephant, more leisurely, then another one leading a baby whose trunk held her bushy tail.

After Wickett Hall, side trails led west to various academic buildings, the redbrick amyloid Joseph Ramos Hall of Literature, the classical Harding Hall of Social Studies, and the postvirtualist Reagan Hall of Science, an opalescent sphere sprouting giant colored jelly beans. As she walked Jenny searched deeper in Toynet for the professor's plant. *"Arabidopsis thaliana,* var. *sapiens,"* came up at last in a window of the Levi-Montalcini Brain Research Institute. **"Forms human neurons. Model system for nerve function and development."**

Rafael's window opened. The drums were now deafening, drowning out speech. **"Jenny and Mary,"** he texted, **"Ricky and Reesie. The line starts here."** There was still no sign of Mary. The new students had all lined up along Buckeye Trail, most with their laces trailing behind their shoes, some red, some lemon, the year's "in" colors. Jenny looked down upon all their heads, then beyond. Beyond the racetrack rose the northern cap of the cylindrical spacehab, cupped like a hand.

Just ahead an escalator climbed to the powwow ground atop the Mound. Giant drums ringed the ground, each pounded by seven tribal elders. The broad grassy hill enclosed several underground tiers of slots and games. Flag-waving taxplayers gathered outside to watch the college opening ceremony extend the daily powwow. The first of the spacehab casinos, the Mound was now considered retro compared to New York's Towers or Mississippi's Rapture.

A window winked open, Reese and Ricky Tsien, then Fritz somebody, then another. Half the students were Reese or Fritz, the "in" names. Many were cultured Newmans, blond and black, male and female. Their tiny windows glittered with skaters and violinists, warworlds and danceworlds. "Visit Gloriana—my Elizabethan court." "Come visit my Candyworld—be a gumdrop!"

Soledad squeezed Jenny's hand. "Go ahead, dear," she said, barely audible above the drums. "We'll find our way up with the others." Jenny watched her parents head off, her heart pounding. Then their two windows blinked open in her box.

"Jenny," texted Rafael. "Have you seen Mary Dyer?"

"Sorry, no." Perhaps Mary, too, got off a waitlist.

The students stood around trailing their shoelaces, some looking dazed, as if they'd stumbled into someone else's toyworld. Others chatted up their neighbors. Ricky and Reesie pointed this way and that as if they owned the place.

"Did your high school have a Young International Leaders Program?"

"Where'd you get waitlisted?"

"Swarthmore and Amherst. What about you?"

"Forget Amherst—they took a DIRG by mistake."

"Hey, all our family DIRGs went to Berkeley."

"Through Toynet, you mean. Amherst actually accepted one residential. They tried to send it home but—"

"My AP calculus teacher was a DIRG at MIT."

Jenny cleared her box and zoomed to center stage. The stage was decked with purple coneflowers and Indiangrass. A handsome arrangement, the pots well watered and artfully placed. Two teddies fussed busily about the podium, some last-minute glitch, while below the stage a maintenance worker in power bands pounded a stuck block of amyloid.

Dean Kwon again. "All frogs please line up promptly behind the professors."

Rafael pointed. "Frogs line up here. Jenny, you can pair with Anouk Chouiref."

Anouk was a dark *parisienne* with a high-bridged nose, her nose ring sporting a ruby. A floral headscarf artfully hid her hair; tight black skirt to her ankles, her feet turned out in ballet flats. With a smile, she made a *plié*. Her cheeks shone with sienna skinglow, the most expensive kind. "Anouk Chouiref, daughter of the Euro finance minister." A clip of herself in her white veil and tulle, dancing *Giselle*. She leaned confidentially to Jenny's ear.

"*Somers, chez l'éléphant. Enchantée.*" She caught Jenny's hand. "Of course . . . my condolences."

"Thanks," Jenny whispered dutifully.

Anouk texted, "**We'll share the same Life class.**"

How did Anouk know that, Jenny wondered. She had sent Professor Abaynesh a course list, but had posted nothing in her toybox window. Jenny made herself swallow, like the mental always said. She looked at her own shoes, laces tied like a dwork. She texted, "**I raise orchids. Do you like chemistry?**"

"**Especially orbital theory. We'll be lab partners; I'll do all the calculations,**" Anouk offered loftily. Her window flashed, "**Visit my Lims in Series World.**"

"**Thanks.**" Jenny eyed Anouk with interest, her scarf the height of *haute couture*. "**Is your brother here?**"

Anouk's face slipped, just for a moment. The wrong thing to ask, Jenny reproached herself. But the *parisienne* recovered, with a delicate shrug. "*Enfin* . . . he had other plans. Oxford." She squeezed Jenny's hand and whispered. "We're going to be great friends."

Jenny blinked Anouk's window to confirm this new member of her ten thousand playmates. It would be a change having a "sister," and one so sharp. Jenny had always done Jordi's math for him.

In her toybox, the two teddies behind the coneflowers bumped fists, then scampered offstage. Lining up in two columns, the students climbed the Mound toward the stage. "**Watch your step,**" texted Dean Kwon as they approached the risers surrounding the powwow ground. "**Remember, you feel lighter as you rise.**" The pairs parted, and the students filed up singly. At her seat, Jenny turned in time to see the Shawnee elders with their great fans of feathers lead the line in. Across her box scrolled, "**No animals were harmed for this ceremony.**"

Elders carried the American flag, the Ohio state flag, then the eagle staff with its proudly hooked beak. "**Veterans of the Antarctic Farmland Defense.**" Black and white feathers fanned out from their backs, swaying in the breeze. They planted their flags at the stage amid the coneflowers.

After the elders came the first black-robed professor. "**Dean of the Faculty, Helen Tejedor.**" Jenny looked forward to Tejedor's frog seminar on "Postvirtual Cuba." A tall woman with long auburn hair, Tejedor carried a colonial ax, a round blade big enough for Paul Bunyan.

Whistles and toychat from the owls.

"¡Diosa!"

"¡Hasta la victoria siempre!"

"¡Viva Guantánamo!" The famous return of the naval base, when Cuba had joined the States. Or, Cuba *venció los Estados,* as Jenny's grandfather insisted.

After Tejedor's ax followed two columns of professors, all in black robes like bats hanging in the attic.

A brilliant ball of light drew attention to the podium. There stood a priest in the embroidered vestments of First Church Reconciled, the Roman-Anglican church. **"Chaplain Clarence Flynn."** Father Clare was Uncle Dylan's spouse, a longtime visitor at Soledad's fundraisers. Here on stage behind the Indiangrass, he looked more like a prairie preacher.

The drums stilled. Jenny's ears still rang. From the naked trees she heard a chorus of chirping. The peeper frogs.

"The chaplain—he's the man. You get in trouble, go see him."

"He runs Homefair—we build homes in Mount Gilead."

"He teaches Renaissance Art—get done your art requirement. What are you taking?"

"English Poets."

"English, that's so middle school." Frontera had no English department.

"Nueva Cuba. **Tejedor's hot."**

"Political Ideas, with Phil Hamilton. Super hot—don't miss him."

"God the Father and Mother," intoned Father Clare. "We humans call upon You to bless the undertakings of all of us here in orbit around our precious Earth; our Shawnee hosts, our neighbors in Mount Gilead, and especially our new students and their parents. For we, along with all of our unknown fellow creatures of distant stars whom we may yet encounter, all of us, however great or low, are creatures of time. We begin at our beginning, and place ourselves in Your loving care unto the end. You alone, the Unknowable Creator, protect us in our endeavors and aspirations, and grant us peace in our universe. Amen."

Above the stage, about halfway up to Mount Gilead, hung a bright patch of purple. The purple square began to float down. Students gasped and pointed as the square expanded, a luminous parachute, striped purple and white. At first it seemed to float forever, then it descended rapidly as the centrifugal pull grew, its silken billows stretched above lines of anthrax. At last the silk collapsed, depositing a man upon the stage. As purple-shirted owls rushed to carry the folds of silk offstage, out stepped a tall man in a lunar Formula One racing suit. The Frontera College president.

"Students, parents, Shawnee elders, friends." Receiving a black academic gown from the chaplain, President Chase draped it over his racing suit. Chase had a nut-brown complexion, a small endearing nose, the kind of earnest good looks and full voice that won immediate trust. Jenny knew Uncle Dylan, an old college friend of her mother's, even better than his spouse, the chaplain. Always there at her mother's fundraisers, Dylan Chase somehow managed to know everyone very well. "As Teddy Roosevelt would have said, I am *dee*-lighted to welcome the class of 2112 to Frontera College, the first institution of higher learning on the high frontier. Let us give thanks for today's fine weather and awe-inspiring sunset to our spacehab engineers, especially our chief engineer Quade Vincenzo."

Applause erupted, with shouts and whistles from the owls. "Elephant Man, Elephant Man!" Jenny craned her neck, but Quade Vincenzo was not to be seen.

"Welcome to our pristine habitat," the president continued, "a radical venture in the project of human civilization. Our very air is composed to a premodern standard—the same composition breathed by our Founding Fathers." Before carbon emissions had risen off the chart.

Jenny took a deep breath. Frontera air did feel special, exceptionally pure and wholesome.

"Frontera is home to birds and deer, free of mosquitoes and yellow plague, untouched by drought or flood. Indeed, all Earth's rivers could dry out, and all Earth's oceans could swallow her shores, while our pristine habitat of Frontera would remain untouched." His voice intensified. "But remember—no matter how perfect our habitat, it remains truly a frontier, the leading edge of human-kind's venture into space."

In the sky above appeared a mile-high vision of Theodore Roosevelt, the old frontier president on his horse in the Sierras. "Teddy" was Uncle Dylan's specialty—he could lecture for hours. Then Teddy's image faded into that of Toynet founder Gil Wickett. The giant Gil Wickett grinned and waved like a child.

"If education," continued President Chase, "is the highest calling of the human race, as we believe it is; and if Frontera College is the world's finest liberal arts college, as we know it is; and if you, the entering class, are the most creative and best qualified class of students ever to enter Frontera, as indeed you are; then we can all look forward to a generation of the finest leaders in the academy, in commerce, in public life, and in the arts, that our nation has ever known." The president raised his arms in a gesture encompassing the spacehab. "And where better to start than *alta frontera*? What better place for an undergraduate college? The Old English *frontera* meant 'forehead'—the high frontier of the human body, facing the world with thought and reason."

Dylan paused, his gaze sweeping the audience. "Frontera was built by the greatest minds of our day, stocked with the healthiest parts of a biosphere, settled by colonists of the highest purpose. College is where each of you will face the world's frontiers with your own. Parents, you face good-byes to your sons and daughters. Students, you face the entire world with your own mental frontier—your own great ideals. Be practical as well as generous in your ideals. Keep your eyes on the stars and your feet on the ground." Pause for dramatic effect. "And if there is any one subject you fear the most, like the dire wolves our first Americans found by the Ohio River—take a course in that subject. Don't stay in the pits—tear out and race your best. Take on your fears, and your dreams will become real. Face your frontiers at Frontera."

Jenny shivered; the air had cooled quickly. This high frontier was different, she told herself, with its hundred-year plans and quality controls, its teddies and habitat engineers.

A shout behind her, and someone screamed. Startled, Jenny jumped and half turned; the stage area was lit, but beyond she could scarcely see. Her toybox filled with student text. Some animal let out a sound between a growl and a squeal. Then a black shape like a medium-sized dog clambered out, rearing on two legs before it trotted off among the trees. "*Ursus americanus minimus*, black teddy bear."

"Someone's hurt."

"His leg—it's *bleeding*!"

The students fell back, stumbling into each other; two of them collapsed on the ground in a tangle of luminescent shoelaces. In Jenny's toybox, her mother's window opened. "Jenny, are you okay? *¿Seguro?* Jenny?"

Jenny steered around the fallen students, her foot slipping on a squashed peeper. She found the victim, a tall *chico* with football shoulders. The *chico* sat on the ground with a dazed "Whose toyworld am I in?" expression. His skin looked pale, not good. From her pocket she pulled a scanscope and snapped it around his arm. The data scrolled through her toybox. "What's your name?"

Someone muttered, "Read his window, *tonta*."

Respiration shallow, scalp circulation low-normal, pupil size normal. "It's okay," Jenny told him. "Take a breath. What's your name?" The standard formula, she could ask any stranger.

"Charlie," he said faintly. "Charlie Itoh." Good, that matched his window.

"Lie down." Jenny put a hand behind his neck to help him down. She looked up. "Towel or blanket? Anyone?"

A tall *chico* pulled off his own shirt and handed it to her. Jenny folded the shirt and placed it beneath Charlie's head, as she helped him lie down. No airway obstruction, pupil size normal. His ankle, though, had a nasty gash. She plastered a wad of amyloid over it. "Charlie, tell me, who's the president of the United States?" The next standard question. An elderly man with a stroke had once replied, "You are, Rosa."

Charlie swallowed. "Bud Guzmán."

Raucous sneers all round. Few here were fans of the president who'd canceled the Jupiter program, sent troops to Antarctica, and solarplated the Death Belt.

"Charlie, what happened?"

He grimaced. "Stuck my leg in a hole, and that critter came tearing out."

"Does your ankle hurt?" She felt the ankle carefully, below the gash, which would do fine under amyloid. "Wiggle your toes."

Charlie winced in pain.

From above, a medicraft whined as it descended. The students fell back as it landed and a small round DIRG emerged. No human operator? *Dios mío,* that was against EMS regulations.

Dean Kwon crouched down beside Jenny. "Charlie, help is here. You'll be okay."

In Jenny's box, a window opened. It was Uncle Dylan. "Jenny, dear, how is he?"

"A sprain, I think, but he'll be okay."

"Calm, everyone." From the podium the president's voice was hypnotic, completely reassuring, like Governor Carrillo that time at her rally when a banner caught fire. "If we pursue a true frontier, as indeed we do—what's a frontier without a few teddy bears?"

Nervous laughter rippled through the audience. Dean Kwon shook her head. "I told Quade to clear out that bear's den."

5

Jenny returned with her parents to Wickett Hall. The toy locomotive was just chugging past the alphabet blocks. Jenny's steps slowed and her throat caught. Soon her parents would leave her here, perched alone like the Somers elephant, while they returned to Earth to cope with ultraphytes, oceans, and mosquitoes.

A crowd of parents and students had gathered, shoelaces pointing in all directions, milling around President Chase. At last he found Jenny's family. "Soli, dear! *Dee*-lighted to see you." A hug, and a kiss on both cheeks. To her father, he called out in Mohawk, *"Niyawehkowa katy nonwa onenh skennenji thisayatirhehon."* Great thanks now you have safely arrived.

"Dylan," her mother reminded him, "you pulled the same trick at our commencement." They had graduated together from the top liberal arts college in swing-state Ohio.

"Ah, *recuerdo*. But today, the real hero was Jenny." Clasping her shoulders, he kissed her forehead; the only family friend tall enough to do that. "You saved the day for us already."

Jenny smiled and briefly closed her eyes. "The coneflowers were lovely."

"I knew you'd notice."

"How's Fritz?" The president's own son.

"Fritz left early for Berkeley, plotting to save the seals or something. If he were here, he'd be demanding your first date."

Soledad sighed. "You dreamed of founding the first college on the high frontier. . . ."

"A college for all," Dylan reminded her. "I just endowed two more Chase Scholarships."

". . . with altogether too much wildlife."

Dylan laughed. "Goodness, my dear, we're *adultos*. So we risk a nip now and then. It comes with the scenery."

"Scenery, security, swing state." Soledad smiled. "That's how we got the final November debate here—at Frontera!"

Frontera was legally Ohio, Ohio's high frontier. But a presidential debate—it would be the first in a spacehab.

"Soli, you always think of us." He clapped Soledad's shoulder. "And we always think of you. Your acreage is secure. Did you check it out?"

Jenny's eyes widened. So her parents had bought land in the spacehab. A Centrist thing to do. Were they that pessimistic about Earth? Would they too try to leave? Like the old Cuban saying, *todos se van.*

"Jenny," added Uncle Dylan, "be sure to sign up for my frog seminar. You'll have to list it first; it fills quickly." With a wave, he moved on to the next family.

✦·

Behind Wickett Hall, the elevator light came on.

"Jenny, there is something I need to say." The letters in Jenny's toybox were so deep blue she could barely see.

"I know, Dad." She couldn't say it either. She hugged him, and they held each other a long time.

"Ten minutes till departure," warned the elevator.

It was her mother's turn for a hug. "Remember, dear." Soledad's voice had fallen, a trifle unsteady. "I know you'll study hard."

"Yes, Mama."

"Attend Clare's service every Sunday."

"Yes."

"And join the right garden club." She emphasized the word "right."

"Of course, Mama."

"And tonight, don't forget the green jello. Anna needs our help."

"Of course."

"No," her father announced flatly, as if to a toyroom. "It's all wrong." He flapped his hands nervously. "There should be two of them."

Her mother's face paled. "It's all right, George." She cradled his head. "Everything is fine. Envision your quiet place."

Jenny texted, **"I've got my housemate, Mary Dyer."** Wherever she was. **"And my new friend, Anouk."**

"A sister never leaves the longhouse," her father insisted. "Especially a sister without a brother. A sister must always have a brother, the most sacred bond."

"George—be appropriate."

That word "appropriate" caught his ear. The most important of all words, that word meant the difference between free life and the blue room.

Soledad added, "A cool glen of pine trees, the Tree of Peace. You're walking there right now. *Enjeyeweyendane.*" We will be comforted.

Jenny stroked his arm. "I'll see you in Iroquoia."

"At the Condoling Council," he reminded her. "Till then, beware. Here are thorny trails and falling trees, and wild beasts lie in wait. Above all, beware the Salt Beings." Salt Beings, what the Iroquois had called white men.

"This fall will be hard," Soledad whispered to Jenny. "With you away; and all his extra stress at work, running ToyVote." All the voting ran through Toynet, and any glitch was a national crisis. "Stay in touch, *hijita.*"

"I will, I promise."

For a while George looked lost. Whatever momentary Toynet glitches were happening on Earth went unattended. At last he spoke, in a low voice with great dignity. *"Wakenekheren. Hiro kone."* One will be missed. I have spoken.

Her father's words filled her heart as Jenny found her way back down Buckeye Trail, gravel crunching beneath her shoes. The south solar was dark, the north solar fading. The southerly breeze quickened. The axial row of clouds had expanded like a sausage, obscuring the slanball court and Mount Gilead beyond. A drop of water cooled her arm, then another. Light rain fell, enough to turn the gravel trail to mud. She'd have to print out hiking boots.

"ToyNews—From our box to yours." National again. "Clive Rusanov, here in Havana with Governor Guzmán." The Centrist governor of Cuba, now Gar Guzmán, was running for president. For most of the past decade the president had been Bud Guzmán, and now there was his cultured hopeful Gar. All the Guzmáns had a chromosome 3 deletion that kept their intelligence below that required to wreck financial systems or solve urgent societal problems. "Governor, what do you think of Betsy's chances in tonight's debate?"

Presidential candidates watched the pollmeter so closely they always reached a dead heat. But their wives were the wild card. Everything else—ultra fears, coastline loss, skin cancer—could be spun with one plausible line or another, but the First Lady candidates, and the response they drew, remained largely beyond control. And wives had complex feelings about their spouses' ambitions. A wife's unscripted response could send a campaign down a new track.

Gar Guzmán's majestic profile could have been chiseled on Mount Rushmore. "Clive, I'm confident Betsy will reassure the American people that we're winning the War on Ultra. And more important, the War on Sin. The Flood is coming; only the faithful will survive. My first acts in office will be to double our solar output and build ten more ultra-free spacehabs." Gar had beaten Jenny's aunt in the Centrist primaries, by less than a hundred votes. Just as well; Jenny would have felt bad in November, voting against Aunt Meg.

"Winning the War on Ultra"—Clive nodded—"that's good to hear. And now, from Salt Lake, the Unity candidate, Governor Anna Carrillo. Governor, how do you think Glynnis will do in tonight's debate?"

Anna was coming off a bad week, with the ultraphyte biofilm spreading across Utah. "Clive, I know Glynnis will share with our fellow Americans our vision of recapturing the American dream: a secure financial future, and genetic health for all. And to save Earth by putting our solar plants and factories in space." The Earth's one hope; at what cost, no one dared say.

Jenny sighed. Anna's wife Glynnis was smart, but Betsy Guzmán knew how to get under her skin. It would be a tough contest. Meanwhile the rain was done, the clouds shrunk to tiny puffballs, and the chocolate hillsides glowed sheer pink. The north solar above the Mound offered a spectacular "sunset," lemon center peeling into fractal curves of orange. Instead of "setting," however, the orange filled the center, turning scarlet. The scarlet hue stretched the entire length of the spacehab to touch the Ohio River, ringed by a rainbow. The glow slowly faded, like embers of a dying fire. Overhead glimmered the lights of Mount Gilead and the cords of the slanball court.

A red racing car screeched around the block puffing steam, its huge wheels kicking up pebbles, one of which hit Jenny in the ankle. "¡Vaya!" She watched their headlights streak across Castle Cockaigne. How could the college admit such *chusma*?

The car stopped and a door flew open. Out jumped a blond *chico* with a purple headband and a prominent nose ring. "**Fritz Hoffman, pledge educator.**" He put up an arm with a muscle the size of his neck. "Hey, Jenny. Don't miss our Bulls Blowout, Wednesday night." An invite popped up, Red Bulls Blowout and Pig Roast. Wednesday, the second day of class, after faculty advising Monday. Fritz winked. "We're signing up voters. We'll count on you." His toybox had a full Unity campaign layout; apparently the Bulls ran Frontera's Unity Club, campaigning for Carrillo.

Jenny managed a gracious smile. For Unity, one had to work with all kinds.

The Buckeye Trail led her back to her Virginia East cottage. The porch light was on, and she paused. On the porch, in the hanging chair, rocked her *compañera*, Mary Dyer.

Jenny stepped toward Mary and leaned on the porch rail. "Hi there, I'm Jenny. You must be . . ."

No toybox window appeared. At Mary's feet, a brown-striped lizard skittered across the porch. The lizard flashed a blue tail, like the one that had climbed the shakes.

Mary nodded slowly, her chin jutting firm, a gold ring in her right nostril. She wore her tie-dyed shift, and her left hand held a water bottle. Her right hand flexed, the fingers in continual motion as if trying to creep away. Her arms and face glowed brightly, the most luminous skinglow Jenny had ever seen. "Mary Dyer," she said. "We picked it from a name garden. Do you like it?"

"Sure, it's a lovely name." Mary smelled faintly like a marina, as if wearing trimethylamine perfume. She must really be into fish. "Did you get here okay? How do you like Frontera?"

Mary said, "We need shorter light."

Jenny nodded, as though she understood. "I hope you get your fish back. I printed out my stuff in the living room, but feel free to add yours. I screened for TPIs." Toy-print infections. "Did you miss the powwow? The president dropped in on a parachute—he's *chulo*." Talking to Mary was easy, she realized. She picked up right away that this Mary was a lot more challenged than herself.

"We missed the powwow. We were delayed." Mary lifted the water bottle and took a long swallow. "The vote was close."

Jenny blinked. "The what?"

"Twenty-one to twenty-two. It took a long time."

"I see." Autism, Dean Kwon had said. Maybe this was one of those incomprehensible jokes.

"We avoid crowds. Someone might notice we're . . . not like them."

"Sure, I understand," said Jenny. "That's why my dad avoids cocktail parties. So, you're from Long Beach?"

"We came ashore there."

"Your parents still live there? What do they do?"

"We don't have parents."

"Sorry." Jenny bit her lip, remembering.

"We're sorry," Mary said. "We're really sorry about all the poisoned fish."

"Did your fish not make it through?"

"Poisoned by ultra."

"Oh," Jenny sighed. "Ultraphytes make cyanide—but only when stressed." That poor squirrel back in Somers. "Ultras can be beautiful. Like poison frogs." She recalled the yellow ultraphyte huddled in her basement, her project for the science fair. And now they were morphing into new forms; if only she could learn more. "Well, I know how you feel. I raise plants—but the quarantine took them."

"We raise plants."

"You do? Aquarium plants?"

Mary's luminous eyes widened. "Humans make poisons too. And humans are beautiful." She held up her water bottle and swallowed again. Then she offered Jenny something in her hand. "Will you be our friend?" Some kind of round white pills or candies.

"Uh, no thanks."

"They're . . ." Mary searched for a word. " 'Genuine.' "

Jenny looked again, and took one of the round pills between her fingers. It gleamed translucent in the porch light. A pearl. She peered closer at Mary's face: smooth as a pearl, without pores. "**Prosthetic**," suggested her toysearch. Prosthetic graft, perhaps for ectodermal dysplasia. *Qué lío*, what a mess this *chica* must be. "That's okay, Mary," she said kindly. "We'll be friends."

6

As soon as she got back to her room, Jenny printed out new clothes, a shirt of fashionable lime green with a loose, draping neckline, and a pair of black pants with a tiny moonhole on each seat. Next, smart black shoes with meter-long lime-green laces. Then she set her toybox to erase the moonholes, and the laces, for all public transmission. In her toybox, her parents' two windows were closed, her father's named **Iroquoia**. She sighed; with all her studies, she doubted she'd have much time for toyworlds.

Anouk's window opened. "*Écoute*, Jenny; where are we going for supper?"

Jenny blinked. "The dining hall."

The *parisienne* looked disappointed. "The campus has several nice cafés. Never mind, *chérie*—see you at the dining hall."

She looked around for Mary. A tentative knock on the bedroom door produced no response, and no window opened in her box. With a shrug, Jenny left.

The dining hall looked like a draft printout, with long plain tables and benches in between. Returning students exclaimed at each other, windows winking and toyworld invites flashing. "**Vivian Hatley, Hostess, Begonia Club.**" A stylish *chica* with a Newman chin and Monroe lips caught Jenny's hand. "Call me Viv, dear. I'm so glad we caught up at last. Those orchids of yours— stunning." At Viv's shoulder perched a creamy begonia with a yellow center and a leaf with an interestingly asymmetric heart shape. Viv's window popped an invite to the Begonia Club Reception, Sunday afternoon.

Anouk, the Parisian math genius, was already seated next to Reesie, the slanball twin from the shuttle. Anouk lifted her hand, her thumb curved out from her exquisite fingers. Jenny pulled her legs over the bench, feeling awkward; there was no graceful way to sit.

"**Who brought the DIRG?**" texted someone.

In the corner stood a Monroe-faced DIRG. Jenny's scalp crawled. Had her own mental printed itself out? It could do that if needed, if she ever tried to harm herself. But not this one, she realized; it was not her own mental, but someone else's Monroe-style family DIRG. Some other *chica* who'd lost the fight with her parents.

"The Brazilian solar heiress; it's her bodyguard." Solarplate covered most of the Amazon Death Belt.

"No, it's the Chinese banker's son."

"*Tonto*, no *chico* would have a Monroe."

"Did you see the new toyflick, *Meet Me in Shanghai*? Newman and Monroe were *estupendo*."

A quarter to seven already; nearly debate time. The menu appeared in her box. Jenny blinked chicken and green beans. They printed up from the table, including gravy for the chicken and butter on the beans. For dessert, Jenny found green jello.

The bench thudded as Yola sat next to her, with Kendall beside. "Ready for practice?" Yola's braids bounced, and she caught Jenny's arm to wrestle.

"Focus," warned Ken. "Got your courses? Pick a tough load, or Coach will send you packing."

Yola frowned. "She's taking Life, Kennie-boy. With Abaynesh. You want to kill her?"

Jenny smiled. "So what do you recommend?"

"Chaplain Flynn's Renaissance Art," said Ken. "Amazing. That Sistine chapel—it should be a slanball cage, so you'd float at the ceiling."

Viv leaned forward knowingly. "Tejedor," she recommended. "The *estilo cubano*—you'll see the world with new eyes."

"Hamilton," added Reesie, nodding her own Newman chin. "My owl says he's the top."

The food was chicken-flavored amyloid, and the beans were faintly bean-flavored. All came from sewage processed by the shell microbes and pumped back up. Jenny looked over at Anouk, who pursed her lips. "*Next time, let's try a café.*"

Yola flashed her an EMS logo, the snake climbing a pole. "Nice job, out on the powwow ground. You got there before the heli."

"Are there many student volunteers?"

"We'll get in touch with you, once we see how you handle classes and slanball."

"ToyNews—From our box to yours." Clive's voice boomed as the toy-wall lit up. Within the toywall stood the ToyNews anchor and two armchairs seating the First Lady candidates.

Cheers and whistles came from the students, especially the two motor club tables up front. The Red Bulls all wore red racing jackets and purple headbands. At the other table, the Ferraris wore black suit and tie, with just a gold ribbon at the lapel. Rafael was there, applauding politely.

"Live from sunny Orlando." A spliced tour of the refurbished seawall encircling the city, and Disney's new cactus park. "Thanks to all our ToyDebate contributors. . . ." Soledad appeared with the Centrist cochair, Jeremiah Stone. "And now the ground rules . . ."

The two First Lady candidates sat in their chairs with their legs crossed. In the dining hall the students quieted, but their windows filled.

"**Glynnis looks out of date—that was last year's color.**"

"**No, that's on purpose, to show she wears stuff more than one year.**"

"**What kind of cookies?**"

"**The cookies,**" texted Fritz Hoffman from the Red Bulls table. "**No nuts, please.**" Analysts said the nuts in the cookies had doomed Unity's bid four years before.

Clive leaned forward ingratiatingly to Anna Carrillo's would-be first lady. "Glynnis," he began, "I know you have something special to share with our studio audience."

Glynnis smiled with all her sparkling amyloid-plated teeth. Jenny crossed her fingers; Glynnis was known for sounding too sharp now and then. "Why, Clive, as a matter of fact I do." She held up a plate of nicely browned cookies. "Oatmeal chocolate chip."

The studio audience clapped appreciatively. The Red Bulls cheered and tossed napkins in the air, as the cookies were handed around through the studio audience in the toywall. "**Healthy but sweet,**" texted Fritz. "**Great opening.**"

Clive had turned to her opponent. "Betsy," he began. "I know you have something good to share too."

Betsy smiled, a bit more carefully, managing to look homey and seductive all at once. "Clive, I want to make sure everyone in the studio gets one of my paradise butter cookies."

"**Righteous and rich.**" The Red Bulls jeered, and Fritz tossed a fork at the toywall. The Ferraris applauded with ostentatious politeness.

"Now, Betsy," Clive went on, "you've won the coin toss for the first question. Tell us why your husband will make the best president."

Betsy Guzmán leaned forward confidentially. "Clive, I'd like the audience to know," she began as if imparting a great secret, "that my husband, Gar Guzmán . . . is a real man." She lengthened the word, nodding. "A man who will go out and get the job done, do what a man's got to do. Especially—most especially—in today's most urgent issue, the War on Ultra."

The studio audience applauded steadily, and the pollmeter rose. A strong opening; it would be hard to counter.

But the anchor had already swiveled to his left. "Glynnis, can you tell our audience why your wife will make the best president?"

For a moment Glynnis tensed, then she recovered. She had to get over that, Jenny thought; this was the big league, now, not just a governor's wife in a western state full of Mormons and Death Belt refugees. "Well, Clive," Glynnis began, crossing and uncrossing her legs. Her voice grew quiet. "I'd like the American people to know . . . that my wife Anna Carrillo is a real American."

The Red Bulls jumped up and applauded, so that Jenny lost the rest of what Glynnis said. Whatever it was, the pollmeter rose; her answer had hit the mark.

Clive nodded sagely. "A truly heartfelt response. Now, Glynnis, it's your turn for the next question. Can you share with our audience an incident in your everyday life that shows us what your life will be like in the White House?"

At that Glynnis smiled, with just a hint of mischief. "Well, Clive." Not your doctorate in solarray engineering, Jenny urged silently, don't mention that. Not how you launched the first solarray beyond the Kessler cloud. "One day last summer, I was preparing a bowl of nice cold punch for our family. A special recipe I call Antarctic punch."

The studio audience hushed, and so did the cafeteria. The pollmeter bounced uncertainly. "Antarctic" was not a word people wanted to think about just now, with half a dozen armies vying to control the emerging farmland.

"Now, my little daughter was in the kitchen, and by mistake she happened to put the punch bowl on the stove."

Beside the armchair, a punch bowl appeared on a hotplate. The punch bowl was half full of ice. The ice was melting.

"Luckily, I saw the punch bowl when only half the ice had melted." Like the Antarctic ice sheet, only half gone. And the warming wouldn't stop. "As soon as I saw it——" Glynnis caught the punch bowl and held it up. "I took it right off the stove." She faced the audience. "And that's why we need Anna for president. Someone's got to get that punch bowl off the stove." Before punch bowl Earth came to a boil.

✦

As the debate wore on, Jenny tried to stay awake, exhausted by the long day's journey up from Somers. When Clive announced a break, she sat up straight.

"Now," said Clive, "we bring you an exclusive live interview: Jenny Ramos Kennedy, descendent of three presidents including her culture source Rosa Schwartz, at her first day at college. Jenny never expected to attend college in the Firmament, but after the tragic death of her—"

All eyes were on Jenny as she struggled to extricate her legs, her bare skin in the moonholes peeling off the bench. One shoelace had caught beneath, and she yanked it out. Just in time, she remembered the green jello.

In the toywall Jenny's image appeared, carrying the plate of green jello. The moonholes in her black pants were filled in, and her laces were neatly tied.

"Jenny." Within her toybox Clive addressed her, while in the toywall his image spliced with hers, heights even. "Tell our audience what it's like for a presidential scion on her first day at college. You've already managed to save a life, haven't you?"

Jenny smiled, keeping her eyes wide. "Well, Clive, I've made so many wonderful friends already." She blinked at her namelist. "There's my 'owl,' Rafael, and my best friend Anouk from Paris. My fantastic team captains, Yola and Kendall; my fellow 'frogs,' Ricky and Reesie, and my welcoming upperclass friends Viv and Fritz. And my *compañera* Mary, and brave Charlie, and there's—" That tall *chico* who'd given his shirt for the pillow, what was his name?

"A wonderful first day," concluded Clive. "I'm sure, Jenny, you'll be leading the local campaign for Carrillo."

"As a first-year student, Clive, I'll be too busy with my studies to lead anything. But—"

"And the food." Clive nodded confidentially. "Tell us—how's the cafeteria, compared to home?"

Jenny held out her plate. "They make the best green jello I've had outside Utah."

+—

Above Buckeye Trail, as new students followed their owls south for the Frogs Chorus, the lights of Mount Gilead made a cluster of stars. The north solar had deepened to twilight purple, like the purple of the light-drinking microbes in the saltwater that filled the spacehab's outer shell. As the hab rotated, all sides of its marine shell received light. Solar microbes now provided a quarter of the spacehab's electricity and hydrogen, while recycling its waste into amyloid. Another fifty percent came from solarray, an array of solar collectors in space; impressive, though not yet enough to survive without Earth. Farther "south," the farmlands gave way to forest, naked trees discreetly screening the homes of those who could afford their own plot, reserved for the day when Frontera was independent and Earth too hot to handle. Even her parents now had their "safe home" here, Jenny realized with a twinge. *Todos se van.* But everyone from Earth couldn't fit here.

"Slanball starts tomorrow," Yola reminded Jenny, "as soon as you hear from Toy Land." Toy Land was the school's Toynet hub, which distributed all the course lists after sorting requests approved by the faculty. Jenny had to meet her advisor Abaynesh first thing in the morning.

The woods now filled with a chorus of crickets and peeper frogs. The frogs were deafening; there must be thousands. "Are they always this loud?"

Yola grinned. "Just wait till you join them. My year, our owl made us peep till we tossed him in the river."

Anouk sniffed. "Frogs call in the spring." Her Hermès headscarf displayed seashells on the beach.

Yola shrugged. "Animals can't tell the seasons out here. They just breed all the time."

"Don't you entrain them by timing the daylight?" Anouk must have had an advanced Life class. Jenny wondered if her own public school had been a mistake.

"Their circadian clock genes were adjusted. Ask Elephant Man," said Yola. "That's Quade Vincenzo, the ecoengineer. He stocks all the wildlife in the hab."

Rafael appeared, nodding courteously to Jenny and Anouk. "The Frogs Chorus is a harmless tradition," he assured them.

"'Tradition'?" Anouk raised an eyebrow. "What 'tradition' can such a young school have?" Frontera had just passed its tenth anniversary.

"You shall be amused," Rafael promised in a tone that managed to take charge while disowning responsibility.

The Monroe DIRG had followed, at a discreet distance. Jenny eyed it, still wondering.

"It's mine," said Anouk. "Berthe, my family retainer. To preserve my honor."

"Oh, I'm sorry." She hastily looked away.

Anouk shrugged. "Not so bad as one inside your head."

Jenny wheeled and stared. How could Anouk know about her mental? Of course she'd know, it was out there; ToyNews hid the scars on Jenny's arm, but the story had leaked.

"This way, if you please." Rafael nodded. Herded by their owls, the new students collected in the darkness at the Ohio River. The "river" actually flowed in a ring encircling the southern cap and drained out centrifugally to the space-hab's outer shell, bringing minerals out to the solar microbes. Fireflies danced all around like stars let loose from the sky. Above the "peep, peep" of the frogs, some other creature called, "Oo-oo-oo *oo-aw*." Some hidden denizen of the trees.

"*Vamos,* little frogs," called Fritz Hoffman, the Bulls pledge educator. His call was echoed by the other owls. The new students clustered at the riverbank, craning their necks for a look. From her height, Jenny looked above the crowd toward the river.

Out of the river emerged a man in hip waders, the ecoengineer Quade Vincenzo. Vincenzo had an interesting face, a bulbous nose and cheeks that Jenny had to admit were indeed reminiscent of an elephant. Like the Mount Gilead colonists, he wore power bands on his arms and legs, devices that reclaimed energy lost from motion. In one hand the ecoengineer carried a large muddy bullfrog; in the other, a small bright orange frog. "Good to see all you new frogs join our chorus." Vincenzo's words filled her toybox. "Frontera is proud of all our fauna, but especially proud of our frog collection. . . ." He held up the bullfrog. "From good old *Rana*, Mark Twain's favorite, to the *Dendrobates* poison dart frog." The bright orange one. "A dart frog lays her eggs one by one in separate treeholes, then climbs up each tree every day to feed her tads. Don't you ever touch one, though." Vincenzo nodded as if to himself. He put down the two frogs, which soon hopped off.

Jenny took a wary step back.

"Now, our most popular, that is to say most prolific frog, is the spring peeper. As you've noticed." Wiping his hands on his waders, Vincenzo put his fingers to his lips and called, "Peep, peep," exactly like a peeper frog.

"Frogs!" Fritz called out to the new students. "Time to join the chorus, frogs. 'Peep, peep.' "

One of the new frogs tried a half-hearted "peep." Others joined in.

Jenny hated group icebreakers. She took another step backward, tripping against Charlie with his foot bandaged from the bear attack. She caught his arm. "Sorry."

Charlie smiled, a tough-guy smile like he was still in pain but wouldn't let on. One of Uncle Dylan's Chase Scholars, he came from Minnesota, with no twin. "Hey, Jenny, that's okay. 'Peep, peep.'"

"Oo-oo-oo *oo-aw.*" From the sky something swooped down to the ground, then back up again. A bird? Now that she'd seen it, her eye caught sight of another, and another one swooping to the ground. She aimed her window and zoomed. *Strix varia,* **barred owl.** The owl had swooped down and caught something, then flitted back up to a tree where it perched, fluffing its brown-striped feathers. Now the owl had something in its mouth to feed its nestlings. It was a frog. Like all tranquil nature scenes, the river bank was a killing field. The barred owls were swooping down all over, feasting on the thousands of tasty spring peepers.

7

Jenny awoke Monday in her printout Lincoln bed, thirty-six thousand klicks from home. Her head was a jumble of dreams, so many new faces that she barely recalled Jordi. She took an R-patch from the familiar shelf, and slapped the diad on her forehead.

In her toybox loomed the pouting Monroe. "Good morning, Jenny," purred the husky voice of the mental. "Do we need any help today?"

"Go away." She called up Frontera's course list to fill the toybox, overlaying the mental. The mental departed, letting her off more easily than usual. Jenny really hadn't dreamt much of Jordi. Still, she would visit him, perhaps that evening when she could sneak in the toyroom. The toyroom—that would be nearly as good as having him alive.

In her bedroom, everything was a middling amyloid copy, not quite her bed from home, not quite the same blue coverlet with gold flowers, a bit stiffer material; nearly the same dresser, almost like oak. But there was exactly the portrait she'd carried up, Great-Grandma Rosa Schwarz smiling from the Oval Office. Jenny smiled back wistfully. Rosa had swept into office after the first methane quake swamped the East Coast. Her wife Mimi had said, "This mess needs more than a woman—it needs two." Rosa had put the jobless to work building windmills, and convinced the UN to ban carbon emissions, earning a Peace Nobel. She'd built a hundred solarrays, and the first space habitat. And got swept out after one term.

The sitting room now displayed Jenny's favorite Kahlos, especially *The Two Fridas*, the two women joined by a vein of blood. She recycled her nightgown and printed out clothes for the day. The printer printed out yogurt and grapefruit, all amyloid. Jenny wondered about that café Anouk had found.

"ToyNews—From our box to yours. Good morning!" Clive looked even perkier than usual. Spliced next to him, President Bud congratulated candidate Gar Guzmán on his wife's performance. "Gar, your Betty did one heck of a job."

Clive temporized, "The pollmeters show that Glynnis and Betsy came out even; a dead heat." The anchor nodded for emphasis. "Looks like we're in for a long, hard-fought election; a real cliffhanger." The kind ToyNews loved best. The last election had been so tight it drove Jenny's father to the blue room, trying to sort out every last stray ballot through ToyVote. Court challenges took up the next two years. Yet the Centrists had won three presidentials in a row, no matter how close.

Jenny recalled the water boiling on the hotplate. She swallowed hard. What if this were it—their last chance to turn back? She barely heard as Clive cycled through the rest of the morning news, how Congress planned to solar-plate a Nevada-sized expansion of the Death Belt, and Earth's population had declined again that year. At last she blinked him out and turned with relief to the *Orchid Times*. Someone had bred a *Trichoglottis* to look like a humming-bird. The cross diagram was a marvel, with a triple hybrid. She couldn't wait to get her Blood Star back from quarantine.

"Good morning, Jenny." Her mother's window popped open. "Did you get back to your cottage all right? No more bears?"

Jenny wished she could give her mother a hug. "No more bears. And you, back to Earth?"

"Perfecto. I just got due diligence from a hurricane start-up that needs launch fuel. Hurricane power is just the thing. Don't you have class this morning?"

"My classes have to get approved first. I have to see my advisor." In person, at her advisor's office, a quaint college custom. "Mama, I'm worried. My friends know so much more than I do."

"Didn't you win the Science Talent Search? The 'Baby Nobel,' they call it. I told you, don't let anyone put down your public school." Her mother had refused private school; the Ramos Kennedy twins had to grow up knowing their electorate.

George Ramos appeared in Iroquoia, as a smooth-chested Mohawk elder with two heron feathers in his long lock of hair. *"Nyawenha skanonh."* The Haudenosaunee greeting rolled sonorously from his lips around the ceremonial pipe.

"Good morning, Dad. 'Thanks for the gifts of life.'" The Haudenosaunee translation went out to him. If only she could be there to pat his arm, and her mother to touch up her hair.

Soledad asked, "Are you taking Dylan's class?"

"His frog seminar on Teddy Roosevelt."

"The Salt Beings," warned her father, "always spoke bitter words about the People."

"And there's Father Clare's Renaissance Art." At least two profs she knew she could talk to; a new teacher could just make her freeze. "And Life Science 101, with Sharon Abaynesh. Then there's Helen Tejedor's Cuba seminar, and Political Ideas, with Hamilton."

"**Phil Hamilton**," texted her father. "**A good man.**"

"You know Hamilton?" That was curious. She'd never heard her parents mention the politics professor.

"Learn your Cuban roots," advised Soledad. "We've got to clear out the Guzmáns and the Creep, and get Cuba purple." The "Creep" was the vice president, a secretive "ultra warrior" not seen in public since the last election. "Jenny, dear, you wouldn't miss our Aspen chalet too badly, would you? You never were much of a skier."

Jenny frowned anxiously. "Is the market that bad?"

"We've done less badly than most. *Ahora,* Colorado's no longer the swing state it used to be." They kept a home in every swing state, then decided where to vote at the last minute.

After her parents winked out, Jenny left to meet her advisor. The air breathed of fresh-mown grass, and the cardinals chirped, "What cheer, what cheer." The tree-lined carpet rolled up in the distance to Mount Gilead, where the little homes shone like rows of lollipops, and the Ohio River flowed overhead, a gleaming thread of silver across the quilt of farmlands. By her wall outside, the bear's hole had filled with water. The water shimmered in the mud, reflecting the bright gold of the south solar and the branches of the maple. Jenny frowned, puzzled. The spacehab "rained" at four in the afternoon, then again at night, on Vincenzo's schedule. Yet everywhere else was dry by now, just this one muddy dent full of water.

From her cottage, an elephant squealed. The donkey-tailed elephant had got up on the porch, its trunk sneaking some kind of treat from her *compañera* Mary, who was seated in the porch swing with her water bottle. Beyond her, two more little elephants trotted up, squealing with interest.

"Mary, *¡vaya!* Remember what the dean said."

Mary's glowing face seemed to look beyond the elephants. "What did the dean say?"

"The dean said to stay away from elephants. *Oye,* you'll just attract a whole troupe of them."

"She wants *to go* to class."

"What? Mary, elephants *nunca* go to class."

Mary thought this over. "Are we an elephant?"

"No, Mary. We are students; we go to class." Aspie or not, this Mary wouldn't last long. Then Jenny thought of her own R-patch and the mental. Caught off guard, her memory of Jordi hit her just so, flooding her with pain. How long would she last herself?

Something twined around her leg. It was the trunk of one of the elephants attracted to Mary's food. "*Vaya*—get off me!" Jenny tugged at the trunk, disgusted by its squishy feel. She had never had live pets; she'd been kept away from animals all her life. In her toybox, she blinked her "safe" button. The elephant squealed in pain at the mild electric shock.

Just then, her aunts called.

"Good morning, *sobrina*." California Governor Meg Akeda, the Centrist primary runner-up, grinned from her toybox. "Glynnis did well last night," she graciously allowed. "How's college?"

"*Chulo*, thanks, Aunt Meg."

"It seems only yesterday you were the birthday girl, showing us all the cups and balls, and the disappearing coins."

"How's the Firmament?" asked Aunt El, the other head on her aunts' shared body.

Jenny returned, "How's the Milky Way?"

Peering beyond her, Aunt El's head gasped with pretended shock. "Really, Jenny, not there a day, and already molesting elephants."

Jenny gave a pained smile and turned to the head of the governor. "Thanks, Aunt Meg. Sorry you lost the nomination." Meg had lost a close primary fight with Gar.

"That's nice of you to say so." Meg and El Akeda had no chromosome deletion, nor were they bred that way like "paulines" bred to keep quiet. Natural twins, their condition, like Jenny's mutation, was unplanned. The first conjoined person to govern a state, Meg's head stood nearly straight whereas El's jutted to the side, her hair aslant across her face. Each head controlled half their body. In a campaign commercial, they rode a bicycle down Lombard Street.

Aunt El told her sister, "She thinks you'd have been easier to beat."

"No, honest," Jenny protested.

Meg sighed. "El, I can't take you anywhere." Their standard tagline—El could say anything the governor's head couldn't. Californians loved it.

"I would have voted for you, Aunt Meg," said Jenny sincerely. "If I were Centrist." Both heads professed belief in the Firmament.

"Really," said Meg. "We may take you up on that someday."

"We sure will." El smiled. "Played your taxes yet? Or made them 'disappear'?"

Jenny was silent. President Ramos had replaced the tax system with tax-players. He was still the most popular Unity president.

"I just vetoed a bill," Meg reminded her. "It would have let someone marry a dog."

"Man's best friend," added El. President Ramos had been carnally challenged. "You see," El went on, reading Jenny's face, "you're more Centrist than you think."

"El, don't pick on our niece, or you'll get banned from Sacramento."

El rolled her eyes. "Please. Sacramento is death."

"Jenny," said Meg, "if you ever need help, remember us, okay?"

"That's right, *sobrina*," said El with a wink. "Blood is thicker than politics."

Professor Sharon Abaynesh had her office on the ground floor of the Ronald Reagan Hall of Science, beneath the outsized jelly beans. When Jenny first entered, the professor was not there. Above her desk the giant DNA spiraled upward as far as the eye could see. The desk was sprinkled with potting soil. By the desk stood a smartcart carrying Jenny's Blood Star, its red trumpets still blooming, along with the purple vanda and the vanilla. The sweet vanilla fragrance made Jenny sigh with relief.

Abaynesh came in from the laboratory, the rows of *Arabidopsis*. She wiped her hands on her jeans. "There you go," she told Jenny's orchids. "You all can go home already."

Jenny pressed the soil around the vanda. The new soil had been packed carefully around each root by someone who knew what they were doing. "Thanks for all your trouble." She spoke toward the plant, not meeting the professor's eye. It took her a while to face a new person. "I brought my course list." She blinked the list over.

The professor picked the pot of "Ari" off her chair and sat, clasping her hands, her skin as brown as the potting soil, her shirt Milena. Above her desk hung the mortarboard that Ari had pointed out, next to an MIT diploma. Like her father, Jenny thought, feeling more at home. In the side wall loomed various virtual models of plant semiochemicals, signal molecules labeled PRIDE, RELIEF, and ANGER. Each tagged a stick molecule full of carbons and nitrogens. The tag WISDOM was blank.

Ari's stalk waved again. The professor looked up as if she'd just remembered something. "I'm supposed to offer you those printout brownies. How about some baobab fruit? It's real," she assured her.

"Thank you." The baobab fruit had a thick yellow pulp. It tasted like grapefruit from another planet.

The professor's head tilted, and the braided arches of her hair twisted like DNA. "So why'd you come to Frontera?"

Jenny blinked. Why indeed? Because Frontera was safe, above any flood zone; because the school was small and protective for a brotherless *chica*; because her mother's best friend ran the place; because the slanball team was hot; and besides all that, what an adventure to live off Earth in a spacehab. She cleared her throat. "I came to study plants."

The professor nodded. "You've come to the right place." She tapped a finger absently on the edge of Ari's pot, and two leaflets leaned forward as if to examine Jenny. "Your ultra project wasn't bad," Abaynesh added. "We knew that ultraphyte genes were not DNA, but RNA." On Earth, only viruses had genes of RNA. Living cells used RNA for copies, like printout. "But how could ultraphyte RNA survive space flight, with the cosmic rays? You found the RNA-binding proteins that protect it. Quite elegant."

"Thank you, Professor." Jenny frowned. "Space flight?" The original seed was said to have drifted at random through space until it landed in Great Salt Lake.

"The first ultra picked a place on Earth salty enough to sprout. What do *you* think?" The professor gave her an unsettling stare. She added, "I won a grant to study ultra, but the college won't sign." Her gaze rose to the wall behind Jenny, the "blind wall" not shown where the office spliced a toyroom. Jenny turned to look. Half the wall was full of Great Bear slanball, coached by the professor's husband, Alan Porat. Coach Porat was also the college rabbi; Frontera staff all seemed to hold two jobs. Gazelles grazing at the Tel Aviv Zoo, tokens from Towers and Quake, and a collection of crayon drawings. The drawings looked like various plants and monsters.

"My daughter Tova drew them," said Abaynesh. "Tova loves invasive species."

"I see." A large warty frog; a Cuban tree frog, Jenny guessed, the kind that came from Cuba's remaining forest and now ate squirrels in Somers. Bulbous green cells underwater: those were sea grapes, *Caulerpa racemosa*, which had taken over California's coastal shelf. *Caulerpa* was terrestrial, although its giant complex cells resembled those of ultraphytes. Next, a monster with six crayon scrawls for legs and two long wings. "Mosquito?" Jenny recalled dengue fever all too well.

"*Aedes albopictus.* Tova drew that from a microscope; a fixed slide, of course, no live specimens allowed. The bushy sex combs—a male."

From beneath the professor's desk slid a large black snake. A toypet, Jenny thought, although it looked quite real, its stretched scales showing white in between. The toy had two heads, jutting at an angle away from each other, each flicking a red tongue.

"*Elaphe obsoleta,* black rat snake."

Jenny startled. The snake was real enough to convince her taxa link. Not a python, but still—a real snake. With two heads. *Dios mío.* Jenny's grip tightened on her chair, as the two-headed snake coiled itself around the professor's seat.

The professor leaned forward and clasped her hands. "So, your courses. You've picked all the *chulo* professors, I see. All students rank their choices, and you each get one round at a time. *Chulo* courses fill on the first round."

Jenny shook herself, looked away from the snake, and tried to answer what Abaynesh had just said. "Oh, but I picked yours first, Life Science 101."

"You can put Life last; I let in everyone. But the frog seminars are limited. You might get one if you list it first."

She thought it over. "Uncle Dylan, I mean President Chase, will save me a place."

The professor's eyes widened, appalled. "You'd pull strings?"

A misstep; she'd have to be careful. "I mean, I'll . . . list the Roosevelt seminar first, then the Renaissance Art, with Tejedor as alternate; then last, Hamilton." A lot of good that would do; it sounded like she'd get none of them. Jenny shifted uncomfortably in her chair. She'd call her mother, that's what; Soledad always fixed things, at Somers High. No, *tonta,* this was college, not high school, and family ties were not *chulo.* "So what else can I take?"

"Whatever you like—toyclasses from any affiliated university. Harvard, if you wish."

"I see." Harvard, after all. She smiled to herself. Wait till Jordi heard that. Meanwhile, the two-headed snake had wrapped itself around a chair leg and was climbing into the professor's lap.

"Your art class will cover one requirement," said Abaynesh, "and Life, another. You're running for president, aren't you? Why not Speech 101?"

Jenny shook her head. "I have a disability," she told her orchid. "I'm excused from oral reports." The professor should have it on file, but she blinked to send a copy.

"A disability? Weren't you cultured?"

"It was post-zygotic. In the embryo, a cell got a mutation on chromosome 18."

"Really." The professor sounded intrigued. "You're not perhaps a pauline?"

Speechless, Jenny stared. She could not believe the rudeness of this professor with the two-headed snake, to ask if Jenny were made a pauline like one of those Centrist wives, bred to keep quiet according to Apostle Paul.

Abaynesh stroked the snake. "Don't mind Meg and El, they won't bother you."

Jenny let out a breath. "You named the snake . . . after my aunts."

"A dozen physicians cover the governor; I interned with them. Two-headed snakes are actually common, sometimes more than one in a clutch. I'll show you my collection. Take off your diad. I don't reveal this on Toynet; too many activists."

Reluctantly Jenny peeled the diad off her forehead. Cut off from the world, stuck in an office with a professor and her two-headed snake.

The souvenir wall slid up. Behind it were tanks full of snakes: black snakes, a garter snake, a king snake. Each had two heads with varying degrees of separation, the garter had two on short necks that swung apart, whereas the king snake's two heads were fused.

"Are they . . . mutants?"

"Most are errors in development. My playmates find them in the woods, and ship them to me. A research question: What if we all had two heads?"

Jenny blinked. "I thought you studied plants."

"The plant is my model system. Before that . . ." Abaynesh turned to the wall, the light shining beneath her arched hair. On the wall was a portrait of a woman, her hair in an elegant past-century coif, her smile slightly asymmetrical, and the most expressive eyebrows Jenny had ever seen.

Jenny blinked the image through her window. "Rita Levi-Montalcini. The Nobel Prize for nerve growth."

"Precisely. Levi-Montalcini found the first protein to make nerves grow. In chick embryos. Today, we grow nerves in plants."

On her desk was the pot of *Arabidopsis sapiens*. Jenny eyed the plant warily, its little leaves erect like mouse ears. "But plants are completely different . . . from . . ."

Abaynesh waved a hand. "Animals are just plants with wanderlust. Listen: Half a billion years ago the Cambrian explosion left polycephalic fossils, three-lobed creatures with five eyes and a long snake-like nose. Why do we vertebrates have it all in one head? Ever since we evolved, we pigheaded vertebrates have messed up the world, refusing to see anything outside our single heads. But Ari, here—"

The *Arabidopsis sapiens* strained two stems forward to listen.

"Ari has a nervous system with ten or twenty flower heads. Why not us? If we had two heads—might we see two points of view? Wisdom in stereo?" She turned to Jenny as if remembering something. "You wanted research. When can you start?"

8

After lunch, Toy Land sent her course schedule. Life Science came through, as promised, and Uncle Dylan's Roosevelt seminar. No luck with Father Clare's course, nor Tejedor, though she got a Cuba survey at Harvard. To her surprise, Hamilton's Political Ideas came through, though she'd picked it last. How did that happen? Jenny wondered. Hamilton was the most popular professor. At any rate, her classes started bright and early Tuesday, with Life at seven.

She'd scarcely read the list when Kendall popped in her toybox, his long black hair floating in all directions. "Got your courses? Time for practice."

"I thought practice was two o'clock."

"Coach expects us a half hour early, warming up. Never be late. If you got your courses—as soon as kosher, get yourself up here."

Jenny complied, though she wondered about the rules. This was a small college team, not Division One.

To reach the court, Jenny climbed the cloud ladder from Buckeye Trail. As she climbed, her weight ebbed away and with it, as always, her many mental burdens lifted; the best part of slanball. Below, the college shrank away to a cluster of residences south of Wickett Hall, notably the castle with its waving purple pennant. Farther north rose the jelly-beaned globe of the Reagan Hall of Science, followed by the Spanish and arts halls. The breeze from the south freshened, on its way north to the air filter at the Mound.

A ten-minute climb, the safety nets falling away, and there hung the cage of anthrax. The cage extended eighty feet, just shy of a basketball court, a tube with two hemispherical ends, each capped with a goal. Within the cage crawled the players in their Great Bear jerseys. One launched himself to zigzag across.

As she arrived, Jenny hooked her bag to the gate and took out her microgrip shoes and her slancap. The slancap fit snugly on her head, where it amplified her brainstream to broadcast the regulation slan signal. A pickup game was in progress, five players to each side plus a goalie, launching themselves back and forth across the court. One jittered a slanball, brainstreaming it to move forward and back, while setting up to slan. Near the equatorial line, Yola aimed herself north to intercept. Yola's braids flexed unpredictably—a good distraction, Jenny thought. Invisibly Yola yanked the ball out. Then her brain focused and slanned the ball out toward the goal. Yola was the Bears' top scorer.

But at the cap zone, just before the goal, the ball deflected. The goalie, Xiang Jones, must have great "reach" of his brainstream, as well as top reflexes. The ball bounced twice off the cage, until Xiang caught it; the only position allowed to physically touch the ball. He tossed the ball back in play.

Yola waved Jenny over to replace one of the five players on her side. Jenny crouched, then leaped out into the court. The other players on the north end included Charlie Itoh and Fran Pezarkar, a junior from Mumbai. Fran's Illyrian twin David covered the south goal. Outside the court, the entire spacehab in its greenery, its patchwork farms and tiny block homes, appeared to rotate around the cage.

Charlie approached the ball, gamely ignoring his bear-torn ankle. He found himself blocked by Kendall. Kendall approached until his nose nearly brushed the ball, then it shot out across the equator to the south end. One-on-one defense. Jenny sized up the players; their teamwork looked rusty. When she saw an opening, she launched herself easily past her guard, Reesie Tsien, to intercept the ball.

The slanball gleamed silver in the light from the south solar. The trick was to let it come as close as possible without a foul, for the inverse square law meant that the closer it came, the more steeply one's power rose. *Ping*—her brainstream slanned the ball.

The ball shot over to Charlie. Charlie hesitated just too long, startled perhaps by the speed of Jenny's pass. The ball brushed his temple before he slanned it toward the goal.

"Foul," called Yola. "Charlie out, Ricky in."

Ricky Tsien launched himself in, while Charlie glided out, and Jenny landed opposite. Fran retrieved the ball and jittered it before taking a long-shot toward the goal; too tempting, Jenny thought, for most to manage. Out of nowhere, Kendall intercepted. He jittered the ball for just under the regulation three seconds, then slanned it back south, where a forward deflected it past David Pezarkar. The ball sailed into the goal.

"One point for North," called Yola.

In Jenny's toybox a window opened: Coach Porat. She looked down, slowly turning until she saw him at the ladder gate. Modest height, with compact features and crew-cut hair beneath his rabbi's cap, the coach had come to

Somers High to recruit her with his promises and penetrating questions. Jenny recalled Professor Abaynesh's wall, with all the slanball loops and the crayon drawings. And here was Tova, the five-year-old invasive enthusiast, climbing the cloud ladder with her dad.

"Line up," the coach texted.

In an instant, all the players launched themselves toward the equator. About thirty students lined up all around, twice the regulation limit for a college team. How did Coach get away with that? Jenny wondered. A couple of late arrivals hovered outside the cage, trying to get in, but apparently the gate was closed. Everyone stilled. The "ground" was too far off to hear even a bird or a frog. Then the drumbeat of the Mound powwow rumbled in her ears. It was two o'clock.

"Welcome to slanball," announced Coach Porat above the drums. "The game of mind force. Sport's highest frontier." He raised an arm. "Let's welcome all our new players. Ricky Tsien from Sacramento Country Day School, where he broke the ten-year record for goals and assists . . ." A rousing cheer for each frog; it took a while to get through them all. Then Fran and David, and the other returning players. "Now, your team captains have some things to say."

Kendall walked several steps north, his microgrips rasping with each step. Then he turned to face the students lining the equator. "Slanball is a tough game. You need your mind and body working at top capacity. 'Nothing is so dark as enslavement of the human mind.' So, rule number one: No mind-enslaving substance. Anything that takes the edge off—alcohol, stimulants, sleep loss—is out, till October break."

A few frogs looked surprised. Reese raised her hand. "You mean, before a match?"

"I mean twenty-four/seven, all the weeks we're in season. Patch test every morning. We can't have hungover kids falling out of the sky. And by the way," Ken added, "from now on, practice starts at five A.M. Great warm-up for class." Life with Abaynesh at seven; how convenient, thought Jenny.

Yola trudged out beside her brother. "Rule number two is, we have fun. Having fun means teamwork—help your fellow player. You all were stars in high school. We're a team, not a bunch of stars." The ball flew up and jittered above her head. "And in October we take a break from it all for King Mark's Feast of Fools—at Castle Cockaigne."

"*El castillo mysterioso,*" someone texted. "**Orgies with knights in armor.**"

Outside, in a safety harness, Tova was slanning balls into the cage, one for each player. Each player zigzagged across the cage, jittering the ball, keeping possession for just under three seconds, then slanned it across the court. Yola slanned fastest, although Charlie did better now that he relaxed. All balls eventually reached the far end, though none came near the goal; they'd need a forward to shove it in. The breeze freshened, tugging Jenny's hair; she calculated the compensation factor. She launched her ball straight to the goal, though not as fast as Yola.

The players drilled, one ball after another. Meanwhile Coach Porat drifted casually along the equator, making a private comment now and then. When he reached Jenny, he planted his feet on the cage and stayed for the next five minutes, watching her slan after slan. Feeling nervous, she stopped. "Hello, Coach."

"Jenny Ramos," the coach said aloud. "What's keeping you?"

Surprised, Jenny's lips parted and she stared. What was wrong?

Seeing something was up, Yola came over. "Jenny's good," she said. "A good team player."

"Too good." The coach nodded. "Jenny, we had a good talk back in Somers last year, didn't we?"

She nodded.

"Can you tell us: What is the job of every player?"

Her throat dried up. "To do your best," she texted. "To be the best player you can be."

"That's right. Go do that, now. Or you're off the team."

Yola stared in surprise. "Coach, what's up? It's her first day."

Jenny stared without seeing, her heart pounding. Shock, and anger, and above all turmoil inside; what to do . . . She looked back over her shoulder, but Jordi wasn't there. Nobody would disrespect her like that in front of Jordi. Jenny paused a moment, then trudged slowly along the equator, past the players jittering their slanballs. As she approached Kendall, she paused. Ken's jaw was set fierce with concentration, his hair streaming around, while the slanball hung before him, moving ever so slightly.

The ball shot out. It sailed forever, past the quarter line and the goal zone. It did not stop in the goal zone but flew straight into the goal.

The players cheered and hugged Kendall.

"What the—" Kendall shook his head. "I did nothing."

"Sure you did," said the coach. "Time out. Ken, Yola, Jenny—All of you, over here."

An umbrella-like shelter ballooned out of the cage. The players floated inside with the coach. "Caps off, bands and diads too. Other teams scout us," Porat explained.

Yola nodded. "Tourists in Mount Gilead; it's easy enough."

"Who did it?" demanded Kendall. "Who's the sleeper?"

"Ask Jenny."

Jenny looked away.

"You did it all those years," said the coach more softly. "Your team must have known, but no one let on."

Kendall's eyes widened. "You mean all those goals that Jordi Ramos—"

Yola elbowed him. "Shush, Kennie-boy. Hey, Jordi was the greatest."

Jenny had started young, at her father's knee, before most people even heard of brainstream. Kids who started young overtrained certain parts of the brain. Nowadays, at Tova's age they all did, but in Jenny's cohort, her brainstream ranked two standard deviations above average. She could brush past Jordi, and no one could tell who'd slanned the ball. It was common for a new player to slan for a forward, the first couple of games, until opponents caught on. But Jenny and Jordi were such a tight pair, and Jordi was a natural star; for years they'd played as one, like her aunts on the bicycle, and nobody cared to know.

"Jordi is still the all-time great," Coach promised. "None of those records will change. But now it's our turn. Jenny, we need you." He paused to let her think. "Suppose you go ahead and slan for Ken."

"What?" exclaimed Kendall. "No way I'll take credit for a frog's slan."

"Just for now. Just till we play Whitcomb. Their goalie, remember, is impossible; he gave up no goal for three games straight."

"Hey, this trick's in the playbook," said Yola. "Play number twenty-nine. Why not? A great idea—really throw off those Centrist suckers."

"Then she can slan for you," said Kendall.

"Fine with me," said Yola. "I'll be the 'star' for the next two games. What a hoot."

Coach shook his head. "Yola slans hard enough already."

The players held their breath and looked away. Kendall's brainstream ranked below average; his strength was defense, where he took more hits than any other player.

Jenny swallowed. "I'll do it. For the team."

"That's the spirit, Jenny," said Coach. "We'll have to practice that move in secret. The first couple of games, you go in once or twice and nail the goal for Ken—not too often to raise suspicion. But if we pull it off, then for Whitcomb you'll go in and slan for yourself. To shake the devil into them. Understand?"

✦✦

To avoid the cafeteria, Jenny tried the Ohioana Country Diner, a Mount Gilead franchise just north of Wickett. A twelve-point buck loomed over the dimly lit table, a slab of wood with genuine splinters. Colonists in power bands served up sliced turkey covered with gravy, with tomatoes actually grown in the spacehab. Students crowded around, knocking elbows, and voices could barely be heard.

Anouk tried the salad, with a nod of approval. "Life at seven—see you there, *chérie*." She added thoughtfully, "President Chase—he's not bad, for an American. As for Hamilton—" Her eyes rolled, and her perfectly spaced fingers spread dramatically. "Hamilton thinks the sky is a ceiling," she whispered condescendingly. "It's a Christian thing." The Firmament movement had begun at Whitcomb, based on Genesis: "And God made the firmament . . . and called the firmament Heaven." But the notion had since spread from Christians to conservative sects of Moslems, Hindus, even Wiccans.

How did Anouk know all Jenny's courses? Jenny had raised her toyguard to the highest level, but Anouk seemed to know everything.

"Of course, all my math courses are at MIT. The grad school," Anouk emphasized.

Jenny wondered again why Anouk had come to Frontera. At her right sat Yola, squeezed in with Kendall, who ordered plankton stew. A "microvore," Ken never ate plants, let alone animals. Next to Ken sat Charlie, while Mary showed up at the far end. Mary had only her water bottle and a bowl of pretzels.

On the windowsill perched one of those blue-tailed lizards, trying to consume a beetle. The lizard kept biting and swallowing; its teeth were dull.

"A lizard—indoors," someone exclaimed.

Charlie shot his arm forward and snatched at the lizard. He caught it by the tail, but the blue tail came away in his hand and fell to the table, still writhing.

"Ooh, how gross!" A student squealed and backed away.

Yola shook her head. "The tail will grow back."

Reesie yawned. "August seems awfully early. Couldn't classes wait till Labor Day?" Ricky was out at rush with the motor clubs. "The no drinks thing, when does that start?"

"Yesterday," said Yola. "From now till mid-season. See you at five in the morning."

Kendall nodded sagely, chewing a yeast cake. "'When your opponent rises against you in the morning, rise up and get him first.'"

"*Hombre*," muttered Reesie. "My school had no such rule, and we won the league title."

Charlie seemed more relaxed since the slanball workout. "Jenny, you sure slan hard. Where'd you train?"

"At Towers." Two weeks for slan camp every summer, then the Somers PTA funded the team travel to New York's spacehab. It was *chulo*, training in view of the storied towers as they collapsed and grew back every day. At night, you could take in a symphony or a show from Up-Broadway. Jenny turned to Anouk. "Could you join me at the Bulls pig roast Wednesday night? I won't drink, but I'll need to stop by." To support the Unity voters drive.

"I'll neither drink nor eat," Anouk emphasized. "But of course, I'll accompany you." She patted Jenny's arm. "And Berthe will stand by."

The DIRG. Jenny's heart sank; she wished she hadn't asked. Meanwhile, her head was spinning over all the day's events. The Life prof with her two-headed snake, and the coach who'd found her out. Nobody had challenged the Jordi-Jenny combo, all those years. And now—she had to find Jordi.

✦

In her sitting room, the printer had formed a delicate pink rose in a vase. It was from Charlie. Jenny smiled; a good-hearted *chico*, but she wouldn't encourage him too much. She went upstairs to check her orchids, now installed in their new home. The vanilla smelled sweet, and the Blood Star's white petals spread from the red trumpets. She brainstreamed the mister to set its timer. The mister began to spray; she moved the vanda closer. The vanda even had new buds opening—that Abaynesh must have done something right.

She headed downstairs to the toyroom. The toyroom closed around her, cutting out the nightly racket from the spring peepers. The tree house appeared, Jenny's default world, with the eight doors placed all around. She could not call up Jordi straight off; that would draw her mental right away. She stepped forward and opened one of the doors. "China."

Eight new doors appeared—Beijing, Shanghai, Guangjou. Shanghai offered a long virtual tour; she went in, zigzagging amid the early-morning crowds on Nanjing Road. She lost herself amongst the tall bright-lettered signs, the shoppers loaded with shoes, chickens, and sewing-bots, the commuters trudging to work; the scent of juniper and peonies and crispy rice cakes, and of the sea from beyond the world's tallest seawall. Above all, the acrid odor of newly poured carboxyplast from the factories that had packed carbon dioxide to build Frontera's shell.

After jogging for some minutes past signs and shoppers, she called back the doors. The doors now shone as eight blue outlines hovering in virtual space.

"Entertainment—Strings." The doors opened to eight different stringed instruments, the two-stringed *erhu*, the *guqin* zither, the *pipa* lute. The lute door opened virtual seating for a concert in Hubei, seven performers in pink robes with bright-colored sashes. Then eight doors to concert programs in eight different countries: the Vienna Symphony, the Sydney Opera, the São Paulo Symphony. No sign of her mental; hopefully the virtual team of therapists would lag a few doors behind. The São Paulo Symphony had an oboist from New York. The New York oboist had once performed in Somers, a chamber concert in Bailey Park. A door to Bailey Park opened the Somers Historical Society archive. Jenny plowed through town governance minutes on child safety, kudzu control, and the summer concert series. The events calendar included speeches and rallies from the midterm election. The final door opened.

There stood Jordi's sim, like Newman or Monroe for the toyflicks, only so much more accurate, since practically every moment of Jordi's life had been recorded. Jordi was there for all the public to "meet and greet," at a Unity rally in Bailey Park, the summer before senior year. Morning light glinted off random kudzu leaves, streaked by a laser to cut back the day's growth from the white gazebo. Beneath the roof hung a white placard, Hachaliah Bailey Memorial, flanked by two elephant silhouettes. Jordi leaned over the white picket fence rail between the columns, and faced the surrounding crowd in their folding chairs.

"And so I say to you, from my generations of family service to this nation: No matter how dark the hour, no matter how late the moment of truth, it is better to light a candle than curse the darkness. Just as we chose to bury our carbon in carboxyplast, we can choose now. We can choose to save our water and shrink the Death Belt. We can choose to build ships to Jupiter, a boundless source of fuel." Hydrogen planet—the ultimate gas tank.

The cheers of the crowd threatened to drown his voice. Jordi spoke quietly, and the crowd quieted again. "We must make our sacrifice now, not wait until the menace of global drought appears. If we hesitate, it will be too late." He took a breath. "We all breathe the same air. We all cherish our children's future. And we all are mortal."

The crowd erupted from their seats. Purple balloons, hats, and TO JUPITER—AND BEYOND! signs flew into the air. Then gradually the crowd faded away, into history. Only Jordi remained, the archival Jordi, in his starched white suit leaning over the white fence rail. The Jordi Ramos Kennedy who lived on forever in the Toynet archive.

Jenny came forward, her heart beating too fast. Seeing her, Jordi smiled, the old smile that used to say, "It was all for you." His features had that square Mount Rushmore look, like his grandfather's; his eyes expressive though just a bit flat, already the seasoned pol. "How'd I do, sis?"

"Fantastic, as always." She swallowed. "The Jupiter line always drives them wild."

"Jupiter. We'll get there," he said with the trademark Jordi conviction. "It won't be easy."

"It will be hard. It was hard enough for me, going to . . ." She mustn't mention Frontera; Jordi hadn't lived to know about that, and if he'd lived she wouldn't be here. "Jordi, I'm taking a Harvard course. About Cuba."

He grinned. "That beats Somers High, I'm sure. I'm off to Havana next week; you can draw up my talking points."

"Jordi—I have to ask you something." Her voice rushed on; the mental could crash through any moment. "Coach wants me to assist someone else; another . . . team captain. Do you mind?"

"Another captain . . . not sure what you're driving at, but of course, whatever Coach says goes. You know that."

"Yeah, I do." She'd known he would say that, but still she needed to hear it.

"You're the best operative there is." His eye glinted. "Today, the Somers town board. Tomorrow, the universe."

"Yeah." She looked away. "The week after, in New York. I'll be there with you."

"Of course you will. I have this new angle I want to try out on you; my plan for inner-city education."

"Although I wish you wouldn't go at all, Jordi . . . not to Battery Park."

Jordi froze. The entire landscape froze, the kudzu leaves, the shadow flickering across the fence rail. The scene faded away. In its place was the giant up-close face of Monroe, taking up the entire toyroom. The six-foot-wide lips pouted in displeasure.

Jenny screamed. She extended both arms straight to touch the walls. The walls turned gray, and she rushed out the door. Tearing across the hall, she raced into the living room and pulled the diad off her forehead. The room was dark and still, the only sound her frantic breathing.

But it was too late. The printer glowed, the unearthly glow of a processor working overtime. An object pushed slowly up from the glow, the top of a head. The head of a DIRG, printing out with the face of her dreaded mental.

Jenny caught her face in her hands. "¡Vaya! Get out, or I'll—" From her desk drawer she pulled a scissors. "I'll slit my wrist."

"That is why you need me." The chin of the DIRG had just cleared the printer. Already the Monroe was moving, talking to her in its ghastly way. "After viewing the sim of your deceased brother, you always try to harm yourself."

"Not this time."

"This cottage was built to meet your needs. We need to keep you safe."

The scissors softened and melted in an amyloid puddle. The whole room was amyloid, she realized. What if the power failed, and it melted around her? "I'll quit college and go wait tables."

"That would be a healthy choice, Jenny. In fact, we recommended that choice to your parents: Why not let her wait a year?"

"I'll go live with my aunts." Slapping the diad back on her forehead, Jenny blinked frantically to Sacramento.

The DIRG stopped at the waist, half emerged from the printer. "Really, Jenny." The Monroe half pouted, half smiled. "You'd go help elect Aunt Meg? Who doesn't believe in the universe?"

"She doesn't believe in mentals either."

Now the mental was stuck. Jenny was of age; she could go where she liked, even live with her Centrist aunts. Her mother would not stop her, would avoid a family row, but would vent her rage on the therapists. Jenny envisioned the entire team of them now, holding an emergency session, debating what to do about the troubled Ramos Kennedy *chica*. "It's our job to keep you alive," the mental said at last. "One way or another."

"I didn't hurt myself."

"We didn't give you the chance."

"I did nothing wrong."

"You know you're not to revisit your deceased brother's sim. You signed your outpatient behavior contract."

Jenny was silent. She'd crossed her fingers on that one.

"We'll give you one more chance. Remember, if you do harm yourself, it's a trip back to the blue room." The cuckoo's nest. The horror ward she'd spent a month in.

9

At seven in the morning, munching amyloid toast after slanball, Jenny rushed to the toyroom for her first Tuesday class. The eight doors of her tree house spliced out to eight different students. Above and below were more rows of eight; she lost count. Most were set to a standard style, like hers. Charlie had the "little red schoolhouse" setting. He shared his toyroom with another *chico* who lacked a nose ring, tall with whipcord muscles. As tall as Jenny herself, she vaguely thought she'd seen him before. At her left appeared Anouk. Anouk's toyroom was all black-and-white checkerboard; she must have made a fancy custom design that took extra time to splice. At last Anouk's design came in, a multicolored tangle of numbered ribbons. **"Series World. Enter at Your Own Risk."**

In the middle, surrounded by the eight rooms, an endless cylinder rose from the depths to the heavens. The students exchanged uncertain looks. "What do you think?" muttered Charlie to his neighbor.

Anouk stepped forward, her eyebrows arched, the very portrait of nonchalance. As she reached the cylinder, she vanished.

Charlie took a sharp breath. In the circle above, another student stepped forward. Jenny figured, with time-honored classroom logic, that peers who seemed to know what they were doing probably did. Heart pounding, she stepped forward into the cylinder.

Within the cylinder, all the spliced toyrooms fell away. All around stretched a vast windswept savannah. The grass was dotted with dark scrub by the side of a lake. Before the lake rose a tall misshapen tree. The tree had a huge bottle-shaped trunk topped by branches extending at right angles. A baobab, *Adansonia digitata*. Beside the tree stood Professor Abaynesh.

A light breeze lifted a torn flap of the professor's jeans. All around her, various students winked in one by one, about forty *chicas* and *chicos* in their svelte tops and trailing laces. Seeing the landscape, Jenny slapped on virtual hiking boots.

"Welcome to Life 101." Abaynesh raised her arm and made a horizontal sweep. "Human life as we know it began here. Here on the Central African plain, amid the baobabs, something happened to DNA—the DNA of certain inquisitive apes. From these inquisitive mutants evolved the one being in the universe that can read its own DNA."

Was that true? Jenny wondered. Might there be other DNA readers out there? She wondered about that other biosphere somewhere across the stars, the one ultraphytes came from.

Abaynesh turned toward the tree. "The baobab has its own DNA, as do the scrub grass and the fish in the lake. What separates us all from our common ancestor is just a few billion years of mutants." As an afterthought, she looked over her shoulder and around at all the students. "Come along."

At the base of the baobab was a dark opening. The professor went inside. Anouk immediately went after, and other students dutifully followed.

Inside the tree, a gigantic double helix extended to the heavens and down into the deep. The "atoms" were colored spheres the size of a slanball. Around the atoms, students stumbled, trying to figure out what they were standing on, if anything.

Abaynesh tapped an oxygen atom of a phosphate. "You all remember the phosphates in the DNA backbone," she told them. "Remember their negative charge. They're sticky. See?"

Jenny touched a phosphate oxygen atom. The red sphere stuck to her hand like a magnet.

"The backbone phosphates connect to what?"

The professor's first question, in their first college class. Everyone straightened and tried to look as though, of course *they* knew the answer but they weren't going to rob someone else of the chance to give it.

"Phosphate connects to a five-carbon sugar." Anouk made her own model sugar appear, twirling between her hands.

"Thanks, Anouk. Sugar, phosphate, sugar. Now the sugars hold the base pairs, the 'steps' of DNA." The professor climbed up over a phosphate and sat upon the round, black carbon atoms of the base pair. "There are four kinds of base pairs, making the four 'letters' of the DNA code."

A student's light blinked. It was the tall *chico* sharing Charlie's toyroom. His name read TOM YODER. He said, "Aren't there just two kinds of base pairs?"

Contradicting the professor. The other students, clinging to "sticky" phosphates, wondered what kind of inferior school this *chico* came from that he would miss something so basic and contradict the teacher on the first day of class. No one would dare help out with an answer, lest they reveal that they too came from such an inferior school.

Anouk said in a bored tone, "There are lots of kinds of bases. RNA has uracil and inosine."

"Thanks, Anouk," said the professor, "you may bring that up when we visit RNA."

Jenny sent Tom a private text. **"Each base pair can face up or down."**

"That's right, Jenny," announced the professor at large. "If you take apart the DNA . . ."

Jenny's stomach squeezed. Her message wasn't so private as she thought. The teacher watched everyone.

". . . you find only two kinds of base pair, AT and GC. But if you string them together in a duplex, they can face either way. So the DNA code has four letters." The professor lifted her arms and slid down a "step." "Now we'll slide all the way down, reading the bases along one strand as we go. See how fast you can read A, T, C, G . . ."

Jenny stepped cautiously up onto a nitrogen of the base pair. The blue sphere of nitrogen was slippery, not at all sticky like the phosphate. Someone collided from behind; she found herself sliding even faster downward in the spiral. She fought the instinct to reach out and halt the toyroom; it couldn't be as bad as it felt, it had to end sometime. All around her students were sliding down the spiral, some with looks of terror, others clutching their stomachs.

She landed with a bump at the bottom, a plain floor. She hurried to crawl out of the way, before someone's image collapsed with her own. Charlie was sitting on the floor, his face white. Half the original students were missing; they had probably stopped their toyrooms and transferred to toyHarvard.

"Before you leave," called the professor, "here's your homework."

A coin appeared in Jenny's toybox.

"Review these three Nobel-winning experiments and come to class Thursday prepared to conduct them."

Someone extended Jenny a hand. It was Tom Yoder, the *chico* who had asked the question. "You okay?"

She touched his hand, though her fingers felt only brainstreamed toy-force. She got up and faced him. Tom was just her height; their eyes met level. Blue eyes, a plain Euro face with no hint of fashion, yet there was something familiar about him.

"A, T, T, G, C," announced Anouk from behind as she sedately slid to the floor. "Just keep your hands on the sticky phosphates to control your speed."

Then Jenny recalled: The *chico* who'd given her his shirt for a pillow for Charlie, that night on the powwow ground after the bear attack. He'd looked *chulo* with his shirt off.

✦

Returning to her cottage, Jenny paused. The bear gash was still full of muddy water. She wondered where the water came from, since the rain was so light and everything else was dry. Could there be a break in the water line? She'd noticed bits of maintenance that went undone, and no lasers trimmed the grass. The college appeared to skimp on landscaping.

In the sitting room, her *compañera* had yet to add anything to the décor. She noticed Mary's bedroom door ajar. "Mary?" For safety, she should check, she told herself. She stepped inside.

The walls were bare as the day the students had moved in. "Mary?" Still no sign of luggage, only the bed with a bare mattress. On the windowsill was a bowl full of pearls, and on the floor a large box of pretzels. The giant aquarium bubbled, and light banks glowed purple overhead. But no sign of fish, nor of plants. Just sand with brownish scum. Poor Mary, she still had not got her fish back from quarantine. Around the tank was a crust of sea salt; a marine aquarium.

A window popped up, the dean of students, Nora Kwon. Jenny stumbled and rushed out of Mary's room, closing the door behind her.

"Jenny?" Dean Kwon sounded solicitous, fully in control of everything for eight hundred students. "I'm just checking in with you, to see how things went, your first day of class."

"No problem, thanks." Jenny added, "The birds are beautiful."

"We're so proud of our birds. If you put up a sugar bottle, you'll draw hummingbirds."

"*Guao.*" She ought to tell the dean about Mary, she thought, but what could she say? They must know what a mess the *chica* was.

"No problems with the grav? No headaches or balance trouble?"

"No, I've trained for years in micrograv." Then she remembered. "There is this puddle outside that won't go away."

"Must be a leak in the water line. Maintenance will get right on it." The dean nodded smartly. "Anything else, just let us know, okay?"

✦

After lunch was her next class, President Chase's history seminar. The frogs-only seminar met in a square room with amyloid wood panels and a toywall at one end. Jenny brought her Blood Star orchid and set the pot before her on the polished seminar table. The amyloid chairs around the table were just comfy enough to relax, but not fall asleep. Uncle Dylan towered over most of the students, greeting each with a handshake. "Reesie, from Sacramento—your team won the league tournament, didn't you? Congratulations! Charlie, camp counselor at the Minneapolis Camp for the Junior Blind? A growing population, alas; so inspiring of you. And Jenny—the international science fair winner, here saving lives for us! Such an honor!" He tapped her flowerpot gracefully.

Jenny smiled, trying not to laugh. Somehow he would always sound like that; he made everybody feel he was their "Uncle Dylan."

"Please—have a seat anywhere, put your feet up." Uncle Dylan wore a rumpled brown jacket with patched elbows. Two *chicos* wore suit and tie, Ferrari-rushed frogs with twenty-four-carat double-X earrings who weren't about to put their feet up anywhere. Others included Charlie, Reesie, and Ricky, but not Tom. Just fifteen in all—Jenny was indeed lucky to get in.

"If a nation may be known by the mark of its greatest leaders, as indeed it may, and by the courage and compassion of its grandest statesmen, as indeed it shall, then to know Teddy Roosevelt, the twenty-sixth president of the United States, is to know America. In the year 1901, Roosevelt was inaugurated after an assassin's bullet. The youngest president ever— 'A very heavy weight,' the press observed, 'for anyone so young as he.' "

Uncle Dylan looked around the table, giving each frog an earnest look in turn. "Roosevelt became our first 'modern' president, the first president to cross the whole country meeting fellow Americans, who reelected him with one of the widest margins. Our first 'imperial president,' the best herder of emperors since Napoleon. Won the Nobel Peace Prize. He conquered—and conserved—the West, a territory then as treacherous as our high frontier seems now. The most national parks to his name; and the most bears bagged by his own rifle."

Dylan shrugged. "But you're not here to listen to me. You're here to ask questions—to think for yourselves. So let's meet the great man in person."

The toywall filled with light; Jenny covered her eyes. She breathed the sour salt smell of the sea. The sea; where her brother had vanished. Her grip tightened on the pot of her orchid.

As her eyes adjusted, a grassy slope rose up to a house with steep rooftops fronted by a broad porch. Roosevelt's "summer White House" in Oyster

Bay. Inside, there was some kind of commotion. A door banged open and a man in a black frock coat ran out onto the porch. Short as a Mount Gilead colonist, and rather stout, he bounded over the porch rail and ran halfway down the slope. Teddy Roosevelt's fierce eyes behind pince-nez glared at the class. "How the devil did you fellows get here?"

From the left, a much larger man appeared and aimed a rifle at the class. Jenny involuntarily shoved her chair backward.

"Never mind, Big Bill." Roosevelt waved the guard aside, though he patted a gun butt protruding from his own holster. "Can't imagine how you all missed the tripwire—it foiled even the dowagers from the Oyster Bay Needlework Guild." He grinned. "So you're those reporters come all the way from our great 'frontier.'" He emphasized the word. "Here this morning to interview me at my summer home. *Dee*-lighted to see you all. Just don't call this campaigning." He smiled mischievously. "A president doesn't campaign for himself—that's for the Republican National Committee. So—fire away."

No one said a word.

"What do you gentlemen know about the 'frontier'? Did you ever sleep beneath sequoias, a cathedral more majestic than any built by the hands of man? Did you ever wake upon a glacier and find yourself buried beneath four inches of snow? Did you ever feel a bear's hot breath on your face before you dispatched it?"

A student raised a tentative hand. "I once shot a sixteen-point buck."

Roosevelt waved an arm dismissively, and his coat fluttered. "Bears are different. Now, there are savage bears and cowardly ones, just as there are large and small ones. And sometimes bears of one district will have a code of conduct which differs utterly from that of bears in another district. You must read my book on the subject."

"Mr. President," asked Reesie, "what do you think of conservation?"

Roosevelt jumped with excitement, and his boots dug deep in the muddy grass. "The conservation of our forests is a primary duty of our great Republic—the mightiest Republic on which the sun has ever shone. You can build a prosperous home by destroying a forest—but you cannot keep it. Woodlands and grasslands prevent flood waste and provide irrigation, that we may raise the crops for such modest repasts as our family breakfast." Behind him, servants were setting a lavish table. Odors wafted over: roast chicken and fresh bread, soon followed by plates of potatoes, asparagus, fruits, and berries with pitchers of cream. A child cried out and toddled across the porch after some small animal.

"Besides," Roosevelt observed in a voice barely audible, "we shall not turn into shingles a tree which was old when the first Egyptian conqueror reached the Euphrates. Pray the people don't realize just how much land I've put away for their grandchildren."

"Mr. President," called one of the suit-and-tie *chicos*. "What do you think of the five-to-four decision on the Northern Securities case?"

Roosevelt's eyes flashed. "It ought to have been six! That Justice Holmes—I could carve out of a banana a justice with more backbone." With difficulty he restrained himself. "The Northern Securities case is one of the greatest achievements of my administration. Monopoly must be crushed. Absolute monopoly is the death of freedom, whether Standard Oil or Tobacco Trust. Remember that, gentlemen, long after I'm gone."

Toynet, thought Jenny with a twinge of unease. She'd heard the word "monopoly" whispered now and then, always out of earshot of her father. But she had a question of her own, one she knew would needle Uncle Dylan. "Mr. President, what do you think of native Americans?"

"Americans are the world's greatest nation," said Roosevelt. "We Americans are one native people, not a hodgepodge of foreign nationalities. We must insist upon a single nationality, one flag, one language, one set of national ideals. We must all of us be Americans—and nothing but Americans."

"I mean, the Indians?"

He shook his head. "Much sentimental nonsense has been talked about our taking land from the Indians. The Indians never had real ownership. Where the game was plenty, there they hunted, until the game moved off, or until they left to butcher some other people. No doubt wrongs have been done; but now, we must treat the Indians with understanding and firmness, until they become citizens. Each Indian is an individual, like ourselves."

Jenny hid her smile. She glanced sideways at Charlie, who was clasping and unclasping his hands. She texted, "**Go ahead; ask.**"

Blinking rapidly, Charlie half raised his arm. "How do you like being president? I mean, are you happy?"

The suit-and-tie *chicos* rolled their eyes, exchanging looks of disdain for such a simple-minded question.

Roosevelt laughed in a paternal way. "Indeed, although the weight of this great office is enough to sober any man, I've been happy. A small, shallow soul can obtain the bridge-club standard of happiness; but if you are to have great happiness, you must face the risks, overcome every obstacle and trample it underfoot. I could say I've been happy as a king; in fact, I've been infinitely happier than any of the kings I know, poor devils!" He turned toward the porch, where a young woman in blue silk walked sedately down the hill. "And I'll be a damn sight happier when I've had breakfast. Alice, dear, have you come to charm the reporters?"

Alice stepped in front of her father. Her young face held a beauty like porcelain, her nose and chin lifted as though she'd never seen the ground. Her silk flowed into her cinched waist like a waterfall down to her feet. She planted her left fist on her hip and raised her right arm, the sleeve falling wide. "Gentlemen, as you know, I am more interested in my father's political career than anything in the world." Out of her right sleeve crawled something green. A green snake, flicking its tongue and twining around her wrist. The green snake caught the silk of her bodice and slithered up her breast to her neck.

At the end of class, Jenny lingered after most of the students had hurried out. Drums reverberated from the daily powwow at the Mound. Uncle Dylan had managed to draw out Charlie, nodding understandingly.

"I don't know how I got into Frontera," Charlie confided. "I never even heard of Northern Securities. My last class on government was tenth grade. I must have got in by mistake."

Uncle Dylan patted him on the back. "Now Charlie, I know you belong here. How do I know? I know, because our admissions director, Luis Herrera Smith, is the finest admissions officer in the country. Luis personally selected you, based on your outstanding qualifications—and he never, ever makes a mistake. So that's how I know, Charlie, that you belong here, at Frontera."

After Charlie left, he at last turned to Jenny. "So how'd I do? B plus?"

"Chulo." She asked curiously, "Was that true, about the snake?"

"The Roosevelt children had all kinds of pets. Snakes, rabbits, dogs, a raccoon, even a badger." Uncle Dylan had never shown that part in her mother's house. "You do understand, about the Indians?" he added anxiously.

"Sure." She half smiled, recalling the time her father got so worked up at Teddy it took his mental all night to calm him. "Roosevelt never knew about the smallpox and all."

"He knew. It made no difference."

"What do you think? About what he said?"

Uncle Dylan looked down thoughtfully. "With any one person, Teddy would be absolutely right. All that matters is two souls touching. But as a leader of a hundred million souls . . . does that always work, do you think?"

Jenny did not answer. Her heart pounded faster. "There's something else . . . I think about." She swallowed. "The smallpox, how it spread among the natives ahead of the colonists. Thousands died before they ever saw white men."

"Yes."

"What if . . . today . . . that's ultra? What if ultra is like smallpox—just the edge of something bigger?"

"Jenny," he sighed. "Teddy was twice your age when he became president. You don't need to save the world right now. You have time to be yourself at Frontera."

Jenny hadn't gotten the art class, but still, she could stop by the chaplain's office and check about the Sunday service. She hesitated just a moment outside his door, recalling his benediction: *". . . all of us, however great or low, are creatures of time."* The door opened.

Father Clare had the lanky Appalachian build of someone who'd spent countless hours hammering nails into studs. Jenny knew him as Uncle Dylan's relatively reserved spouse, who generally spoke little at fundraisers but retreated to a corner texting with her father. Here he sat in his black vestments, before a full-size floodlit replica of Michelangelo's *Pietà*. The white marble Christ, limp as a drowned youth, head fallen back, legs hung over his mother's marble knees.

Jenny stared, transfixed. Jordi—the view of Jordi she would never see, the body forever lost. For a moment she blacked out. Then she was aware. The chaplain's face was very near hers, the large blue eyes.

"I—I'm sorry," Jenny stammered. "They never let me—that is, I just don't want to call the mental." The dead Christ in his office, for goodness' sake. "More Roman than Anglican," her mother would say.

"No mentals here," Father Clare told her. "My office is a mental-free zone."

"What? Why?"

"In case a mental goes bad, you have somewhere to go."

She blinked, disconcerted. A mental gone bad—one more thing to worry about. She glanced furtively at the marble.

"You can touch it."

There was a thought. She took a step toward the statue and tentatively brushed the fingers of Mary's outstretched left hand. Cool, solid amyloid, just a sculpture. Mary, sculpted tall as Jenny, looked down upon her fallen son with infinite repose. So young a face, she seemed more his sister.

Recovering her manners, Jenny turned to the chaplain. "I tried to take your class," she told him apologetically. "I didn't get in."

"That's all right. Better luck for next year." On his desk lay the *Book of Reconciled Prayer*, and another curious book that was dog-eared and blackened as if by fire. "Jenny, before you go on, I have a task for each visitor."

Off to the side, a table held a vast jigsaw puzzle. The pattern looked vaguely abstract; she could not make it out. Above the puzzle rose shelves full of pieces, sorted by colors: reds, yellows, greens.

"Please place one piece. Any piece you like."

Jenny took a closer look at the puzzle. "The pieces," she said carefully, not wishing to sound impolite. "They don't all fit."

"None of them fit. They come from hundreds of different puzzles."

"But—" She picked up a piece tentatively. "There are holes showing through. And some look . . ."

"Shoved in." Father Clare smiled broadly, and Jenny noticed that his teeth were imperfect. Random-bred, raised in Appalachia. "Life takes a lot of shoving."

Suddenly Jenny felt uncomfortable, impatient. A brownish section showed some holes; she picked up a piece and placed it indifferently.

"Thanks so much, Jenny," he said, as if she had made his day. "So what can I do for you?"

"I was wondering about the Sunday service. What time does it start? Does the sanctuary need flowers?"

"Sundays at eleven, and yes, we always appreciate flowers. We also appreciate help with Homefair."

"Homefair, yes, that's such a good program." Hammering nails wasn't exactly her thing. "Are there 'homeless' here, in the spacehab?"

"Homeless on Earth. Homefair is for would-be colonists who can't afford amyloid. All amyloid homes have a monthly maintenance fee."

"And if you miss the fee?"

The chaplain's lip curved. "If you miss a payment, your home melts down."

"*¡Oye!*" Like the melting scissors.

"Homefair builds homes of carboxyplast, sequestered carbon dioxide, like the shell of the hab. Once built, carboxyplast lasts forever. If you're interested, we meet at Wickett every Saturday morning, at the pound-a-peg door."

"I already volunteered for EMS." She'd filed Yola's forms for the squad but hadn't yet heard. "Well, I have to go now; I have Life work." As Jenny reached the door, she stopped.

"What else?" he asked. "What is it you need to know?"

"I was wondering if . . ." A mental-free zone, he'd said. "Father Clare . . . do you really believe Jordi is up in heaven, now, looking down at us?"

The chaplain clasped his hands and leaned forward on the desk. "Jordi is now outside of time. He is out there, along with your grandfather, and your great-grandmother. And so are all your descendents, your unborn children who will die in their time. They're all out there, all pulling for you, Jenny."

The north solar cast its crimson south, lighting up the ring of Ohio River, as Jenny walked north to her cottage to freshen up before meeting Anouk for supper. She hoped Tom might show up at the Ohioana, though she wasn't about to call him.

"ToyNews—From our box to yours." Clive floated above Cross River Reservoir, a kudzu-lined lake near Somers. "Ultraphyte poisons have now reached Cross River, the major water supply for New York City. A dozen people sickened before the reservoir was closed for all drinking, boating, or swimming . . ." Jenny frowned. Ultraphytes never lived in fresh water; it must be human pollution. It was too easy to blame everything on ultra. Still, she hoped her parents had kept the cellar stocked with bottled water. And their plot of land on Frontera.

Something pricked Jenny's arm, an insistent itch. Instinctively she slapped the arm. As her hand came away, there lay a long-legged insect, crushed but still recognizable. She gasped with shock. Dengue and malaria—anyone from Somers could recognize a mosquito.

10

President Chase sat at his desk in the executive conference toyroom. "*Gracias*, Nick," Dylan sighed to his assistant who brought him his coffee with Quade's latest report. A sandy-haired Newman-chinned senior, Nick Petherbridge epitomized the Board's image of a happy alumnus, well educated, well mentaled, and largely unscathed by terrestrial misfortunes. "And could you please get out this letter to Homeworld Security?" Homeworld Security had just announced a plan to scale back their Kessler debris surveillance. For the solarray, a few collectors knocked out would only slightly degrade performance. But Frontera—it wouldn't take much of an old rocket chunk to crack the hab.

The coffee helped Dylan focus on Quade's report splashed alarmingly across his toybox. Alas, Quade's report only confirmed the worst: Alien invasion.

Around the toyroom spliced sixteen different virtual slices of desk, one for each member of his senior staff. Dylan was proud of his staff, and he hated having to break bad news, especially at the height of Highest Frontier: the Tenth Anniversary Campaign for Frontera. Back when he first founded the orbital college, with Gil Wickett's money, old Witherspoon at Harvard had warned him that fundraising was not the truest mark of a great college president, though certainly the most visible. The true mark was how one faced a crisis, like the one he faced today.

The slice of each staff member's desk revealed much about its occupant. The tall true-oak desk, larger even than Dylan's own, belonged to the vice president for finance, Orin Crawford, husband of the dean of students Nora Kwon. Orin taught a seven A.M. course on wealth creation, always full. Behind Orin's desk hung a Persian that Dylan's father would have envied, beside a large framed cartoon of medieval invaders ramming a castle gate with a giant wiener dog, which aptly depicted Orin's view of college finance. Orin himself had not yet arrived; he generally managed to arrive last, by just a minute, as if daring Dylan to start without him.

The fullest desk belonged to the dean of faculty, Helen Tejedor, holder of the José Martí Chair of Humane Studies. One could tell the time of year by the height of toyprints and tenure review dossiers that accumulated on Helen's desk beneath the colonial ax hung on the wall. At present, summer's end, there lay only a *Times* toyprint topped by Helen's latest book, *Nueva Cuba: A Postvirtualist Reading of Self and Society.*

The most inviting desk belonged to toymaker Zari Valadkhani, who ran the local Toynet and trained the Toy Land teddies. Upon Zari's desk sat an original Steif teddy bear, surrounded by Phaistos disks and Chinese puzzles. In the early days, the college had nearly folded when they couldn't recruit Toynet staff out to the spacehab. Zari and her wife, the college physician, had pulled their own two children from elementary school to fill the breach. Then they'd adopted orphans from vanishing islands: the Maldives, the Marshalls, the Andamans. For the college, Zari taught Developmental Arithmetic.

Orin arrived and settled his imposing bulk behind his towering desk. The morning chitchat subsided. Dylan cleared his throat. "We'll review the budget, *por favor*, then move on to *un problema* in the spacehab." He hoped this hint got Orin through the accounts swiftly.

Unruffled, Orin reviewed the year's balance sheet. "Investments are up eight percent, despite the black-hole trading climate." Orin prided himself on his knack for the market. "Expenses are down, thanks to thoughtful economies shared by all divisions of the college. But income was still not what we'd like to see." His eyebrows worked up and down as he spoke, and he gazed pointedly at the dean of admissions, Luis Herrera Smith.

Luis adjusted his sunglasses and leaned back on his poolside chair, out recruiting on the West Coast. Everyone had read Luis's op-ed with their morning coffee; Frontera was "hot" with *Times* reporters, thanks to Luis's connections. Hired the year before, the fresh-faced snub-nosed Angeleno still looked like he'd wandered off Sunset Boulevard. "We met our quota," Luis reminded Orin.

Luis had filled the last spot with Mary Dyer, a late applicant from a reclusive West Coast family with a fortune in pearls. The *chica*'s guardian had paid cash for a custom residence with extra fees that covered half a dorm on financial aid. Frontera's housing policy, of course, was another brainchild of Orin's. Orin had predicted that parents willing and able to shell out a million a year for a "high frontier" education would come up with another few hundred thousand for custom accommodations, which subsidized more needy applicants. The Kearns-Clark twins, cocaptains of the slanball team, got their castle complete with drum towers and a moat with a drawbridge. Their parents would announce the new Kearns-Clark Library at the next Campaign

Brunch. And for the Ramos Kennedy girl, her greenhouse; dear Soli had raised the endowment ten million. Thank goodness the girl had her parents' brains, an easy admit.

Still, it was unsettling to be so fee-dependent year after year. A college took generations to build a strong donor base; alums had to reach a certain age. A patent, that's what Frontera needed. One good patent could set up the college forever. Couldn't those science faculty come up with something?

"Very well, Orin," Dylan concluded, "thanks so much for the financial update. As you know, our staff retreat this year will focus on admissions. Helen?"

Helen Tejedor folded her hands upon her book. "I'm pleased to report that all positions are filled, and all faculty have returned on time for the start of class." Helen was implacable; Dylan could always count on her to get all the grades in, to get the tenured faculty back from their summers at the Louvre, and to make them spread their courses throughout the day from seven A.M. to midnight. "Two colleagues have earned major awards." The names flashed in midair above her desk. "Ten million from the Wellcome Trust for Sharon Abaynesh to study plant cognition . . ."

Dylan smiled through his teeth. The funds were welcome, all right; science was expensive. But from student grade appeals to sit-ins against cruelty to plants, one mess or another involved Abaynesh.

"And the American Association for Political Ideas has named Phil Hamilton their Teacher of the Year." The one Centrist on the faculty, and students adored him.

"Dee-lighted," exclaimed Dylan. "Such honors, for our small faculty." Fifty full-time professors serving eight hundred students; half their courses were still piped in from Earth. This fact was not advertised. "Might this be a good time," he ventured, "for the faculty to consider . . . requiring frog seminars?" Every first-year student would be guaranteed one course in a cozy room with a live professor to pat your back. It was Dylan's cherished dream for his college.

"Six new positions." Helen's penetrating eyes commanded attention, concentrated by the blade of the colonial ax. "That's what it will take."

Orin shook his head. "Three would do it; I've done the math—"

"And the academic division has other urgent needs." Only a full professor would dare cut Orin in mid-sentence. "Frontera has a growing digital divide," Helen continued. "We valorize technology as empowering students; yet our discourse disconnects with the economically challenged students in our residence halls. Many lack adequate access to Toynet."

Zari's long Iranian brow furrowed, as her fingers twisted a 3D puzzle of fiendish complexity. "Universal access remains our goal," assured the toymaker. "Today, half our students have private toyrooms; but the Erie and Huron residences have just one toyroom per floor. Frogs have to share classes, or beg access from a senior."

Orin gave Zari a wide-eyed look. "Do you know what it would cost to outfit the rest? Do you have that in your budget somewhere?"

"Now Orin," Dylan interposed smoothly, "we all know you're the conscience of the college; our conscience, Orin, I've always said." A record ten years operating in the black—despite playing out this same scene each September, barely making ends meet after all the divisions made agonizing cuts. Then each October, lo and behold a surplus appeared, at a time when everyone was too busy to spend it. The trustees adored Orin. "Nora," Dylan asked, "what do you think? Do our dorms need more toyrooms?"

"It would help morale," Nora admitted. "Myself, I still like the conventional classroom where you can squirt napping kids in the eye, but we've got to move with the times. Orin, have you checked the Witherspoon account? Its securities have appreciated, and the interest must get spent on technology."

Orin nodded sagely at his wife's suggestion. Much of Frontera business was smoothed by family ties; one couldn't very well keep a spouse on Earth, thirty-six thousand klicks away. The president's own marriage to the chaplain offered great symbolism. Parents could rest assured that good old Anglo-Roman morality informed college affairs.

"Besides," added Nora, "the more virtual outlets, the better. Too much time on their hands, and they're off molesting elephants. We've just had our first complaint."

Dylan sighed again. Why couldn't the bros stop with tipping mini-cows; one could always pay off the homesteader. This new generation, with their unspeakable tastes. *"Ahora,"* Dylan hurried on, "I'm afraid we must share some challenging news." He turned to Quade. "Something we've always known could happen—would happen someday."

The ecoengineer had introduced the miniature elephants, along with the mini-deer and teddy bears, and all the other spacehab flora and fauna. Behind Quade's desk hung his waders, while the toywall played a mini-wolf nursing cubs. Quade cleared his throat. "We have a wolf introduction plan. Minis, of course. The insurance premium is manageable, and wolves will control deer, just as owls control—"

Dylan clenched his hands beneath his desk. "Some other time." Wolves indeed; teddy bears were one thing, but a president had to draw the line.

Quade cleared his throat again. "Our hab's been invaded."

Heads turned in each wedge of the virtual pie. Zari asked, "What species?"

"Aedes albopictus."

From his beach chair Luis sat up straight and pulled off his sunglasses. *"No puede ser."*

Nora looked grim and shook her head.

Dylan said quietly, "We always knew this could happen someday, though we hoped not in our lifetimes, but today it has. 'Tiger mosquito,' they call it, right, Quade?"

The ecoengineer nodded. "Tiger mocs carry dengue, yellow fever, meningitis, among other things." From kudzu to Asian carp, long-horned beetles to yellow plague—every terrestrial habitat endured the curse of exotic alien species. The infamous mosquito carried some of the worst diseases humanity had ever known. But spacehabs such as Frontera were planned, seeded, and stocked according to precise planning and maintenance—designed to be free of exotics, never marred by pest or pollution. Indeed, that was Frontera's claim to fame, perhaps its strongest selling point: No cancer-causing UV, no criminal element, and no mosquitoes.

"How could this happen?" demanded Helen. "How'd they get here?"

Orin leaned forward above his expansive desk. "Probably those unsterile orchids."

"Of course not," said Dylan quickly. "We were most careful about that, weren't we, Nora?"

Nora pursed her lips. "Those plants practically went through a sieve. Who knows how the gnats hitched their ride? Probably in a Red Bull tire."

Dylan winced. Motor clubs were a perennial bone of contention, though his own Lunar pastime pulled in major gifts from donors.

"Well now," grinned Orin, "we'll just have to put up with a few Windsor Bombers buzzing us."

Dylan smiled through his teeth. "However they got here, *la cuestión ahora* is how to get rid of them."

Behind Quade, the mini-wolf and her cubs gave way to a clutch of small brown furry animals with pointed ears and snub noses that hung from a branch with their wings folded. "Brown bats will consume more than a thousand mosquitoes per day—"

"I said get rid of them, *de golpe*. How?"

Quade ticked off his fingers. "Drain or treat all water systems, from river to treeholes. Hypercarb insecticide, delivered through our central precipitation. Recombinant biological larvicides, though that takes longer and never fully eliminates the target. If all else fails—" He paused. "Evacuate the spacehab, and put it in deep freeze." That would mean losing all the farms and woodlands developed since the hab was founded, thirty years before the college. The Mound and the Mount Gilead colonists all displaced; that would do wonders for town-gown.

Orin shifted his bulk meaningfully. "Have you any idea how much these schemes will set us back? How's your budget, Elephant Man?"

"I've identified potential economies," said Quade without hesitation. "There's our annual restocking of the Ohio River. We've put that on hold."

"Let's not be hasty." The president's annual Senior Class fish-off and beach party was legendary, essential to inaugurate new alumni. As a child, Dylan himself had fished the original Ohio, before the riverbed dried and the forests died. One summer you could hear the parched branches crashing, night after night. Fire swept through, leaving only blackened trunks, a charcoal desert. Dylan still dreamt of those fires raging down the valley, and he woke choking for air. But the new Frontera, the college he'd built with Gil Wickett's money, would remain forever pristine, a drop of God's country restored, safe from fire and drought, untouched by "the divine dice game" of terrestrial climate.

"The Shawnee," asked Luis. "Won't they help?" The Shawnee built and owned the spacehab, legally a tribal reservation, but they didn't care about the fauna so long as they could pack players into the Mound. They let the college run the biosphere, in lieu of rent. It was best not to bother the Shawnee.

The president straightened in his chair. "As Teddy would say, 'Ninetenths of wisdom consists of being wise in time.' Whatever it takes, the Board will help," he promised. "I'll head down to Gil's."

Everyone looked relieved except Orin, who hated going hat in hand to the Board. But Dylan knew the time had come. A spacehab lived in dread of alien invasion. Gil Wickett would understand.

Zari put down her puzzle, now a solid cube. "Don't some of our faculty have expertise we could tap?"

The faculty were full of expertise, but they could be unpredictable—and unlike administrators, they couldn't be fired when their schemes went awry.

"Good idea, Zari," Dylan replied after a slight pause. "Consult the faculty. We need all the help we can get."

✦

Dylan arrived home at his amyloid-oak study, where Clarence Flynn sat on the ebony amyloid couch before the virtual fireplace. He felt as if he had just extricated himself from the car after an eight-hour Formula One Lunar Grand Prix. With a sigh Dylan sank onto the couch next to Clare. "If I were a drinking man, which I'm not, I sure would have one now."

Clare looked up from his book, a well-worn tome that Dylan recognized, an exegesis of the Gospel of John. "Your day was that bad?"

"Disastrous." The end table always held a bowl of apples; Dylan reached over and took one. As he munched, he glanced overhead. The ceiling projected the Sistine Chapel, zoomed to view panels which slowly cycled through. The Expulsion was just cycling out, poor Adam sheltering Eve from the angel's sword. "Quade found a mosquito."

"*¡Qué va!* Here in the hab?"

"No doubt about it." Dylan took another bite and chewed thoughtfully.

Clare nodded slowly. "It had to come."

"What do you mean, 'had to come'?" His frustration boiled over. "We spend *millones* to keep the hab clean."

Clare clasped his hands behind his neck and looked away, stretching his hammer-toned triceps. "Do you know how the first human-sucking mosquitoes reached the Americas?"

"From Africa?"

"On the slave ships."

"We have no slaves here."

"Only slaves to sin."

Dylan pulled away. "This is serious. If mosquitoes could get in here, what else?"

"There was poison ivy. We survived that."

"Mosquitoes are more personal. A direct hit on our brand."

Clare stroked Dylan's shoulder. Dylan's arm went around him, feeling the taut ripples of his chest, always a comfort. His eyelids closed. Clare asked, "Have you talked to Sharon?"

Dylan's eyes flew open. He would never forget his last encounter with Professor Abaynesh. He'd called her in, ever so nicely, right there in his own office, for just a chat about how she'd posted the college hepa-Q infection rates on Toynet. She had stormed out, with some rhetoric about free speech and "honest mating signals"—whatever that meant. Afterward a two-headed snake—a live one, no toy-thing—had emerged from beneath his desk.

"Sharon took care of the deer," Clare reminded him.

The deer, the bears, and several other fecund species, were kept reasonably in check by Sharon's genetic engineering. But mosquitoes—even one was too many. "The parents are clamoring about dengue fever. Don't know how much longer I can put off Clive."

Clare shrugged. "It could be worse. Could be flooding."

Dylan frowned. "Clare, that's no joke. Half our students are from New York."

"Where d'you think I got it?"

Dylan tilted his head. "So how was your day? Counting nails for the blitz build?" The blitz build always attracted new frogs for Homefair, raising a home in Mount Gilead for penniless colonists. It brightened his day, that Frontera drew the kind of billionaires' kids who'd dent their thumbs to help the homeless.

"We poured the foundation," said Clare. "The rest of my day was about pachyderms."

Dylan's heart sank. "So I heard." The ethics of molesting elephants. Thank goodness classes had started—the whole staff felt that way. "I just don't understand this generation. Hitting on *chicas*, that's been done since time immemorial. But elephants—these kids, from billion-dollar homes patrolled by DIRGs? It's—it's bestial."

"A lot of things have been called bestial," the chaplain pointed out. "The wrong chromosome, or the wrong melanin content."

Dylan waved a hand. "Teddy nearly lost the election after Booker T. Washington dined with him at the White House." So much for individuality. "That was then. This is now—this *is* bestial, literally."

"Kids will be kids."

"Clare, sometimes you're just too forgiving."

"Lucky for you."

"That's hardly fair. In my day, I stuck to guys." In his first three years at college, before he met Clare, Dylan had managed to sample nearly all his house bros, and then some. Extremely nice memories; they remembered, when he came calling for donations. "Kids today—it's beyond the pale. To say nothing of the infectious consequences."

"I seem to recall a hepatic incident."

Dylan shuddered; along with several bros, he'd undergone a liver transplant junior year. It wasn't hepa-Q back then; a virus earlier in the alphabet. "At least we got human diseases. These kids need a veterinarian."

In Frontera's first year, the faculty had nixed the Greek system. After all Dylan's courting his old bros, he'd naively assumed his charm would push it through the faculty. Surely the professors would understand how getting funds for their precious endowed chairs required alums who'd spent their four years having a good time, while helping hold down grade inflation. The faculty vote went down, and half a billion in gifts evaporated.

Then he'd come up with the scheme of motor clubs, named for his beloved Formula One teams. He'd gotten the scholarship boys to propose it, the ones from disappearing Pacific islands. The motion had passed the faculty by one vote.

The motor clubs went off well enough, no more than their share of drunk runs and parental lawsuits. But then came those zoophile initiations. How could he have imagined? At least the greeks had standards.

Clare looked overhead. Noah's ark was receding in the distance; interesting, how Michelangelo had focused on all those left behind, clinging to tree trunks with their doomed children. "Why does Student Affairs send them my way?"

"Kids trust you, Clare. They see you on a rooftop, hammering slates. They know you're for real, not just some toy-shrink."

"Just for once, couldn't they ask me something really controversial. Like, 'Is the Word truly God, or only *with* God?'"

Dylan smiled. "Which is it?" he asked softly.

"Ask me on our next vacation."

There was a hint. "Winter break. How about Lila's Beach?" Gil's private island in the Maldives; it had maybe twenty years left.

"No," said Clare firmly. "Not Lila's."

"Just for once? No clothes and no cameras—Gil promised."

Clare gave him a look. "No cameras—on Gil Wickett's island? You sweet innocent."

A shaft of light flooded Dylan's toybox. "ToyNews—From our box to yours." Clive Rusanov grinned triumphantly, smoothing his oily black hair. "And here we are, at last, live from 'Ohio-in-the-Firmament.'" Clive's most irritating epithet for Frontera, his revenge for getting put off all day. "President Chase comments on our breaking news: bugs in paradise."

11

In the office of Professor Abaynesh, Jenny and Anouk hovered over the crushed insect. Dengue fever—all Jenny could think of was eye-breaking pain, pain in the bones, delirium. She zoomed her toybox. Each of the long legs had three little white segments near the tip. The dorsal side had prominent white stripes.

The professor nodded. "Distinctive, I'd say." She glanced over by the window, where her daughter Tova sat on a carpet square playing with blocks and casino souvenirs. Meg-El glided lazily over the child's leg, the late-afternoon light glinting on the snake's scales. "Tovaleh? Come give us your expert opinion."

The five-year-old got up and came over, carrying a Twin Towers with the two planes stuck in, the kind you could win at the kids' level. "The two towers—they were not the same." Full of nervous energy, Tova hyperventilated as she talked. "The second tower had warning." She pointed her finger like a miniature professor. "But a voice told them all to go back up."

"Yes, Tovaleh, that's another invasive species. Now give a look here. What is this?"

Tova leaned over and stuck her eye close to the insect. "A tiger mosquito. No bushy antennae—it's a girl."

"Indeed." The professor looked at Jenny, almost accusingly. "Did you have to kill it?"

Jenny blinked, then exchanged a look with Anouk.

"Professor," observed Anouk, "these mosquitoes carry every plague you can name, especially chikungunya." A viral fever like dengue, with higher mortality, chikungunya had spread throughout Europe.

"I have a license for invasives," said Abaynesh. "Whenever they show up here, I remediate them. I can't very well breed dead ones."

Before Anouk could reply, Jenny quickly asked, "What other invasives are here?"

"*None* is what there should be." Anouk sounded like a customer demanding her money back. "Not as advertised, this school."

"What in life is as advertised?"

Anouk's eyes widened at the disdain in the professor's voice, then narrowed, simmering with displeasure.

"There's poison ivy," Abaynesh went on. "We bred a form that doesn't make the allergen. Then there are Quade's poison frogs; still on my list, remind me."

Jenny asked, "Don't the DIRGs control what comes in?"

"If it slips through, what can you do? To destroy a species is a crime against science."

Another look exchanged with Anouk. Endangered species were one thing, but mosquitoes?

The professor probed the insect with her dissecting needle. "If you find any live ones, let me know. I'll breed them to avoid humans. Or you could do it, as your research project." The intro lab course was all virtual, but Honors students could start research their frog year.

"Thanks," said Jenny politely, "though I prefer plants."

"Then you'll like Ari." Abaynesh waved her hand over the little plant. The stalk swayed, and at its base the leaves lifted. Behind it, in the toywall, a virtual stalk expanded to giant size, its color seeping away, a transparent tube. Within the stalk grew lollipop cells, each extending a long axon. "The leaves secrete nerve growth protein. The nerve growth protein induces neurons. The neurons interconnect, and undergo Darwinian selection. That means the ones with active synapses survive; those with nonworking synapses wither." The lollipop cells ramified and connected like interlocking fingers. One cell turned red and failed to connect, then it withered away.

Anouk took a step closer. "Is the neuron selection entirely stochastic?"

"With a built-in bias for receiver inputs. See this paper by my grad-school mentors, Ng and Howell." The link for Ng and Howell appeared in Jenny's toybox.

Jenny eyed the swaying stalk. "What is the aim of your research?"

"We build models for human cognition. Human complexity arose from simpler models. For example, simple eyespots formed the basis of eyes; startle-laughter originated the sense of humor, and so forth. Calculation ability, there's something easy to measure. Intelligence—everyone wants to increase it. But where did intellect get us? Destroying our planet." Abaynesh shook her head. "My project addresses something tougher: wisdom." She tapped the plant's stalk. "Call it wisdom, judgment, the ability to make 'the right choice.' It's one thing for Ari to find my mortarboard when I need it. It's quite another to know, is it right for me to go out and wear it today?"

Jenny avoided looking at Anouk. "Is this related to, um, your two-headed project?"

"Another approach to the same end. A two-headed person might be twice as wise."

"**Or twice as foolish,**" Anouk texted Jenny.

"True," admitted the professor, "that's how it works in snakes."

Anouk startled, caught out for once.

✦✦

As Jenny returned south with Anouk, three goldfinches took off from a maple, while overhead a hawk soared. Anouk's DIRG kept to the side, in the shadow of the trees.

"Mosquitoes," exclaimed Anouk. "How shall I sleep at night?" She wiped her arms as if brushing off insects. "That professor—because of my religion, she treats me so rudely."

"I don't think so," said Jenny. "She talks like that to everyone. She's just . . . socially challenged." Aspie, for sure.

"American," Anouk sighed. "One must make allowances."

"What do the other Life professors work on?"

"Professor Semerena studies the DNA of pile worms, which burrow in the sand off San Francisco. Professor Needham studies the ecology of liverworts. Of course, you can always work at a Harvard lab." Anouk smirked. "I'm doing cryptography at MIT."

From between the trees a deer leapt out across the trail, tail flashing and hindquarters pumping up and down with every leap. Shrieks split the air, as two mini-elephants trotted after, one followed by a baby struggling to catch up. The donkey-tailed elephants seemed to amuse themselves by flushing the deer. Now, mosquitoes would hunt them both. Jenny shuddered.

"ToyNews—From our box to yours." The anchor was back, his black hairstyle slick as always. "Clive Rusanov for ToyNews, live from Frontera, the world's first college at the Firmament. . . ." Jenny brainstreamed her dose to the pollmeter. "Attended by such celebs as the Anthradyne heir and the surviving Ramos Kennedy twin. Now joined by a less welcome guest—the *Aedes* mosquito."

An outsized mosquito filled the window, spliced with Uncle Dylan's smiling face. "No cause for alarm. We find isolated individuals, no breeding population. None of the pathogens that mosquitoes could carry. Nonetheless, it's a good reminder for students to make sure your HIV is up to date. As a precaution, your room will print out repellent patches until further notice."

Jenny eyed her mother's window, but restrained herself. She had sworn she would not call home at every mishap.

Clive then turned to Professor Abaynesh in her laboratory. "Professor, as Frontera's expert on invasive species, can you tell our ToyNews audience how the college will cope?"

"Biocontrol," said Abaynesh. "We'll release terminal reproductives, that is, male individuals engineered to propagate Super-X females which mate only with females in the next generation, thus failing to reproduce."

"My, these scientists use long words," observed Clive with his most winning "don't click out yet" smile. "And now for the college ecoengineer . . ."

Quade Vincenzo, with his elephantine face that never cracked a smile. In his hand squeaked a furry brown creature. "Bats," he offered. "A single brown bat consumes a thousand insects per day—"

A window opened, amid the student windows announcing new parties or seeking lost nose rings. It was Rafael. "Jenny, how are your classes? I hope you got the professors you desired."

"Yes, thanks. The Roosevelt class is *chulo*."

"Excellent. May I have the pleasure of your company for dinner? Please join us this evening at the Ferrari club."

She could get her homework done after dinner. "May Anouk Chouiref come too?"

Rafael made a slight bow. "Absolutely. I'll drive by for you both at six."

Anouk smiled. "Thanks, *chérie*. The Ferraris, they have at least some manners. I hear also that a new place is opening, with a Paris-trained chef, Café de la Paix. Next time, I'll treat you there."

At six, a black convertible glided silently up to the cottage. Wheels splayed out racing style, the chassis had road-hugging skirts and rear wings shiny as Abaynesh's snake. Jenny came out wearing her moonholes and a Fifth-Avenue blouse. The car door waited for her to tuck her laces in by her feet before it slid shut.

Rafael wore a dark Euro-cut suit, fine woven wool. "Magnificent evening. You both look well; excellent adjustment to the spacehab." He added, "Not to worry about the mosquitoes. Elephant Man will take care of it." Beneath the car the path slid back without a sound save the crunch of gravel. The car glided south, into the river-ringed orange of the solar. Nothing manual, only brainstream.

"Nice wheels," observed Jenny politely.

Rafael patted the door. "Solid anthrax. Superb air flow; we could drive upside down on a ceiling. Of course, its full force can't be used here. I spent the summer at Valencia."

Jenny thought, there were more useful ways a well-off *chico* could spend his summer, but then there were worse. A string melody arose, as if someone were playing a violin from within the car. A harpsichord joined in, and chorus, a Bach cantata.

Anouk's residence was a geodesic dome with no apparent door or windows. A hexagonal panel flashed open and Anouk stepped out. She wore a shimmering gold lamé headscarf and a dress that wrapped her from neck to toe in a design of interlocked stars. Heads would turn, thought Jenny, wishing she herself dared dress like that.

As Anouk reached the back door, Berthe plodded behind her. Jenny cringed; she'd forgotten this embarrassment.

"A retainer," observed Rafael approvingly. "Sign of a good family." Both rear doors opened.

The car glided south past the Reagan Life and History buildings, and the students trailing their laces toward the dining hall, including Yola and Kendall with the slanball team. Jenny looked away, hoping they didn't see her. At last the car slowed before the Ferrari club. The club house was top-grade amyloid marble with a porch of Ionic columns. Two angels with trumpets faced each other across the cornice. Rafael got out and came around to her side, although the doors opened themselves. Empty of passengers, the car drove itself forward onto a platform, which dipped down to an underground garage to pipe up microbial hydrogen.

On the porch a senior leaned against the column. "Rob LaSalle," introduced Rafael. "Our club president." The LaSalle family, industrial solarplate.

Rob smiled. "Just back from my weekly chat with Chase. Quite a day, with all the invasion."

"Indeed. Does the college have a plan?"

"If Quade has his way."

Rafael permitted himself a smile. "This way, Jenny."

The dining room was fitted with near-authentic hardwood floors. The damask table linens had acanthus swirls. Anouk's DIRG stepped back to the wall.

At the table, Rafael pulled out a chair for Anouk, and Rob pulled one out for Jenny. A menu scrolled down her toybox.

"Extensive, as you see," observed Rafael. "Anything you'll find in New York."

In other words, amyloid. Jenny picked "veal parmigiana," which wouldn't be too bad; then just to see, she added "fresh asparagus," which never printed out well.

Anouk asked, "What does one do here for the arts? Is there any . . . theater?"

"Our club has virtual seating at theaters throughout the world, from the Biltmore to the Opera Bastille."

"And the finest symphonies," added Rob. "Season virtuals at the Kennedy Center."

The lip of a wineglass appeared in the table, then rose slowly, followed by the stem, just like the Monroe had risen out of Jenny's printer. Rob tasted the wine, then nodded to Rafael.

"We hold our own social at the Mound," Rafael told Jenny. "Monte Carlo Night—the week after classes start. *We* don't preempt academics." As their rival club presumably did. "We enjoy ourselves, while serving our country." The Centrist ban on games of chance didn't apply off Earth. "Do you play blackjack? Or the wheel?"

"Um . . ." She looked to Anouk.

"Blackjack," said Anouk, with a gleam in her eye. "A game for tough players." Apparently her rules didn't either.

A fine glow suffused the table, while all around the light had gradually dimmed, revealing a pattern of stars. Constellations filled a night sky, above and below. It was as if their table floated, a planetoid amid the void. It left Jenny's insides oddly unsettled.

Rob said, "We do service in Mount Gilead. Easter egg hunts for the children."

"The children," murmured Rafael. "So important; the future of our world." He sent a clip of himself amidst children scampering with their Easter baskets.

The veal parmigiana was quite good. The asparagus tasted good as well, although no one could mistake its texture for true vegetable fiber. As she ate, Jenny felt her brain play tricks on her. Were these two *chicos* really amyloid as well; or perhaps hosts of a toyworld? "Children," she repeated aloud. "I wonder what it's like for children, growing up in a spacehab."

Rob looked up, his fork suspended above his plate. "Frontera is fantastic for children. Free of crime, free of infectious disease. Only the best moral influences."

"Would children of a spacehab ever dream of going out beyond? To Jupiter?"

A look passed between the two young men in their suits. Behind them the Great Bear was rising and turning around the pole star, as the heavens revolved around the table. "Humanity comes first," Rob asserted. "Children deserve a world that revolves around them. Don't you agree?"

"Perhaps they won't believe in Earth either, if they've never been there."

Rafael looked alarmed. "Of course not, that is not what we believe."

Rob laughed, while catching Rafael's arm as if to still him. "I heard a little boy say that last year at the egg hunt, 'I don't believe in Earth.' A trip down the anthrax will cure that, I'm sure. Jenny, at this college no two of us agree on everything. Everything is up for discussion."

"Indeed." Anouk's silken shoulders lifted in a delicate shrug. "Nothing in Frontera agrees with me."

✦

"You needn't have been short with them," Anouk told her afterward. "They were extremely nice."

"Doesn't it bother you, a mathematician, to be told that the universe revolves around your nose?"

"*Enfin*, they're young; they'll outgrow it." She added pointedly, "My people are good astronomers. And evolution was discovered by al-Jahiz in the ninth century."

"I have to do my homework now." A DNA sequence, three Nobel-winning experiments, and the Northern Securities case.

"Of course, *chérie*. Let me know if you need help." From Anouk's window flashed a golden key. "This bit of code will write your DNA automatically." She winked out.

Jenny went to open her toyroom. She would build the DNA herself, atom by atom, to make sure she understood before using Anouk's shortcut.

"Open Life lab," she told the toyroom.

To her surprise, one of the eight doorways in the tree house showed a stranger, a squat man in a green frock coat and top hat with a gold buckle, lounging against the trunk. "Top o' the evening to you, miss. Surf's up at Quake—won't you try your luck?"

Jenny frowned. "Clear out."

Instead of disappearing from the toyroom, as any dismissed visitor should, the green-clad apparition stepped forward and brushed her with a four-leaf clover. "Holy Trinity Special at Rapture." The Mississippi space-hab, where Whitcomb played. "Say your prayers—it's your lucky day."

"I said, *clear out.*"

The man vanished, then reappeared in another door. "There's the Life-boat Special at Iceberg—luck o' the Irish—"

Jenny called Toy Land. Layla Vimukta, the little Andaman girl, appeared in door number three, braids tossed over her shoulder. "Ooh, you've got a ghost. Been surfing the toys, have we?"

Jenny smiled sheepishly. "Not much." The door chain to Jordi must have let something slip in. "Can't you raise my protection? A friend of mine hacks my toybox."

Layla put down her Phaistos disk. "Okay, but close your eyes and put your fingers in your ears. This will take just a teeny-weeny minute."

Curious, Jenny half closed her eyes. In an instant the doors all went blank as if consumed by white flame. A thunderclap filled the toyroom. Jenny cried out and held her hands to her ears, her eyes now closed but still full of light. After what seemed forever, the light died and the forest bird calls returned. Cautiously, Jenny opened one eye, then another. The tree house had returned to normal, with only Layla standing in door three.

"Bye-bye ghost." Layla waved cheerily.

12

After Wednesday morning slanball, Political Ideas was not till ten. With no early class, Jenny had time for a shower and a leisurely breakfast. The Ohioana stacked pancakes would not be bad, she thought, as she strolled north past the coneflowers. Just past Wickett Hall, there stood a small storefront she hadn't noticed before. Out front, below the awning, a freshly painted sign read CAFÉ DE LA PAIX. A framed chalkboard stood on an easel, next to two small round tables with folding chairs. The chalk was real, a fine dust fallen onto the frame. Jenny sat on a chair and read the chalk letters. *Brioche—Café— Petit Dejeuner du Jour.*

Out of the hut came a student in a white chef's toque and jacket. It was Tom Yoder.

Startled, Jenny felt warm all over. She smiled and her eyes closed.

"Tinúviel," she heard him whisper.

Her eyes flew open.

Tom shook himself. "Excuse me," he said. "Are you ready to order?"

"I'll have the *'du Jour.'*"

"You're sure? You have time?" The price popped into her toybox, fifty dollars.

"Sure, I have time. I hear you have a Paris-trained chef."

Tom said nothing but disappeared into the kitchen. On the maple tree, two squirrels chased each other up and down, and a cardinal sang at the top of its lungs. To the south, the light source brightened, round as the sun; and north, past the Mound, Lake Erie lit up blue before the chocolate peaks. By eight o'clock, a few students straggled down the trail to the dining hall or to class.

At length Tom returned with a tray. Belgian waffles formed a crisscross star pattern, their crust topped with powdered sugar and fresh strawberries indented with real seeds. On the Limoges china plate, a butter pat was molded in the shape of a frog. A boiled egg in a cup, its shell sketched with a rose. A cup of *chocolat* with a cinnamon stick. A pink grapefruit carved as a swan. *"Citrus paradisi, red grapefruit."* The grapefruit looked and smelled so fresh it activated her taxa link, the cut pulp swollen full beneath the swan's wings.

Jenny ate the waffles first, thinking she would hate to break open the painted egg. She chewed slowly, the crust and strawberries melting in her mouth.

"Is everything all right?" Tom asked, stepping outside the door.

She nodded. "Did you . . . make these?"

Tom nodded. "The ingredients were all shipped up this morning. Except the eggs, those are from Mount Gilead."

She did not want him to leave. "The swan looks so real."

"Thank you. Was the egg not done as you wished?"

"I don't want to break the rose."

"Never mind, I'll make you a blown one."

Her pulse raced. "Why don't you sit down?"

Tom cast about, as if checking for other customers. He pulled over a chair backward and sat on it, legs to either side, and crossed his arms upon the back. He had light brown hair, with the bluest eyes she'd ever seen. "How'd you like our class?"

"Life?" Her lip twisted. "I'll never forget those phosphates. Did you get the homework?"

"Yes. I need to check which carbon ends with the phosphate."

"Always the five-prime carbon. The other end stays free to grow more DNA." She opened the egg, trying to leave the rose intact. "What else are you taking?"

"Flynn's Renaissance Art. We'll get to make our own frescoes."

"That's amazing. I sure wanted that class."

Tom thought this over. "I could drop out, and then you could get in."

She looked up, puzzled.

"Sorry." He shook himself. "That wouldn't work, would it."

"Anyhow, I have Uncle Dylan's seminar. He's *chulo*."

" 'Uncle Dylan'?"

"President Chase. He's a family friend."

"I see, of course."

"Could we be playmates?"

"Sure, thanks." Tom's window moved to her playmate group, along with Anouk, Tusker-12, and a Chinese student who'd just posted the molecule of the day. Two hundred comments already.

"So, you're French?" Jenny asked.

"Nope. I was born Amish and grew up near Danville."

Amish. Inbred, genetically challenged. Her view of Tom blew up in the air and came down in fragments that had to be pieced together. He certainly looked healthy enough, though he could use more of a tan. He'd asked a good question in class. She hoped her expression had not changed. "Well, I think I'll come here for breakfast every day."

"I'm open just three days a week, that's all I have time for."

"I see." Supplementing his scholarship. He'd have no Newman genes, though somehow he felt more like Newman than those who did. "What are you doing Saturday?"

"The Homefair blitzbuild, then cooking for Saturday night."

"Homefair, that's nice. I guess being Amish, you know all about building."

Tom withdrew, looking away as if she'd said something wrong. "I never built a house." He got up and disappeared inside the café.

For Political Ideas, they had to print out a book, Aristotle's *Politics*. Jenny tried to remember the last time she'd printed one out, instead of scrolling in her box. The pages came apart like puff pastry, and the black lines of text undulated like the surface of the sea. The content had little to do with the politics she knew, the trading of votes and promises.

The class met in the same Harding Hall seminar room as Uncle Dylan's class, but now furnished with plush maroon chairs. Jenny set down her orchid on the table, which was now inlaid wood, Louis something or other, with rounded ends and legs. The toywall was covered by a curtain.

Professor Hamilton turned from the two students seated already. Not quite her height, he wore a dark suit and tie, like the Ferrari *chicos*. A degree in baraminology at Whitcomb, doctorate from Chicago. "Jennifer Ramos Kennedy." He spoke her full name, like at graduation. He extended a hand to shake hers. "Such a pleasure to have you, Jenny. I made sure to save you a place."

Jenny nodded, though surprised. She recalled that her father knew him. Her mouth suddenly froze, conscious of the other students arriving and this professor she didn't know. Looking down at her plant, she texted, "**My father speaks highly of you.**"

She looked up just in time to see Hamilton's face shift, a hint of alarm, as if surprised she knew of her father's connection. Then he relaxed. "You are an award-winning life scientist. Aristotle invented life science, as well as politics."

Among the other students, fifteen in all, Jenny knew only Ricky and

Mary. Mary Dyer, her odd *compañera,* sat there with her water bottle and her box of pretzels. Jenny tried to text her a warning not to eat during class, but Mary still had no toybox. Mary's fingers groped the table unnervingly.

The professor went and stood behind a table podium. "Aristotle was born twenty-five centuries ago in an ancient city of Greece. And yet, in your first year at college, all of you have something in common with the man whose book we are reading." Hamilton paused, scanning the faces. "From his home city on a northern peninsula, Aristotle sailed the Aegean Sea to attend Plato's school in Athens. The sea was then a dangerous place, a place of angry gods and sudden storms, where even the most advanced tools of seafaring might not save a stricken ship. Like Aristotle, each of you had to leave the city of your birth and cross a great sea, the sea of air and space, in order to reach your school." Space within the moon's orbit—Centrists claimed to "accept" that.

Hamilton placed his book on the podium and opened it. The students all took out their books. The pages rustled as they opened, like the sound of opening presents. "'Book One. Every state is an association of persons who intend some good purpose. And that type of association we call 'political.'"

Jenny fingered the flexible pages. Back in ancient Greece, Aristotle wrote upon animal skins, in a language long gone. How did this amyloid book in the twenty-second century relate to what he wrote? She tried to imagine a world where you had to kill animals to write, let alone eat.

The professor looked up from his book. "Aristotle became the greatest student, and the greatest teacher of all time. He taught the child who became Alexander the Great, the world's greatest conqueror. He returned to Athens to found his own school, ultimately a school to the world's rulers for centuries to come."

Hamilton leaned forward on the podium. "But the school of politics is not an easy school, nor one to make us comfortable. Politics is about how rulers rule, how leaders lead and governors govern. And, in every *polis* the principles of governance are understood only dimly by most of those who are governed. To lift the veil and behold those principles may shock us, may transform what we think we know about the world. Tell me: As you read Aristotle's first pages, did anything . . . surprise you?"

The dreaded first question. It hovered like a cloud drifting around the table from one student to the next. The crunch of Mary's pretzel marred the silence. At last, a hand lifted, a Newman-chinned *chico* with tousled black hair. "I was surprised that we're reading Aristotle without Plato first. I mean, isn't Aristotle obviously quarreling with his old teacher?"

Nervous looks. Half the students sat up straighter, their stance assuring everyone that they too had read Plato first, while the others slouched back in their plush chairs, desperately hoping to avoid being called on.

"Enrico, that's wonderful that you've read Plato. You can help point out those parts where Plato is engaged." **Enrico Peña,** from San Juan. His home had finally become a state paired with Cuba: one purple, the other gold. That kind of politics Jenny understood. "Who else was surprised by Aristotle?" the professor asked.

A *chica* with a prominent nose ring raised her hand. **Priscilla Cho,** said her box. "Like, I read *Uncle Tom's Cabin.* So, this Aristotle says slaves and women are just tools?"

Hamilton smiled. "Tools, yes; but different kinds of tools, Aristotle says. Not an all-purpose Delphic knife. Only barbarians fail to distinguish women from slaves." He looked around the room. "What about us, today? Which of us are not 'tools' of a state?"

Another long pause.

Ricky raised his hand. "We all play taxes."

"Very good, Ricky," agreed Hamilton, "we all play taxes."

"Only if we want to," said Priscilla.

"The rule of desire," muttered the professor, as if rehearsing some ancient argument from elsewhere. "The ultimate end of democracy. But Aristotle begins way before democracy. 'Every state' he aims to describe, from tyrannies to democracies. Every state consists of ruler and ruled. And who is the ruler? 'For he that can by his intelligence foresee things needed is by nature ruler and master.'" Hamilton smiled, his eyes darting toward one student, then another. "Is this view so unfamiliar? How were you all chosen for Frontera? Is not 'foreseeing' what the 'forehead' does?"

Priscilla insisted, "We don't own slaves."

"Slaves, indeed, we shall return to that presently. First, let's not miss a crucial step. According to Aristotle, what makes a man a man? A human being?"

The Newman-chinned Enrico said, "Man is a political animal. By his nature, man lives in a state."

"That's right, Enrico, a man must live in a state. So, is a man outside a state not a human being?"

Silence. Jenny thought irritably, A human being is a human being.

Mary asked, "What about elephants?"

Jenny swallowed, suddenly tense. She hoped Mary would not act too much out of place. She felt at once protective, though resentful of her *compañera.*

"That's a good question, Mary. What about elephants?"

Ricky raised a hand. "Speech," he said. "Speech is what makes us human."

Everyone seemed to let out a breath. Elephants couldn't talk; only humans could talk, they all learned that in kindergarten. That was the trouble with Aristotle, Jenny thought; one moment he sounded like kindergarten, the next he went off a cliff.

"You're right, Ricky, speech is most important. Speech makes the state possible; makes humanity possible."

"But," said Priscilla, "this book says, like, the state comes before the person? Actually, the state is just to help people get along."

"And what is a person outside a state? What is a hand removed from the body?"

Mary said, "A hand removed from a body can be a person. It just has to grow."

Silence, a silence deeper than before, more awkward. Two other *chicas* exchanged glances with raised eyebrows.

Jenny felt bad for Mary. **"What she said would be true of a colonial animal,"** she texted to the class, watching her plant. **"A sponge. A piece broken off a sponge grows into a whole one."**

"Jenny, how observant." The professor smiled triumphantly. "Aristotle observed marine sponges. 'A sponge responds to attack by contracting to protect itself.' If a sponge could speak, and if it lived in a state, then it would be a person, wouldn't it?"

◆◆

After class, Hamilton drew her aside. "Jenny, I'm so glad you joined this class. You show a true gift for leadership."

"Thank you."

"Jenny, I would like to get to know you better, and help you make the most of this class. Would you stop by my office?"

"Thanks, I'll make an appointment." She felt flattered, though surprised. Getting to know a professor was part of college. But why would this Centrist professor seek her? She remembered something. **"The Greeks didn't deny the sea just because they lost a ship."**

Hamilton bowed slightly, as if to a fencing opponent. "The Greeks, though, had gods and monsters, and a cliff where the world ended. I can see you and I shall have much to discuss."

13

Back at her cottage, Jenny found an egg carton on the porch. Inside were a dozen blown eggs, each with an individual hand-painted rose. She flushed, feeling warm all over. She admired each one before setting the carton down on the table. She went to her bedroom to start her homework; a mistake, for she soon nodded off.

She awoke to an ear-splitting crash. Dazed, she sat straight up in bed, trying to remember where she was. Something was crashing through the next room. Her living room. Blinking at her contacts for emergency, she crept to her bedroom door. There she stopped, afraid to look out.

One final crash, as if every last window in the house had caved in. Then silence. Cautiously, Jenny crept out to the living room.

The room was a total wreck. Window shards littered the futon, *The Two Fridas* lay black and crumpled on the floor, the painted eggs scattered. A trail of blood led outside the fractured picture window. In the peach-colored light of early morning, Jenny glimpsed a blood-spattered deer limping back to the pines.

From the hallway came her roommate. Mary Dyer smelled oddly of something like chlorine, yet her face and arms still glowed all over. Her eyes held an intense questioning look. With a quick step she was at the window, her fists raised, pounding on the glass. The glass, what was left of it, flew outward, piece by piece.

Jenny's hands flew to her face. "*¡Dios mío!* Mary, what are you doing!" She grabbed Mary's shoulders from behind, but, surprisingly strong, her roommate kept pounding until the glass was gone from the sill.

Then abruptly Mary stopped. Her fists still fluoresced clean, no trace of blood. She turned and studied Jenny's face. "I was trying to help."

"Help? Are you crazy?"

"The window is clear now."

So it was. A breath of azalea floated in on the breeze, and the frogs peeped like crazy, while an occasional "oo-aw" rose above their chorus.

"If we need to do better," Mary said, "tell us how. Tell us how to be human."

Jenny sighed. "Look, *I* didn't break the window—it was that deer. It bounded in here, and out again."

"Deer are eighty percent human." Mary's face never changed expression; it almost seemed painted on. "Can you explain to us, what is the function of deer?"

Jenny shook her head impatiently. "Deer have no function. They have creampuff tails, and they look cute. How will we ever clear this mess?"

"Deer look cute," echoed Mary. "So do humans. It won't save them."

From outside came shrieks and squeals of elephants. A gray trunk probed the window, then the elephant slunk inside, surprisingly agile.

"Get out!" demanded Jenny.

A second elephant clambered in over the broken window, cleverly avoiding a scratch. It had herded the deer into the window, Jenny guessed. Now it sidled over to the printer, as if it knew what to do. To Jenny's astonishment, the printer put out peanuts.

"Who's there?" A man stepped in, his height about Jenny's chin level, in a plaid shirt and denim overalls with the rocking-horse logo. Bands of amyloid circled his biceps and his calves, the energy harvesters worn by Mount Gilead colonists to eke every bit of power they could. **"Travis Tharp, College Security,"** read his window. He gave a low whistle. "Looks like the track at the Lunar Circuit."

The elephants withdrew their trunks and lumbered out in a hurry. Apparently they knew College Security.

"Thanks, Mr. Tharp. How can we clean this up?" It was a good thing they'd put her greenhouse on the roof.

"Never you mind, we'll take care of the venison. And beef up their contraceptives." Tharp glanced at her torn futon, the shattered windows. He called out, "Code forty-two: restore."

The window fragments melted and slowly seeped into the floor. Meanwhile, the outer frame of the window grew panes slowly creeping toward the center. The Frida poster puddled away, but a new one took shape on the wall. The torn futon merged itself together. It made Jenny queasy to watch, as if she herself might just melt away. Only the scattered eggshells remained on the floor, irreparable, although two miraculously survived in the carton.

"It's nice having you young folks back," observed Tharp. "The hab gets mighty quiet in the summers."

Remembering her manners, Jenny extended her hand. Tharp walked stiffly; a hemiprosthete, Jenny realized, his whole lower torso and legs replaced. His toy window showed a Purple Heart and the ice-blue Antarctic Defense ribbon. "You live here all year round?"

"I'm a homesteader," Travis explained. "One of the first in Mount Gilead. Came to stock the spacehab with Quade." Travis nodded as if to himself. "Deer, I could see, they're good hunting—arrows only, of course. Wouldn't do to have bullets shooting across the sky." His gaze strayed outside to some shards of amyloid from the window that had failed to rejoin the structure.

"You may glean them," Jenny offered.

"Much obliged." Travis picked up a shard and applied his left-leg power band to draw what little energy remained. Colonists had strict energy quotas, and appreciated whatever extra they could get.

Jenny was thinking of what he'd said about stocking the hab. "Why elephants? I thought the hab stocked only Ohio native creatures."

Travis shrugged. "The mini-elephants were made originally as guides for the disabled. A few donkey genes got mixed in. Smarter than dogs, and tamer than monkeys. But then a couple escaped." Adam and Eve pachyderms. "They're all over Ohio now, down to the Death Belt."

Mary moved closer, turning her face toward the man, yet she gazed slightly past him, as she did with Jenny. "Are elephants human?"

Travis laughed. "They sure think they are."

Mary asked, "How would you exterminate them?"

Jenny blinked and looked hard at her *compañera.*

"Oh," Tharp said cheerfully, "that depends. Smartshot wouldn't take but a couple of hours to clear the hab. Kinder way is to max their contraceptives."

Mary asked, "Would that work for humans?"

Alone in her room, Jenny reached her mother. "The hab has mosquitoes, my place is a wreck, and my *compañera* wants to exterminate humans."

In her toybox, thirty-six thousand klicks away, Soledad nodded soothingly. "Never mind, *hijita,* your furniture code is up on Toynet, even Grandma's picture."

"But Mama, my *compañera.* What if she's an ecoterrorist?" Those fists pounding the glass.

"*Hijita,* who does not contemplate human extinction? It may yet happen." If the Centrists won another four years, they'd scrap the few global protection laws and solarplate the Death Belt from Alaska to Alabama.

Jenny swallowed, reluctant to voice her worse fear. "What if . . . she's a DIRG?"

"A DIRG? Accepted at Frontera? *Dios mío,*" her mother muttered.

Her father actually smiled. "I played jokes like that on your mother's school. Hacked the registrar, then changed all the As to Fs."

Soledad rolled her eyes. "Just to impress me with his smarts, the MIT brat."

If only she were home, Jenny thought. Home where her mother could squeeze her hand, and Jenny could pat her father's arm.

That evening Jenny set out with Anouk to the Bulls Blowout at the Red Bull clubhouse. She still had her last two Nobels to read for Thursday, and now she had a Politics paper due Friday. The trail had softened after the late afternoon rain, and she grimaced at the condition of her laces. She'd print out new ones as soon as they reached the Red Bull house. Anouk lifted her hem from the mud, her Monroe following at a distance.

From ahead boomed heavy music, drowning out ToyNews and the spring peepers. Scarlet race cars lined the curb, their rear wings extending halfway across the trail. From all directions, students converged to the music's source, a square textured-stucco building with *chicos* hanging out of open windows and doors. Glitter-haired *chicos* and *chicas* milled around watching as a giant hog carcass rotated on a spit above a laser grill. Real pork; it smelled wonderful, though she felt bad for Anouk.

The music boomed so loud she could barely hear. Several frog *chicos* were standing around in slash-cut shirts, anxious but friendly. A *chica* arrived in glittering tights, a tattoo of coupling dogs showing through her moonhole. Text crowded Jenny's toybox.

"Has anyone played *Meet Me in Shanghai,* with Newman and Monroe?"

"Pong, anyone?

"Let's shag the mosquitoes."

"Blast the mocs out of the hab."

"Drown them in beer."

Everyone's cup was full, and some had the glazed eyes of pregamers. An elephant sidled up among the students, lifting its trunk to beg. One student held out a cup; the elephant dipped its trunk and slurped. Everyone laughed.

"Jenny!" Fritz Hoffman came out from the clubhouse, his hair brushed up full of glitter, biceps polished to a shine. He pointed to a table inside, draped in purple. "Voter registration, tonight and tomorrow morning. We avoid scheduling classes on Tuesday and Thursday, so we can volunteer service."

Jenny texted to Anouk, "I just need to say hello inside."

Within the clubhouse, the air had a stale yeasty smell. Anouk followed close behind Jenny, politely smiling, while Berthe stopped just inside the door.

"Jenny," called Charlie, weaving his way through the crowd. "What a great practice that was today!"

"A great team. Remember what Ken said," Jenny warned.

"Oh, I can handle that." Charlie had no cup yet. "These bros are real great to me; they make me feel at home. They even hold study sessions."

Someone bumped into her. "Hi, tía. Dance?"

Jenny smiled but looked away, trying to inch closer to the draped table.

"Don't miss the Frontera Grand Prix."

"Ferrari whipped our ass last year, but this year we've got new Anthradyne engines."

"Fingerprints?" someone asked at the desk. "To register to vote?"

"It's an Ohio thing," the chico behind the desk explained. "Fingerprints, or else a retinal scan. You want to save the planet or not?" Behind him, the amyloid wall blinked in purple, CARRILLO FOR PRESIDENT. A virtual globe showed black areas for the solarplated death zones: the western USA, Nevada through Tennessee; the Amazon; the Sahara, the Australian interior. Unity candidate Carrillo pledged a halt to solarplate.

Behind her back, someone pinched Jenny through a moonhole. "Qué jeta." Jenny pulled away, but the chico caught her arm. She wheeled around. Glazed eyes, a pregamer. "Excuse me," she said very clearly, "I need to leave."

The glazed eyes stared, and the grip lingered. Jenny blinked her "safe" button. At the shock, the chico withdrew his hand, with an angry utterance.

From the doorway, Anouk's Monroe moved forward, her face pouting prettily. Reaching the pregamer, the Monroe grasped him by the back of his shirt and lifted him a couple of inches off the ground. Turning him to face her, dangling from her hand, the pouting face shook her head.

"Dios mío." Jenny pushed her way through the crowd, now just desperate to get out. She ran out the door, dodging students lined up for their plates of pork. The elephant was now tottering unsteadily on its feet, while more students gathered to laugh. Passing the red cars, she tripped on her laces and fell in the street. Mud all over, she picked herself up and paused to catch her breath. Above amid the black gleamed the stars and the church cross in

Mount Gilead, and north, the golden haze of the Mound. A ring of lights beyond marked the motor track.

"Jenny!" Anouk called, running after her. "Are you all right?"

"Get away from me, you and your DIRG."

"Berthe was just trying to help."

"I took care of myself. I just had to put in an appearance; but now, Clive will have an incident to report on." Jenny tried to wipe the mud off her clothes.

"But your honor—you should not allow—"

"Who are you to say what's honorable? What are you doing all the time, snooping in my toybox?"

"What do you mean?" Anouk's voice chilled.

"If you snoop in a dealer's toybox—in America, that's ten years in prison."

"I don't need to snoop, I just count cards."

"Well, you won't count my cards anymore."

"*Écoute*—You don't understand." Anouk's face drew close to hers, wisps of hair straying from her gold headscarf. "It's a disability. I can't help it—I'm compulsive."

Jenny's jaw fell open. "You're what?"

"A compulsive hacker. A form of OCD; it's all documented."

"*Qué historia,*" Jenny muttered.

"It's the truth," Anouk insisted. "That's why I couldn't join my brother at Oxford," she added bitterly. "The *gendarme* told my parents I could go to the pen, or leave Euro, one or the other. So they sent me off-world." She lifted her chin. "How would you feel, to be banned from your own planet?"

Jenny looked away. Drunks, ghosts, mosquitoes, and hackers. How was she to get any work done?

"Not that it matters, I can hack the Pentagon from here. But I didn't harm you. Just got to know you, that's all. That's how I know that we'll be great friends."

Some friend.

"Look, I—I'll keep Berthe away next time. And I can help you lose your mental."

Jenny turned on Anouk, blinking fast. "You can't do that." She swallowed hard. "I need the mental."

"But you could lose her, now and then, just for a bit. Just long enough to see Jordi."

14

From the slanball court, the south solar was a peach, pale and luminous, ringed by the blue Ohio River. The "sunrise" gradually whitened. The players were practicing a one-two pass, in pairs with paired guards, zigzagging all the way down the court. Yola jittered the ball ahead of her, as Jenny crawled the cage at an angle, behind the back of guard David Pezarkar. Yola slanned it back to her—but David nearly hit it out from under, before Jenny jittered it away. David had good "eyes in the back," Jenny thought. She slanned the ball back to Yola; but then out of nowhere came Reesie. Reesie got in just near enough to slan the ball out of Yola's range.

"Great job, Reesie." Coach Porat hung overhead, like a bat from a tree. "Don't run all the way; pass."

Reesie jittered the ball past Jenny, then she slanned the ball hard. But her footgrips came loose, a sign of inexperience with the cage; she extended her arms and legs but continued sailing slowly across.

Meanwhile, Jenny caught the ball, letting it jitter for a moment before her eyes. Then she passed it to Kendall. Guards Fran and Ricky converged on him. Jenny crossed over to play her part, trying to get her head in the mix without fouling the defenders. She scrabbled like a monkey along the rungs of the cage, till she had the right angle to launch. Launching herself just right, she passed by Kendall's shoulder and slanned the ball out from him. The ball crossed half the court and sank into the goal, despite a late deflect by goalie Charlie.

"Way to go, Ken!"

Everyone cheered Ken, in case of spies. Indeed a suspicious heli sailed around outside, at some distance from the cage.

Fran took a moment to launch herself to Reesie and nudge her toward the side, recovering her grip.

"Time out."

They could use it, thought Jenny, wiping the sweat from beneath her slancap. Coach Porat had climbed over to Reesie to advise her.

"Hey." Yola caught her shoulder. "Nice catch—and nice pass."

Kendall came over, hand over hand. He did not look Jenny in the eye. "Cruising the clubs already, are we?"

"Chill out, Kenny-boy." Yola punched him. "She didn't drink anything. We all need to work on passing."

"I *know* that, Yola-babe." Then he smiled, as if remembering something. "'The wise man learns from everyone.' Good job, Jenny. How's the roommate? The classes?"

"*Muy bien.* We're building DNA." Jenny avoided comment on her *compañera.*

"You haven't dropped Abaynesh yet."

"Ken, I like your sayings," Jenny told him. "Are they all Quaker?"

Yola laughed. "The Talmud. He likes to butter up Coach."

"I like the Talmud," Kendall insisted. "Quakers can go to hell."

"Ken tried to convert," said Yola, "but Coach wouldn't let him."

They turned as Coach Porat ambled over, along the cage; he usually walked with footgrips, not bothering to use hands. "That's more like it; hustle on defense. Never let up on your opponent; confuse them, whoever's got the ball. But what happens when three of us go after one slanner?"

"Other players get left unguarded," said Fran.

"And Melbourne's man-on-man defense is lethal." The Melbourne Uni Scorpions—just over a week till their first Sunday game. The first game of the season was always tough, Jenny thought with a tightening in her gut.

"But we're the greatest," called Yola, "aren't we, Coach?"

Porat put his hand out, and everyone put theirs together. "Together, we're the greatest. Our opponents are as feeble as we are formidable. We beat the Scorpions last year; we'll do it again. Show them what the Great Bear is made of."

Tuesday-Thursday classes met twice a week, but Thursday was the three-hour Life lab. The class had dwindled to about twenty diehards, still including Tom and Charlie. "**Thanks for the eggs,**" Jenny texted Tom.

Tom smiled back, like a burst of sun through the clouds.

Within the baobab trunk, the DNA strand plunged downward forever. Abaynesh surveyed the class. "So what does DNA do? It receives signals, for your cell to do things—like grow a nerve fiber. And it makes copies of RNA." RNA was like DNA's Illyrian twin: nearly alike, but not quite. "If you've read all your Nobel experiments, you should be ready for the quest. Pick your partner, then step out. Always remember two things: observe, and cooperate."

The students paired off. Jenny and Anouk followed the professor out a narrow doorway through the trunk.

As she emerged, Jenny blinked in the sun. A couple of trees dotted the savannah, near a shallow river. Anouk was there, but where were the professor and the other students?

Anouk nodded smartly. "We're on our own."

"So what do we do?" In Jenny's toybox appeared an inventory. It held a laboratory notebook, a flaming torch, and a clean baby's diaper.

In the distance rose a cloud of dust. The dust came nearer, revealing four men on horses, their hooves pounding. Jenny caught Anouk's hand and reminded herself this was all just a toyworld. Just when she was about to get out of the way, the horses pulled up short.

The nearest horse reared with a whinny, raising a hoof the size of her head. The rider was space-black, in a leather costume decorated with beads and a lion's mane on his head. He pulled out a long trumpet and blared a flourish. "In the name of the Queen of Sheba, sovereign of the Cushite Empire, I proclaim your quest. The Queen's baby is missing. The baby must be found—the future of the Cushite people is at stake. The aim of your quest is to find the royal infant."

The lion's mane leaned down from the horse, whose flanks still panted in the hot sun. From his hand dangled a large bronze key.

Jenny looked questioningly at Anouk.

"Accept the quest," Anouk whispered loudly.

She took the key. "We, um, accept the quest."

"Be warned—beware the Convolvula. It has a copper deficiency." With that parting shot, the four horses galloped off, tails waving. Jenny was left holding the key, which had a couple of teeth and a curious twig-shaped rune.

Anouk rolled her eyes. "This is worse than Middle Earth."

"So what next?"

"Observe." Anouk cast around, looking this way and that over the clumps of grass. She zeroed in on a rock. "Look there."

The rock had a bronze keyhole. Jenny fitted the key into the hole. The rock began to slide with a grating sound. As it came to a halt, a new object appeared in Jenny's inventory: a fresh hen's egg.

Beyond lay dark. So Anouk produced a lit torch. Jenny blinked her inventory and pulled out her torch as well. The torchlight revealed a stairway down. The two students stepped gingerly down the stairs. Jenny scanned the corridor walls, wondering how all this would help find the Queen's baby.

The students emerged in a forest, no more sunlit savannah. The trees were so dense that only glimmers of sun came through. Birds and insects called unseen. As Jenny's eyes adjusted, she saw a glowing tablet held up amid a tangle of vines. The tablet showed the genetic code of DNA.

"Convolvula." Anouk reached for the tablet. "Ow! Jenny!" Anouk was pinned to a tree by the vines. "Keep off," she yelled as Jenny approached. "*Merde,* every toyworld has a scene like this. Go back and get the torch."

Jenny hurried back down the stairs and retrieved her forgotten torch, still lit. She brandished it at the vines surrounding Anouk. The vines blackened and smoked with a foul stench, but still clutched Anouk. One snaked around Jenny's legs and bound her too. Fighting panic, Jenny tried to think.

"It must be something else," muttered Anouk. "The key! It's bronze, that includes copper! *Tout de suite!*"

Jenny blinked at her inventory to retrieve the key. Immediately the copper-starved vines let up and converged on the key, tangling around it until it vanished beneath the leaves. Anouk withdrew, the tablet in her hand. As they backed off from the vines, Jenny wondered uneasily how the rest of the class was doing. She clicked Tom's window.

The window opened. There lay Tom entangled in the vines, with Charlie caught behind him.

"Hi, Jenny," said Tom, trying to sound unconcerned. "I'm sure we'll figure it out. How are you doing?"

She smiled. "Give it the key."

"I can't—we left the key behind in the stone."

Anouk gave him a withering look. "Just a minute." Her eyes scanned back and forth, writing code. Another rune key appeared before Tom. Jenny didn't ask how, although she suspected this work-around broke the rules.

"Thanks," called Tom, and Charlie waved heroically. "We'll see you later." The window winked shut.

Ahead, a patch of light poked through the trees. A path led to a small wooden cottage. Jenny and Anouk approached cautiously. A broken road sign read, TORINO 10 KM.

"Italy, of course." Anouk knocked on the door.

The door opened, revealing a young woman with expressive eyebrows, elegantly coifed hair, and a long floral dress. Her smile was kind, though infinitely sad. *"Buon giorno. Avete portato le uova?"*

"*Buon giorno,*" replied Anouk, going on in Italian. She told Jenny, "Doctor Levi-Montalcini wants the egg."

The first Nobel Laureate—long before she won the prize, Jenny guessed. Jenny blinked the egg from her inventory.

"Thank you," replied Rita Levi-Montalcini in English as she closed the door behind them. "I hope there was a rooster in the henhouse, so the egg will be of use. I wish I could say 'Welcome to Turin,' but 1941 is not a welcoming time in Europe." Her fingers clenched for emphasis. "Now if you'll both come this way, I have some embryos prepared."

The chick embryos were set in a glass incubator, with two round openings for arms to manipulate while maintaining the temperature. The incubator stood on a small side table, crowded next to a Zeiss microscope and a microtome. The rest of the room contained a dining table set for four and a china closet.

An elderly man with red-tinged white hair came to the microscope. He adjusted the focus and peered intently at a slide.

"Our great teacher, Doctor Giuseppe Levi," she introduced. "No relation, but he taught three who won Nobels." A Nobel Prize from a country dining room.

The table jarred as Giuseppe Levi rose too fast, bumping into it. He lifted his large hands. "*Scusi, starò più attento.*"

Levi-Montalcini reached into the incubator and held a large magnifier above one of the culture dishes. Upon the egg yolk grew an embryo, a red disc of twining blood vessels and limb buds. "In the chick embryo, I cut out a wing bud and saw the loss of nerve growth, an experiment devised by my German friend Viktor Hamburger. Viktor thought that removing the wing bud stopped new cells from becoming nerves."

Giuseppe Levi raised his arms and spoke excitedly, his arm waving perilously near the microscope.

"Yes, dear," she assured him, "of course we thought differently." Her hands rose and fell as if conducting an orchestra. "I argued that the nerve cells degenerate, in the absence of a signal—"

From outside, overhead, came a whining sound. The whine fell in pitch, like distant fireworks, ending with a muffled explosion.

Her eyes flew open. "Extinguish your torch," she hissed. "And crawl under the table." Grabbing the Zeiss microscope, she cradled it protectively and climbed under the dining table.

The torch would not go out; Jenny fumbled, fearing to burn herself or set the cottage on fire. Anouk whispered, "Return it to your inventory." With a wink the torch vanished, and Jenny joined them under the table. Another descending whine, and an explosion shook the floor. The explosions continued, growing in intensity and tumbling one upon another. She froze in panic, trapped like the ultra in the tree. A final explosion deafened her; it must surely have destroyed the house. But afterward, all was still.

"As non-Aryans," Levi-Montalcini explained under the table, "we had to hide in the country to pursue our work. Here, I found the first clues for a signal to grow nerves. Nerve growth factor." Her eyes widened at Jenny, scrunched by the table leg. "Nerve growth factor grows, when your life changes. For instance, when you fall in love."

Startled, Jenny looked away.

Rita Levi-Montalcini climbed nimbly out from the table, helping the two students up. "After the war, Victor invited me to your country, the University of Washington, St. Louis."

Light flooded the room, which was now a comfortable laboratory with several microscopes and incubators. Outside the window, a bell rang twice. In the city street a trolley car rolled by, while men in top hats and women in long dresses strolled the sidewalk. Levi-Montalcini now had lines in her forehead, and she wore a lace blouse with pearls.

"In St. Louis, we began our experiments to isolate the mystery signal that made nerves grow." She gave Jenny and Anouk a closer look at the chick embryos, each with a head, a long curving backbone, and limb buds, all pulsing with new blood vessels.

Out of the corner of her eye, Jenny saw something move. A large black handbag sat by the incubator. She couldn't help notice that the handbag was moving and stretching; something was happening inside.

"We asked: Can a foreign tissue producing the right signal make a nerve grow?" The doctor drew out a set of slides and placed the first one under a microscope. "I used my new technique of silver staining to mark nerve axons in the chick embryo. In this embryo, I implanted a source of the signal: a mouse tumor."

"A mouse tumor in a chick embryo?" wondered Jenny.

Anouk shrugged. "Mouse and chick DNA are two-thirds the same."

"I learned that much later," observed the doctor, "though in retrospect, I'm not surprised. Tell me: What do you see in this embryo?"

A tangle of nerves blackened by silver grew everywhere. Jenny could scarcely make sense of it. She and Anouk took turns at the microscope.

"Any nerves in the mouse tumor?" hinted the doctor.

"Not in the tumor," said Jenny. "But here, in the chick veins just outside the tumor, there are lots of new nerves." Bundles of axons, creeping out from the neurons. "Where you wouldn't expect nerves to be."

Anouk was ticking numbers in a column of the lab notebook from her inventory. "You must compare numbers with the control, which lacks the tumor. A t-test shows the growth of chick nerves is significant."

"Excellent," observed the doctor. "The nerves grew. But what signal caused this growth? I had to isolate the signal from mouse tumors." She opened her handbag. Out of the handbag crept two white mice. The mice sniffed the edge of the bag and cast their noses this way and that as if discovering a new world. Each mouse had a large misshapen lump on its back.

Levi-Montalcini pointed to each tumor. "Extracts of these tumors contain a signal that makes nerves grow. But this experiment was hard to do in the whole chick; we had to use chick neuron clusters in tissue culture. I had no tissue culture facility in St. Louis, so I boarded a plane with the mice hiding in my handbag—to visit my friend Hertha Meyer in Rio."

The doctor went to the window, drew the blind shut, then thrust it up again. A cacophony of music filled the room, as if several bands competed in the street. The street was full of dancers in colorful costumes, adorned with outsized masks and mock genitals. "I believe Rio's Carnival inspired an exuberant growth of nerves. Look!"

In each dish treated with the tumor extract, a black halo of nerves surrounded each chick neuron cluster. An urgent outgrowth, relentless like Convolvula. It made Jenny's hair stand on end. If plants, now, grew such nerves—if they escaped, what then?

Anouk said, "The replicates look good. But where's the control?"

"The control—good question. There's a problem." Levi-Montalcini produced several more dishes. "Instead of a tumor, this embryo was treated with a control: plain snake venom."

A hissing sound. Jenny looked up. Levi-Montalcini withdrew a snake from a nearby terrarium. To her horror, Jenny saw it was a rattlesnake. With gloved hands, Levi-Montalcini held the snake's head by a covered beaker. The head lunged, its fangs struck the cover, squirting venom through.

"It's just a control," Levi-Montalcini assured her. "Snake venom has an enzyme we use to degrade contaminants. It's always around the lab; a good control. Compare the tumor-treated embryos with these controls, treated only with snake venom."

They observed one dish after another. Anouk concluded, "The tumor works best, but the venom controls all grew some nerves."

"Precisely. Even snake venom contains this nerve growth factor. The signal is made by many different animal tissues. Of course—many kinds of tissue need nerves, do they not?"

Chick embryos, mouse tumors, snake venom. All made the same signal, the same protein made by the same gene. And always told the neuron's DNA to grow an axon. Axons that made your brain do a hundred different things—even fall in love.

The doctor rose and checked her watch. "I wish you could stay, but at last I came back to Rome, where I was named Senator for Life. The assembly is about to open." Outside the cottage window rose a sunlit building with marble columns and statues. Levi-Montalcini's face was now lined, like Rosa Schwarz when she became president; her hair white, her eyes keen as ever.

Jenny swallowed. "Could this protein . . . make nerves in a plant?"

"That comes after my time. Meanwhile, this will help you." The white-haired senator gave Anouk and Jenny each a bag full of coins imprinted with polygons. "How does the signal work? It tells DNA to make RNA. You will traverse half a century now, so hold on tight."

Wishing she could stay, Jenny put the coins up in her inventory. "Could I come back sometime?"

In her inventory quivered something new. It was a mouse with a lump on its back, curiously sniffing around her toybox. "Certainly, my friend. Just send me sarcoma thirty-seven."

The cottage was already dissolving. Jenny hurried out after Anouk, and she blinked in the bright sun.

An enormous model of a molecule towered in the blue sky. The molecule looked much like DNA, but only a single strand that doubled back on itself in fiendish helical twists.

"It's RNA," exclaimed Anouk. RNA was the long chain of atomic "letters" that copied the gene to make a protein. "It must be the RNA to make proteins that grow the nerve."

This RNA was not a straight line of bases, like she recalled from high school. Its bases doubled back to pair in short DNA-like helices. The helices made hairpin turns and hunched-over loops, forming helices to pair as many bases as it could. From the nearby end of one strand hung a car with little seats and bars to hold down the rider. With growing horror, Jenny realized what it was: a roller coaster.

Anouk took her hand. "Just hold on tight."

"But—all those turns and loops."

"*Enfin,* keep your eyes shut."

They got into the nearest car, and pulled down the bar. The car started out slowly, chugging its way up the exposed strand. Then it took its first sickening plunge into a helix. The car looped over and over again, coming out just long enough to veer in another direction, into an even longer helix. Anouk laughed. "I'll make Rafael ride this someday."

After endless loops and turns, the car came to rest at the far end. Jenny knew she was still, although the world still rushed around her head. As her head came together, she became aware of a wooded hill and a large hospital complex. Beyond the hill, a brick-colored seawall held back the blue Pacific.

From one of the hospital towers, a woman in jeans came running out to meet them. Nancy Ng, the author of their homework paper—she'd won her Nobel the year Jenny started high school. "Welcome to San Francisco," said Ng. "UCSF always needs good grad students. Hope you'll consider us."

The elevator took them up to the lab on the fifty-fourth floor. "My postdoc Lee Howell," Ng introduced him.

"From Ole Miss." Howell nodded in a friendly way, his face bronze, with rounded lab-rat shoulders. "Nan does the neuro. I'm the green thumb." Today, a decade after the Nobel he'd shared with Ng, Howell ran a large neuroplant institute back at his alma mater.

Anouk looked admiringly around the lab, with at least half a dozen unfamiliar forms of apparatus. "Impressive."

"We're quite proud of our lab. It held up even through the quake of ninety-seven. Some say another is due."

Jenny clapped her hands to her head. "No way," she exclaimed. "I've been strangled by vines and strafed by artillery; I will *not* have an earthquake."

Howell laughed. "Don't mind our little jokes."

"No towering inferno? No meltdown? No Godzilla?" Jenny tried to recall all the disasters that might befall a toyworld.

He laughed even harder and slapped his knee. "They'd melt us down, all right, if they knew what we're up to."

"No more disasters," Ng assured her. "Well, just one . . . let's get done before that."

Behind a glass panel grew rows of *Arabidopsis,* the little green leaves poking out just like in Professor Abaynesh's laboratory. "Rita found the first nerve growth factor," said Ng. "But Rita's protein turned out to be one of hundreds, perhaps thousands, of signals controlling nerves. Their effect is a combinatorial problem."

"Combinatorics—yes!" exclaimed Anouk. "It was all in your paper the professor gave us." Jenny had made it about halfway through. "Ng and Howell."

"Growth factors need receptors," Ng explained. "Receptors made by genes. I engineered a plant with the genes for nerve growth factor receptor. With those receptors, plus nerve growth factor, the plant grew a nervous system."

"Sounds simple, doesn't it." Howell nodded. "Did she mention the combinations?"

A window to one of Ng's instruments opened in Jenny's box. Anouk saw it too, and her eyes lit up. "I can do this."

Jenny felt lost; a t-test was one thing, but combining hundreds of genes was beyond her.

"Remember, Anouk," said Howell, "you don't actually find one 'right' combination, just select about a thousand plausible sets. Then we'll transform the plants and grow them all."

The instrument was running scenarios for each gene, which receptor it made for which kind of neurons, sensory and motor, and so on.

"All right," said Anouk, "I've picked a thousand combinations. Can you grow the plants?"

Behind the glass, the thousand plants sprouted and grew. "Don't get the wrong idea," observed Howell. "This part took decades."

"My hair turned gray," agreed Ng. "But in the end, look what we found." She opened a glass panel. Behind the glass, the plant looked just like all the others. But when she touched a leaf, it flexed and curled. "A motor reflex. Your combination of receptor genes produced a reflex arc."

Jenny stared. "Is that . . . *Arabidopsis sapiens?*"

"Sapiens came later. Sharon's work." Sharon Abaynesh, her own professor.

Anouk's eyes narrowed. "By the way . . . Which experiment won the third Nobel?" She hated to admit she'd missed something.

Ng rolled her eyes. "Sharon figures she will someday."

Howell chuckled. "Sharon was always the uppity New Yorker. Good luck in her lab."

"Time's running short." Ng hurried on. "Uh-oh. What's this?"

A form appeared, from the National Institutes of Health. A termination notice.

"After your great-grandmother lost reelection, the first Guzmán invaded Antarctica, and all the research labs lost funding."

In the laboratory, a light went out, then another. At last they were in darkness. Jenny produced her magic torch. In the torchlight, the four faces shone like moons.

"We scraped by—"

"Others didn't," put in Howell.

"Scientists ignore politics," said Ng. "My own postdocs were too busy to vote."

"I voted," Howell insisted. "Others—" He shrugged. "After that, the only government funding was for anthrax. Weapons-grade anthrax."

"To test defense, of course."

Jenny's scalp crawled. She couldn't imagine working in a triple-sealed biodefense lab to make life-forms you never planned to use.

"We turned it into anthradyne," said Ng.

"That's *chulo*," said Jenny. "My mother financed the first anthradyne plant in space. The one that grows anthrax cords for the space lift."

"Nowadays," said Howell, "if you lose your grant, you make weapons-grade ultra."

Jenny's jaw fell. *"¿Qué?"* Ultraphyte bioweapons?

Ng shook her head. "That's classified. So tell us, what's Sharon up to these days?"

Howell added, "They say Sharon gets plants to sing and dance. Even pray in church."

Despite herself Jenny smiled. Then she realized he wasn't laughing.

Back on the savannah, Jenny and Anouk found themselves on horseback, wearing chain mail with a helmet, and holding a shield and a jousting pole. Jenny barely noticed the toyworld paraphernalia. "Weapons-grade ultra," she muttered. "To make cyanide?"

"Americans," exclaimed Anouk. "They'll make a weapon out of anything. *Zut*, Jenny—look out!"

Ahead of them, two armored knights guarded a tall gate before a river.

Waving her pole, Anouk trotted up to the knights. "Let us pass, *s'il vous plaît.*" The helmet muffled her words. "What may we give you? Gold coins? Diamonds? Health spells?"

The two knights raised their poles and held them out threateningly.

"If that's how you want it." Anouk rode forward and jabbed one of the knights. But he only lifted his shield, and the pole slid aside. Anouk's horse reared up before running into the other knight. Jenny warily joined Anouk with her pole, with similar result. No jab of the poles could break the knights' defense.

"Wait," Jenny called, "look there." From upriver, two more knights bore down on them, poles pointing forward.

Anouk drew up her pole and stared. "Whose side are they on?"

The two strange knights lost no time attacking the guardian knights. Emboldened by reinforcements, Jenny and Anouk redoubled their own attack, jabbing at the knights' shields. While Anouk occupied one, Jenny and the two strangers all jabbed at the hapless companion.

At last the one knight was unhorsed. His companion trotted over to help him up, but the incident convinced both to retire in ignominious defeat. As the defeated knights trotted off, the newcomers raised their visors. They were Tom and Charlie.

"¡Hola!" Jenny pulled off her helmet. "How'd you get here?"

Charlie laughed, his hair tossing. "To the rescue! Huzzah!"

Tom explained, "We knew we'd never beat them on our own, so we tried cooperation."

"Did you ever get your plants to move?"

Charlie said, "We guessed random numbers. Dr. Ng got annoyed and told us to take a math class. But darned if one plant didn't move, just a bit."

Anouk sniffed. "There's always a false positive. Wait—quiet, everyone. Do you hear that?"

A sound of crying, like a baby. The cries came from ahead somewhere behind the gate. Charlie galloped on ahead, trying to find another entrance. "No way," he shouted back, "the wall goes clear around."

Jenny got off her horse, threw off her armor, and rushed to the gate. The gate displayed four rows of disk-shaped imprints. "The genetic code! The coins!"

Each of Levi-Montalcini's coins had a symbol for a protein building block. Everyone contributed coins, while Jenny fit them in. The unseen baby's cries rose to shrieks.

As the last coin fell in place, a crack appeared in the gate, and a hinge creaked. Charlie leaned on the gate and pushed it open. Everyone rushed through.

In a basket surrounded by high walls lay the baby, its blanket fallen off, furiously waving its arms and legs. The baby was unclothed except for one badly soiled diaper. Tom already had the fresh diaper out of his inventory and set about changing it, as if he'd had lots of practice.

From behind, a distant trumpet sounded. Through the open gate, an enormous procession appeared. It snaked toward them, with horsemen in lions' manes and musicians followed by the Queen of Sheba in a canopied chair upon a camel.

In Jenny's box a window opened. "You finished in time for lunch," observed Professor Abaynesh. "Grade A."

Grade A—after all that? Jenny was stunned. In high school, she'd never earned less than A triple plus.

15

Dylan had just confirmed his Friday appointment with Gil Wickett, with ten minutes to spare before his son was to call from Berkeley. But a window popped up; Nora Kwon, dean of students. She had that grim "thought you ought to know" look about her.

"Nora, what's up? Tell the parents we're taking care of the mosquitoes—"

"The Pentagon," she began. "They traced an attack to one of our student accounts. The Chouiref girl." The Euro minister's daughter. "Thought you ought to know."

"Can't Toy Land turn up security a notch?"

"Zari says no one can fix the holes this student found. Luis never told us she's compulsive. And a banished criminal." The sarcasm made him wince. "Admissions accepts these kids, then expects us to deal."

"A compulsive hacker?"

"It's a recognized syndrome, listed on the APA. We've got Twelve Step, AA, and Taxplayers Rehab, but this one is new to us. We're all boning up on it, got her in therapy, Zari is on her case, but—"

"I'm sure Clare will help." A change of pace for Clare. "Now if you'll excuse me, could we—"

"And the Dyer girl." The one with the pearls, from Long Beach. "Mary Dyer shows up for just one course, Phil's seminar, and she spooks people asking them how to exterminate humans. She's an omniprosthete—yet she can't use Toynet? Within FERPA, can't Luis give me more than that?"

An omniprosthete had total body replacement, only a human brain inside somewhere, typically the "chest" region. A few brain cells away from a DIRG. Dylan checked his notes. "She had childhood osteosarcoma that spread. Her doctor's well known; his clients include the White House." The vice president had become an omniprosthete after a hunting accident. Only his original head and hands remained. His hands had a habit of creeping away from himself, hence his nickname, the Creep.

"Osteosarcoma," Nora breathed. "And no parents. What survivors these kids are."

"I can give you the clinic's Toynet window."

"That's a help. Don't go yet—"

Dylan let out a breath, willing himself to be patient.

"A young taxplayer at the Mound sold his ticket home, now he's stranded. We put him up in an empty dorm room. Thought you ought to know."

"But—a nonstudent, that's not our problem. And it's not supposed to happen." The Mound sponsored taxplayer rehab, of course, the standard 10 percent mandated by the original Ramos bill. But that was down on Earth, in a Dayton facility.

Nora gave him the "whatever you say" look. "The Mound won't return calls."

Of course, they couldn't just leave the kid out in the cold. Bad for Frontera's family image. "Couldn't he just wait tables in Mount Gilead until he pays it off?"

"Father of three, a grocery clerk from Peoria."

Dylan sighed. "Put him in our rehab." The college ran their own taxplayers rehab; it had long ago surpassed alcohol and eating disorders. At present, an art history professor and a philosopher were in rehab, along with about forty students. "I'll talk to Bobby." Bobby Foxtail Forrester, manager of the Mound—their landlord, Dylan reminded himself.

Thankfully that was it. He managed to settle on the couch with Clare, just in time for Fritz to pop into his toybox. They'd originally picked his name because it was least popular in the name book; then that year, all the boys were named Fritz. Dylan had wanted to culture him from Clare, but Clare had wanted him like Dylan, so they'd gone retro, split the genes fifty-fifty. Their son's mop of hair, fair and wavy like Clare's, was ringed by a native swastika headband, while his nose and mouth echoed Dylan's. He looked gorgeous, despite his perpetually serious expression. "Fritz! How are you, tío?"

"¿Qué haces?" added Clare. "What are you saving this week?"

"Groundhogs," Fritz answered, all business as usual. "Marmota monax. They're endangered—nearly gone." He stared at Dylan. "What are you going to do about it?"

"Groundhogs?" repeated Dylan halfheartedly. "I'll have to look up groundhog preservation. Ask Quade—"

Fritz rolled his eyes. "Dad—you know, groundhogs? Groundhog Day, and Punxatawny Phil? Do you realize there are no groundhogs left in all of Pennsylvania and Ohio? Doesn't the history loss even bother you?"

Clare said, "Of course it does. A field without groundhogs would be un-thinkable. I'm sure you're holding a benefit."

"The biggest ever. It will be, but we have to raise funds up front."

A pitch for funds—that Dylan understood. "Sure, *tío*. How much do you need?"

A look of pain darkened Fritz's face. "I told you not to call me that."

Dylan bit his tongue. This was his third term of endearment crossed out, and he was at a loss for another.

"Fritz, you know we'll send what you need," added Clare. "Just make sure it's effective, remember? Effective philanthropy, I always say."

"Sure, Pop," said Fritz, "I know what you mean. Just don't let Reesie hear you use those gender-exclusionary words."

"Reesie?" Dylan asked. "Do we know Reesie? Caroline was a nice *chica*—"

"Caroline was last week." A moment's pause. "Don't look at me like that, Dad. What do you expect—a man my age to settle down?" He pointed an accusing finger. "Look at your own elite college, a raft full of hedonistic rich kids. Thinking you'll all outlive spaceship Earth."

"Okay, okay." Dylan raised both hands. "Never mind. I love you . . . son, no matter what."

Fritz's brow wrinkled, the way it looked when he would have said "I love you," if he could. "Babylon," he muttered. "Your school's got quite a rep, you know. Everyone knows. Just remember—I'm keeping an eye on you." A momentary glare, then his tousled head vanished.

Silence lengthened. Dylan held Clare's hand. "Why did we make him hetero?"

"It was your idea," said Clare. "Greater mate choice, you said."

Dylan winced. "He doesn't appreciate it. He thinks love is . . . disposable."

"At least he'll never have to go through what I did." Abdominal implan-tation.

"Was it so bad, the Swedish clinic? Nine months on your back, the pool every day, the masseur, the chanterelles?"

"The preboiled potatoes—the memory still makes me sick."

"Groundhogs," muttered Dylan, shaking his head over his son. "What'll he be saving next? Mosquitoes?"

Clare looked up. "What's the latest? Any help from Life?"

"From chemistry." An estimate had already come through his toybox.

He didn't like the total. "I'm out to Gil's in the morning, to spring a few million for smartspray."

+-

Early Friday morning, on his way out to the anthrax, Dylan paused at the door. Clare came over and grasped both sides of his jacket. Dylan took a deep breath, feeling light-headed. Clare eyed Dylan's tie, the one with the alphabet blocks, a tricycle, and a mallet with colored pegs. "Heading down to Gil's?"

He nodded.

"A big ask?"

"I wish." Dylan loved fundraising; to connect earnest donors' assets with the dreams of highly talented students was his greatest satisfaction. But just to kill bugs—what a waste.

Clare thought a moment. "Have a safe trip. Don't do anything I wouldn't do."

Something in the way he said it made Dylan blink rapidly. "Of course not, sweet. God forbid." A long kiss.

The space lift left on time, but it stalled halfway down to Earth; one of its anthrax cords got clipped by debris, and they had to wait for Anthradyne to slide in another, always in reserve. After a two-hour delay, at last he got below, to find Gil's solar shuttle waiting. The shuttle streaked down to Ohio, above the brown windswept plain just a hundred miles north of the Death Belt.

The Toynet Corporation Headquarters stood outside Dayton, not far from where the Wright brothers first played with bikes and kites. The headquarters took the shape of a gigantic alphabet block, the letter A, of course, and the number 1. Well-watered lawns surrounded the colossal cube, though they could not escape the tumbleweeds blowing in.

As the shuttle landed, a transfer car came up to dock. The shuttle door opened, but the car's snout came forward just too late to engage. Through the door came an oven blast of outdoor air. The blast caught Dylan in the face. His lungs choked, and his eyes streamed. For a moment he was back in the charcoal desert of his Ohio childhood.

"Excuse the error," apologized the shuttle. The door engaged the car, restoring conditioned air.

Catching his breath, Dylan wiped his eyes and stepped into the car. The air cleared; he took a deep breath, as the car sped into Toynet Headquarters through the base of the A.

Outside the office of Chief Executive Officer Guillermo Wickett, Dylan paused to adjust his tie. The doorway shimmered, then the entire wall evaporated. A carpet of amyloid grass with a swing set, and a large soft-fleshed man of boyish proportions riding a rocking horse, the one that adorned the college crest. "Dillie!" The man waved so hard he nearly fell off. He dismounted and hurried forward, pumping his arms vigorously. "*Mucho gusto.* Can we do the Lunar again? Please?"

Dylan laughed, with his best donor-greeting smile. "Someday soon, Gil. Today—"

Around the room tooted the famous toy train, snaking through villages and tunneling through amyloid mountains. "How is good old Clare?" Gil asked. "When *are* you coming out to Lila's Beach?"

"Very soon, I hope." If only Clare would go; what a treat that would be.

"And how's your good school, all the *chicos* and *chicas*?" Gil rubbed his hands together. "Such a wonderful school. If only it existed back then, I would have gone there." Gil had quit primary school to found Toynet. His eyes darted back and forth, no doubt answering all his windows.

Dylan patted Gil's shoulder. "Frontera is thriving," he assured him. "All the *chicos* and *chicas* are well. Your little world in the sky has bloomed in ways no one could have imagined."

"It's too fun." Gil rubbed his hands together. "I 'visit' all the time, you know—without telling."

"But this insect problem—" Dylan shook his head. "It could be the death of us, Gil."

Gil waved a hand as if batting a fly. "Don't sound like my auditor. Frontera," he sighed dreamily, his fantasy come true. "If only I were born there. Well, come, Dillie, let's talk about your problem." Turning toward the back of the room, he climbed into the sandbox and picked up a shovel. With the shovel he carefully adjusted the texture of an Egyptian pyramid in the desert. The pyramid had a tunnel carved through, for a train engine and caboose.

Dylan recalled Clare saying, "Don't do anything I wouldn't do." Of course, Clare would not hesitate; he'd jump right in the sandbox and sketch the Mona Lisa with his finger. With a smile, Dylan stepped in, knowing the routine. The smartsand would not bother his suit; or if it did, the suit was disposable. He took up a handful and idly started shaping an elephant's head and trunk, the smartsand fading in rainbow hues. Then he thought better of it, hurriedly shaping a maple tree instead.

"What to do," muttered Gil. "Are the bugs so bad? Why not re-form your hab as a desert? No mosquitoes then."

"Trees and grass," Dylan rejoined apologetically. "The parents, you know. They like green."

Gil looked up. "Trains don't need grass. I just installed an 1880 Baldwin steam engine on my track! A joy to ride—you must come out and see."

Dylan grinned. "Dee-lighted, Gil, I'd love to ride your train. As soon as this insect problem is off my mind—I value your judgment, you know I do."

Gil's shovel paused above the pyramid. His eyes darted back and forth, scanning his toybox. "Those Super-X flies—no mate with males, no more flies. What a neat scheme."

"Ingenious," admitted Dylan. "But we really need to avoid generations—"

"And bats to prey on them." Gil shook his hand in the air, an excellent imitation of a bat in flight.

"Gil, we need to wipe out the mocs now, before campus visit season. Orin's identified a highly effective smartspray, which only targets mosquitoes. They use it on golf courses."

"Are you sure, Dillie?"

"*Seguro.*"

Gil sighed. "I suppose you're right. Well, here you go."

In Dylan's toybox a window flashed a ten-million-dollar credit. "Thanks *so* much, Gil; I can't tell you how much this means for Frontera."

Gil rose to his feet. "Can we ride the Lunar now?"

Dylan rose and stretched his legs, brushing the smartsand off his suit. "The train," he corrected. "Sure, let's go."

"Oh, but the Lunar Circuit—Dillie, you promised."

"Someday," he emphasized. "I promised Clare I'd be home for supper."

"Oh, *Dillie.* Your new Anthradyne is just too *chulo.* And the way you handled the Tycho pin curve—what a finish."

Dylan bit his inner lip. Actually he'd promised Clare that he'd quit racing for good, after the crackup in Mare Crisium. "Gil, let's chat about this again real soon."

"The frog seminars," announced Gil. "You said you'd need three positions."

Startled, Dylan looked up at Gil's innocent face. Seminar courses reserved for frogs were Dylan's most cherished priority for the curriculum. But he had only just broached the idea in Senior Staff, and consulted the chairs of Spanish and History. Helen said the faculty would need six new positions to offer live seminars for every first-year student, but Orin had shown that three would do.

"Three endowed chairs." How did Gil know—of course, he "visited" through Dylan's toybox, Dylan indulged him that way. "But it's not been approved. The faculty has yet to—"

"You can have the three chairs, after the Lunar Circuit."

Dylan had planned to ask for the chairs next spring, but now his plan was preempted. If he declined now, he could hardly come ask again.

16

Stunned by her mediocre grade, Jenny trudged home. Other students had actually got Bs—the grade Somers High gave "sit-ins," delinquents who sat in study hall just to keep their public funding. Anouk claimed the Life professor never gave frogs more than A.

Back outside Jenny's cottage, the old bear gouge was still collecting water. A few feet away, a new depression had opened, a dead lizard floating in the murk. It smelled like sewage.

In her toybox she called for Maintenance. As she waited, the tumor mouse from Levi-Montalcini crept about her box, sniffing like a toypet. At last Travis Tharp appeared in her window.

"Dean Kwon promised to fix the leak," Jenny reminded him.

"We did fix it," Tharp assured her. "Did it fill again?" He smiled and gave a wink. "Don't you fret; I'll be over for a look."

In her greenhouse, the vanda had already put out new leaves, glistening with drops of moisture from the spray. And three new blossoms had opened, five purple petals outstretched like fingers, each central column pointing upward. Surprised, Jenny looked closer. In just six days since Abaynesh took her plants, the main stalks had grown the length of her hand. How could an orchid grow so fast? Blood Star, too, had grown maybe six months' worth. She already had to divide and repot it. She'd never seen anything like it, not even in the orchid growers' toyworld. She'd have to ask that professor, with her two-headed snakes and innervated plants.

The Café de la Paix was closed until Saturday night, as Tom had to do his homework. Jenny was torn between going to the dining center, where Tom went, though the amyloid all tasted the same; or the Ohioana where the slanball team and Anouk went. The dining center was a big *gazpacho*; would she ever find him there? Homefair, Saturday morning; he said he'd be there.

At the Ohioana, the students all celebrated their first Friday. There were mugs of beer all round, except for the slanball team and Anouk. Charlie was thrilled with success. "That Life toyworld was *chulo*. I hope we have more classes like that."

Anouk wrinkled her nose. "Those knights—they were *Crusaders*. How dare that professor mock Europe's foremost religion."

Kendall exchanged a look with Yola. "The Arabs got their revenge," he told Anouk. "They invented math."

Yola punched him.

"Well," observed Anouk, somewhat mollified, "that happens to be true." She turned to Jenny. "I heard today from Dr. Valadkhani at Toy Land. She invited me to assist teaching her class on Developmental Arithmetic."

Jenny pushed with her fork at the gravy she had specifically asked the server to omit. In her toybox popped Viv, from the Begonia Garden Club. "Just a reminder, Jenny: We can't wait to see you at our Sunday afternoon social in the club conservatory."

"The college is going to spray." Yola was outraged. "Spray the whole hab, just for those poor mosquitoes." Flipping her braids, she glared up at the antlered deer head, as if it were President Chase.

Jenny itched just thinking of the mosquitoes.

David Pezarkar took another bite of meatloaf. "They say the spray's very specific to mosquitoes. Smartspray."

Kendall frowned. "It's the principle," he insisted. "Humans should never use our higher powers to wipe out an entire population of another species. It's species cleansing."

"Species cleansing," agreed his sister. "First, the mosquitoes; next, who knows what? Bears? Poison frogs?" Yola nodded decisively. "We're organizing a protest. Who's in?"

About half the team raised their hand, with varying degrees of enthusiasm. Jenny stared at her plate, suddenly very interested in the gravy.

"ToyNews Ohio." The large-necked state news man again. "Several Ohio House races are in play this year. Contesting the eighth district, we hear from both candidates."

The Unity candidate: "Poverty is the number one issue in our district. My opponent will cut our community gene clinics, while sending more troops to Antarctica. 'Cut and pray,' the Centrist way."

The Centrist: "Depravity is our number one issue, the decline in moral values. My opponent will legalize zoophily and put Win Now in your toybox. I will never vote for any game of chance on Ohio soil." Only off-world. "'Game and spend,' that's Unity."

❖

The solar filter's last scarlet rays tinted her cottage pink. The bear gouge now held a green amyloid tube snaking up, only to bend down again plunging deep into the soil. The second puddle, too, had sprouted a tube that snaked up, around, and down. The green tubes faced each other like some kind of modern art form.

Nearby stood Travis Tharp, chin in hand, surveying his handiwork. "It's just a temporary fix," he promised. "Don't you worry, miss; it'll hold real good."

Jenny frowned. "Why can't you just replace the water line?"

"It's not that kind of leak. Not the line to your house, that's fine."

"Then what is it?"

Adjusting a power band on his leg, Tharp looked reflectively at the tubes. "When they first built the hab, the main bulk of substratum was designed to be just a tad less dense than the seawater in the outer shell, where the purple solar microbes grow. Well, they underestimated the compression by centrifugal force. Within a year or two, the substratum settled in a tad denser than water. So the water tends to seep upward, through a crack here and there. Of course it's always filtered clean by the time it gets here."

Jenny's mouth fell open. "The water from the outer shell? You mean, the microbial saline?" She blinked. "It . . . seeps up? All the time?"

"Very slowly. It always gets pumped back down. Pumps are all over, throughout the hab, like a sump pump in your basement. No problem, really."

"What if the pumps stopped?"

"Well, now. If the pumps were to stop, eventually the whole hab would have a mess of water to clear out, maybe two meters deep."

For a while Jenny could only stare in numb silence, alone except for the tumor mouse in her toybox. The last rays of light died, closed by the filter, while the lights of Mount Gilead came on, a central cross-grid with streets outlined in dotted constellations. Not as advertised, Anouk would say. Frontera was no Old Bet perched safe atop a post. Frontera was a new bet, and not a good one. An over-engineered disaster waiting to happen.

Up the walk came Mary Dyer, her enigmatic *compañera*. Water bottle in hand, Mary paused at the green tubing. "Bears were here digging."

Jenny was puzzled. "Bears?"

"Digging, and planting those things."

"People were digging," Jenny corrected wearily. "Maintenance workers." How much longer could this Mary last? she wondered. "To keep the water down."

"Down?"

"Out in the shell of the spacehab, where the microbes grow. If all the water comes up here, we'll all drown."

"The water needs more salt."

"What do you mean?"

"If the water held more salt, people would float." Float—like in Great Salt Lake. There was Aspie logic all right.

Mary was useless, but who else could Jenny tell? Her mother—what could her mother do; withdraw her from college? Her aunts; Aunt Meg would always have something sensible to say, but Jenny hated to call her. Professor Abaynesh? The professor was too unpredictable.

Jenny went to the toyroom, the eight-doored tree house. This time she posted Anouk's code, the bit that would keep the mental away. She tapped the Jordi archive, and waited. No sign of the Monroe. A twinge of fear—she thrust it away. She picked "Poverty in Somers," Jordi's last and most famous Unity rally in Bailey Park.

The gazebo stood in the distance, half in shade, half in the blinding sun. The light dimmed a moment as a cloud passed, then was bright again. A crowd filled the park, larger than before. High school kids had climbed up into the trees, peering out through the kudzu. Jordi could barely be seen as the Somers town supervisor introduced him. Jenny blinked to zoom in. His face appeared, already beaded with sweat. That day had been blistering hot.

" 'The poor you will always have with you.' " One of his favorite lines. "I know you think young people don't listen in church, but you see we do." A few chuckles in the audience. "So today let's talk about poverty. Poverty may sound like a surprising subject, for us in Somers. We all know—our real estate board boasts—how the poverty level in Somers is below half a percent."

Jordi paused, a pause timed precisely, just long enough for the audience to start feeling uncomfortable. "How is that possible, that our poverty rate is so low, when our neighboring counties have poverty rates so high? In fact, some say we in Somers did years ago what Centrists would have us do today: Leave poverty behind." He nodded. "The Centrists would have us leave poverty behind—leave the poor behind, in their poverty."

A few boos from the audience, especially the kids in the trees. Few fans of Centrists were here.

"Kind of like the 'Rapture,' when all the 'saved' will be called to heaven, they say, leaving their shoes behind. Well, the Centrists would have us take off and leave our whole trashed planet behind. Bringing only our virtual memories, for a fortunate few in a spacehab." The homes in waiting, down by the river, *todos se van*. "Spacehabs, for the fortunate few. How many of us will there ever be room for?"

Not many in Frontera; barely a village, Jenny thought. At night you could count the lights in Mount Gilead. Even with the latest tech, it took an Oklahoma-sized range of solarplate to build and sustain one spacehab. Or a space solarray—but those took years to build.

"Yet some say that we in Somers have already done the same thing. We left our own poor behind decades back. Behind zoning rules and ultraphyte patrols." Jordi nodded. "Ultraphyte patrols are designed as much to keep out the poor and the homeless. And zoning—no one who can't afford a million-dollar home need apply in Somers."

In the audience a shoe scraped, a fan swished, cicadas hummed above the kudzu.

"But I see a greater Somers. I believe in the people of Somers. I believe in a Somers that can save our planet. That fights for clean energy and a future for all our citizens, for the next seven generations. That's what Unity stands for . . ."

In the end, as the audience dissolved away, there stood Jordi alone in the gazebo. Alone, outside time, Father Clare had said. Yet Jordi never seemed to know it; he was always caught there, in that moment. "They took it well, didn't they," Jordi told her. "Better than I expected."

"Of course, Jordi, you knew they would. Everyone knows you."

He was shaking his head. "It just seems hopeless, sometimes. Everyone means well, and yet . . ." Wiping the sweat from his face, he looked tired. "What we're up against." Recollecting himself, he smiled. "That was a good line of yours, about the ultraphyte patrols."

"Yeah, I know." She'd seen it on call, how the ultraphyte patrol would pick up a homeless man and dump him in the next county. "Jordi, listen— Those spacehabs, they aren't how they're supposed to be."

"I know."

"Even Uncle Dylan's spacehab. You know, the one he used to tell us about."

Jordi grinned and pulled his hand through his hair. "Remember how Uncle Dylan used to let us drive the Lunar? How mad Mama got when she found out?"

"I know, but Jordi—if the spacehab lost power, it could flood any time."

"Tell the squad. You're in EMS, you always know the right people."

That was true, although she hadn't heard yet from the local service. She would ask Yola again.

"The speech went well," Jordi reflected. "It will go even better next week, in Battery Park."

Jenny pulled out. For a moment the toyroom went blank, little colored dots against white snow. Then the tree house with the eight doors. A mirage, a tree house that could flood any time and sweep her away, like Jordi in New York Harbor.

Her mind fell into a deep hole, the lowest she had fallen in months. A knife cutting, again and again; the only relief from that feeling. Summoning all her strength, as if swimming in slow motion, she made herself blink for the mental.

The Monroe did not appear right away. For a moment, Jenny panicked; had Anouk's code banished the mental for good? Then at last the timeless face appeared, the sweeping eyelashes, the perfect cheeks. "Are you sure you need me, Jenny?" purred the Monroe. "You've been doing so well on your own."

"It's not me, it's the spacehab. I just found out it could flood."

"You're right, Jenny. That's not about you. You're physically unsafe— and no one told you, did they."

"That's right."

"So you're right to feel upset," the Monroe assured her. "And angry. Remember, feeling anger is normal."

Jenny nodded. "I do feel angry." Especially at Uncle Dylan—how could he have kept this from her? "But what can I do about it?"

"That's for you to figure out—and you will. You can do it." The Monroe added, "I'll watch over you tonight. Remember, I'm here for you. You and nobody else but you." She pouted and blew her a kiss.

There was one thing Jenny could do—she would not sleep on the ground floor again. She brought her sheets up to the greenhouse and turned off the mister in one corner. The Homefair build was the next morning; she set her toybox early. Above her stretched the orchids with their blossoms, purple and blood-red with the white star. I wish I could just be a plant, was her last thought before she fell asleep.

17

Saturday was the slanball team's one day off, then a week to go till their first Sunday game. Jenny arrived early at Wickett Hall where volunteers gathered for Homefair. Above the window, the amyloid mallet flexed and pounded each colored peg through the hole, then turned the bench over and started again. Jenny had come up with several sound reasons for being there, besides seeing Tom. None of them changed the fact that she scarcely needed another distraction from work—five more neuro papers to read, plus a math tutorial; an entire book on the Northern Securities case; a toytour of Cuba, for her toyHarvard class; and for Hamilton, an essay on "Is man's foremost aim to govern the *polis?*"

"ToyNews Mount Gilead." The local ToyNews had finally found her box. "A dairy cow belonging to the Lazza family at Raccoon Run fell into a ditch and is just now being hauled out." Three men with ropes were struggling to help a cow up a bank without fracturing her legs. Even a hundred-kilo mini-cow was quite something to handle. A real cow—Jenny hoped the cow's milk would get to Ohioana. "The First Firmament Church announces a Tuesday evening seminar by an eminent baraminologist on the subject of 'Heliocentrism: A Christian Response.'"

Father Clare emerged from a truck, wearing worn jeans and a blue T-shirt. Jenny realized she had never before seen him without the collar. A battered old convertible pulled up, its electric motor popping loudly. Out of the car jumped Fran and David, who opened a sign-up window in Jenny's box. Others arrived in assorted ancient vehicles, or walked over from Huron, the scholarship frogs' dorm. A scarlet sports car disgorged four Bulls in red shirts, including club president Fritz Hoffman, with dark marks around his eyes as if he'd had a long night. Priscilla Cho she recognized from Hamilton's class; then Charlie; and at last Tom.

Jenny smiled, her pulse quickening. But for some reason Tom turned away, as if he thought she didn't belong here. Puzzled, and feeling silly, she looked the other way, as if she just happened to show up.

David surveyed the crowd, over two dozen in all. "*Guao,* what a turnout.

Okay, everyone, pile in somewhere. Follow Father Clare's truck out Raccoon Run to the build site, twenty-six and a half Methuselah Lane."

Jenny got in the back of David's car, holding her ears from the noise. The cars trundled off slowly, with students hanging out the sides. Ahead, the truck turned west off Buckeye Trail. The cars lurched down a dirt road along a stream, while the college rolled upward behind them, until Jenny could just make out Wickett Hall and the parapets of Castle Cockaigne hanging down from the "sky." Always solid overhead—no wonder children raised here could so easily believe outer space was a "firmament."

Along the stream rolled fields of wheat and soy, dotted with red farmhouses. In a pasture grazed mini-cows, thick power bands encircling each leg. The cars turned again onto Methuselah Lane. The students piled out at the build site, a concrete slab about the size of Jenny's family room back home. From the truck David was distributing hard hats, while Fran introduced the future homeowner, Sherri-Lyn Robins, a mother of three from West Virginia. "Sherri-Lyn was sponsored by Homefair to settle her family here. Last year, she put in a hundred hours on the Tharp home. This year, it's her turn." Fran raised Sherri-Lyn's hand. The upperclass students cheered; the group seemed to know each other well. "We always take donations. Thanks to the First Reconciled Church for materials, and to First Firmament for providing today's lunch."

Father Clare held out his hands to clasp. Everyone gathered in a circle for the opening prayer. "Almighty God, our heavenly Father and Mother, we ask your blessing to build the Robins family home, for 'unless the Lord builds the house, its builders labor in vain.' Open our hearts, and bless our foundation. Let us be like the wise man who heard your word and built his house upon rock. Above all, guide us to build safely and to build a safe dwelling, here on this hollow rock amongst the stars. In the name of Jesus your son and Mary our mother, let us all dwell in your heavenly mansions forever. Amen."

Jenny nodded at his mention of the stars.

Out of the truck came hard hats, aprons full of nails, and wall frame sections of gray carboxyplast, numbered to fit tabs on the slab. While Fran and Fritz hauled out the sections, David lectured on safety. Hard hats, hammers, how to climb a ladder—it was a lot for everyone to remember.

"Why no floating tools?" Jenny rarely used her hands.

"Floating tools consume too much power," said Fran. "Homefair builds on sweat."

The juniors and seniors seemed to know what to do, dividing into groups, each group assigned to a wall section. The first gray frame of carboxyplast went up quickly, posts buttressed with a long plank at an angle out from the slab. Jenny's group raised a section at a corner. Tentatively she positioned a nail in the middle of the corner. The first blow of her hammer went thud on the carb, three inches past the nail. Embarrassed, Jenny was aware of Sherri-Lyn Robins working next to her, and one of her small children watching from off-site, finger in his mouth.

"Hold the hammer close, at first," advised Sherri-Lyn. "Get used to where it hits."

"It's my first time," Jenny admitted.

"It took me a week to hit the first nail."

Jenny glanced sideways at Tom. He was driving special long nails through the base plate right into the slab; a tap for each one, and the whole wall was done. He said he hadn't built houses, but he sure knew a thing or two.

Before long the entire home was framed in. The posts and crossbeams and diagonal braces traced open spaces all around, making pretty shapes against the rolling land. If the braces held stained glass, they'd make a cathedral. A house was born "all windows," she realized, until all but a few got boarded in.

The wall boards were a different kind of carb with a lighter, porous texture. They went up fast with a volley of nails. One board covered a door, so David had to saw out a piece. Then a spider bot went up the walls, crawling over every board to check for hidden flaws.

David dropped his hammer. "Walls are done," he called. "The bot will report back after lunch. With luck, we'll put up the roof."

Everyone cheered, as much for lunch as for the walls. The morning had gone fast. Jenny found herself wondering if there wasn't some other way, like couldn't they just print out whole homes in carb?

Lunch was not printout; it was prepared and served by two ladies from the Mount Gilead First Firmament Church. Each woman wore a long pioneer dress with a round bonnet, arms power-banded. Jenny tried not to stare, horrified yet fascinated to see ordinary people who really believed the stars were pasted on the sky. The younger one smiled and said hello to everyone. Her companion, Leora Smythe, about the age of Jenny's mother, was more reserved. A pauline, Jenny thought, knowing the look. At any rate, she was grateful enough for the sandwich. Real bread and fresh cheese from Raccoon Run cows were a treat. As she left the table, she turned. Beneath her bonnet, Leora was watching her.

Priscilla sat down on the slab next to Jenny. She wiped a damp curl of hair out of her eyes and took a bite of her sandwich. Jenny did the same. From the north, the racetrack beyond the Mound, came the faint drone of cars practicing for the Frontera Circuit. In her window she could see them, the scarlet Red Bulls and the black Ferraris.

Drums boomed, a rock beat reverberating from Buckeye Trail. Too early for powwow; it must be the live band the Kearns-Clarks had hired up for their Save the Mosquitoes rally. Jenny opened a toybox window to see. A fair crowd of students had collected to hear the band, in the soccer field behind Reagan Hall. Above the stage a giant virtual mosquito hovered in mid flight, its wings rainbow colored. After the band warmed up, Yola came out to address the crowd.

"To destroy any species is a crime." Yola's words echoed from the up-curving fields. "Mosquitoes and other insects feed frogs, and the frogs feed owls. None of the diseases they carry are even found here. We can breed the mosquitoes to avoid humans altogether. Who is the real danger to earth's survival? The danger is us, human beings. We need to learn to live with our biosphere, not trash it."

The last part drew applause and whistles.

"Now here's our petition to the college trustees to withhold the smart-spray until we give biocontrol a chance. We need everyone here to sign this petition. Check it out—it's right there in your box. Sign now to prevent species cleansing."

Kendall stepped forward on the stage, looking grim as death. "You don't have to know life science to see that it's wrong to destroy nature's precious creatures. According to Genesis, God gave humans dominion over all the creatures of the air and earth. With dominion comes responsibility to do it right. And we messed up. First we got kicked out of Eden, then we drowned in the flood. If we mess up this time, we could lose Earth altogether." Applause at that line, for who didn't worry about losing Earth. "Saving insects is a start. If we expect God to save us."

The band picked up again, echoing through the spacehab.

Priscilla looked up curiously. "What do you think about the mosquitoes?"

Jenny shrugged, reluctant to undermine her team captains. "What do you think?"

Priscilla looked reflectively at her sandwich. "I'm not sure. Like, I'm still thinking about it." She took another big mouthful. "What about Hamilton's homework?"

"Aristotle?"

"Yeah." Priscilla chewed again until she swallowed. "I mean, if we're all here to govern the *polis*, then what's the *polis* here for?"

Jenny wondered the same, although she doubted that response was what the professor wanted. She wondered about this Professor Hamilton, how his mind worked; what she might find out about Centrist leaders and how they held on to ordinary citizens like Leora Smythe.

"Bear!" called Fran suddenly. "A bear's headed this way. Clear out the trash."

There ensued a hasty scramble to gather all the leftover food and napkins into the recycler. Everyone stared across the field, where a black furry creature lumbered over. It looked like a medium-sized dog, although its plodding gait was unlike a dog's. The little bear approached to within a few yards of the students huddled together outside the house frame. It reared on its hind legs, as if for a better look, a piece of sandwich wrap in its jaw. Then, spooked by the crowd, it turned and took off again across the field.

"Newbies over here," David called out to the frogs. "We'll go over the frame and fix the issues found by the spider. Not too many," he assured them, "you all did great. Owls with experience, follow Fran to raise the roof."

Out came the triangular roof trusses, all laid in a stack. Father Clare climbed a ladder to raise the first truss, steadied by students at both ends. His biceps stood out like cords of anthrax as he centered the peak, lithe as a student and a lot more expert. A nudge at one end, then at the other, to align the overhangs and nail it to the frame. For the next truss, Fran soon followed up the ladder, looking as secure up there as she did in the slanball cage. The red-shirted Bulls followed too. From the north came the rumbling drumbeat of the two-o'clock powwow at the Mound.

Soon the peaks of the trusses reached halfway along the length of the roof. By now, the few spider issues had been resolved, a loose nail here, a misaligned plank there. Now the frogs were regarding the growing roof with interest. Tom and Charlie ventured up to align a truss, guided by Fran. Tom had his shirt off, and his chest gleamed in the light from both solars. Then Priscilla went up, nailing and creeping monkeylike through the web beams. Before long, the frogs up there outnumbered the owls, and the air rang with a dozen hammers. A lot of people clambered along a lot of narrow beams.

The rafters went up quickly, boards of lightweight carb filling in the slopes of the roof. Ladders went up all around, and people were crawling all over the roof, nailing boards and drawing guides for shingles. Jenny sat on a windowsill, feeling she'd had enough for one day.

A shout; someone cried out, and others gathered around. Priscilla lay on the ground, just below the roof overhang.

The chaplain knelt beside her. "Keep still."

"I'm okay," Priscilla insisted. "I just slid off the edge." She winced.

"You must keep still. The medic will get here."

Jenny pushed past the chaplain. "Lie down, all the way." With her hand she eased Priscilla's head down, took her pulse, and felt her arms and legs. "What's your name?"

"Priscilla Cho," she sighed.

"Who is the president?"

"Like, Chase?"

"The United States." I'm out of practice, Jenny thought.

"Guzmán, a hundred forty-one days to go."

She put a test patch on Priscilla's neck. The patch would dig in and sample her blood. "What happened?"

"I just reached without looking, and my foot went off the edge."

"Only experienced volunteers were supposed to go up."

"Duh, how should I get experience? Like, I'll know better next time. I didn't fall that far."

"Can you wiggle your toes?"

In Jenny's box several numbers blinked red, for molecules that leaked out of broken bone. There must be a cracked vertebra. Jenny pulled out a piece of amyloid and set it on Priscilla's neck. The amyloid liquified and spread about her neck, then solidified.

"Hey, now I can't move."

"You move, you're dead," Jenny replied, more crossly than she should have. Totally worn out, she sat back on the ground and momentarily closed her eyes. Overhead a heli whined, descending with the medic. Her eyes opened; there was Tom at her side, watching gravely. She looked up at Father Clare. "Why don't you have EMS standing by?"

"We prayed for a volunteer. Now we have one."

The heli opened, and a medibot trundled out. "**Where's your human operator?**" Jenny texted. "**EMS rule, no bots alone.**"

"**We're short-handed,**" the bot replied. "**Why did you not call in this event according to regulations?**"

"**I applied for the squad but never heard.**"

"**Show up Monday at twenty-one hours.**"

In her toybox next to molecule-of-the-day a new window appeared, the

EMS snake twined around a pole. The window bore the name of Eppie Uddin, M.D. The college physician, Jenny recalled, Doc Uddin was married to the toymaker, Zari Valadkhani, who ran the local Toynet with all their adopted teddies. The tumor mouse sniffed the new window curiously, amid all the rest; there was barely room for another.

+-+

Back at her cottage, Jenny had to drag herself up to the greenhouse, where she'd put her mattress. She let the mister play on her face. She thought she'd lie down for just a minute before a shower.

The next thing she knew, Anouk was calling. "Jenny? Jenny, are you all right?" Anouk's scarf had an elaborate pattern of blue and gold tiles. Next to her sat Yola and Kendall, at Café de la Paix. "Did you forget?"

It was past seven, when they had all agreed to meet for dinner. She must have slept three hours, and still done no homework.

At the café, Jenny found Anouk and Yola enjoying an appetizer of *crottin de chavignol roti*, roasted goat cheese with honey and sautéed apples arranged in a swirl, while Kendall enjoyed spirulina salad. "We saved some for you," said Anouk. "And some of the bread—fresh from Paris." The bread was a wonder, a crust that crunched just right, and the inside melted in her mouth.

Yola nodded. "Congratulations on joining EMS. I'll know who to call."

"Thank you." Jenny tried the *crottin*. Crumbling on her fork, its flavor was delicate, piquant. "How was your . . . event?"

"Fantastic," exclaimed Kendall. "The band was awesome—you could hear it all the way to the Mound."

"We collected fifty-eight signatures," said Yola. "Impressive, for a species with such a bad rep."

Anouk nibbled her bread and kept quiet. Outside the café, Berthe kept watch, her Monroe face just visible through the window. "The Homefair house looks nice," Anouk observed at last. "Most charitable."

Jenny sighed. "I just wish I'd got my Life done." Those neuro articles were as impenetrable as kudzu.

Kendall groaned. "I'll trade you my chapter on 'The Reconciliation of the Apostolic Succession.' Pope Leo ruled that King Edward messed up, then Pope Sebastian ruled the Anglicans back in." The foundation of First Church Reconciled. "Pope, pope—I feel like a peeper."

"Hah," crowed Yola, "Christian history, for a change."

"It's required for the major. Never postpone requirements till senior year."

Anouk said, "I completed my homework, on the coding of Legendrian submanifolds."

The door to the kitchen swung open, and Tom brought out a silver tray. Clearly he hadn't come back to sleep for three hours. Out of the tray came plates of *sandre au beurre d'écrevisses*, pike-perch in crayfish butter surrounded by parsley and shallots.

Kendall tasted his triple mushroom pâté. "Not bad. Do you suppose we could get him at the castle for our Feast of Fools?"

Yola said, "Let's see how he does with the *boeuf en croûte*. It always comes out soggy."

Jenny put down her fork. "Since I'm on EMS now," she ventured, "could I raise a point of . . . safety?"

"Sure, sis. What's up?"

"The water seeping up from the shell." Her pulse raced just to think of it.

"Why that in particular?" Yola wondered.

"Well, the hab could flood any time. And nobody knows about it."

"Sure we do. We all signed the form."

The form from Frog Preorientation popped into her box. A phrase was highlighted, "substratum overflow."

Jenny said, "I had no idea what that meant."

Anouk crossed her silver on her plate, as usual leaving just a morsel un-eaten. "I didn't know what that meant either," she said, "until I found it in the secure archive. Not that I was surprised." No Frontera deficiency would surprise her.

"EMS runs a flood drill," said Yola, "let's see, every other year. Or has it been three years? We're really more concerned about Kessler debris."

Tom returned to take the trays and refill the water glasses. Jenny smiled but did not catch his eye. She turned again to Yola. "At least everyone could sleep on an upper floor."

"What good would that do? The hab would flood only in a power-out, and the amyloid would all collapse."

"Really?" Jenny recalled the broken amyloid melting. "There's no solid frame underneath? No carb?"

"Wickett has carb underneath, and so do the frog residences," Yola ex-plained. "For seniors, it would be too expensive to cut down all that carb every year when new students come in. It releases carbon dioxide."

Her greenhouse, everything would collapse. Jenny's scalp crawled. The next dish arrived, the *boeuf en croûte* with asparagus, artichokes, and red peppers. The pastry formed the Frontera College crest, complete with the colonial ax and Gil Wickett on his rocking horse. But now Jenny could scarcely eat.

Yola took a forkful from the crisp crust. "You're right, Kennie-boy, this will do for our Feast of Fools."

Kendall looked up. "Our castle's got lifeboats," he remembered. "Why don't we hold a Flood Awareness Day?"

"'Flood Awareness Day'?" Jenny repeated. "How would that work?"

"Ask the chaplain, he's Student Events Coordinator. He'll send you the form."

"He approved our event," said Yola, "the band and all."

"A band," exclaimed Kendall. "A New Orleans band—I can see it. 'What do we have to do to send the river in reverse . . .'" He snapped his fingers. "We could hold it at the castle. Next Saturday, after our annual tour. Demonstrate the lifeboats in the moat."

Yola nodded. "People are always curious about Castle Cockaigne. We hold an open house, early in September."

"Hey," said Kendall, "we'll open the moat and *flood* the castle. And paddle the lifeboats out."

That would draw attention, all right. "Can we do a flyer—a map of all the flood-safe locations?" As they planned, Jenny got back to eating. The beef was excellent, as were the concluding profiteroles with Côte d'Ivoire chocolate.

As the group rose to leave, Jenny hung back. "I'll see you tomorrow," she told Anouk.

Anouk nodded. "I understand. If you call, I'll send Berthe to walk you home."

"Um, I'll be okay, thanks."

After the others left, Jenny paused at the door to the kitchen. Her heart suddenly beat fast, so fast she thought she would faint. The door swung in. A steel sink was piled with spoons and copper kettles, amid a rush of onions and tarragon. The onions made her eyes tear.

Tom looked up. "Something wrong?"

She wiped her eyes. "The food was wonderful. I just thought maybe I could . . . help with the dishes."

Tom looked confused. "But you paid in full." Seeing her look, he added, "That's okay, I'm nearly done. You can hang out while I finish."

Jenny got to work with the soap on the pots and spoons, having had long practice after all those campaign suppers. "You must have done a culinary course." She nearly added "in Paris," but caught herself just in time.

"No, I'm self taught. On Toynet."

"Did you always like to cook?"

"Always had to. It was something I could do," he added cryptically.

"You're good with the hammer too."

"I made furniture. Mostly pine, I never worked carb before. The nails don't set as well. Hey, it's good you were there for Homefair. You're almost a doctor."

She smiled, her eyes briefly closed. "I really want to breed orchids."

"Really? An orchid breeder for president."

"I'll never be president."

"Why not?"

"I can't speak in public."

"I never noticed."

That was true, she thought. She never had the least trouble talking with him. "What do you want to be?"

"A doctor, of course. To fix things my people have."

"Like what?"

"We're all sensitive to light. Blind by age thirty." The UV through the lost ozone. "My mother died of melanoma soon after I was born."

"I see." She swallowed hard.

"After that, they decided to keep me indoors. I was the one who'd get to see for an extra decade." Tom shrugged. "In the daytime, I looked after babies, cooked meals, built furniture. I went out only at night, under the stars."

Jenny kept rinsing one plate over.

"I never went to school, but one day the social worker brought me a solar tablet. I hid it on the roof to recharge. Then, at night, when everyone was asleep, I surfed Toynet until the charge ran down."

"So that's where you learned French cooking."

"And everything else. News, history, medicine. Chemistry was my favorite subject, all the colored atoms. But the only chemistry I could do at home was cooking. Eggs turning white as the proteins came apart—that was *chulo*."

She smiled. "Did you get the molecule of the day?"

"I think it's anthocyanin. The doublet shifts in the NMR."

She put the plate in the drain board and leaned her elbows on the counter. "So how'd you get to Frontera?"

"They told me that on my sixteenth birthday I'd have to go outside. My father was blind by then, and we all had to earn a living." He leaned his chin on his hands. "The night before my birthday, I left home. Walked by moonlight, all the way to town. The social worker took me to the gene clinic for treatments, until the state funds ran out. Then I heard about Frontera. The 'solar' light sources exclude UV."

"That's right, the light is all artificial." No way to get a tan.

"So here I am."

"And your family?"

"They wouldn't see me again." He looked at her curiously. "What about you? You came here for the adventure? A step toward Jupiter?"

"After Jordi drowned, my head was messed up. I couldn't go to Harvard; too close to Boston Harbor. I thought Frontera was as far from drowning as you could get."

Tom nodded.

"But today, I just found out the whole hab could drown. If the power goes out, it will flood two meters deep." She swallowed. "I know it sounds silly, but I feel as if I could drown in my sleep. It's a scary way to die."

Tom thought this over. "I could sleep downstairs and look out for you." Then he shook his head. "Sorry, just a dumb idea."

Jenny smiled. "I could adopt you as my brother."

He laughed, just how Paul Newman would laugh. "You could at that. Say, I know you're all busy but what time do you go to the dining hall?"

She said carefully, "I usually go somewhere quiet." So as not to insult the food that all could afford.

"There's Lazza's Diner in Mount Gilead. We could go there."

The two of them, away from it all. Jenny felt warm all over.

18

Sunday morning at All Saints Church, the campus chapel, Jenny brought flowers for the communion table, white dendrobiums nestled with maidenhair ferns. The stained-glass windows depicted lives of the saints: St. Peter with the key, St. Francis, St. Clare. The hues were shaded in Renaissance style, yet the borders looked decidedly contemporary, a row of jigsaw pieces. Jenny wondered who'd designed them. Then she thought about Tom the night before, and at Homefair, how he'd looked on the roof. She had dreamt of him all night, and she couldn't stop thinking of him.

"Remember, God's answer to the problem of evil is compassion." Father Clare's sermon drew to a close. "God is good, and all-powerful, and He and She will deal with evil. Our task is to love God and love our neighbor. Through our love, the barriers that divide us will crumble; and our divisions being healed, we may live in justice and peace.

"But what is love? Love is patient and kind. Love bears all things, believes all things, hopes all things, endures all things.

"Where is love? Colonists, you came up here leaving loved ones behind, farther than any immigrants before left theirs. If love feels distant now, as distant as Earth, keep looking here. Students, the toys of Wickett Hall remind you of your loving parents throughout childhood. When I was a child, I spoke like a child, I thought like a child, I reasoned like a child. When I became a man, I gave up childish ways. For now we see only a blur in the glass, a puzzle, like a funhouse mirror. But then, when perfection comes, we shall see face-to-face.

"Above all, hope. 'For in hope are we saved,' through Jesus Christ our Lord. Amen."

Jenny recalled a funhouse mirror, how it had stretched her four-year-old arms, hobbled her feet, and doubled her nose. So long ago. With a start she realized that the students, faculty, and about an equal number of colonists in power bands were all up from their seats and passing through the pews. So Mount Gilead wasn't all Firmament. She waited in her seat during the organ postlude.

When the others had left, she asked Father Clare about Flood Awareness Day.

The chaplain regarded her reflectively. "Did one of the staff suggest this?"

"No, but my cottage has a leak. It must sit right on top of a crack in the substratum."

"I see, Jenny. I'm so sorry. Has Maintenance addressed your problem?"

"Yes, but it could happen anywhere, and nobody thinks about it." Father Clare seemed oddly reluctant, Jenny thought; why? "We just want people to know. Kendall will hire a band, and demonstrate lifeboats in the moat."

The chaplain nodded. "So long as it's all students, sure, you can do it. Just fill out the form."

Jenny blinked through the Toynet form, checking off the items they'd need, including Maintenance support; perhaps Mr. Tharp would help. As she finished, it occurred to her to dip into the Toynet archive about the church. To her surprise, she read that Father Clare himself had designed the windows. She took a closer look, admiring the St. Francis with his hand outstretched holding a bird, alongside St. Clare in her black robe. Something about St. Francis caught her eye. The face; the features were definitely Uncle Dylan.

As soon as she stepped outside, squinting in the filtered sun, a flurry of delayed campus memos popped up.

"I want the campus to know," began Fritz Hoffman indignantly, "that we had *nada* to do with the Ferrari car compacted into an F sign on their roof last night. The Red Bulls condemn all such acts of vandalism—"

Blink.

Rob LaSalle appeared, with a self-satisfied smirk. "Of course, the Bulls will say they had nothing to do with this act of hooliganism, as if they didn't order their pledges to wreck one of our cars every fall for the past ten years. As usual, the Ferrari men forgive our brothers in Christian humility—"

Blink, and blink to the rest of them. She had just two hours to get some Life done before the Begonia Garden Club reception. The Life articles were the kind where every sentence had to be read twice, then a third time after getting through the paragraph. In the first article, certain groups of *Arabidopsis sapiens* neurons connected in a feedback loop, which maintained a steady state. Others made feed-forward loops that amplified their signal. A combined circuit of twenty neurons could release a powerful semiochemical. For instance, moth eggs induced the plant to release an insecticide. Moth eggs— would she have to subject plants to that? The thought of worms anywhere near her orchids made her scalp crawl.

"ToyNews—From our box to yours." Clive again. "President Guzmán thanks Homeworld Security for 'doing a heck of a job clearing shipping lanes to the Firmament.' The off-world casinos are taking bids on the selection of vice-presidential running mates for Anna Carrillo and Gar Guzmán . . ."

Jenny listened on her way out with Anouk to the garden club. Of course, Guzmán would pick the Creep again, the same secretive vice president picked by the previous two Guzmáns, always tucked away in a secure location to fight ultra. As for Carrillo, hopefully she'd avoid picking the Connecticut senator who'd made his fortune running zoophile toyworlds.

The Begonia Club reception was an exclusive affair for potential recruits. The club maintained a spectacular greenhouse, with windows of self-cleaning amyloid. At the door, Viv introduced the club sisters. "Our recruiting director, Suzan Gruman-Iberia."

"Call me Suze, girls." A sophomore with Monroe cheeks and lips, a round salmon-colored flower opened at the shoulder of her slash-neck blouse. Suze gave Jenny and Anouk each a pink begonia bud to pin. The bud sat prettily on Anouk's shoulder. Suze admired Anouk's dress, a floor-length tessellation of interlocking triangles, beneath which her toes turned out in third position. "The pattern is quasicrystalline," Anouk explained.

"My goodness," Suze exclaimed at the sight of Berthe. *"Caramelo."* She playfully pressed the DIRG's arm. "I hope she'll submit a bid too."

To Jenny's relief, Berthe stayed outside, peering discreetly through the greenhouse glass window while the frogs went in. Inside the greenhouse stretched rows upon rows of flats and light banks, with a surprising variety of begonias. Not Jenny's favorite, but the range of colors impressed her: golden, red, pink, and white. And the leaves varied intriguingly, from serrated green to filamentous silver.

Suze took her hand and gave her a tour. "We raise all kinds of begonias, from tuberous to dragonwings. Each sister selects her own variety. Mine is the Springtime Elatior." Salmon-colored petals, large inviting flowers with handsome leaves. Viv's Butter Praline had creamy blossoms with yellow centers. The leaves had interesting asymmetric heart shapes with a wrinkled texture. Beyond the last row of flats was a furnished lounge with a bar where the sisters gathered.

"Of course, we keep professional help to maintain our plants, while we focus on our studies. James is our full-time horticulturalist."

The gardener James stood by in a neat cap and uniform, nodding deferentially to each guest. Beyond the garden rows strolled several older students,

in the latest slash-neck blouses. Reesie Tsien greeted each sister with an ex-
clamation and a hug, as if she'd played their toyworld for a month. This club
might be okay, Jenny thought. A place she might bring Tom; with the right
haircut, he could pass for a Newman.

Viv was explaining the club's virtues to a group of *chicas* with buds on
their shoulders and strawberry daiquiris in hand, all Monroe lips and Newman chins, with gold rings through their perfect noses. "Academic excel-
lence is our first priority," she assured them. "To help, we provide a large
study archive, including exams and essays from the past decade of classes.
Hamilton especially, all his Aristotle assignments with grades and comments. 'Is man's foremost aim to govern the *polis*?' Ten years' worth of that
one."

Jenny's eyes widened, suddenly curious. She'd love to see what Hamilton
wrote on a decade's worth of papers.

Reesie asked, "How's your career network?" She twirled her daiquiri,
hopefully without rum or she'd be in trouble with Coach.

"The best," Viv assured her. "The Cleft Palate Investment Fund," she
ticked off, "they donate reconstructive surgery. The Islands Fund, they re-
settle refugees. And start you with a six-figure income."

"*Chulo*," said Reesie. "Can you get us an internship?"

Anouk asked, "A stint at the femtosecond toytrade?"

"Whatever you want, through our growing network of sister alumnae."
Viv added in a whisper, "We're affiliated with the Alphas."

Another frog asked, "Which motor club do you date?"

Viv shrugged. "We keep our options open. Remember, if you earn the
paycheck you don't have to catch one. You can date whoever's hot."

Suze chuckled. "And ditch them when they screw up. Speaking of hot,
don't you think it's time for our show?"

Music filled the room with a Times Square beat and the voice of a male
crooner. In the lounge at the end, the Begonia sisters pulled back the chaises
for more room. James pranced languidly up to the lounge, apparently a gentleman of multiple talents. *Chicas* with their drinks gathered with nervous
giggles. As the tie came off, they squealed and caught each other's arms. One
caught the tie and held it up like a trophy. A drink splattered droplets in
the air.

Jenny looked around for Anouk, wondering how she would take this.
Then she caught sight of Berthe in full view, just outside the greenhouse window. She clapped her hands to her face. "*Anouk!*" The last thing she needed

was a scene with a disapproving DIRG. She texted, "Get out of here with Berthe."

Anouk was off to the side, explaining the quasicrystalline pattern to sisters admiring her dress. She looked up, seeming confused. Then she caught sight of the stage.

"Viv, my friend and I need a restroom, quick."

"Out the door, to your left. Stocked with underwear."

Jenny grabbed Anouk's arm and dragged her down the greenhouse rows. At last they got outdoors, breathing quickly.

Berthe took a step toward Anouk. "Are you all right, *chérie*?"

"Of course, no problem. That was close," Anouk added to Jenny. "Berthe would certainly not allow me in the presence of—*enfin*, it's too bad," she concluded. "Such interesting connections. Well, I can find my own job in toy-trade, thank you."

Jenny sighed. Times Square shows were not really her thing. "Well, I'll just stick with the team."

"Oh, but Monte Carlo Night, next month—you'll see, the Ferraris are different. They wait till classes are under way. They are most civilized."

"Campus Bulletin." Quade Vincenzo on Toynet. The ecoengineer cleared his throat, seeming more subdued than usual. "The college has decided to commence smartspray for mosquitoes, starting at seven A.M. Monday. The sprayers will cruise along the axis, emitting spray in all directions. The spray will appear in the form of pink rain, most of which will dissipate before reaching the habitation surface." Vincenzo paused before continuing. "The community should remember that the mosquitoes in our hab, about a thousand so far, constitute just a tiny fraction of their entire world population of mosquitoes, estimated at a billion billions. Elimination here won't endanger their species. It's just culling them where they don't belong, like weeding a garden or trimming a hedge. Hopefully they'll be gone, and we won't have to do it again." His face brightened as he held up a furry winged creature. "Still, we'll establish a bat colony, just in case."

19

That Sunday, Jenny got her homework done by midnight. But Monday morning, she was up at five for slanball. She reached the court with seconds to spare. The faintest of light dribbled through the sausage-shaped cloud.

Coach strode along the cage on his footgrips. His long smile had lines that betrayed strain; players got to know the slightest nuance in a coach's moods. When he reached Jenny he slowed to a halt. She clenched her teeth against a yawn.

"I should send you back to bed."

"I—I slept." She'd learned to fall asleep in an instant, anywhere, on any campaign bus.

"Not enough," he said. "Sleep deprivation is a drug. My players don't play sleep-drunk." He raised a finger. "You've been warned."

After Coach moved on, she turned questioningly to Yola. "Where are . . ."

Kendall crossed his arms and set his chin. He looked grim as one of those old stills of an Inuit elder. "Rickie pledged Ferrari. And Reesie, Begonia."

Yola shrugged. "Frog attrition is always high. That's how we get our team down to regulation size."

Charlie looked downcast, hiding his face. "I gave up the Bulls," he told Jenny, after the captains had left for drill. "The bros had checked in with me all month before—they really made me feel welcome. I never had brothers before."

Jenny patted his arm. "Hey, you'll be okay. Look at the team—we're your brothers and sisters."

"Pair up and jitter down the cage."

They each picked up a ball and jittered it, zigzagging from side to side while crossing the ball right to left, front to back, head to toe. To evade a guard the ball could jitter in any direction, straight up, down, or backward. Jenny crossed, then double-crossed the ball, at unpredictable angles and intervals, showing off her dexterity despite her short sleep.

At last Coach gathered everyone to strategize for their first game. Frontera hosted the Melbourne Scorpions the next Sunday. Yola was center, of course. "For forwards, we're fielding Fran and David; and guards, Ken and Iris." Iris was a solid sophomore; both she and Ken were guards able to take a beating. "Xiang covers goal for the first half, then we send in Charlie. The Melbourne players don't like change; they'll be rattled. Charlie's as quick as our opponent is slow."

Everyone cheered, and Charlie looked as thrilled as when he'd bested the knights in DNA World. It was hard to believe they'd really be ready; the first game always came too soon. But somehow, a good team always got to where it needed to be, just in time.

Coach added, "Jenny rotates in later at a critical point, to execute Play Twenty-nine. Not to overuse it—we need to hold off suspicion as long as we can." Until Whitcomb, the last game before October break, followed by the Feast of Fools at the castle.

Jenny paired up with Ken for wall passes, slanning across the court. Then she moved out at a new angle to receive the ball again. Guard Fran was surprisingly slick; she almost seemed to read which direction Jenny would take. For her final slan to the goal, Jenny took care to "assist" Ken only twice. The spying helis were out of sight, but they could always be hiding in the long axial cloud that pulsed and billowed, orange in the morning light.

"How do you always know, Fran?" Jenny asked, catching her breath during time out.

Fran gave a crooked grin. "You always glance that way. Frogs often have habits like that."

She smiled ruefully. "I need to get used to the cage."

"You won't always be in home cage. The Whitcomb Angels play at Rapture." Rapture, the Mississippi spacehab. Where every day was Judgment Day.

From the cloud emerged a saucer-shaped floater crawling with spider bots. Another appeared, a dark menacing shape, farther south. "**Sprayers**," texted someone. The mosquito sprayers were moving into position.

The sprayers slid back and forth, their shapes dipping in and out of the cloud like plates loose in a washer, as the south end gradually brightened. It was just after six A.M. when one sprayer moved slowly up to the cage. The metallic surface stopped outside.

"**EVERYONE OUT.**" Outsized text invaded her box, and a loudspeaker blared. "**CLEAR OUT AND DESCEND TO SURFACE LEVEL.**"

Jenny caught herself in midair, floating slowly to the side. Everyone stared, unsure what to do. Nobody ever dared interrupt slanball.

"NO TRESPASSING," Coach Porat broadcast back. "GET OFF MY CAGE."

The students stared, exchanging furtive glances. A breeze whistled through the cage, then died, and shadows shifted in the cloud. At length the rim of the sprayer slowly backed off. Jenny reached the side of the cage, grabbing a cable, her pulse getting back to normal as the players got back in line to complete their drill.

+

As Jenny left her room, having showered and changed for breakfast, the pink rain was just starting. Starbursts of pink exploded silently along the morning cloud, breaking up into spots like cherry blossoms drifting down. The petals floated and dispersed, spelling doom for the dreaded mosquitoes. A lizard skittered up the porch rail.

Just around the corner, at the bear gouge with the pipe loops, stood Mary Dyer. Mary was leaning down to fill her bottle with the brackish water.

"Mary, ¿qué haces? There's clean water from the tap, inside the cottage."

Mary looked up at her but said nothing. She always wore the same tie-dyed shift, and her face had the same iconic look; not Monroe, but something vaguely familiar.

"You cannot drink that water," Jenny tried to explain. "It's full of salt. And it needs to be filtered." Like sewage, a microbial stew.

Suddenly Mary smiled. "What a good idea! Thank you!" Her voice lilted exactly like Dean Nora Kwon.

Jenny smiled. "Have you been seeing the dean?"

Mary stood up with her bottle. "We're having therapy. We learn to say things."

"What things?"

Mary's face lit up, expressing executive confidence. "'Hello, how are you? That's a pretty necklace.' 'Professor, may I ask a question?' 'Oh, I'm sorry. I hope you feel better soon.'"

Jenny bit her lip to keep from laughing. "Hey, Mary, that's okay. Catch you later."

Along Buckeye Trail the gravel crunched beneath her feet. Her soles picked up so many pebbles, she had to print new shoes every night. Meanwhile she was famished, and looking forward to Café de la Paix. That morning the Belgian waffles were great, but Tom was kept busy with Orin Crawford's investment committee. The investors sounded like her mother's office crowd, all about An-thradyne and the falling markets. Her own trust fund had lost some, not that she'd ever spend it. She thought of Wednesday, when she planned to meet Tom for lunch in Mount Gilead.

"ToyNews Mount Gilead. We have a candidate for mayor." Mount Gile-ad's mayor had died in office the previous spring. Apparently the town of a thousand had managed without one since then. "Phil Hamilton has just filed for the ballot, with a petition containing fifty-seven valid signatures."

Jenny stared in surprise. Her professor, running for mayor? There in her news window stood Professor Hamilton, looking just like he would lecture on Aristotle. "Although no one can ever fill Dick Smythe's shoes, I am truly humbled to be considered for service to this God-fearing community beneath the stars. I thank members of my congregation for encouraging me to run, and for collecting the signatures on my behalf."

The voiceover added, "We asked Mrs. Smythe to comment on Hamil-ton's nomination."

Leora Smythe, the lady in the pioneer dress who had served the lunch for Homefair. So she was the mayor's widow. Leora kept her eyes downcast, the typical pauline. **"Dick would be pleased to know that Phil will be shep-herding our village in God's name."** They seemed to assume the election was done. Were there no other candidates?

"Another week till the filing deadline. The mayoral election is Tuesday, October ninth. All votes are cast at the courthouse, between six A.M. and seven P.M."

A special election, a month before Election Day? At the courthouse? Why not through ToyVote? All on one day? The second Tuesday—that was Fall Break, when most students would be away.

Jenny was tempted to ask Hamilton in class about the election, but she lacked the nerve. Her paper from Friday returned to her toybox with an A^{+++}, and a reminder of her private conference with him scheduled for Tues-day. He returned papers quickly, she thought, a sign of a good teacher.

In the plush seminar room, Hamilton left the podium to pace back and forth as he lectured; it was good neck exercise to follow him this way or that. But never for long before he shot out one of those dreaded questions. "Should the possessions of citizens all be equal, as in the Regime of Phaleus? What do you think?"

A couple of students leafed through the crinkly pages of their books, as though the answer could be found there. The professor's penetrating eyes stared at Enrico.

Enrico ventured, "Before you can have equality of possessions, you need equality of desires."

"Equality of desires. Enrico, I believe you've hit upon a profound problem with the Phaleus regime." When Hamilton liked a point, he always made the student feel like the first to ever make this discovery.

Priscilla, in her neck brace from her Homefair misadventure, was hard put to follow Hamilton's perambulation but nonetheless waved her hand so high that he could not ignore it. "Slaves by definition are owned; like, they own nothing, desire or not. So if there is slavery, then Phaleus's regime doesn't just have a problem, it's a logical impossibility."

A pretzel crunched between Mary's prosthetic jaws.

At the Ohioana, servers in power bands passed gravy dishes right and left, while the evening peepers chorused outside. In Jenny's toybox, a thousand playmate notes scrolled down. **"My best class is Antarctic Studies. What's yours?"** Her Somers friend Tusker-12 attended virtual University of Miami, in a toyworld that re-created the submerged city. The real Miamians had long since fled, most to Havana.

"I've lined up the music for Saturday." Ken was planning the Flood Awareness Day. "An authentic Jackson Square tribute band. The castle tour starts at noon, then afterward, the flood."

Jenny nodded and smiled as she ate. The only way she'd get her work done was to keep at it every available minute. So in her toybox she resumed reading her first chapter on Cuba. In her toyHarvard class, she'd hoped to learn more about her mother's roots, about the revolution and Guantánamo, how the rebel island had rescued thousands from flooded Florida, and how it become the fifty-second state. But so far, the course was all ancient history— how the highlands had formed from sedimentary rock, and how pretribal peoples left petroglyphs in the caverns centuries before Aristotle. At this rate they'd never get to the present, how *los cubanos* today combined revolutionary fervor with retro Romanism. Many Cubans still couldn't see Archbishop Eliza on equal terms with the Pope, whereas others still worshiped Che. The ultimate swing state.

Yola nudged her arm. "You awake?"

She looked up, startled. "Um, about flooding the castle?"

Kendall said, "I asked, will you help row the lifeboat out of the flooded castle?"

"Um, thanks, you can do that part. I'll prepare the handout."

Yola shook her head. "As if anyone will read it. Jenny, you've become a dwork."

"A what?"

"A dwork is someone who reads all the time and thinks everyone else does the same."

Charlie looked up. "Hey, Jenny's okay. She's an honors student."

Kendall leaned forward, remembering something. "Watch out for that politics class," he warned. " 'Warm yourself before the fire of the wise, but beware of their embers, lest you be singed.' "

"Politics," muttered Yola. "That's for motor clubs."

Anouk was fuming and muttering under her breath. "It's an outrage," she abruptly exclaimed. "They told me," she hissed, "to meet with the *Christian* chaplain."

"You must be a hard case," said Kendall. "Like the guys that hump elephants."

Anouk's silverware clattered on the table. "I knew this abominable college would try to convert me. The Euro minister will hear of it."

"Why don't you see Coach instead?" offered Kendall. "Coach won't convert anybody. Believe me, I've tried."

Jenny said, "Father Clare won't convert you either. Look, Anouk, you've just got to quit hacking the Pentagon." And all your friends, she nearly added.

"I cut way back. I only . . . explore once a week."

Yola eyed her with interest. "You hack the Pentagon? Really?"

Anouk gave a modest shrug.

"Ever hack the Creep?"

At the mention of the Creep, heads turned. The Creep, originally an Idaho senator with ties to the solar industry, had been vice president since anyone could remember. Every Centrist candidate picked some rifle-toting blonde to drum up the votes, but always ditched her at the last minute, ending back with the Creep. Obsessed with the war on ultra, the Creep never appeared in public, but he ran much of the government; how much was never known for sure.

The *parisienne* pursed her lips. "The Creep is tough," she admitted. "I've gotten close." It pleased her to have the attention of the entire slanball team.

"Well," said Yola, "let us know whoever he plans to invade next." They all had high school classmates serving in Antarctica, Earth's last source of new farmland. Yola turned to Jenny. "EMS tonight at nine, dwork. Don't forget."

+*+

The emergency medical volunteers met upstairs in Wickett Hall. Along with Jenny and Yola, there was one other Frontera student, Nick Petherbridge, Uncle Dylan's senior assistant. There stood Travis Tharp, and a cattle farmer, Frank Lazza, who had helped pull the cow out of the ditch on Raccoon Run; and two older men in power bands, one of them Judge Bart Baynor. Baynor was the town's morality officer. One of those posts always down there on the ballot, along with county auditor and dogcatcher. Frank and the judge were peering with a penlight into the carapace of one of the medibots. Medibots outnumbered the volunteers two to one.

"Welcome, heroes!" Doc Uddin had long gray-streaked blond hair in braids down her back and a scanscope slung around her neck, the round cuff resting on her overalls. She nodded at Frank and the judge. "Thanks for taking time from your Labor Day barbecue." The college seemed to ignore most holidays. "And welcome Jenny, our new volunteer. We could use more," she told Yola hopefully.

Yola nodded. "We have a couple other frogs interested, but they need to complete training."

Frank Lazza looked up from the stalled medibot. "Could the college maybe train entering frogs the summer before? We're always short-handed, first semester."

"We're working on that." Doc Uddin grimaced. "The admissions transition . . . has been a challenge." Every lack seemed to get blamed on the new admissions director, Luis Herrera Smith. "But we're doing better. Our human-attended call rate is up over fifty percent."

"That won't last, when call volume rises."

"I know last Wednesday was rough, but now that classes are in full swing, things should quiet down."

"Wednesdays," sighed the farmer. "Couldn't the college just require Thursday-morning classes?"

"Sure—like Mount Gilead could make skybikers wear helmets." Doc Uddin turned to Jenny. "Jenny, please arrange a full tour and tutorial, Friday at the Barnside." The Barnside Clinic was the hab's one medical facility, installed in a barn at a local farm. The doctor looked around the group, her thick braid swiveling around her back. "Three flu cases already, in Huron." The first-year residence hall where Tom lived. "A new strain printed out somewhere; Zari's fixing the filter, but you know we can expect more from those common-room printers." Ghostwriters were always coding new flu strains, a scam even worse than a leprechaun in your toyroom. "Make sure you all download the update to your scanscope. Jenny, here's yours."

The doctor handed Jenny her scanscope, and the connection blinked in. To check, Jenny clicked the scanscope around her wrist. The ring of amyloid molded to her arm, where it could find a vein. Blood meter, microscope, dialysis, drug injection.

"A reminder." Doc Uddin looked grim. "Any recreational use gets you expelled and deported. One strike, you're out."

Jenny nodded. "So when am I on call? What's the rotation?"

"You're on call twenty-four/seven. Whoever responds first takes the call."

"What if I'm in class?"

"Someone else has to go."

Jenny looked around. Six volunteers, plus a dozen medibots. "What if no one else is available?"

"Bots are always available." Bots responding alone. Unthinkable back in Somers.

Nick offered, "I'll take the morning calls; my classes are all afternoon."

Yola tapped Jenny's arm. "You can miss a class. You're super smart; you'll catch up."

20

Tuesday morning Jenny made it to slanball on a full night's sleep. With five days left, the team was coming together: one-on-one defense, blocked shots, and above all they pulled up their slanning percentage. Coach Porat was pleased. "Great Bears are the oldest team in the league, and we're still the greatest," he told them. "But remember: the Scorpions are tougher, so we need to get smarter."

At Life, it was Anouk's day to present. Back on the toyworld savannah, student models were winking in. Some had morphed their appearance into a film star or a monster, but most models showed up as themselves, bleary-eyed after their full weekend. Charlie looked bright and enthusiastic, much uplifted by the morning practice. Tom looked as usual, like Newman on a horse, ready to face whatever rode over the hill.

In the middle of the lake, some monstrous thing was rising from the deep. A swirl, and a colored shape breasted the waves. Up rose a gigantic tangle of an RNA. The molecule resembled the RNA that had taken Jenny for a wild ride to Ng's lab. It looked simpler, though, Jenny thought hopefully; this RNA had only four stem-loops.

As the molecule emerged, Anouk stepped forward in a fiendishly tessellated dress, the pattern so fine and sharp it made Jenny's head swim. Anouk turned to face the class. "Ribonucleic acid is the most ancient of life's molecules. As you know, the first cells on Earth were all made of RNA—"

Professor Abaynesh waved a hand. "And ultraphyte genomes still are."

Anouk rolled her eyes. "And ultraphyte genomes. No DNA for them." Anouk brainstreamed parts of the molecule to light up. "Now the messenger RNA code consists of four main letters like DNA; but this transfer RNA which you see here, a relatively small molecule, also uses the so-called 'unusual' bases such as pseudouridine—"

"And methyladenine," interrupted the professor. "The ultraphytes still use methyladenine in their RNA."

With an exasperated glance, Anouk muttered something in French.

Jenny quickly asked, "Could you please point out the pseudouridine?"

To her relief, the students got to climb and check out the atoms without riding or sliding. Jenny lost her footing just once, when she failed to grasp a phosphate. Charlie slipped into the lake, where he had a great time splashing. By the end of the hour, half the class was splashing around in the virtual lake.

After class, Anouk ran off to assist toymaker Valadkhani's Developmental Arithmetic class. Above Buckeye Trail, the air still sprouted pink fringes of smartspray. Jenny stopped by Abaynesh's office beneath the outsized Reagan jelly beans.

"Good job marking the RNA." The professor spoke while brainstreaming the transfer bees that hovered about her *Arabidopsis* plants, sniffing hormones and inserting genes here or there. "How are your orchids?"

"The orchids are great," Jenny admitted. "They grow so fast here. Is it the spacehab?"

Abaynesh kept her eye on the bees. "I gave your orchids a semiochemical to boost their motivation. It's temporary, it'll wear off."

Jenny frowned, hoping not to sound dumb. "Motivation?"

"How else do you boost production?" The professor blinked another paper over to Jenny, adding to the stack she struggled through. "Better yet, transform their genes to make the semiochemical. Then all the plants motivate each other." She cast a dark look outside at the sky, still aggrieved about the spraying. "Different inputs stimulate the plants to form different neural networks." She pointed to a row of plants with a profusion of flower buds, more than Jenny had ever seen on *Arabidopsis*. "This strain has a production network. They want to work hard. Very productive—I have a grant from the National Association of Wheat Growers."

Jenny opened her mouth, then carefully shut it again.

"You won't find it commercially, not yet approved. Now here—" Abaynesh reached across to the next row of plants. "We are making a 'wisdom' network, nerves that can be organized to guide wise and cooperative behaviors. Suppose different plants possess effective defenses against the diamond-back moth, the beet armyworm, or the cabbage looper. Each plant releases enzymes to combat different worms. Will the plants develop a 'wisdom circuit' directing them to share the light and grow equally, rather than overcrowding?"

Jenny winced at the thought. "I still don't follow what these 'networks' are."

"The networks are made by cloning a set of genes into *Arabidopsis*. For example . . ." She rose and headed out to the greenhouse, still talking. "This variant of *A. sapiens* has a laughter network. It detects a stimulus and finds it funny."

The plant sat there, about a dozen leaves radiating from the base, a stalk projecting upward about a foot high. The stalk had a few flower buds. It didn't look particularly amused.

Professor Abaynesh touched a leaf. The whole plant shuddered for a moment, and the stalk swayed back and forth. "See, it's laughing."

"Really?" Jenny viewed the plant skeptically.

"It lacks discrimination," Abaynesh conceded. "The network has less than a thousand neurons. It can't always tell what's funny. It laughs at me no matter what." She pointed to the next plant. "This other strain has a depression network. Much simpler; only fifty neurons."

The depressed plant looked similar to the laughing plant, except it had fewer leaves, and they drooped; it could use a good watering. When the professor touched it, several leaves fell off. "The depressed strain is very hard to grow. This one probably won't survive being touched. I have to plant a whole flat of them to keep a few going. Usually I end up having to start over and engineer a new line." She moved on to the row of plants. "Now here, we have a worship network."

"Uh . . . a what?" The plants looked very ordinary, nearly picture perfect *Arabidopsis*.

"They sense a higher power and respond. Don't leave your mouth open, something might fly in."

Jenny shut her mouth and swallowed. "They sense . . . when you touch them?"

The professor shook her head. "This strain hears only an inner calling."

Remembering Howell's question, Jenny asked, "Do they pray in church?"

"Of course not." The professor moved on. "They pray in shul."

Suddenly Jenny realized how late it was. "I'm sorry, I'll be late for my appointment with Professor Hamilton."

Abaynesh turned and looked at her curiously. "Hamilton? What for?"

Jenny frowned, reluctant to say. "To help me. Anyway, thanks for all the . . . examples. I think I have a better idea now of what I'm reading."

"You should be careful around Professor Hamilton."

Jenny wondered how to take that. She herself was suspicious of Hamilton, but one professor should not speak ill of another.

The professor's eyes widened. "You've got your own greenhouse. Why don't you take some plants home to play with?"

"Well, I don't know—"

"You could try behavioral conditioning." She summoned a cart, whose surface opened like the mouth of a bag. She picked up one of the laughing plants. "These are easy to work with. Here's the training protocol." A new window joined the jungle of windows in Jenny's toybox.

"Um . . . orchids are so delicate. I have to keep them free of any pests, like those cabbage loopers—"

Abaynesh looked shocked. "We would never have cabbage loopers in here." She whispered, "I just scare the plants with their semiochemicals."

"I see. Well, if you're sure . . ."

The professor had kept Jenny's orchids here, after all, and they came through okay. She arranged two flats in the cart, which extended a cover. "There you go. The cart will follow you right home."

Jenny hurried out to Buckeye Trail, narrowly avoiding a spring peeper squashed in the gravel. The cart moved along, its tractor tread comfortably negotiating the ruts and race car skid ruts. She hurried over to Hamilton's office, wishing she had time to drop off the cart at her room first. "**Sorry I'm late,**" she texted quickly.

He waved his hand with a dismissive air, ignoring the cart. "Have a seat, please."

The chair was the kind you could sink into and never get up. Hamilton's office had the same feel of plush elegance as his classroom. The desk was full of souvenirs from various think tanks, the Heritage Foundation, the Rand. An end table held a statue of a Greek discus thrower, and a curious round token imprinted with the letter Z.

"Jenny, I cannot tell you what a pleasure it is to have a student who's actually read the Founding Fathers. 'Life, liberty, and the pursuit of happiness'—you certainly addressed profound points in your essay."

"**Thank you.**" She felt cautious, self-protective, and curious all at once. Why would this professor run for mayor? she wondered. Mayor was a busy job; you had to keep the streets clean and the water flowing.

"Especially the pursuit of happiness. That all men form governments so as to free them for individual pursuit of happiness—that's so American," he added. "And yet . . . is that what Aristotle was about, I wonder. Aristotle's *polis* was a modest-sized world of gentlemen, about the size of Mount Gilead, perhaps. Gentlemen who'd grown up together, who knew each other intimately. Trust can be extended only to a small circle of friends, fellow citizens. Such things as love, affection, friendship, and sympathy are the grounds of political life; a life in which men care for one another. Isn't that what the *polis* is about . . . a political community small enough for affection?"

Jenny wondered what he was getting at. If Aristotle was only for small-town mayors, then why was he quoted in the halls of Congress? Maybe that was their problem, the hacks who treated Congress like a playground for their friends.

"Shared trust comes from shared values. Values expressed through speech, *logos*. It is *logos* that makes us political. Through speech we become fully human. Speech or reason; they amount to the same thing. For instance, shared praise of the heavenly bodies placed in the Firmament—"

"There is no such thing."

Jenny's heart pounded so hard she could scarcely hear. For a moment the room swam around her, then her head cleared. The professor was still sitting there, and her statement hung in the air. He nodded appreciatively. "You certainly expressed your point."

Above the desk appeared a projection through a brain. The sight of the toyview startled her, incongruous amid the antiques. The frontal and parietal lobes shone transparent, and within lit up regions of color. The colors flexed even as she watched.

"Here is where your brain lights up when you speak; not just Broca's area, but these other regions as well, courage and fortitude perhaps?" Hamilton smiled apologetically. "Not that I would know, of course, but you can train these regions."

He'd scanned her own brain. Her scalp tingled. "**Brain scans I've had before.**" The specialists had tried for years to train her brain to get around her problem.

"This is new technology," Hamilton assured her. "I always get the latest."

Technology; was that how he knew her father, Jenny wondered. Out of the corner of her eye, she noticed something moving. The cover of the cart was flexing, as if under stress.

"Even so, Jenny, I'm surprised your own clan hasn't helped you before. Did they prefer to keep you the quiet one?"

"That's a lie. I'm no pauline."

The brain scan pulsed red in the same spots as before.

"There, your pattern is developing. Perhaps it's a new experience for you to face ideas you really disagree with."

Jenny kept silent. She'd heard plenty of Centrists before. But rarely in the same room, breathing her own air.

"You may keep the system running in your box. With a little practice, you can train it to stimulate your key regions as you need, just so—" He stopped, his eyes wide with consternation.

The cover of the cart was straining, as if something were alive underneath, like Rita Montalcini-Levi's handbag. Out of the cart poked the two heads of Meg-El, Professor Abaynesh's black snake. The two tongue-flicking heads batted back and forth a moment as if quarrelling over which way to go. They seemed to decide, and a loop of their body pressed outward and down the side of the cart in a leisurely way.

Jenny stared. This could not possibly be happening; it had to be a toy-world joke of some sort. But there it was, slinking down onto the plush carpet of the professor's office.

Her mind clicked into emergency mode, like on EMS call. How to recapture a snake; the answer must be out there on Toynet. A couple of blinks led to a method: Catch the tail first, then behind the head. A stick would help, but there was none.

By the time she decided to act, Meg-El had slid nearly her entire bulk out of the cart. Jenny grabbed for the tail. As she held it up, the rest of the body stiffened. The two heads strained to flee in opposite directions. That made it easy for her free hand to grab behind the shared neck. She stuffed the whole snake back where it came from, then shoved the top onto the cart, hoping it would stay shut. Mortified, she turned to face the professor.

Professor Hamilton had retreated to his desk, where he stood upon the chair. His face was white, his arms limp, like someone about to faint away.

Jenny shoved the cart back into Abaynesh's office. "I'm switching advisors."

The professor looked up. Behind her, Tova was back from kindergarten, sitting amid a pile of crayon drawings of alien invaders.

Jenny blinked over the change-of-advisor form. "You did that on purpose," she added, keeping her voice down.

"Did what?"

"Sent me off with a dangerous animal."

The snake found its way out of the cart again and slithered to the floor. Seeing it, Tova got up and ran over. "There you are, Meg-El, I missed you." She gathered up the snake around her neck. Why did the girl have no twin? Jenny wondered. It was as if the snake were her twin; unnatural.

"I'm reporting this to the dean," Jenny added.

"What else is new." The professor sighed. Her face looked downcast. "I thought you would be different."

Jenny swallowed. "Just sign the form."

The seconds ticked by. The professor tilted her head this way and that. Then at last the form pinged back, with the line signed. "By the way," she asked, as Jenny turned to go, "what did he do when Meg-El came out?"

Without answering, Jenny left.

At her cottage, Jenny went up to the greenhouse to calm herself amid her orchids. She was still shaking all over. She was fed up with both professors, whatever their game. Above all, she was furious at Uncle Dylan. To hear him tell it, Frontera was always "the best college" in the universe, with the best faculty anywhere. But these professors were nuts. They probably couldn't get a job anywhere else.

She called up the form in her toybox, wondering how to find a new advisor. Maybe the one with the pile worms.

Then she caught sight of Blood Star, the fresh buds starting to open. Abaynesh had taken care of those plants all right; and the vanda had grown twice as tall with her special treatment. The professor packed a lot into class; *adiós* high school. Jenny thought again how Hamilton had looked, the mayoral candidate, cringing on his chair. Abaynesh had wanted her to see that. She didn't want Jenny to end up an acolyte, like the Ferrari suits.

And yet, Hamilton's speech system was intriguing. If Centrists had new technology, why not use it for her own aims? He thought he could use her, try to make her Centrist like her aunts; but two could play that game. Campaign operatives always stole tricks from the other side.

She blinked to place a call. Hamilton appeared in the window, none the worse. "Professor, I'd like to apologize for—"

"Never mind." He waved his hand. "It's my pleasure, Jenny."

"Professor, I was thinking, I would like to do a second major, in Politics. Would you be my advisor?" She called up a second-advisor form. Meanwhile, she put away the drop-advisor signed by Abaynesh, without turning it in.

Hamilton smiled with delight, thoroughly pleased. He'd be off his guard now, Jenny thought, and maybe divulge a few Centrist secrets. At the same time, she'd keep Abaynesh as her advisor for Life. She'd keep on learning about plants—and maybe ultra. These professors were nuts, all right, but she could still learn plenty.

21

Wednesday morning, ToyNews was full of disaster. "A major fall of Kessler debris, on the solar array in the Death Belt, just west of the Texas border. Homeworld Security nudged the object just past the habitable region. The trail of radioactive debris stretches toward—" An old mid-century station for space tourists. Thousands of such decrepit objects floated aimlessly around Earth and moon carrying bits of plutonium. Cleaning them out was not easy, not that the Centrists really tried. President Bud Guzmán praised Homeworld Security for doing a "heck of a job" steering the landfall.

"A major failure of Homeworld Security," proclaimed Anna Carrillo at a rally in Indianapolis. "Expanding the Dead Zone and poisoning our children. America deserves better leadership."

Her opponent, Gar Guzmán, was more sanguine. "Homeworld Security effectively steered the object to land in the Dead Zone, away from habitation," the Centrist candidate told Clive. "This shows why we need to maintain a steady Centrist hand at the helm. Remember, Earth itself has its limits; someday we'll all rise beyond."

The scene cut to Rapture, an idyllic misty spacehab. In the distance rose its gaming center, the Holyland Hotel, a scale replica of ancient Jerusalem. Above rose a giant cross flanked by seraphs. In their slanball court, in October, Frontera's Great Bears would meet Whitcomb's Angels.

But neither Frontera nor Rapture could ever hold all the populations fleeing Earth. Had the poison reached New York? Jenny called her mother.

"We're fine," Soledad assured her. "The radioactive cloud will pass by New York, but we stepped up our HIV just in case."

"Is the Death Belt still expanding?"

"The Death Belt is expanding, all right," her mother assured her. "Drying out more every year."

"Do they really think they can put everyone from Earth out in spacehabs?"

"Not if they do the math. We've reached a turning point on global drying—I truly believe this election is our last chance." Her mother shook her head. "But the plutonium fall throws a wrench into the vice-presidential selection. Anna will have to pick someone who knows space security."

Jenny absorbed this. "Not Sid Shaak." The Connecticut senator was a ranking member of the Space Defense subcommittee. Shaak's family fortune derived from the Schaghticoke Tribal Nation, who owned the third largest casino empire. He was under investigation for running a child porn toyworld.

"Nothing's final yet." Hardly reassuring. "As for Guzmán, you know, he's stuck; he can't just pick some pretty face this time." A pretty face to trade out for the Creep. Soledad smiled reassuringly. "*No te preocupes,* I shouldn't distract you from your studies. How are your classes?"

"*Chulo,*" said Jenny. "I'm growing plant nervous systems, and arguing with Teddy Roosevelt, and Professor Hamilton is training me to speak."

"Public speaking?" Her mother pounced. "Really?"

"Well," she muttered, "he'd like to think so anyway."

"*¡Muy bien!* We'll put you down for the convention." The Unity convention was scheduled for the following Monday.

Jenny frowned, wishing she had not let it slip out. "I told you, I can visit the convention but I can't do a speech."

"Sure you can. You speak for Clive."

"Clive is like family. He always cleans it up."

Soledad waved her hand. "Clive cleans up for everyone—it's his job, to keep up the ratings. Jenny, you've got to do it. For Anna. For the world. For the family." For Jordi—the first convention since his death. "And don't forget, the final debate at Frontera—October twenty-fifth."

Presidential candidates in the hab—*fantástico.* Still, Jenny shook her head. "You're sure you and Dad are okay?" The news was all so bad.

Soledad gave a sigh. "Your father misses you."

Jenny swallowed. "I know."

"I'm getting him out for a few days at Lake Taupo." Their remote New Zealand hideaway. "Our last bit of rest before the convention."

"I'm sure the rest will do him good." Toynet could be all-consuming.

"Remember Iroquoia—the Condoling Council. He'll feel so much better."

"October break," Jenny agreed. "I'll play then, I promise."

"And bring some of your new friends. They'll enjoy it."

Jenny shuddered. Iroquoia was no place for her friends. Her mother's clients, and her father's Toy Land engineers—they played hard.

+-+

For lunch at last she set out to meet Tom in Mount Gilead, at Lazza's Diner. Tom had said he had business in the village, and would meet her there. She wondered what to wear—not moonholes, of course, but certainly no pioneer dress. At last she printed out overalls like Doc Uddin, and pulled on her heavy boots, mud-streaked from Homefair. Her Fifth Avenue flower-print blouse would soften the look.

By eleven she trudged into the village down Raccoon Run, the same dirt road the Homefair crew had taken. The college grounds rolled away behind her while the village grid straightened as if by magic, a trick of the eye. The steeple of the college All Saints Church now pointed down, while the Firmament Church pointed "heavenward," with the college way up there. A purple pennant flickered upside down from the Kearns-Clark castle.

Along the road flowed a stream toward Scioto Creek. The stream grew increasingly turbid and soapy, with floating bits of carb and anthrax fiber. It seemed to get worse the nearer she approached the village center. This could hardly meet regulations. For a moment she stopped to dip her scanscope in, wrinkling her nose at the smell. Coliforms, manure minerals, and amyloid waste—the scanscope recorded high levels. All headed for the Scioto, and at last the Ohio River. The entire drainage must be polluted. Waste cycling in a spacehab was always a challenge, but this—how could it be?

She blinked the EMS snake to file a report. Then she hurried on to find Lazza's. The squat storefront stood in the main square, pigeons clucking in the street with tiny power bands on their wings. Pigeons flocked across the street to the redbrick courthouse with classic pillars. And next door to Lazza's stood the Smythe Power Bank, run by the late mayor to bank energy from all those power bands.

Jenny had arrived early at the diner, but never mind; a chance to watch people. She might as well get to know Lazza's, as she was bound to end up there sometime on call. The diner was built of roughly finished carboxyplast, with a long bar and tables imitating knotty wood. Jenny found herself a stool and leaned her elbows on the counter. Several men and women in overalls lounged at the toywall watching football, all half a head shorter than she. One tipped a server with a few watt-hours from his power band. At a table sat two women in pioneer dresses and bonnets, with three small children. Even the children wore power bands; not good, as too much load could stunt their growth. Where was Tom, and why couldn't he have come out along with her?

On the back wall a blue-tailed lizard skittered up across a beer ad, and an elk jutted out with mugs dangling from its antler points.

Someone coughed loudly, right by her ear, as if to get her attention. On the stool next to Jenny sat a woman in a pioneer dress. Leora Smythe—the mayor's widow, who had served lunch for the Homefair volunteers. Jenny smiled. "**Thanks for the Homefair lunch.**"

"**Homefair,**" texted Leora. She eyed Jenny intently. "**At the college?**"

"**I'm a student,**" Jenny returned. "**My first year.**"

Leora's eyes widened and she touched her bonnet. She took a deep breath. "Castle!" she exclaimed. "There's a castle up there."

Castle Cockaigne. From here in Mount Gilead, the castle must be the most striking landmark above. Jenny smiled. "My team captains live in the castle. There's a tour this Saturday."

"A tour of the castle? Really?"

"At noon it opens. Then at one is Flood Awareness Day. We're flooding the main floor from the moat, then Kendall demonstrates the lifeboat."

"Flooding?"

"In case the water ever leaks in from the shell." It occurred to her that Mount Gilead colonists would be in trouble too. "Are your homes all carb?"

"Only Homefair homes. The rest are amyloid." Leora nodded slowly. "Dick would have wanted people to know about flooding."

"Well, why don't they all come?" Jenny blinked her announcement. "Here," she offered. "You're welcome to pass this on."

Leora accepted the file, then popped a playmate request.

Jenny confirmed her playmate. "I'm sorry about your husband," she added.

"Thanks," said Leora. "It was a Wednesday," she said. "So I come here now, every Wednesday. Just to get away."

Jenny swallowed and nodded.

"I'm glad you joined EMS. They need people." Suddenly Leora pressed Jenny's hand. Then she slid from the stool and glided out, her long skirt brushing past a chair.

As Leora left, Tom sat down on the stool at Jenny's right. "I saw you, but I didn't want to interrupt," he explained.

"That's okay." She smiled and closed her eyes, feeling warm all over and enjoying it. When her eyes opened, he flashed into view, blue-eyed and smiling, just like Newman in a toyflick.

A server approached, smoothing her overalls. "Can I tell you the specials?

Hey, Jenny! How're your thumbs?" It was Sherri-Lyn, the Homefair home-owner.

"*Bien*. How's the home?" Jenny asked warily. "Still standing, I hope."

"The home is fabulous. I'm just so glad to get this job right off—tide us over till our farm makes a living."

Jenny picked from the menu in her toybox. "Hope we don't mess up too bad."

Sherri-Lyn nodded. "When I first arrived, they told me the college was all snooty faculty, and students tipping cows and getting their stomachs pumped out at the Barnside, but I'm sure glad to see it's not true." She blinked at her box. "Today's special is the ribs. Fresh from the hog."

When Sherri-Lyn had left with their orders, Jenny stole another look at Tom. She kept thinking how he had looked without his shirt. She reminded herself how back in high school, a *chico* who looked so good could suddenly do or say something incredibly disgusting.

"How is Priscilla?" Tom asked. "Is she okay?"

"She'll wear a neck brace for a while, but she's okay, thanks. How's your café?"

Tom looked away, his face shut like a clam. "It'll break even."

Jenny thought she'd leave a bigger tip next time. "Teddy Roosevelt's admirers once sent him a possum. He had it 'well browned, with sweet potatoes.'"

Tom's face softened. "I'll put that on the menu."

"How's your art class?"

"*Chulo*. Dante and Donatello. Figures that step right out of stone."

"Father Clare made his own stained-glass windows for the chapel."

"Really. The professors here are amazing."

"Are you sure you weren't cultured?" she suddenly asked. "You look like a Newman."

Tom laughed. "If only everyone thought that, I could sell my genes." He added, "You look just like your great-grandmother. Even your expressions. Whenever someone mentions the 'Firmament.'" He smiled slyly.

She looked away, abashed.

"How's Life going for you?"

"Life? You mean, the class?" Jenny thought a moment. "It all . . . comes at you at once."

"I'll say. Have you started a laboratory project?"

"I have these laughing plants in the greenhouse. I'm supposed to train their neural networks."

"Train them? To laugh at a joke?"

"When they detect a semiochemical," Jenny said. "After I master that, we start the wisdom networks. That's frontier research; no one really knows what's going on."

Tom nodded understandingly.

"So what kind of plants are you researching?"

"I'm not doing plants," he said. "The combinatorics—I don't yet have the math."

"I don't either," Jenny admitted. "I've had two years of calculus, but none of this modeling. I'm depending on Anouk." A good partnership.

"Charlie and I are doing pile worms."

"I see."

Sherri-Lyn brought their orders. The ribs tasted fresh, after Jenny pushed off the gravy.

Jenny asked, "What are pile worms?"

"Pile worms are these long, jointed invertebrates with over a hundred pairs of legs. They live in intertidal mud and eat detritus. They survive a wide range of salinity, up to sixty-five percent."

"*Guao.* So what do you do with them?"

"DNA sequence," Tom explained. "We explore their genomes."

"That takes math too."

"Statistics I can manage. Their genomes have some really weird genes."

"Weird? Like what?"

"Like ultra."

Jenny's fork froze. "Ultraphyte genes? That can't be."

"The math says they are. Some of the pile worm DNA is from an ultraphyte."

"But—" Jenny looked around at the colonists, hoping no one overheard. They wouldn't understand anyhow. She leaned closer and whispered, "Pile worms are terrestrial, right? Ultra comes from some other planet. Ultraphytes don't even have DNA, they have RNA."

"But their bases correspond to the four DNA bases," Tom pointed out. "Comparing pile worm DNA with ultraphyte RNA, you find sequences that share an ancestor."

She absorbed the implications. "So pile worms and ultraphytes have a common ancestor? A few billion years ago, on some other planet?"

"Maybe," said Tom. "Or maybe they transferred genes more recently. Remember, ultraphytes grow in saltwater."

"Not open ocean, it's too dilute and lacks iron." Ultraphytes preferred the saturated Salt Lake. They flourished there, even formed towering bio-films. How could they have got there by chance?

"Intertidal zones have plenty of iron; and when they dry out, the salt concentrates. Ultraphytes growing there could have put their genes into Earth creatures."

"By accident? Or on purpose?"

"On purpose? How could that be?"

Earth creatures, Jenny wondered. What about humans? Human genomes were already full of parasitic DNA.

Sherri-Lyn returned with a bushel of string beans. "Thanks for the help, it was a busy morning. We had these extra; thought you could use them." She left no bill. Tom had worked there that morning to pay for their lunch.

As they got down from the bar, Jenny brushed against Tom's side. She felt lightened, like micrograv. She barely noticed how they left the diner. Her hand touched his hand, tentatively clasping two fingers. They held hands and walked together all the way home.

That evening the Ohioana crowd was thin. Charlie was gone, as well as all the scholarship students on the slanball team. "The dining hall might be more convenient," Jenny suggested to Yola.

"I suppose," Yola sighed. "I'm tired of gravy, anyhow. The dining hall serves amyloid crap, but at least it's an infinite variety."

"Where's Ken?"

"The High Holidays start tonight, Rosh Hashanah. Ken is at service with Coach, along with David and Fran."

The holidays would take extra time and energy for them, and Coach. Jenny resolved to be extra attentive, and get to practice well rested. "Do Quakers have holidays?"

Yola shook her head. "For Quakers, every day is holy."

"Really. Are there special, like, observances for 'everyday' then? Like, things you don't do?"

"Lots of things. No drinking, gambling, or voting."

She blinked. "No voting?"

"The early Quakers abstained from 'the infernal practice of elections.' Politicians are so gross. Sorry," Yola added.

"What about gambling? Do you play taxes?"

"Never," said Yola shortly. "Ken and I, we fund a foundation for disappearing islands."

"That's a great idea. Wish my mother would let me do that."

"Hey, you're an *adulta*. Parents are idiots—do what you want."

Mary Dyer was eating her pretzels. "Jenny, are we socializing tonight?" Dean Kwon's voice again.

Yola gave Mary a look. "Not if she can help it."

"So much work," Jenny sighed. "I have to read the Northern Securities case, and Aristotle's 'Regime of the Spartans,' and train plants to laugh."

"Dean Kwon wants us to socialize," Mary told them. "Is the 'Midweek Melee' socializing?"

The Red Bulls' regular Wednesday party, for those without Thursday classes. This one promised bear pit wrestling. "Um, I wouldn't go," advised Jenny.

"You're always welcome with us," said Yola kindly. "Stick with our crowd."

"Sure, Mary. Just go where we go." Jenny smiled, feeling guilty that she wished she had a more normal *compañera*.

+−

A beeping alarm roused Jenny from deep sleep. Three A.M., two hours till slanball. Struggling to rouse herself, Jenny slapped the diad on her forehead. The EMS snake was pulsing. Jenny blinked back.

Doc Uddin appeared, the thick gray braid down her back, hunched over a stretcher outside the red-shingled Barnside. "There's another call, out on Buckeye Trail. Can you take it?"

Jenny blinked rapidly. "I have a morning class—and I haven't yet had the EMS tutorial." She thought she had shut off the call alarm.

"It's you or the bot."

Jenny stumbled to get some clothes on, no time to print out fresh, grabbing her scanscope on the way out. Outside waited the heli, beneath the lights of Mount Gilead and the church spire pointing down from the darkened curve of the spacehab. She got into the waiting heli with the medibot. Her window reported three calls in progress, two at the Bulls' clubhouse and this latest out on Buckeye Trail. Her EMS window showed a *chico* sprawled facedown, one arm at an odd angle, laces dragged in the mud.

As the heli landed, the door opened and she followed the medibot out. A whiff of ethanol and vomit. His headband was inactive, a worrisome sign.

The medibot shined a light on his face. "Luke Reid, first-year." A Bulls pledge from Hocking. Jenny pushed aside his hair. "Can you hear me?" Face pale and cool. No use asking his name, or the president for that matter. She pulled his eyelid open; the dilated pupil showed no reaction. She dragged his wrist from the mud: pulse low, respiration faint. Jenny gave the medibot an uncertain look, hoping she missed nothing in the local routine.

"Run the scanscope," texted the medibot.

Jenny worried about his breathing. "Could I have a tube first?" She gently turned his head aside, concerned as well for his neck after the fall. The medibot snaked a breathing tube down the *chico*'s throat. Then at last she clicked the scanscope rings around his wrist.

A dozen columns of numbers flowed down her scan window: oxygen low-normal, glucose low, ethanol 400 mg percent. "*Guao*. He may need dialysis."

The medibot, receiving the same stream, was already back to the heli, returning with the dialysis rig.

By now, several other students had collected round, evidently returning late from the Melee. One knelt anxiously at his side, Enrico Peña, the well-spoken *chico* from Politics class. "Is he okay? I'm his roommate, I'll help him home."

Jenny shook her head. "Thanks, but he won't go home for a while."

Another partygoer came by, his body pitching unsteadily. "Hey, total wipeout. That's what you get from 24-24." Twenty-four shots in twenty-four hours, a common pledge prank. "That's the way—filter and back for more." The unsteady one half fell, just missing the medibot bringing the backboard.

"You can take *that* one home," Jenny told Enrico.

From the unconscious student, the scanscope showed no signal of broken bones. The medibot deftly slid the backboard under him, and the amyloid molded to his form, holding him still. **"Take him to the Barnside."**

"He needs glucose, and thiamine." At such a high dose, Jenny wanted these treatments just in case. The medibot deftly inserted the patient into the heli, with breathing tube, dialysis rig, and all. Well built for these functions, Jenny was relieved to see.

The Barnside clinic had several treatment modules, including detox and surgery. Doc Uddin was there, with two other students stabilized. A nurse in power bands was setting an IV. "Good job," Doc Uddin told Jenny. "Next time, check the blood for bone signals before moving him. But you're right, he did need the tube. It's touch-and-go when they're this intoxicated."

Four fifteen, Jenny checked. Her teammates would be rising soon. The sleep test—she dreaded to see Coach's face. "May I go now?"

"Nick and Travis are tied up at the college, and we just got two more calls. One fell out of Ferrari's second-floor window. The other, a blue baby in Mount Gilead."

"A blue baby? Newborn?"

"It's not congenital, I delivered her four months ago. She was healthy last week."

Jenny swallowed hard.

"I can't take either call; the one you brought is still critical." Doc Uddin looked her in the eye.

She swallowed again. "I'll take the baby."

Out she went in the heli with a medibot, while another medibot headed alone back to Buckeye Trail. She found herself shaking, at the verge of tears. *Hola*, she thought, pull yourself together; this is no way to be a first responder.

Jenny peered into the dark interior of the amyloid kitchen. A single dim light revealed a cross above the mantel, a pot simmered on the stove. Like in a Rembrandt, the light illuminated the face of a woman in a pioneer dress and cap cradling a baby, her face creased with fear. "She was fine this morning. What's wrong with her? Is she going to—" The mother stopped her mouth with her hand.

"She'll be all right," Jenny said soothingly, hoping it was true. Beside her, the medibot turned on an examination lamp. The baby was limp and drooling excessively, fingers grayish with blue nail beds, like the pale blue of blank windows. But what could bring on cyanosis so quickly? Some clue pricked her mind, just out of reach.

"I'm so glad you came," the mother told her. "Leora told us, never get sick on Wednesday night; the squad is always stuck at the college."

Jenny sized down the scanscope to fit the baby's leg. "Has she been feeding?"

"She feeds well," said the mother. "I'm weaning her to the formula Doc Uddin recommended."

In her window the figures scrolled down. Methemoglobin—the level was out of sight. Hemoglobin with the iron oxidized, so it couldn't bind oxygen. What caused that?

At her side, the medibot was already snaking the oxygen line. The scanscope followed up with an enzyme that reduced the hemoglobin, removing whatever displaced the oxygen. One minute passed, then the next. The methemoglobin number went down, then again, a steady decline. The baby pinked up and began to breathe.

Jenny took a long breath. "I think she'll be okay." She turned to the mother. "What else did you feed her?" Antibiotics, antiseptics, even certain dyes could cause methemoglobinemia.

The mother shook her head. "I made up the formula with clean water, just like the doctor said."

"Where'd you get the water?"

"Our tap, of course."

Nitrates. "From that stream? It's polluted." Nitrates from fertilizer runoff could turn to nitrites in a baby's stomach, then oxidize the hemoglobin.

"That's what the doctor said. So I boiled the water an hour, before using."

Jenny closed her eyes. "That's the worst thing you could do. It only concentrates the nitrates. Didn't the doctor tell you to use bottled water?"

"How could we afford that?" The mother looked around her, at the room. Her shoulders collapsed, and she stared at the floor. "We can barely keep up the house payment. As it is, we're three days from meltdown."

22

Thursday morning, Dylan was at the Mound for his meeting with Bobby Foxtail Forrester, manager of the Native American Mound Casino and Worship Center. Dylan came early for a few hands of blackjack with Nick Petherbridge plus a couple of alumni online. Dylan never won in the long run, but he kept ahead long enough to give the alums a sense of his management skill, assuring them that their gifts were in good hands. The dealer was an amyloid DIRG, whose flourish around the table was just for show, as the cards melted up from the table surface. In the air, floating feathers glimmered red, green, or blue, carrying drinks and self-cleansing cigarettes. The dealer's up card was a ten; Dylan blinked "hit" for another card. The dealer ended up going bust, while Dylan won the hand.

"*Guao*, President Chase," exclaimed Nick, "your luck is running high today."

"For the scholarship fund," said Dylan with a winning smile.

The manager sailed over, so smoothly his feet might never leave the floor. Impeccable tie, his generous round face always conveyed the aim of enriching every player.

"Bobby! *Muchas gracias* for the opening drums. They were awe-inspiring, as always."

"No trouble. Please, do me the honor . . ." Bobby drew Dylan by the elbow into his office. His desk was flanked by American and Ohio State flags between spiral-sculpted evergreens in marble pots. Above soared the famous two-hundredth-anniversary mural of Shawnee warchief Blue Jacket charging to victory against the army of the Northwest Territories. "I do hope all the classes are going well."

"Our strongest class of frogs so far."

"Our classes too," agreed Bobby, "particularly for blackjack and three-card poker. Students all want to learn strategy."

"Quite an education, I'm sure."

Bobby nodded gravely. "We do appreciate the college. So well mannered, so patriotic about their taxes. Alumni bring their families back. Enhance our brand."

Dylan spread his hands. "I'm glad our students do credit to their institution."

"No trouble, no trouble at all."

"As you know, our staff are always ready to help out."

"We know you are, no trouble."

"Including that young man who played out his ticket home." The played-out Peoria grocery clerk, now in college rehab.

"Indeed?" Bobby's face went blank a moment as he made a show of scanning his box. "Ah, no trouble, I see. The customer cashed his ticket through a shady Maldivian syndicate, the kind you can't trace. His ticket record literally vanished."

"I understand." A vanished record; the sort of thing to make an executive's hair stand on end.

"We make arrangements of course, but this was the fourth time for this particular customer. We thought he might find your rehab . . . educational."

"Ah, *entiendo*."

Bobby stood straighter and gave a sharp nod. "It's done, no trouble. He'll be sent home straight."

"*Muchas gracias*." Why hadn't Bobby done that right away—he had wanted to call Dylan in here for something. "Bobby, you know the college is fully supportive of our relationship. We do whatever we can."

"Absolutely. Especially the habitat. Photogenic flora and fauna, unique exotic species, just dangerous enough for adventure. It fits our native tradition."

"And prompt pest treatment." Was that Bobby's concern?

"Pest treatment—no trouble at all." Bobby paused, clasping and unclasping his hands. "Perhaps some space treatment? Strings in Washington?"

The new directive from Homeworld Security. The cutback on monitoring space debris, from 99 percent coverage to 96. You didn't need to count cards to figure out what that meant. But if even the Mound, with all their funds and their clout with the statehouse, couldn't get this fixed . . .

The Mound was the only off-world casino founded outside Centrist control. After Frontera's success, the Centrists had found ways to underwrite Towers and Rapture without compromising their earthly values. If Frontera took a hit, they'd make sure to control the next one—and complete their monopoly on the colonial Firmament. Dylan knew what Teddy Roosevelt would say to that. He straightened his stance and gave a brave smile. "We'll get right on it."

"No trouble, Dylan; I knew you would."

Alone outside the Mound, he allowed himself a sigh. Uneasy lies the head that runs a college full of golden-haired children beloved of eight hundred terrestrial families, thirty-six thousand klicks from home. He strode briskly back down Buckeye Trail, stopping only to pick the occasional piece of gravel from his shoe.

Just before his next office appointment, Nora popped into his toybox. "The latest on the F-car investigation. Thought you ought to know."

"Yes?"

"We interviewed every bro in both clubs, and then some. A key witness swears the Bulls' pledge class compacted the car, then engineered a forklift to get it onto the roof. But the forensic evidence shows DNA only from Ferrari pledges."

He nodded. "Sounds like last year."

"Regardless, a Ferrari parent just replaced the car. This year's model, guaranteed to win. As for last night, EMS got five kids detoxed, including one fallen from the cloud ladder, plus they covered an infant in Mount Gilead. A typical Wednesday night," she added with emphasis.

"The infant is okay? I'll have Nick schedule me a visit." The colonists were still upset at how their mayor had died last year with just a medibot on hand, because all the EMS volunteers were tied up at the college. Of course, it would help if the village could shake loose some funding for the Barnside; their state and federal reps were useless.

"The Ramos Kennedy girl is a godsend," Nora added. "Meanwhile, the latest trend this year: flooding residence halls."

"Flooding?" Every new year seemed to sport some particular class of prank. Vandalizing faculty offices, pulling fire alarms, or setting fires; the last made him shudder, thank God that was out of vogue. Whatever it was, there'd be a spate of them, mysteriously ending after that year, while the next year ushered in some new form of mayhem.

"They pull one of the valves and shoot it down the hall. Two cases last night, in Scioto and Huron." The first-year scholarship dorms—usually done by drunk seniors. "No perps yet. And by the way, Alan's on the warpath." Nora winked. "Just thought you ought to know."

Dylan sank into his chair. Meanwhile, into the president's office marched the student leaders of three social clubs: Fritz Hoffman, with his healthy shock of hair and endearing wide-eyed look; Viv Hatley, the well-connected future toytrader; and the suit, Rob LaSalle. It was hard to imagine their three rival clubs agreeing on something, except for a common foe.

"As you know, President Chase," Rob explained, "the college's foremost athletic team discriminates against our social groups. It's a perennial problem, but it's come to a head this year. Our right to freedom of association has been infringed."

Dylan nodded understandingly. "Infringement of rights" of course meant a veiled threat of action that could dip into the college's legal defense fund. "I understand your feelings, Rob. Of course, the constitutional right to associate is a First Amendment matter, pertaining to freedom of speech. I trust no one has interfered with you expressing your views?"

Viv leaned forward. "It's a question of standards, President Chase. As social groups with collegiate standing, we need to uphold our own standards of membership."

"Intimate association," insisted Rob. "The courts have held that fraternal organizations are intimate, familial groups. With the right to choose brothers that meet our standards." In fact, the courts had ruled so many different ways over the past century, the only certainty was it would cost the college one way or another.

"The slanball team has its standards too," Dylan pointed out. "A team needs to be competitive."

Fritz said, "We're just Division Three-A. Our competing schools don't all have these extreme athletic requirements. We put academics first."

This turn of logic perplexed Dylan, and he could see Rob shift in his seat.

"Safety is our rule," Rob pointed out. "The Amethyst Rule: Can recruits drink responsibly? Drink is part of social life."

"Like Wednesday night?" asked Dylan. "Was that 'amethyst'?"

"We have to test the recruits, see what they can handle. We don't want to admit men who can't drink safely."

"Do you exclude nondrinkers?"

"Of course not," said Rob quickly. "Not if they really want to join."

Dylan turned to Fritz. He had a real affection for the Red Bulls, who most resembled the greeks of his own pre-nondrinking days. The first group that had fully accepted him, made him feel like an insider. There was nothing like a group of extremely nice guys with their inhibitions loosened by a few beers. "Anything to add?"

Fritz wrinkled his brow. "I just feel really bad about this one frog, who had to withdraw his bid in order to stay on the team." Charlie Itoh, the Chase scholar.

"He chose to, you mean." Making choices—all the students had trouble with that.

Viv added, "One of our pledges was cut from the team. It's not right."

"Recruits," corrected Rob. Pledging was not till the next week of class, though unofficially the clubs had recruited all summer. "It's discrimination," Rob added. "Discriminating against our group. Our . . . friends will hear about this."

"Friends?" Dylan's eyes narrowed. "You mean affiliates."

"Oh, no," said Viv. "Of course not—we can't have affiliates."

The two *chicos* murmured their agreement. Of course, all three clubs had a greek affiliation under the radar. Greeks with big-gun lawyers.

Dylan sighed. "I am very sorry about this, believe me, and I will certainly have a chat with Coach Porat." A chat he did not look forward to. "To see whether some accommodation might be made. We need to tread lightly, though. Raising such issues is likely to spur our faculty's investigation of the . . . matter of affiliates."

The three all looked suitably alarmed. The faculty were the only ones who might press a principled objection regardless of financial cost. At present, though, the faculty committee on student affairs was moribund; no need to breathe life into it. A good part of the president's job, he reflected, consisted of convincing all parties to desist from actions they'd later regret.

"Your health, Dylan." Alan Porat crossed his legs on the chair, his *kippah* neatly capping his crew cut, a steely grin hiding any hint of displeasure.

"How are you, Alan?" Dylan began. "How's the team?"

Alan shrugged. "How should we be?"

Dylan glanced nervously around the room, hoping for no snakes nor any other unexpected creatures associated with the Porat-Abaynesh family. "Winning, of course. I'm sure you'll have a winning season. Especially with your new recruits, like the Ramos Kennedy daughter."

"Whose time is lost detoxing wasted bros."

Dylan nodded. "You know how badly EMS needs volunteers."

"At this rate I'll have no team left."

"There are the Tsien twins. My understanding is that Rickie and Reesie really want to play."

"The evidence suggests otherwise. Apparently they want to play like a fish wants to fly out of water."

"Alan, that's hardly fair. They both had award-winning records in high school. You recruited them yourself."

"And I explained the rules up front."

"Can't we meet halfway on this?" Dylan offered. "Surely some modest level of imbibing won't hurt, well after any games?"

The coach's eyebrows rose. "I'm training students to shoot around in a cage a thousand meters above ground, and you speak of modest intoxication?" He placed his fingertips together. "Perhaps we should give players the weekend off, and move all our games to Wednesdays."

"What?" Dylan blinked rapidly. "No, of course not; that would never do."

"Wednesday afternoon. Other schools schedule no classes then."

The Frontera faculty would toss out their mortarboards. "Alan, we know that's a nonstarter."

The coach shrugged. "So be it. On my team, there will be as little ethanol in the blood as mosquitoes in the hab."

"Come now," muttered Dylan. "Our own digestion generates a third of a drink's worth daily."

"A third of a drink probably wouldn't show up."

"A third of a drink? Would that be allowed?" A hint of a compromise.

"I'll stick with what I said." Alan rose from his seat. "Now if you'll excuse me, I'm really busy. As you know, Rosh Hashanah came early this year."

"Of course. *Shanah tovah.*"

As he turned to go, Alan stopped, remembering something. "Dylan, I want you to know how impressed I am about Flood Awareness Day. The students are planning it, but I know they had your blessing."

"Thanks, Alan. . . ." Flood Awareness Day? Dylan had not heard of any such thing. The last thing he wanted to hear at Frontera.

Then he recalled that he hadn't yet gotten to Clare's weekly report on student events. He blinked it now. What he read sounded even worse than he feared. He had to find Clare, and clear up this "Flood Day" business. He blinked the window that always connected them. **"Clare?"**

"In the toyroom, sweet." Clare was in their home toyroom, playing golf with Dylan's parents. The fairway stretched to the horizon with putrid-green grass, beneath an absurdly warm sun. Clare stood on the putting green with Dylan's father, the close-shaved black patrician, both of them in impeccable white polos. Clare would look good in anything, but the towel around his neck was just the limit.

"Good putt," Dylan's father was telling Clare, as Dylan entered the toy-room. "You just made par. If only you'd practice more."

"You're right, Dad," Clare was saying contritely. "I'll practice more." Clare hated golf.

"How did you like that latest Persian I sent you?"

"Outstanding aesthetic." The rugs were collecting in their attic. "Such a fine knot count, and the design is clear and crisp."

"Thanks, Clare. You're the artist; I value your opinion."

Dylan's mother took a glass of sherry from a tray held by a DIRG in a white tuxedo. "I'll look into that village in Guatemala," she told Clare. "The one you said needs a new church."

"Thanks, Mom. It's so good of you, founding churches."

"But Clare, you look overworked. You need to take better care of your-self." She sipped the sherry. "I'll send my beautician out on the next lift. He's an excellent masseur—"

"No," objected Dylan. "No masseur." He bit his tongue. Why did he al-ways have to come in on the wrong note.

His mother turned. "Why hello, Dylan. I hope you're not neglecting Clare."

"Of course not," said Clare quickly. "Sorry, Dad, something's up at the college."

Dylan headed out from his office, grabbing an apple from his desk for a last spurt of late-afternoon energy. He met Clare on Buckeye Trail. They strolled south, the filtered afternoon light gilding the trees. A lizard skittered up a trunk, and a hummingbird dive-bombed a rival. "I won't have masseurs, Clare. You're just candy for them."

Clare put an arm around him and crunched reassuringly. "How sweet of you. 'Candy,' at my age."

"You're spoiling my parents again."

"I adore your parents."

"You needn't fawn on them so."

"They could have checked that box."

Dylan closed his eyes and sighed. That box on the gene form, before his conception; the one that would have assured a hetero offspring, instead of letting God's will unfold. "Of course, everyone else checked the box. In middle school, I realized I was a freak—the only one of my kind in all of Westchester. People thought I was a—an accidental birth."

"The natural way," said Clare. "Like we do in Appalachia." He added, "Do you wish they'd checked the box? As you and I did for Fritz?"

"What? No, of course not." Dylan blinked rapidly, avoiding the precipice.

"You'd never have looked at me twice."

Dylan stopped and turned to face Clare. "I detest biology," he exclaimed. "I don't believe in genetic determinism. I believe I was destined for you, no matter what my genes."

Clare smiled. "The beauty of faith."

They strolled on in silence. Dylan took the plunge. "Look, Clare—about this Flood Day."

"So you finally read my report."

"Flooding a student residence? Isn't there enough of that already?"

"We consulted Alan and Nora, and various student groups. The New Yorkers are thrilled."

"It's a distortion," Dylan insisted.

"Embarrassment, you mean."

It was indeed embarrassing, a Frontera design flaw corrected in later habs. "The chance of actual flood is so low."

"All it would take is a power outage."

"Even then, it would take a full day for the water to percolate up. Whereas a dead space truck could hit us any time. And Homeworld Security just cut back on us again, from ninety-nine percent coverage to ninety-six."

Clare absorbed this.

"That's a four-fold increase in annual risk," Dylan explained. "Within twenty years—"

"I can do the math." Stopping, Clare looked reflectively toward the student residences. "There's really not much students could do about a dead space truck."

There was one thing, Dylan thought morosely. One thing students could do but rarely did.

"I don't get it," Clare exclaimed, as if to himself. "If the Centrists want us all to live in spacehabs someday, why do they leave us unprotected?"

"We're pagans, remember." The only hab outside Heavenly control.

"'Pagans,' thanks for reminding me." Clare shook his head. His eyes took on a faraway look. "If only the students would vote."

For most students, politics was a spectator sport. Actual voting wasn't *chulo*, never had been. And the Mount Gilead settlers made sure to keep it that way. Their one guy in Congress kept business regs down and schools teaching the sky was a bowl.

In Dylan's toybox, Gil's window opened. "Dillie, are you there? I'm on my way to Mare Crisium."

"I'll be there tomorrow, Gil—but keep quiet." Dylan had booked the Lunar Circuit and had practiced discreetly in his toyworld. Frog seminars— and maybe Gil could influence Homeworld Security. Feeling bad for Clare, he silently vowed this would positively be his last lunar drive.

23

By the time Jenny got home, she had barely time to change and grab a snack before Life lab. Letting down the team—would Coach cut her? She tried not to think about it.

After the Nobel experiments the previous week in the Cushite toyworld, this week was devoted to their research project: plant laughter. Jenny now had her experimental neural-network plants in her own greenhouse, so Anouk joined her there. "Will twenty replicates be enough?" Jenny asked.

"Too few," Anouk observed disapprovingly. "The reported variance is so high."

"Well, it's a start," said Jenny, trying not to yawn after her disastrous night. "Let's see how consistent they are." Nearby stood a black box printed out from the Research Methods. The box contained the test chamber for the plants.

Footsteps sounded behind. Startled, Jenny wheeled around. It was Mary, in her same old tie-dyed dress; she must print out the same one every morning. Jenny let out a breath. "Mary, what is it?"

"Are we socializing?"

"We're doing homework," Jenny sighed. "You can watch," she added, avoiding Anouk's eye. "Just don't touch anything." She opened a door to the box. "The 'humor' signal turns on in here. An inverted light spectrum—peaks in the red and blue, dips in the green, just the inverse of natural light. I guess a plant would think that's funny," she concluded dubiously.

Anouk tapped the box with her finger. "This humor concept is mechanical: an inverted spectrum. It contradicts an established norm, that of the solar spectrum. It invokes light, a substance crucial to the plant; yet it's harmless, no ultraviolet or X-rays here. It's straightforward enough to engage the thousand-neuron intellect. So yes, I suppose a plant might find that humorous."

One plant started to shake its leaves. Anouk frowned. "What was that for?"

"I don't know, they just laugh spontaneously now and then. Perhaps it thought of its own joke."

"Background noise. We'll have to subtract that."

Jenny opened the door to the box. The interior was completely dark, with no crevice admitting light. She placed one of the plants inside, then sealed it up. A window appeared in her toybox, an infrared signal revealing the plant inside. She blinked the switch. A pale violet light appeared. Within five seconds, the plant began to shake.

"So that one has a sense of humor," observed Anouk. "Five seconds to respond—not bad for a plant." She started to open the box.

"Wait," Jenny remembered. "Don't we have to try it again? If it's really humor, it won't be half so funny the second time."

"Adaptation," agreed Anouk. "We should repeat the stimulus until the response disappears below noise level."

"I'll print out some more test boxes." The twenty plants would take a while.

Suddenly all the plants were shaking.

"Hey, what's that?" Jenny watched in alarm. "If they all adapt, we'll have to wait another day."

"Our results won't be consistent. I wonder why they . . ." Anouk looked curiously at Mary, who had come over beside the plants. Was there something about Mary, something straightforward and obvious to the thousand-neuron intellect, that made the plants laugh? Mary leaned over the plants, as if trying to sniff.

"Mary, what are you doing?" asked Jenny.

"What is 'humor'?" Mary asked in her own voice.

Jenny exchanged a look with Anouk.

"Humor is distinctly terrestrial," Mary added. "Only Earth life-forms have humor."

Anouk looked at her curiously, with a hint of disdain. "How do you know that?"

"We ran an experiment."

"Experiment? On what?"

"On our plants."

Jenny's eyes widened. "Your aquarium plants? Did you get them through quarantine?"

"Indeed," said Anouk. "I'd like to see these humorless plants."

Mary hesitated. "Not enough replicates."

"That's all right," said Jenny. "We'd still like to see them." She'd been wondering about that aquarium ever since Mary arrived.

Mary's face shifted and contorted as if arguing with herself. She's more than Aspie, Jenny thought with sudden conviction. There's something else about her. "All right," Mary said at last. "But the vote was close."

Downstairs in the sitting room, the door opened to Mary's room. Jenny's heart sank, embarrassed for Anouk to see the state of Mary's room. Empty pretzel boxes were strewn everywhere, and there was a faint odor of marine decay. The window was closed, and the only light came from purple-tinted light banks above the large salt-encrusted aquarium. Within the aquarium undulated a snake-like form, a filament of large round cells with eyespots. The color of the creature could not be seen clearly, but Jenny well knew the general shape of an ultraphyte.

She gripped Anouk's arm. The ceiling seemed to turn over slowly; she realized she was holding her breath. Catching herself, she let out the air and breathed deeply.

Her mental popped up. "Jenny, dear," purred the Monroe. "We seem to be having—"

"Go away." Jenny squeezed her eyes shut to block out the scene of the tank. Turning around, she blinked in Anouk's code to evade the mental. Who should she call? Clive? Homeworld Security? To shut down the college? *Tonto,* they didn't shut down Somers for one ultra. But then, Somers was no spacehab. The EMS squad?

"**Call the professor,**" texted Anouk. "**She'll know what to do.**"

Jenny blinked for Abaynesh. "Professor? We found—that is, my *compañera* found something."

The professor took in the scene from Jenny's window. "I should say you have. Don't move; I'll be right there." She rose hastily from her desk. Then she stopped in mid-stride. "And this time, don't kill it already."

The creature was soon ensconced in a large invader-proof amyloid tank in the basement of Reagan Hall. A continual rush of air sounded from the ventilator, to draw off any cyanide. The professor skipped about, brainstreaming this or that connection, while the three students looked on apprehensively. "You're right," she concluded, "it's an ultraphyte. The thirteen cells, the eyespots."

Jenny said, "I've never seen one swim before."

"That's because you avoid water," Abaynesh replied with her usual tact. "Some swim, some don't. Some build towers in Great Salt Lake."

"How can that be?" Anouk wanted to know. "How can one species show so many different forms?"

"Ultraphyte is not a regular species. Even a single individual within several generations forms a quasispecies."

Anouk scanned her toybox to look that up.

"A quasispecies," explained Abaynesh, "starts with one genome, one RNA sequence. But RNA replication makes lots of mistakes—mutations. Much more than DNA would. So the offspring evolve quickly into many forms."

"Viruses do that," added Anouk. "RNA viruses, like hepatitis Q."

"That's right," said the professor, "on Earth, only RNA viruses make a quasispecies. The RNA virus mutates so fast that its variants infect different body parts in different ways. But all forms of the quasispecies keep key traits in common." Her eyes suddenly scanned back and forth, brainstreaming some complex operation.

Within the tank, the amyloid wall extruded a manipulator. The manipulator formed a hand, which reached for the ultra and grabbed it by one end. Caught in the hand, the ultra waved in a whiplike motion for several seconds. Then abruptly it broke off from the trapped cell. Once separate, the single cell squeezed itself out of the manipulator and swam away, zipping around the tank. The remaining body, however, stretched rigid as if stunned. The stunned form vibrated but made no headway.

Anouk recoiled. "*Zut,* just like the lizard."

"Not quite," warned the professor. "The lizard's tail twitches, then it's done. But the lost ultra cell grows and doubles."

They absorbed the implications. Jenny asked, "Can they escape?"

"Certainly not. My facility is licensed for ultra and other invasives. Yet the college still won't sign off on my grant," muttered the professor.

"Why is the larger one stunned?" Jenny had seen that before, in Somers.

Mary said, "The vote was tied."

The other two students stared at her.

"She's right." Abaynesh looked at Jenny. "How many cells did the ultra have before?"

"Thirteen." Jenny had counted them, as she always did. "And now, twelve."

"They're not simple cells, of course; more like 'citizens' of a colony. A colonial organism, in which each individual casts a 'vote.' The whole group takes a vote, a hundred times a second. So, an even number of 'cells' is bound to reach a tie vote soon. Then they're paralyzed."

"¡Oye!" Jenny half smiled. "A good thing they can't filibuster."

The stunned body began to recover. Its form relaxed and began to undulate again.

"What happened?" Jenny asked. "How did it recover?"

"Count the cells."

Jenny zoomed her toybox and began to count. "Thirteen again. The fourth from the end; it fissioned into two smaller cells."

"Precisely. One of its cells must double, to restore the odd number."

"It counts its cells!" Anouk clapped her hands. "What if it has nine cells? Could it split in three factions?"

"That might happen, but eventually they'd double enough cells to restore a prime."

"Of course, how sensible. These cells would fit right into my Series World."

Mary said, "They're getting hungry. They need to feed." No light bank.

"We'll see about that. First—" The professor grew stern, and stared at the three students. "The one non-terrestrial life form to make the Homeworld terror list, and it shows up in your residence? You're all in deep trouble."

Jenny and Anouk stared back, then at each other. The mention of trouble set their instinct for self-preservation against the ancient taboo of betraying a fellow student. "We did nothing wrong," blurted Jenny. "The ultra—like, it was just there."

Abaynesh rolled her eyes. "Woe is me. 'It was just there.' Like all the bros said about the compacted car atop the Ferrari clubhouse."

Anouk drew herself up. "As for me, I'm already banned from Earth; I can't afford more trouble." Turning to Mary, she said sweetly, "No one's hurt your pet, chérie. Tell the good professor where you got it."

Mary's eyes defocused.

"It's okay, Mary," Jenny assured her. "Tell the professor how it got through quarantine."

A purple light came on above the tank, feeding UV. "Does that help?" offered Abaynesh.

Mary said, "I grew them."

"You grew them? An experiment?" The professor shook her head.

"What is it with students today, they want to do research but not take the classes. The least you could do is take Life 101."

Jenny texted, **"She can't use Toynet."**

"Am I to believe our great new *angeleno* admissions director accepted a student who can't use Toynet?"

Anouk said, "She's an omniprosthete."

At the mention of "omniprosthete," something seemed to click for Mary. "Omniprosthete," Mary repeated. "That is what the doctors said. Omniprosthete—we can grow things inside. The doctors said people won't understand us."

The professor listened. She looked hard at Mary, then at the tank, then back to Mary. "You can't use Toynet, but you have exceptional talents to compensate." Abaynesh nodded to herself. "Very well, you may take the Life class with me, in person."

"*¡Oye!*" said Jenny. "That's great for you, Mary." She almost felt jealous.

"We study terrestrial life first," the professor emphasized. "Not the trendy outer space kind."

"Terrestrial life," repeated Mary. "Yes."

"Then sign the add-drop form right away. But how, without a toybox?" The professor went to the printer. Out came a writing stick, and a sheet of crinkly material. "You can sign here."

Mary stared quizzically at the Aristotelian sheet.

"If you can't write either, just mark with an X. Your *compañera* will sign as witness."

Jenny swallowed and flexed her hand. "Um, I don't know." She hadn't hand-written anything since kindergarten.

The professor shook her head. "And this one expects to reach Jupiter."

Anouk extended her hand. "I took calligraphy class, in my *lycée*." She held Mary's hand to form an X, then signed her own name with a flourish worthy of the Declaration.

"You're still in trouble," Abaynesh reminded them. "I have no choice but to turn you in. Your residence will be atomized—who knows if more are hiding?" She stared hard at Mary. "And you'll have to face Dean Kwon."

" 'What a good idea!' " said Mary in Dean Kwon's voice. " 'I hope you feel better soon.' "

24

The Lunar Circuit stretched out in Mare Crisium, a smooth crater basin six hundred klicks across. Just a sliver of sun rose east, but the track gleamed amid glowing billboards, casinos, and zooparks. Their primary colors pulsed against the airless dark of the "firmament," filled with the twinkling haze of sublunary rubble. The rubble nowadays claimed more lives than the track, like that poor French crew last August, rest in peace. A cone of light appeared as an incoming shuttle vaporized the debris ahead of its descent.

Out on the track, a car sailed up into the overhead loop. The circuit, actually a series of tracks and associated entertainment operations, financed the United Nations and the International Monetary Fund. Dylan had driven pro for two years, then later used to take Fritz out to joyride, until the boy got hooked on saving species. Dylan still owned one beloved car, an Anthradyne 500 two-seater, which he shared with very good friends of the college.

Within the terminal, Dylan took an anxious look at Gil, encased like himself in "sausage roll," their term for lunar suiting. Gil was dutifully running the two dozen checks on his suit, the sort of task he loved and was good at. Dylan's attention returned to his toybox.

In the box, Helen Tejedor faced him at her desk beneath the colonial ax. "About the special fellowship program, for faculty recruitment." The blond dean of faculty wore her usual "I've accomplished something" smile. "Faculty Development finally approved it."

"*¿Verdad?* With all the caveats about course load flexibility?"

In the corner, Nora Kwon's window blinked URGENT. Dylan hoped Nora's list was not too long, would not outlast Gil's patience. That aside, he was extremely interested to hear from Helen. Getting a committee of three faculty to agree on anything, even a pay raise, could take months. And something as complex and subtle as a recruitment fellowship—a momentous event.

"*Finalmente.*" Helen's smile lengthened. "It's understood that certain courses will have to rotate." Faculty desperately desired new colleagues they could count on out here. It was one thing to entice a new Ph.D. here for a year's stint to tack on to their resume; quite another to get one to settle for years in the hab. "It's also agreed that we drop the idea of alternating semesters."

"You're quite sure that's agreed?" A pet idea of the humanities faculty, to double-up on courses one semester, the next semester back to Earth. No good for student access.

"Semerena and Hamilton quashed it."

The pile worm biologist, and the Centrist. An unholy alliance had saved the day, thanks as usual to Helen's maneuvering. Dylan sighed with relief. "Helen, I can always count on you."

"And the Antarctic Studies program." West Antarctic agriculture, Earth's southernmost *fondillo* offered their final breadbasket before the seas boiled off. And thus, fought over by forces from six continents. "Enough departments have put in courses to do it."

"Excellent." A new major program to advertise, without costing an extra cent.

"There's just one more thing . . ."

In the corner Nora's window blinked faster. Meanwhile, across the room, Gil had finished his last suit test. He stood and stretched, flexing his limbs of sausage roll.

Helen cleared her throat. "It has been alleged that the student social clubs have secret affiliation with terrestrial extracollegiate organizations. A specific violation of our charter. The faculty committee on student life is obliged to investigate." Helen's face took on the look of a pedestrian coming upon a decomposing skunk.

Alan must have hit the warpath after all. Dylan's heart sank. "Surely the matter will take time to sort out. To hear all sides fairly."

"Time, which our hardworking faculty can ill afford."

"The alumni, of course, have their opinions." Some returned every year for the Frontera Circuit.

"The alumni are your job. We expect you to keep this sort of roadkill off our plate."

"*Claro,*" he hastily replied.

"Thanks, Dylan. We know we can count on you." Helen's window closed. Nora blinked in. "We've had a fire."

"A fire? As in, combustion?"

"Carbon combustion," she confirmed. "Cigarette on a carpet in Huron."

Smoking was not just forbidden; all forms of carbon combustion were out, anywhere in the hab, with the exception of the sealed lower level of the Mound. "You know the rule."

"Expulsion," she agreed. "If you confirm."

"Expulsion." A lifetime opportunity lost, all for a cig ground underfoot. *"¿Qué más?"*

"We've got ultra."

"What!"

"Dillie, look what I can do." By the window to the stark, unchanging moonscape, Gil had turned on his side doing one-finger pushups.

"Just one, in a custom residence. Not a dorm," Nora assured him. *"Gracias a Dios."*

"A—an *ultraphyte?*" Dylan sputtered. "Where there's one, there's a hundred."

"We melted the residence, but found no others." Her voice deepened. "The Dyer girl got it past quarantine."

The one with the pearls. The omniprosthete from the White House doctors. The suitemate of Soli's daughter. *Qué lío.* "Past quarantine? How on earth?"

"We're grilling her."

"First mosquitoes, now ultra?"

Nora shrugged. "Invasives are this year's thing."

"But a terror agent—this means a report to Homeworld Security."

"A private report," she assured him. "An isolated incident. Sharon signed off on it."

He sighed with relief. Then his eyes flew open. "Sharon?" he asked suspiciously. "What's Sharon got to do with it?"

"She's got clearance for ultra. She certified the residence site clean . . ."

"I see."

". . . and took custody of the specimen."

"No way. Vaporize it." Custody indeed.

"Will do," agreed Nora. "One more thing. We've had Ebola, printed out with illegal toyworld downloads."

"Are the kids okay?" Ebola virus could turn the body into blood pudding. "Anyone critical?"

"Three cases, all recovering, thanks to quick EMS work. Nick diagnosed the first one." Where would they be without student volunteers. Maybe when Hamilton became mayor, he'd get the village to fund a backup for Eppie.

Gil was now playing moonpong, bouncing himself from floor to ceiling. Not as safe as it felt—one lost weight, but not momentum. "Nora, hold the rest; I'll catch you later."

+ +

The Anthradyne 500 enclosed them in eerie stillness, its gigantic wheels splayed like giraffe legs, its nose curved like an anteater's snout. Overhead, the brilliant green Solarplate banner spread above the starting grid. Charge, breaks, sensors, all checked out in Dylan's expanded toybox. He heard Gil breathing in the seat behind him, brainstreamed helpfully to his helmet. Getting himself and Gil through this alive, that was the thing. He frowned. Stop thinking like Clare, he told himself. The key thing was to give Gil the time of his life. What else was the point of living? He grinned. "Sure you're up to this, Gil? Thousand klicks an hour?"

"I can't wait. Your seniors would love it; I'll sponsor their trip."

To head off that notion, Dylan hurriedly blinked some buttons in his expanded toybox. The seat grabbed his rear, accelerating smoothly as the car glided out. All control was brainstream, indistinguishable from the simulator. His head and limbs were strapped in completely, with the finest tolerance to withstand whatever g force.

The track was empty, for Dylan had rented twenty minutes. The horizon looked eerily close, like the edge of a cliff that kept receding. At left they passed the Icarus flight hall, a tourist landmark. At right, for the carnally challenged, rose the 666, the Equus, Macdonald's Farm, Dolphin Dayz, and the ultimate Z. Only on the moon were zooparks legal. The greatest off-world playground. Nobody, he hoped, in this round-the-clock entertainment zone would take notice of a couple of guys streaking past in a modest Anthradyne 500.

The long straight led out toward the razor-sharp horizon. Dylan let her briefly reach a thousand, as promised. "You okay there, Gil?" Of course he saw all Gil's vitals from pulse to pupil size displayed there in the box next to his own.

"Just fine, Dillie. Whee—wait till my toymakers all see us!"

That was not the plan; "no cameras," Gil had promised. Dylan sighed as he took the speed down and eased into the first turn. The turn banked nearly vertical, the track rearing right while the universe opened out to their left. Over his left shoulder hung the blue earth, its black solar blotches obscured by lunar haze, and somewhere in between hung Frontera, where a college hummed busily and Clare waited in his church—

Gil shrieked. "Dillie, we're falling off! Off into space!"

"*Verdad.*" Dylan grinned. "Just hope Hamilton's right, there's a Firmament to catch us." Easing out of the turn, he warned, "Next comes the chicane." One devilish turn after another.

"Oh, the loop, Dillie. You can't miss the loop."

The loop loomed ahead, its bright curve cut aslant by a harsh lunar shadow. Drive up and let the whole universe revolve around you.

"Sorry, the loop's out for maintenance." Even with full protection Dylan was not about to drive the Toynet CEO at five g's. "But you'll love the chicane. It's worse than Monaco." Dylan knew the turns well, and he could make them feel more dangerous than they were.

The track turned left. Dylan jumped the curve, the red border line sailing below. Even so, the maneuver yanked the car hard, a sharp contrast to the moon's lack of g's. The car tipped slightly, despite its splayed wheels. Before it fully recovered, the track switched right. Glowing towers veered across one way, then the other, a dizzying pull each way. From behind, Gil laughed. This part was the most fun.

At last done with turns, they headed into the final long straight. The car accelerated gently, the towers streaking past ever faster until they mingled like so much confetti. The nearest thing to flying; even space flight paled by comparison, once you got past liftoff.

In his box a light was blinking. The track light. Dylan tensed. The light was not there before, or had he missed it? Debris on the track, the latest harvest from space. A large flat chunk, too late to swerve around.

The car bumped up, like rolling up a ramp. The angle was slight, but enough to turn the car into a spinning projectile. Over and over the car turned, the lights of casinos and zooparks winking past, again and again. The entire egocentric universe revolved, over and over, around Dylan's flying car.

Counting the turns, Dylan estimated landfall. He blinked the emergency jets, just a tap. The revolutions slowed, until the car at last came level. Several interminable seconds followed, Dylan counting every one. At last the car thudded back to ground. Dylan braked hard, until the tires glowed red. The car steadily slowed, at last stopping just past the finish line. His head still swam while his inner ears adjusted. Outside, all was still. The track walls, the zooparks, the Icarus, all completely still, like the day the first man landed.

For a moment, there was no sound from Gil. Then the Toynet CEO let out a breath, and a high-pitched laugh. "That was too good! I wet myself, but still, it was worth it. When can we go again?"

Outside, people were gathering, their arms waving, sausage-rolled tourists and security guards. The toybox lit up with messages, autograph inquiries, and ToyNews slow-mo playbacks of the last-minute near-disaster, the car rising up and turning over and over again before its agonizing return.

25

Thursday night, as the northern rainbow faded, Jenny had stood outside with Anouk and Tom watching her cottage dissolve. The cottage was surrounded by maintenance workers and coonskin-capped DIRGs. The DIRGs brain-streamed sniffers to crawl up the walls inspecting the doomed amyloid. Outside collected a wider ring of curious students and faculty children, including Tova with her twin towers. Searchlights flickered off their diads. No one else knew exactly what had happened; Jenny's toybox spouted rumors of a drug bust. Her orchids were back with Abaynesh at Reagan Hall. Mary hadn't been seen since the professor turned her in at Wickett Hall. What had become of the omniprosthete, and her smuggled ultraphytes?

The evening sun lit up the clay of the Spanish roof tiles. But now, the ruddy hues began to ebb from the tiles, fading to gray. The curve of the tiles puckered, and the roof peak sagged like modeling clay. The cottage walls buckled outward, and a window cracked open. The window pane drooped over like a tongue. With a thud, the upper story of the greenhouse pancaked down.

Jenny's scalp crawled. She squeezed Tom's hand.

Anouk brushed her arm. "It's all right, *chérie*. You saved your plants, and you'll download the rest again."

Tom asked, "Will you be okay tonight?" Tom was the only one she'd told about the ultra.

"You'll stay with me," Anouk assured her. "Let's be off, and get to our homework."

Travis Tharp poked with a hook at the amyloid subsiding into the ground. Then the ground cratered in, as DIRGs sucked out the sediment. Dust to dust. Only the green tubes of the makeshift pump remained at the substratum leak, where the side wall had stood.

"Sure you'll be okay?" Tom's hand was firm and warm.

In the news window Clive appeared, patting his immaculate dark locks. Hairstyle number nineteen. "Jenny, what's the story?"

"*Nada.*"

"We know there's a story, but we can't locate your mother." Her mother had to okay all her interviews. But her parents were still out of reach at Lake Taupo, thank goodness. Her mother took vacation seriously, especially when she was worried about Dad.

"Mama won't allow it."

Clive hesitated, patting his hair as if slightly nervous. "We can't sit on this. We'd rather not report rumors."

After Clive left her box, Jenny took a breath. "Anouk's right. Let's get our work done." A hundred pages of Cuban ancient history, and for Hamilton, write an essay on political friendship. All to get done by eleven, time for enough sleep not to trip Coach's sleep meter. If he'd even let her back in the cage.

Within Anouk's icosahedral cottage, the sitting room pulsed and evolved. Jenny sank into a chair of black puffed pillows, only to feel it gradually expand around her, sprouting dark bubbles. The bubbles formed a Mandelbrot fractal, in which each sprouting bubble grew into a self-similar chair; nearly the same, but not quite. After about ten minutes Jenny's fractal chair began to dissolve away, as its bubbles filled out into other chairs. Hurriedly she stood up.

Anouk had returned from her sunset prayers with Zari Valadkhani and Doc Uddin. Unperturbed by her dissolving seat, Anouk simply shifted to a newly sprouted chair while pursuing advanced calculations in her toybox. "It's unhealthy to sit in one place too long," remarked the *parisienne*. "One loses blood flow to the lower back. One must keep physically active."

Jenny repressed the urge to observe that ballet turn-out ruined the knees. At last she sat on the floor, where a small woven rug held the only stable spot. The rug had a Persian pattern, red and gold, with angular figures of birds and goats, even a lion.

"A *sumak*," Anouk told her. "Wool and silk, with authentic natural dyes."

"The animals are cute."

"It's about Noah's Ark."

"Really?"

"The Qur'an tells the true Noah's Ark," Anouk emphasized. "The Ark came to rest on Mount Judi. And the olive branch was brought by a pigeon."

"I see."

"The chaplain gave me the sumak," Anouk added. "For a Christian, Father Clare is a remarkably learned man." She frowned. "He said the Qur'an forbids information theft."

Jenny nodded, not daring to comment.

"I don't steal information," insisted Anouk. "I just borrow it."

Jenny swallowed. "Anouk—what happened to Mary?"

"The professor arranged something." Jenny didn't ask how she knew. "Professor Abaynesh put her somewhere in the basement lab."

"A room in the laboratory? That is odd."

"They're two of a kind, if you ask me."

"No they're not." Mary was an Aspie omniprosthete who smuggled ultraphytes. A puzzle in the mirror.

Her EMS window blinked; another Ebola case in Huron, Tom's dorm. Fortunately Nick covered it. She hoped Tom was okay.

"And now we've got an ultra." Anouk got up and moved to a new chair. "Perhaps we could do our project on it. Wouldn't that be fun?"

"Maybe." That's what Jenny had wanted before, to experiment with ultra. But now she wondered. "Tom says ultraphyte genes have gotten into pile worms—and maybe other Earth creatures."

"So?" Anouk shrugged. "Our own chromosomes are full of alien DNA."

"Earth viruses, over billions of years. Ultraphytes have only been here for twenty years. What if their DNA infects us?"

"RNA," Anouk corrected. "They would have to copy it into DNA for our genes."

"They change their own RNA superfast. They form a quasispecies."

"That explains how Mary's ultra got past quarantine. They mutated to a form the DIRGs could not detect."

"Like a virus," agreed Jenny. Hepatitis Q virus changed its genes so often that most of the viruses in a patient were as different as different species. No detector could be made to find them all.

"But most of the virus particles end up defective, n'est ce pas? So how could that be for ultra?"

"Ultraphytes are modular," Jenny explained. "Different modules can take different forms. And they can discard defective modules."

"That goes way beyond viruses. A virus is still a virus, no matter how far it mutates." Anouk stepped out of her chair just as a long dark squiggle crossed the room and bubbled out three new ones. "I think Abaynesh should let us do our project on ultra. Goodness knows we've spent enough time in that dumb toyworld."

+⊦

Friday morning Jenny awoke, her head still spinning fractals, to find her toy-box clogged with inquiries on the "Ramos Kennedy drug bust." Spectacular footage of her cottage collapsing, a dozen different views. Her box overflowed with windows, local reporters who ordinarily would never bother her. Anouk helped her clean them out; but in the process she lost most of her playmates and newsfeeds. Too late to fix it, she slapped her diad on her forehead and rushed to get to practice on time.

Coach did not say a word to Jenny, nor did anyone else comment on her disastrous week. Everyone focused on their upcoming game with Melbourne's Scorpions, their first of the season. After practice, Jenny waited till the others had left. She pulled off her slancap, her hair floating up around her face. Her pulse raced. She hated disappointing the coach.

Coach Porat hung upward from the side door. "So you've had better weeks."

"There was no one else to take the call—" No point in excuses. "It won't happen again."

"Until next Wednesday."

She looked away. A thousand meters below gleamed the river, and tiny skybikers circled like condors. Then she looked back and held his gaze.

The coach reflected, "To save a life comes first."

"That's right."

"So I should save yours."

Jenny swallowed. "I got enough sleep."

"It's only the second week of class." The coach shook his head. "With your sense of duty, you'll be running the squad by fall break. With no pay," he added pointedly. "Students should not be put in such a position. The Mound should hire staff."

"I'm not paid to play either." Her heart pounded; she hadn't meant to say that.

"You're not—and don't get ideas. They always do," he muttered as if to himself. "The ones with brainstream like yours. Don't go pro," he warned. "I've seen them after five seasons, their brains turned to soup. The rest of their lives in the blue room."

"If we're not pro, then why act like we are?"

"You want a good team?"

"Of course."

"A winning season?"

"In our league."

He nodded slightly. "See you next morning."

In Political Ideas, Jenny tried to stay awake. Hamilton paced by the podium. "So, Aristotle compares rule by the many, the one, and the few."

To her surprise, Mary had made it to class. The enigmatic *compañera* sat there as usual, without pretzels, but her water bottle had a white crust of salt around the rim. Mary's hands moved continually, as if independent from her body though connected, like the two heads of the snake. Like another omni-prosthete Jenny knew . . .

The Creep. The perennial Centrist vice president had hands like Mary's that crept along the table with a life of their own. ToyNews always brushed it over, but Jenny had seen the *hombre* in person, at Great-Grandma Rosa's funeral at Arlington. The hands looked creepy, hence his nickname. The Creep, too, was obsessed with ultra.

"Which form of rule does Aristotle favor?"

Enrico raised his hand. "Democracy is better than kingship, because the crowd of people is less corruptible than the one."

Hamilton raised a finger. "An intriguing point, Enrico. As you've discovered, Aristotle argues that the greater number of people share greater wisdom than the one. And in a true city, the greater number of people 'become like a single human being with many hands and feet.'" Hamilton looked around. "Any other arguments?"

Priscilla waved her hand. Hamilton ignored it, but she spoke up anyway. "How could a democracy work if the slaves are never counted among the number of people? Aristotle never saw a real democracy."

Without looking at her, Hamilton nodded indulgently. "Of course, today we think our own democracy is the only 'real' democracy that excludes no one, no 'hidden persons' in our midst. Other arguments?"

Ricky raised his hand. Ricky was now a "suit," one of the *chicos* that followed the professor in a clique strolling down Buckeye Trail. "Isn't the point of democracy majority rule?"

"Ricky, I believe you've got to the heart of the matter. In a democracy, the larger number overrules the smaller. And why must this be so?"

Jenny was starting to nod off, when Mary's voice jarred her awake. "The large number out-votes the smaller. If the two groups are equal, the body is paralyzed."

"What an interesting point, Mary. The body politic is paralyzed. Is that a major problem for democracy?"

"Until one person divides in half."

Jenny froze. Enrico blinked, and other students shared startled looks. But Hamilton merely shrugged. "That would work for a sponge-person, I suppose." Hamilton was never bothered by the craziest remark, Jenny realized, since no one else would take it seriously. "But doesn't this solution raise another problem? A majority of one?"

Enrico said, "Doesn't a majority of one mean that now one person has all the power?"

"Precisely, Enrico. A majority of one is a kind of tyranny. That's one reason Aristotle considered democracy as potentially bad as tyranny."

+-+

After class, Jenny stopped by Hamilton's office to continue their speech sessions. The Whitcomb School of Baraminology diploma hung behind him. On his desk the Z token was gone, but there stood a recent autographed photo of Aunt Meg and El. What did that mean, Jenny wondered, reflecting on her Machiavellian aunts. Was Hamilton reporting to them?

Jenny had brought a speech for practice, an old one she'd once written for Jordi on economically-challenged housing in Westchester. The housing event had been postponed and somehow the speech never got delivered. She spoke more readily now, having mentally shifted the professor into her "well known" category. As she spoke, her different brain regions lit up in Hamilton's instrument, in much greater detail than she had seen before. The instrument sent subtle feedback to her brainstream, encouraging new behavior patterns. She realized it had been five years or more since her therapists had tried something new. They had sought to avoid discouragement. Or perhaps they just found it more rewarding to keep pushing Jordi as far as he could go.

"Outstanding argument, Jenny," Hamilton assured her. "We all wish to see our citizens in housing they can afford. I'm sure your aunts would agree."

"Yes, they would." Probably they'd agree more than most of her Somers

neighbors. Housing—Rosa had gunned through Congress sweeping legisla-
tion on housing reform. After that she'd lost the Somers vote.

"Is this the speech you're delivering at the convention?"

"No, of course that will be . . . different." The "Mutant speech." She had
read the inane script the handlers gave her, for Monday at four in the afternoon with the "family and friends." Anna was keen to plant her roots in the
Ramos Kennedy clan. But there was no way Jenny could do it except to read
woodenly into the prompt.

She focused on the professor. "If Aristotle thinks democracy is tyranny,
then what sort of state does he want?"

"I think you know by now, Jenny. The same thing we all want: A polity
governed by the able few. The few with college degrees," he emphasized.

"But everyone votes."

"Based on what we tell them."

Jenny knew better now than to rise to the bait. "They'll throw us out if
we forget the price of socks." Milk, eggs, a subway ticket; she maintained the
list, updated monthly. Her gaze caught the Whitcomb degree on the wall.
"What is 'baraminology'?"

His eyes lit up. "Baramins are the created kinds of life. I so miss discussing life science. Frontera's busy researchers have little use for me, I'm afraid."
His plaintive tone made it hard not to sympathize.

"What are 'created kinds'?"

"The kinds of life made at Creation, and saved from the Flood. A topic
that interests you; as a candidate for mayor, I heartily approve your public
demonstration."

The flood, the next day, Saturday—she had to find Ken this afternoon.
Had he lined up the band, and got the moat under control? The last thing they
needed was a genuine disaster. "So," she asked, "would 'birds' be a baramin?"

"Birds are created kinds. All the birds together form a baramin. Except
for penguins, according to Marsh and Wise. Penguins were a separate created
kind. But they all migrated straight to the Ark, just in time. No wonder so
many animals migrate today. Did you ever wonder why birds migrate thousands of miles—to find exactly the same tree? How did that ability 'evolve,'
can you tell me?"

"And dinosaurs, are they part of the bird baramin?"

"Dinosaurs constitute a cryptobaramin. A cryptobaramin is a baramin
that is hidden from common view; that is, unseen since the Flood by all but a
very few people. But what's really exciting is what became of the baramins

right after they left the Ark. Of course, each original baramin had to diversify within a few hundred years, to make all the varieties of life we know today. Can you imagine living in the time of Abraham, and seeing all the new species appear around you? A hundred per week, according to Wise."

It didn't sound like any Bible she'd read. She toysearched "baramin." The word was there in Genesis, in an unfamiliar translation. "So . . . you went from baraminology to politics?"

"Like Aristotle," he agreed. "From sponge to man, the political animal. Jenny, who do you think will be the Unity running mate?"

The abrupt turn took her by surprise. "I've no idea. Only Anna knows."

Hamilton nodded as if he had little doubt. Jenny had little doubt either, and was less than thrilled about it. "What about Centrists? Will Gar pick the Creep again?"

He leaned forward confidentially. "Someone new," he assured her as if imparting a privileged secret. "A very serious candidate; someone you'll be pleased to hear. Some of your family will be at our convention," he reminded her.

✦╍

At lunch, the dining hall announced salt restriction. Everything tasted the same. To her relief, most of the windows had reappeared in her toybox, even Levi-Montalcini's tumor mouse. In a far corner of her box, a window blinked; Anna Carrillo. Rising from the table, Jenny stumbled over the long bench and got away to the side of the room.

"Jenny." Governor Anna Carrillo filled her toybox. "I want you to know, Jenny, how much Glynnis and I appreciate all your family's support."

Jenny swallowed and blinked for a neutral background behind her. She tried to ignore the food fight going on nearby, about all the desalted food was worth. "You're welcome," she told the governor. "Glynnis did a good job." The first lady debate seemed years ago.

"And thanks so much for planning a speech for me. It means so much to me, that you're presenting your first speech in public for my nomination."

"De nada." First and last, Jenny figured.

"And you'll be one of the first to know when I announce my selection for running mate. I know you'll be pleased."

Jenny made herself smile.

"You can be sure I'll pick someone to lead the fight for conservation.

Someone who can hold his own against any debater, even the current vice president."

Jenny swallowed. "Gar won't pick the Creep," she blurted. "He'll pick a serious new candidate."

Anna's face froze at this unexpected departure from script.

"And another thing; about ultra—the kind that crawled out of Great Salt Lake." The quasispecies. "We've learned some things—"

"Thanks, I'll have staff follow up. And thanks again, so much." A thousand more calls to make.

The governor's window had barely closed, when another opened: her mother. "Jenny? Goodness, *hijita*, what's got into you?" Even at Lake Taupo, she'd heard. She wore her investment power suit, a sign of her outrage. "Drugs—the second week of school?"

"Not me. It was that *compañera* you made me take."

"The one from the lost island? She did look fishy." Her mother considered this. "Your whole residence wiped out by Homeworld Security—we saw it all. Imagine how your father feels. And right before the convention."

"That speech—I told you, I said *no*."

"We all have to help. The polls are so close." Soledad peered at her closely. "You're absolutely certain you had nothing to do with that drug bust?"

"Nada." Jenny looked away.

Soledad shook her head. "If you can't tell me what's going on, *hijita*, you must tell Marilyn."

"No. Absolutely not." Jenny's heart pounded just thinking of her Monroe.

"Then you'll have to come home. How can I leave you there, already into drugs?"

"I told you, there's *nada* with drugs."

"Well, whatever it is, you have to tell someone."

Jenny thought it over. "I'll tell Father Clare."

"Bien. Clare will set you straight." Soledad paused in thought. "If nothing more comes out, the news cycle will get over it in twenty-four hours. But please—think of your studies. Think of Rosa. Think what you can do for the world."

In her toybox flashed the EMS snake: A colonial father of four had just collapsed in his home. For once Jenny felt relieved to respond, a situation where she knew just what to do.

✦

The man was splayed out in a chair, head back and mouth open, his wife holding his hand. A child poked an anxious face in, then ran out.

Regarding the stricken man, Jenny made the mental switch from stranger to patient. "Can you please raise both arms?"

No response.

"He complained his right arm was numb," said his wife, "just before he collapsed." Donna Matousek, her voice was strong and matter of fact, like Sherri-Lyn's. Her overalls were much washed, and her arms flexed power bands.

Jenny fixed her scanscope around the patient's upper arm. The medibot had the stretcher out, and lifted the man smoothly onto it, bracing his head, neck, and spine. Data poured through her windows, columns of proteins and cytokines. A dozen signs already added up to ischemia somewhere, probably the carotid. Age forty-five; he was young for a stroke.

"Send the nanos," texted the medibot.

She blinked to release the microscopic bots from the scanscope into the vein. Within minutes the cell-sized probes would find their way to the brain, map the arteries, and start dissolving the blockage. The brain map popped up, pulsing red with signs of arterial plaque filling the arteries. Sure enough, the carotid was blocked. As she watched, the nanoprobes broke through, restoring circulation. A textbook case. Somehow it was hard to believe when the most likely thing actually happened.

The man's color improved, and his hand moved.

"He'll be okay," Jenny said. "He still needs help; we need to check him out at the Barnside."

"Thank God," Donna breathed, squeezing his hand. "Gabe, can you hear me yet? We're here, Gabe, even if you can't talk." She turned to Jenny in amazement. "You're a real doctor."

Jenny half smiled. "Maybe someday."

"The Barnside needs more doctors." Her eyes narrowed. "Tell me the truth: Does the Barnside have what he needs to make him well?"

Jenny considered this. "Our team is good at emergencies." When they weren't overwhelmed, they could do as well as Somers. "We got here in time to prevent permanent damage. Beyond that, though, the Barnside's limited. I see extensive plaque in there, too much for these first-responder nanos to clear it all. I'd send him down to a good clinic."

Donna shook her head. "Still saving up for our first flight home. Besides, the lift isn't recommended for stroke victims, is it?"

"You're right, it's not," agreed Jenny, embarrassed.

"Stroke is common enough. Why can't Doc Uddin treat it here?"

Jenny shrugged. "Ask your mayor. Your new one, that is, once he's elected. He can apply for a full clinic; your town meets the specs." Rural Community Health—Rosa had pushed that through, her first year as president. The government would fund the docs; and the local casino would add a point to the house edge.

✦✦

She found Kendall at Castle Cockaigne, working on the drawbridge; the winch was stuck. A couple of bots like dwarves from Middle Earth stood by to help. The dwarves didn't seem much into maintenance, although they ran the daily operation. Inside the ring of the moat stood the crenellated outer walls with four drum towers. Within the outer walls rose the keep; three floors, plus a high lookout where you could walk. Jenny wondered what it was like up there. She wondered how much of a fortune the Kearns-Clarks spent to run all this stuff.

"Is the moat working?" she asked Ken. The water was normally about six feet, but it looked higher than usual, nearly running over the top of the moat's inner wall.

"Sure thing." Ken tossed his long Inuit hair back over his shoulder, so different than at zero g where the strands beneath the slancap flew out all around. "Just plug the outflow, and let it run over. I've raised the water level, so it'll just need a nudge to go over."

"How deep will it fill the castle?" Between the moat and the castle stretched a parterre garden of sculpted shrubs; it seemed a shame to drown it. She was starting to regret this plan.

His arm pointed. "No deeper than the height of the inner wall, *verdad*? Maybe three feet. Chill out; it can't go wrong."

"Don't you have lots of good stuff inside the castle?"

"The keep is mostly printout. But you're right, we have to go through the ground floor, picking up any nonprintout to haul upstairs. And of course what's below, the whole wine cellar. Haven't got to that yet; you can help me in the morning."

Saturday morning was Homefair, with Tom and Father Clare. She'd have to leave early. "What about the band?"

"The finest George Lewis tribute band— *¡Oye!* what a racehorse tempo.

You got the flyer out?" The flyer read, *Tour the Authentic Medieval Castle. Jazz Age Entertainment. Live Flood Demonstration.*

Jenny nodded. "All the student windows, and all the public ones. Even the First Firmament Church." Leora had posted that one.

"Before I forget," added Ken, "Yola leads a required optional practice tomorrow morning. We always do, before the Sunday game."

"Saturday morning? I didn't see it in her window—"

"Word of mouth. No coach allowed; it has to be 'optional,' college rules, but you gotta be there. Especially you," he emphasized, after her missed practice that week.

Jenny reached Father Clare's office just before supper. She picked a piece for the jigsaw collage, a bit of daisy with two knobs that more or less fit within a yellow section. Some parts buckled, but overall it was surprising how ingeniously the pieces from different puzzles had been made to fit.

"A good one, thanks," said the chaplain. "I was wondering how that mass might fill in." Behind him, the Virgin sat eternally with her fallen Son, her left hand outstretched. "I'm sorry you've had a rough week. Any way I can help? You have a good place to sleep?"

"Oh, that's all right," she said quickly. "They promised to reprint my cottage by tomorrow." At a new site, away from the substratum leak.

"So how do things look for tomorrow? Can we expect a good flood?"

Jenny shrugged. "The tour at least will draw people. The castle's a major landmark even from Mount Gilead." She bit her lip. "I'm sorry to miss Home-fair."

"I understand; of course, you need to set up your event."

"There's that, and there's slanball. And also . . ." The EMS took time, and all her homework was behind. And her Life grade was only an A. "I don't know what's wrong with me. I managed twice as much in high school."

"This isn't Somers High. This is college." Father Clare tapped his forehead. "A new level. New competition."

"You think I should quit slanball."

"Not at all. Slanball is, like dance, a form of art you create for the rest of us."

She hadn't thought of it quite that way. "Well, thanks. Look, I was never great with a hammer anyway. But I'll keep your window in my box, and if Homefair ever needs EMS, I'll be right there."

"Thanks, Jenny. You know, that's the biggest help we need." His head tilted. "Anything else? How's your family?"

"They're fine. They're in Lake Taupo, where nobody can reach them." She paused and swallowed. She had promised her mother to tell the chaplain, but tell him what? About Mary? Her gaze caught the hand of Michaelangelo's Mary before her, the marble fingers curled forever, suspended outstretched in empty space.

"What do you think?"

"The hand . . ." She paused. "It's hard to believe it was . . . carved out of solid rock. How could you do that with a hammer?"

Father Clare nodded. "That hand has a storied history. It was smashed twice, the first time by accident in the eighteenth century. Scholars still argue what the original actually looked like, before the repair."

"Really." Hard to imagine how something so important could be . . . unrecorded.

"The second time, a twentieth-century madman took a hammer to it. But by then the form was well documented."

Madmen were dangerous. Jenny swallowed. "No mentals here, right?"

"That's right."

"I'm worried about Mary Dyer. She had those ultraphytes—no one knows how she got them past the DIRGs. And besides—" Jenny gulped, not wanting to say it. "She tries to act like one."

"She acts like an ultraphyte?"

"She always talks like multiple people, and she says a person can divide in two, like an ultraphyte cell. She even drinks saltwater. It's not healthy."

The chaplain's eyes scanned back and forth, reading his box. "Actually, you can drink small amounts of salt, with plenty of water. I'm sure Professor Abaynesh will look after Mary's health. And so will you. Although she's moved out, Mary still needs a good *compañera*."

"Thanks." Jenny felt guilty for wishing she was done with her. "But Mary's obsessed with ultra. Like the Creep, obsessed with the War on Ultra. Her hands—she even looks like him. It's . . ."

"Creepy?" Father Clare smiled. "I don't think Mary wants to fight ultra. I think she loves ultraphytes. Perhaps she . . . identifies with them. She feels different, isolated."

"*Claro.*"

"People often imitate things they love, like their pets."

"That's true."

"There are more extreme cases," said Father Clare. "There's Jerusalem syndrome. People visit Jerusalem and see all the holy sites; they get overwhelmed. A person of unbalanced mind may suddenly think they're John the Baptist. They start running around wrapped in a goat skin, trying to baptize people."

She smiled. "That's pretty funny. I mean, not really."

"Then there's Paris syndrome. People who've studied art all their lives visit Paris and suddenly get overwhelmed by all the Van Goghs."

"¡Oye! Couldn't such a person . . . do something dangerous? " Like that madman who had smashed the *Pietà*.

He sighed. "Students do dangerous things every day of the week. As do college administrators," he added cryptically.

"So you think Mary has, like, ultra syndrome?"

"I can't disclose details, but we're working closely with Mary, believe me. Jenny, I understand your concern, after all you've been through."

"Well, thanks." She'd kept her promise to her mother, and she did feel better. "I guess I'd better go start my homework. Oh, how are things with you? How's Uncle Dylan in Washington? Did his trip go well?"

Father Clare gave her an odd look, as if she ought to know otherwise. He looked somehow much older, as if slipping a mask. "Yes, thanks, Dylan's trip . . . went well."

Afterward, Jenny checked her toybox. Her newstream was still turned off; she'd missed a whole day of world, state, and local news. A whole day without Clive—how Anna Carrillo had leaked her short list for running mate; how several drones had gone down in a dogfight above Ellsworth, and the Amery Ice Shelf had collapsed, the last remaining ice shelf of Antarctica; and how a certain college president on the moon had driven his Anthradyne 500 up into a spin. There it was in her box, amid the gaudy lights of Mare Crisium, the heart-stopping sight of Uncle Dylan's car tumbling over and over at least a dozen times while falling ever so slowly in lunar one-sixth g.

26

The lunar express took Friday night returning to Earth, then Saturday morning Dylan came back to Frontera. On the way, Fritz called from Berkeley. "Dad—how *could* you?" His curly-haired son was the picture of filial outrage. "Just imagine what could have happened."

"Thanks for your . . . concern, *tío.*"

"Think how Pop feels. That car—all through everyone's windows. The whole universe saw it."

Dylan had blocked all his media windows. He hadn't yet heard from Clare. "How was your benefit for *Marmota monax?*"

"The band was fab, especially the Lennon." Fritz shook his head gloomily. "But we may be too late. It's been a decade since a groundhog's been seen in PA."

"Why not send us a breeding pair?"

Fritz's face lit up, the picture of youthful hope. Then he remembered to frown. "You better watch yourself, Dad. Don't do anything I wouldn't do."

As he neared Frontera, Dylan tried again to reach Clare, but he still wasn't answering. *Qué desastre.* Orin called, before the lift had even docked. "Congratulations!" chortled the financial officer. "Three new positions. Wait till the Board hears. Witherspoon bet me you wouldn't do it—he owes me a new set of irons."

Helen called as well. "The faculty will be thrilled." The toyprints mounted higher than ever on her desk. "Three new positions—just what we need for Antarctic Studies."

Dylan winced, recalling that the faculty had yet to approve his frog seminar plan.

Helen added, "There are matters requiring your prompt attention. The ultraphyte in Reagan Hall—"

"Of course. Arrange us a meeting *pronto.*"

Clare's window had disappeared.

Dylan felt a shock, and he nearly lost his footing. What had become of Clare? Was Clare even still here in the hab? He fought down a rising sense of panic. Life without Clare—it had been years since he had imagined such a thing. In college, before his liver transplant, Dylan had been the life of every party, yet inside he felt achingly alone. Then one day Clare had appeared in the bookstore, the golden-haired frog printing out a pile of books that weren't even assigned for class. Life without Clare would be like life without books.

Stuck down below, on outer level, the three screening lines were interminable. After an age he got up to ground level and rushed home. But Clare wasn't home. Wherever would Clare be on a Saturday afternoon?

Feeling light-headed, Dylan sank into the couch. Overhead, the Sistine God separated light from dark. Dylan was famished; the lunar express no longer served food. The bowl by the couch had one apple left, and he bit into it. The rush of sweet juice cleared his head.

How to find Clare?

He blinked for the toymaker.

Zari appeared in a conference room at the Toynet Support Center, the vast hidden labyrinth of toyrooms and electronic hardware that connected all Frontera residents with each other and with planet Earth. The teddies were coming in and out of toyrooms, a couple of them snoozing on their little nap rugs. "Welcome back!" Zari's dark brow arched expressively. "We're in training for Toy-five. It plugs all those security gaps, especially Ebola."

"My, that's something." Dylan flashed his most winning smile. "So sorry, but my box overflowed again. The media, you know."

"Of course. Need a clean-out?"

"I think I fixed it all, except for Clare's window. Would you mind?"

"No problem. Just a minute." Zari's eyes defocused. In a moment, Clare's window returned.

He blinked for coordinates. There was Clare, all the way down at the south end of the hab. He was sitting on the bank of the Ohio River.

Dylan sighed with relief. A quick change of clothes, and he was out jogging down Buckeye Trail. Snatches of student music blended with the birdcalls, then the distant rumble of powwow drums. A group of wide-eyed prospectives and parents, their student guide walking backward while lecturing. A troupe of donkey-tailed elephants staggered drunkenly across the trail. A bear's shaggy hindquarters lumbered off into the wood. At last, amid the foliage, reflections twinkled off the water. There, upon the gravel of the riverbank, sat Clare.

Dylan sat himself down on the bank and threw his arm around Clare. "Goodness, you gave me such a fright."

Clare said nothing. Looking out across the river, he picked up a flat round stone and tossed it with a flick of the wrist. The stone skipped once, twice, thrice.

"Not bad," said Dylan, trying to smile. "Clare, I'm truly sorry. I should have told you; I just didn't want you to worry." He took a breath. "I'm done with racing for good. I sold the car on ToyBay."

Clare picked up another stone. He turned it around in his hand, then tossed it. This time it skipped a full eight times before vanishing beneath the waves.

"Clare, what is it? I come back, I find an arsonist to expel, an ultra to exterminate, and God knows what else. What am I to do?"

"It's all about you."

Dylan paused. "I didn't say that. I said, what is with you?"

"I've lost my faith."

Dylan closed his eyes. He took a long breath and let it out again. "Clare, you have more faith than anyone I know."

"It's not enough."

" 'Faith is the substance of things hoped for, the conviction of things unseen.' "

" 'And if I have all faith, but have not love, I am a noisy gong or a clanging cymbal.' "

"Clare, you have more love than anyone."

"Without you, I can love nothing. If you were gone tomorrow, my faith would be gone. So what good is it?"

"We've been this way before, Clare. You can't live every if; if this, if that. If a dead space truck hit the hab today, what then? We've always lived here like this, on the edge."

"If a dead space truck hit, at least we'd be gone together."

Dylan blinked several times, at a loss for words. A blue-tailed skink flitted amongst the stones, in that curious lizard way: three steps, stop; three steps, stop. Peepers began to sing. Finally, he tightened his arm around Clare and held him close. Clare relaxed at last, just like the old days. The peepers' chorus grew deafening. A breeze blew from the river, and the solar faded from gold to auburn. Light glinted off distant skybikers, heading north. From somewhere cried a barred owl.

The two of them rose together and started back north, strolling slowly hand in hand toward the campus. Students headed toward the dining center dragging their shoelaces, mumbling at their toyboxes, or singing some

Renaissance air in flawless harmony. The front lawn of the Red Bulls' club house sported a purple campaign sign, FLYNN FOR MAYOR.

For a moment Dylan's foot froze in midair. Then he recovered his stride alongside Clare. "Did I miss one of your reports again?"

"Nope," said Clare. "I didn't want you to worry."

The college chaplain squaring off against the Politics professor to fill the shoes of Mount Gilead's dead mayor. That would do wonders for town-gown.

In Dylan's office, Sharon Abaynesh faced Helen with her arms crossed. Helen was on Dylan's side for this one, he knew. She would explain to Sharon why the ultra had to go. Still, he repressed the urge to check for a snake under his chair.

"Sharon, as dean of the faculty, I'm always your advocate," Helen began. "Now, just explain to us why this is a First Amendment issue."

Sharon maintained her serpentine stare. "The ultraphyte is my research subject. I put in for it, I got approved."

"Not by the college."

"So, approve me."

Helen shook her head. "Senior Staff discussed it. This project is not in the best interest of the college. After mosquitoes, it's too many invasives in one year."

"So what should I do?"

"Give up the terror agent to be destroyed."

Sharon sat there in her jeans, considering. Finally she shrugged. "So I'll give it up."

Dylan let out a breath.

"Thanks, Sharon," said Helen. "We knew you'd understand. Next year, you have my word we'll take up your request again."

"Not to worry. I'll just put out salt to attract some more."

Helen stared. Then she turned to Dylan.

Dylan cleared his throat. "The substratum passed inspection. It was cleared by Homeworld Security."

"Homeworld Security?" demanded Sharon. "What do they know? The feds have purged evolutionists for the past decade. Imagine—suppose they purged missile defense of physicists?" She took a breath. "Ultraphyte is more than a species. It's a quasispecies, like hepatitis Q." She eyed Dylan meaningfully, a reminder of their previous run-in. "Ultra evolves even faster than viruses. Like baramins after the Flood."

"But we can still detect hepa Q. That's why we test for it."

"Hepa Q and R, yes. But we can't yet detect hepa S or T. Though half our students probably—"

"Yes, Sharon," interrupted Helen, "we get the picture. So your point is . . . you think our soil's got ultra, and Homeland Security can't find it?"

If that were the case, Frontera was finished. First mosquitoes, now ultra. How could the college survive that, all in one year?

Sharon added, "Their DIRGs didn't find the one the student sneaked through."

The student—there was another dilemma. What to do with Mary, the ultra-obsessed orphan with the pearls? They'd contacted her doctor, the one with the White House connection who'd done her omniprosthesis, but the doctor wasn't returning calls.

Sharon spread her hands. "If our soil's got ultra they can't detect, you can be sure Earth does too. At least if we study what we've got, we may get a handle on what's here."

Seconds ticked by, as all three professors sat, absorbed in their own thoughts.

The lights flickered. **"Power loss,"** came Dylan's toybox. **"Level One systems shutting down."** A burst of windows opened, announcing, demanding, questioning.

Outside, the late-afternoon light dimmed, like the penumbra of a partial solar eclipse.

Sharon got up. "Excuse me, I have to check the Reagan emergency generator."

27

That Saturday morning, Yola had spent half the practice in a toyroom full of Melbourne's Scorpions. "I know Melbourne Uni; my *novio* goes there. I warned him, expect no quarter. Think of them as boiled lobster." The Melbourne team logo was a red scorpion. "They puff up but don't do much."

Fran and David laughed, recalling the match the year before.

"But watch their center, Number six," Yola warned. "He can reach the goal all the way from the midline. I'll need to cover him all the time he's in our half. Keep him out of the cap zone, where he'll try to make us double-team. That leaves a forward exposed . . ."

Jenny could see what Yola meant about the Melbourne players; they moved just a fraction of a second slower than the Great Bears. But the Scorpions had their own plays, and a way of sneaking behind to steal the ball. And keeping that Number 6 covered would be harder than it looked.

"ToyNews Mount Gilead." After practice, the local ToyNews was back in her box. "A new candidate throws his hat in the ring for the job of mayor. The candidate is Father Clare Flynn, Frontera College chaplain and rector of All Saints Reconciled Church."

Jenny's mouth fell open in amazement. Father Clare, who always hung in the background of her mother's fundraisers? Who'd never given a speech outside a church?

Father Clare appeared in the news window, his sleeves rolled up, outside the Homefair frame just raised. "My aim is to assure every citizen a roof over their head, full medical care, and protection from outer-space debris."

For response, there was Professor Hamilton, smiling his most ingratiating smile. "I welcome my esteemed friend and colleague into the race. My aim, as my fellow church members know, is to keep our focus on spiritual values; the kind of values that make Mount Gilead a great town, a part of our great spiritual nation." In other words, avoid any profit-trimming regulations and keep the house edge low.

"And finally," the announcer added, "a response from Mrs. Leora

Smythe. Mrs. Smythe, which candidate do you endorse to fill the position left by your esteemed late husband?"

Leora looked aside as she always did, even when handing out lunch for the Homefair volunteers. "I believe Phil will be a fine Christian mayor." She seemed to hesitate. "And I believe Father Clare is a fine Christian man."

Jenny sighed. Only four weeks left till the special election; Father Clare would have to hustle. She wondered who was running his campaign.

By midmorning, Jenny was at Castle Cockaigne, hauling the last crates of Margaux and Saint-Julien up a winding staircase to the next floor of the keep.

"Mind the trip step," called Ken.

Jenny had no idea what that meant, until her foot hit the top of a step just an inch taller than the rest. Only the narrow width of the claustrophobic staircase kept her from falling headlong and dashing the bottles down the uneven amyloid stonework.

"The trip step repels marauding Crusaders."

Repressing a retort, Jenny returned to the main floor, where brilliant amyloid tapestries of knights and archers covered the four-foot-thick walls. This all had little to do with flood protection; but then, it was hardly worse than assembling hundreds of canapés for a Somers state rep's fundraiser. In back of the hall rested the two lifeboats, built of carboxyplast that would last forever. The boats were moored ominously at the postern gate.

To greet their visitors, Ken and Yola came out dressed in historic garb. Ken was a monk in a brown tunic cinched at the waist, a cowl drooping over his head. Yola was an Elizabethan physician, in a blue tunic and cape, white gloves, and a beaked mask.

Outside, visitors for the tour were already crossing the drawbridge above the precariously overfilled moat. From above came the lively beat of the George Lewis tribute band, staged behind the parapet atop the keep. Not medieval, but old enough. The archway through the curtain wall led across a short courtyard, thence into the keep. The first floor consisted of a large hall with a crude amyloid-wooden table surrounded by rough-hewn chairs. The ceiling was painted with scenes of landowners and their hunting hounds jumping through hoops, shepherdesses in quaint frocks twirling their crooks at the sheep, and monks tending their vineyards.

Leora, in her pink-checked pioneer dress and bonnet, held her little boy by the hand, while her two older children raced around the table, their power bands *click-clacking*. Children's energy; what a power source, Jenny thought with a smile. While the little ones squealed with glee, the mayor's widow inspected the ceiling closely. "**Sheep**," texted Leora. "**Ready for shearing.**"

"Sheep and shepherds," agreed Jenny.

"Any dinosaurs?"

Startled, Jenny blinked at her.

"**Dinosaurs are rarely seen. But the Medievals had sharper eyes than we do.**"

Sherri-Lyn brought her two girls. Flexing her hammer arm, she shook her head at the four-feet-thick wall. "Imagine laying *that* foundation."

Jenny had no idea how the Medievals did it. It was almost harder to imagine building a real castle than finding a real dinosaur.

Sherri-Lyn leaned closer, confidentially. "So sorry, about that 'mutant' thing. It's just gross what those Golds spout on Toynet these days."

Puzzled, Jenny did a quick scan. A Centrist talk show had put out how the "Ramos mutant" was scheduled to speak at the Unity convention. She gave a shrug. What else did the party expect.

Outside, the students were gathering, some more drawn to the music. Anouk in a coneflower scarf, with solicitous Rafael; Fran and David with the whole slanball team, including Charlie; and there was Tom with his tool belt from Homefair. Tom's face held that look of Newman intensity. Jenny stared, then made herself look away. Donna Matousek, Frank Lazza, and other farmers admired the ponderous curtain wall, while children played hide-and-seek in the space between the wall and the keep. Travis Tharp inspected the wall, tapping it now and then with his amyloid tester.

There were Professor Abaynesh and Coach Porat, with Tova on his shoulders clutching her model *Titanic*. Mary Dyer accompanied them; heaven only knew what that omniprosthetic ultra-grower made of all this. Meanwhile, Dean Kwon and Father Clare stopped by to keep an eye on things, as did Quade Vincenzo. The ecoengineer looked up and down the castle wall, with a businesslike air, as if performing some structural calculus.

"Jenny, the lifeboat," called Ken. "Time to get ready."

She shook her head. "That's your job."

"Aren't you going to try?" he demanded. "What will you do when you really need it?"

Jenny froze. This was not part of their plan.

Yola caught her arm. "Don't be a dwork, Jen. This was your idea, after all. Try it—it'll be good for you."

The music came to a halt. A siren wailed, alerting all to leave the building. Jenny blinked open her EMS life finder, a channel that returned the location of all toyboxes and brainstream sources within the area. Townspeople and students gradually strolled out of the keep and back over the drawbridge.

Yola pulled off her mask. "Attention everyone." Her voice was amplified, echoing off the curtain wall. "This year's tour of Castle Cockaigne concludes with a demonstration of what can happen in the event of substratum overflow. 'Substratum overflow'—it was there in the form we all signed as Frontera colonists." A copy of the form blinked into everyone's box, with the key phrase highlighted. "What does that really mean? It means that, in the event of total power loss, the hab's outer substratum—the water layer full of solar microbes—will flow up (that is, inward) above the denser layer of rock and soil. The flow could flood the hab with up to six feet of water. What to do? A simple carboxyplast lifeboat is what every family needs."

Yola turned to Ken for the next part, but Jenny stopped her. "Someone's still inside." Her EMS window showed a signal source.

"It's my boy," called Frank Lazza. "Just a minute." The farmer glared at the castle, presumably texting the boy what he could expect if he didn't get out. Suddenly the child burst through the great doorway, pumping his legs as fast as he could to run down the drawbridge.

Ken threw back his monk's cowl. "'And the flood was forty days upon the earth,'" he intoned from Genesis. "'And the waters increased, and bore up the ark, and it was lifted up above the earth. And all flesh perished that moved upon the earth, both fowl, and cattle, and beast, and every man, died.' But those who heeded God's warning were saved by the ark."

This message dampened the mood of the crowd, which fell silent. Above, the musicians rested their instruments upon the parapet. Ken and Yola started up the drawbridge. "**Come on, Jenny,**" texted Yola.

"**My mental won't allow it.**" Jenny blinked her mental's window.

The Monroe appeared, pouting reflectively. "We think you can handle the Flood. It will do you good. Don't worry, we'll be here for you." The cherry lips blew her a kiss.

At the drawbridge the entire slanball team was watching, and Anouk and Rafael, and even Fritz Hoffman with the Red Bulls. And Tom.

Jenny dragged herself up across the drawbridge, her pulse pounding, as she wondered, how did she get herself into this? She followed Yola through the deserted castle. Ken got into one boat and drew out the oars. She suddenly recalled their old family vacations on Lobsterville Beach, before that end of Martha's Vineyard went under. She got into the other boat with Yola, and found the pair of oars.

"Backwards," Yola reminded her. Rowing wasn't that hard.

The first tongue of water came gliding snake-like over the amyloid. Jenny's skin crawled. Then the water came faster, like tide rolling up the beach, only much faster than it ever had in Lobsterville. The flood rose surprisingly fast; faster than she'd realized.

The boat lifted and swayed, unsteadily.

Yola gripped Jenny's arm. "You okay?"

Jenny nodded, seeing her own pallid arms. She took a deep breath.

Ken was already rowing the other boat, using his oar as a pole to navigate past the table in the hall. There was actually only about three feet of water. Once Jenny got started rowing, it felt rather silly, rowing a boat through a room. Only it wasn't silly; it was everyday life for millions of coastal people, watching the sea claim their homes.

As the boats emerged outside, the crowd cheered. From the parapet the band played "Oh When the Saints" as if to beat a train. Jenny blinked in the light and remembered to smile without closing her eyes. In her window, the Marilyn face beamed. "Congratulations, Jenny!" The mental team would tell her mother and expect a raise.

Suddenly people gasped. Arms pointed back toward the flooded garden. Jenny looked backward, following the arms. Mary Dyer floated there in the deep water of the moat, swimming in a rather vague way. She must have been inside the castle—yet the EMS stream had not detected her as a person. No Toynet for her; that had to get fixed.

Yola tossed a ring in the water, but Mary did not seem to notice. So she pulled off her costume and dove into the moat, leaving Jenny to clutch the rocking boat for dear life. Yola reached Mary in a couple of strokes, and held out the ring. Watching Yola, Mary at last got the idea and caught the ring with her hand, allowing herself to be drawn to the wall.

The music concluded, and the visitors slowly dispersed. Ken and Yola set to draining the moat, while the dwarves came down to clean up. Jenny approached Tom and Charlie, who had stayed discussing some project.

"Tom and I are going to build lifeboats," Charlie told her. "Carb is dirt cheap now, with the slump in Earth housing. We can get surplus carb through Homefair, and build enough boats to supply every dorm."

"And every home in Mount Gilead," added Tom.

Jenny beamed. It felt like the sun came out.

Tom squeezed her hand. "Have to go now; I've got to work on tonight's menu." The Café de la Paix.

"*Chulo.* We've got our reservation." Life was suddenly wonderful.

As the *chicos* left, only the ecoengineer remained. Quade stared at the castle, seeming lost in thought, his unique bulbous profile half in shadow.

"So," ventured Jenny, "what do you think?"

Quade stroked his chin, and his eyes defocused. "What about the animals?"

The minis. Elephants, teddy bears, mini-deer, and all the settlers' mini-cows and mini-sheep. A few would make it out of the water, those near either pole where the earth curved upward into the cap. But most would not get there in time.

"And the plants," added Jenny. Even Noah had saved no plants beyond animal fodder. No maple trees, no wildflowers, no cornfields. The parterre garden might recover from its brief submersion; but a real substratum overflow would be full of salt.

Suddenly the light dimmed. The "southern" cap went black, and the "northern" cap faded to a moonlike glow. The upside-down forest went gray. It was like nightfall, only an eerie brownish tint. The gloom filled the entire length of the spacehab.

Jenny turned to Quade. "What is it?" Her EMS window opened a long checklist: Activate backup lights, check the sewage pumps, shut down the elevator.

"Interesting," Quade observed to his toybox, doubtless feeding lots of windows. "A brownout. We've got work to do."

Jenny's cottage had been restored two blocks away, minus Mary's half, and well away from the substratum leak. Despite the brownout, the amyloid walls held up, although the printer flashed "Empty"—no fresh amyloid pumped up from the outer shell, where the microbes used sunlight to produce it. Nothing else amiss, aside from the penumbral light throughout the hab.

President Chase's office window opened. "We've lost our Earth power," Uncle Dylan explained in his most reassuring tone. "As most of you know, this happens several times a year: Some piece of space debris cuts our connection. Not to worry—Frontera generates eighty percent of our own power, from the infinite rays of the sun." Their purple microbes in the outer shell, making electricity and amyloid; and their solarray out in space. "But Earth, *ahora*, is experiencing Toynet instability, with rolling blackouts all across North America; while at Frontera, we only dim the lights. Our microbial generators continue service, all around the hab. So you see, this is the worst power loss our community will ever face."

An obvious dig at their demo. Jenny wondered about that, as she showered and changed for the Café de la Paix. As she was heading out to Buckeye Trail, her mother's window opened.

"Jenny? How's the college? *¿Está bien?*"

"*Sí, bien,*" Jenny assured her. "So far."

"Your father has gone back to New York to help restore the system. It's done him a world of good; he feels needed."

Jenny thought of her seminar reading, about Teddy blasting the trusts, the perils of Combination. "Mama . . . do you think Toynet is a good thing?"

"*Hijita,* whatever are you saying? Is this what you learn in college? Where would we be without Toynet?"

"I know, Mama, I'm just wondering. The news, the power, the calling—it's all in one now. It used to be different, remember? When Toynet started, it was just, like, games for Christmas."

Soledad waved her hand. "That was then. Your father helped change all that. You should be proud of him."

"Of course I'm proud of Dad." Before Toynet; what were things like then?

"Then don't worry about such things. Keep your mind on your studies. And your convention speech."

"Mama, I told you—I can't do that speech."

"Jenny. Remember Glynnis with the hot plate?" The First Lady debate; it seemed like an age had passed. College life was so full of everything. "Did you see how the last Antarctic ice shelf broke up? This is our last chance, Jenny; our chance to get the reins back, and just maybe get our planet under control." Her voice lowered. "Remember, this is the convention; the friendliest audience you'll ever have. They'll cheer no matter what you say."

Saying it was just the problem, speaking out to a hundred million strangers. She'd look worse than Leora fielding questions by text.

Then her eyes widened. There was an idea.

"And please, *hijita,* no more drug busts till after Election Day."

At the Café de la Paix, Anouk and Rafael basked in the glow of each other's solicitous regard. Yola and Ken had managed a workaround through Asian Toynet to reach their respective *novio* and *novia,* sharing the windows with everyone's toybox. Yola's *novio* at Melbourne was a hunky shark researcher. Yola crowed about how the Bears would clobber the Melbourne team, then closed her eyes and brainstreamed him a long mental kiss. Ken's *novia* was a colonel in the Israeli army. A water engineer, she enthused about their desalination plant. Then she brain-kissed Ken; he nearly collapsed.

Jenny slipped out to help in the kitchen. "What do you think of Father Clare running for mayor?" she asked Tom, while grinding the cinnamon.

"Father Clare does so much for the town." Tom stirred the chocolate sauce, intently watching its consistency. "All those Homefair homes. And he's always fixing someone's roof for free. I'm sure they'll vote for him."

Recalling Leora, Jenny was less sure. "The cinnamon, it goes in the sauce?"

"No, no, that's to dust the napoleons."

"He needs to campaign," Jenny said. "Talking points, and ads on the news. Mount Gilead is small; we should go door to door."

"Really? I've never done that."

"It's easy. And it's important. The town needs so much help." Someone to clean up the pollution, and provide doctors.

Tom nodded. "I could try."

The EMS snake was blinking. A student had called in from Huron. Seconds passed, lengthening. No one else responded.

"I should go," Jenny sighed. "It's my turn for a call." Better now than after midnight when she'd need her sleep for the game.

"I'll save you a napoleon," Tom said. "I'll wait up here for you, whenever you're done."

"Okay, thanks." She took off her apron. Then her heart pounded. As she left, she went by and kissed Tom on the cheek.

The hallway of the frogs' dorm was so narrow, Jenny and the medibot could barely fit the stretcher through. A code violation; she blinked a report. The walls were bare carboxyplast, like the castle lifeboats.

The call had come from Charlie. She found him in the hallway, crouching by a *chica* sprawled on the floor. The *chica* lay motionless, without any clothes. Breathing okay, with the usual sour odor.

"What happened?" Jenny snapped the scanscope around the *chica*'s limp arm. Looking into her mouth, the airway was clear.

"I don't know. I was just coming back from Game World," Charlie emphasized. Toy Land ran an elaborate substance-free game world on Saturday nights. "I just found her here."

The scanscope figures scrolled. Moderate intoxication, along with hepa Q and two other emerging STDs. And her name.

"Suze Gruman-Iberia." The Begonia recruiting director. "Do you know her?"

Charlie shook his head. "A sophomore, isn't she? What's she doing in a frogs' dorm?"

The medibot handed Jenny a blanket. They wrapped Suze up and wheeled her out for a quick trip to the Barnside.

At the clinic, Doc Uddin nodded. "It's the Begonia party. They aim to score as many new *chicos* as they can. But if they pass out, they get dumped out in the hall."

Jenny checked the time, barely eleven. "It's kind of early to pass out, isn't it?"

"Someone spiked the punch. We confiscated the first batch, but not quite in time. Uh-oh, there's another one."

Another call, this time from Knox dorm. No one answered. Frank Lazza was working a heart attack at a southern homestead, and Yola was with a Bull who'd smashed a car into a tree. Jenny bit her lip; she really wanted to get sleep for slanball. She blinked for Nick Petherbridge.

Music blared, and she turned it down. Nick appeared amidst the Red Bulls crowd, his eyes glazed. "Sure, I'm on my way."

"No, I'll take care of it," said Jenny quickly.

When she arrived at Knox, Nick was already there checking out the patient, another Begonia sister.

"Nick! What are you doing here?"

"I told you, I took the call."

"But you're in no shape to—"

"Mind your own business. I took care of myself."

Behind him, the medibot looked confused.

"How, Nick?" The only way to clear ethanol from the blood that fast was the scanscope. But using the scope on oneself was a class-A violation.

"Look out, you're obstructing care."

Backing off, Jenny blinked for the Barnside. In the window, Doc Uddin shook her head. "I'll deal with Nick."

"But he must get suspended." Worse, sent back to Earth.

"Don't have to tell me." The doctor's long braid twisted as her head turned. "But we're shorthanded." She inserted an IV for an elderly patient, an oxygen mask on his face, power-band marks visible on his arm. "You'd think the mayor's death last year would be a wake-up call." She looked up at Jenny. "Make plenty of time for next week."

The Ferrari victory celebration. The Frontera Circuit; they always won.

28

Sunday afternoon, the cords of the slanball cage gleamed in the north-south double sun, the lights casting double shadows. The pounding drums from the Mound signaled two o'clock. Jenny sat with Charlie just outside the cage.

"**Show 'em how to play.**" Tusker-12 was watching on Earth. "**Show 'em for Somers.**"

Jenny had skipped church but still failed Coach's sleep meter, and resigned herself to spend the first game on the bench. Yola's braids swung beneath her slancap, defiantly alert despite spending all night with Doc Uddin stabilizing the Bull from the wrecked car. She couldn't have passed—but Coach couldn't afford to bench her. What a start to the season's first game.

The cage was now wrapped around by a cylinder of seating, crisscrossed with protective chains and holds. The spectators included students, parents, colonist families, and tourists from the Mound, all strapped into their seats. They emitted waves of the usual smells, popcorn and hot dogs mixed with droplets of upset from stomachs unaccustomed to micrograv. "Go Bears!" squeaked a couple of teddies at the top of their lungs. "Bears *go*, Scorpions *slow*!" Melbourne's Scorpions had a small but brave contingent of red shirts huddled at one end.

"Go Bears! Bury them!" From the outer row boomed an enthusiastic dad. Loud enough for fun, yet not embarrassing.

Coach paced the row, taut as a tiger on the prowl. "Don't leave Number six unguarded," he rattled off. "And don't let them crisscross and make you switch defenders. You're switching out, you get clocked." There were about forty different points to remember, every second of the game.

At the midline, Yola faced red-shirt Number 6 for the slan-off. The automated ref system spun a randomizer. Number 6 won.

"North," called Number 6. That meant the Scorpions would face north at first, then south later, when the light was waning in the south but growing at the north end, streaming into the Bears' eyes.

The south half of the cage soon filled with Scorpions. They really did look like boiled lobsters, Jenny thought with a smile. The Bears all wore their white jerseys with the purple constellation of the Great Bear. Their shoe grips crunched along the rails of the cage.

"Slan time," called the announcer, Dean Kwon.

Yola slanned the ball wide, at a shallow angle bounding up around the cage, away from Number 6. The ball should have reached David; but surprisingly, it slowed at Number 40. Number 40 jittered the ball for an instant, then zagged himself across straight at Ken. The impact resounded, and Ken's hair flew out in all directions. Elbow in the gut; Jenny blinked, startled to see, though the ref apparently didn't. Her high school games were rarely that rough. But Ken didn't yield, and Number 40 was confused just long enough for Fran to steal the ball.

The home crowd cheered. "That's it, Bears!" called the dad. "Show 'em your claws!" Jenny clapped, exchanging a quick grin with Charlie.

But seconds later, the ball was down at the goal, the Scorpions batting it around the cap zone. Xiang heroically deflected it three times, but the fourth time it went in.

"Two points for Melbourne," called Dean Kwon. Cheers this time, smaller, from the visitors' side.

"Foul ball!" called the dad. "Reset the ref!"

"**Who is he?**" Jenny asked Wade, waiting on the bench to rotate in.

"**Mr. Kearns-Clark. Never misses a game.**"

The play went back and forth, never long into the Scorpions' half. After the second goal lost, Coach called a time out. Coach Porat was not the yelling kind. He was the fume and spit kind. Like a cobra, he spat right now. "I *told* you not to let them make you switch. What do you expect? Quit daydreaming and *play*. Get that ball in play, and don't let go. When they set the screen, fall back and pass. Once you get a goal, they'll wilt."

The players regrouped, and got the ball forward. Yola at last slanned one in, and the Bears did better for a time. For each goal Jenny rose and cheered, and tried to make mental notes for next time.

By halftime the Bears were three points up. A drumbeat started, and a group of air-dancers came through in Shawnee-inspired feathers and fringes. Their feathers whirled and pulsed as they rolled head over heels, all the while sailing down the cage with apparent lack of effort. *Chulito.*

In the second half, Jenny's concentration slipped. Her eyes defocused. Suddenly, a blue-tailed skink came into view, perched on the cage. However had it got there? Jenny wondered. Did it climb all the way up the cloud ladder? Or did it hitch a ride in someone's pack?

"Jenny, you're in."

Startled, Jenny checked the board. The score was nearly tied; neither side had kept advantage long, but the Scorpions had a two-point edge.

"You're in," Coach repeated. "Do it when you can."

Once her feet grasped the court, adrenaline kicked in. Jenny passed and jiittered the ball a couple of times to get the feel, the sea of faces rotating beneath her feet. *Jordi. . . .* She shook herself. Hand over foot, she cartwheeled toward the quarter line where Ken took a step, trying to escape his Scorpion guard. Ken looked ragged, injured somewhere; he'd rotated out, but Coach sent him back in.

At their cap zone, the Scorpions had their tallest player on Yola, but she got the ball down to Fran who passed it back to Ken. Jenny launched herself from the cage to sail within three feet behind him. Ken's guard slipped between the two of them, but the guard couldn't know that wouldn't matter, that Jenny's mental reach was easily twice that. The ball leapt out from Ken, headed straight for the goal.

"Three for Frontera!"

The crowd roared. *"Way to go, Kearns-Clark!"* called his delighted dad. Several Bear teammates leapt onto Ken for hugs. Jenny kept her smile small, hiding the inner thrill, like an operative whose candidate won by half a point. She zigzagged across the cage, already eyeing the next play. After two minutes more Coach called her out, but the damage was done. The confused Scorpions double-teamed Ken whenever he came anywhere near the ball, leaving open Yola or Fran to clean up.

The Bears exulted in their first win. As they headed off to shower, Coach climbed arm-over-arm to the privacy bell and called Yola and Jenny aside. "Well, ladies." Coach put his hands together. "There's good news and bad news."

Jenny nodded. Doc Uddin had said Ken had a broken rib, and goodness knows how many bruises. He'd be out for at least a week.

Coach grinned. "First the bad news. Yola, you dominated the game— and Jenny, too, for the five minutes you were in. You played fantastic—and now you feel indispensible, no matter what."

Jenny smiled uncertainly.

"So here's the good news. You're suspended from practice for three days. Time to catch up on sleep, and time to think over whether you still intend to play."

Coach locked stares with Yola. Yola's face didn't move a muscle.

Jenny swallowed. "Thanks, Coach."

With a nod, he clapped them each on the shoulder, then left.

As soon as Jenny emerged from the cage, ToyNews windows lit up scrolling all the news she'd missed, including the day's big story, the inevitable Homeworld assault on Great Salt Lake. The ultras could never be wiped for good, of course. But the fed had sent in scores of drones to blast the invading cells into oblivion. For hours the lake was aflame, obliterating all the biofilm towers and strange new stalks and crawling things that had emerged.

After the strike, the lake was a flat sea of mud, not an ultra in sight. Outside in the suburbs, the populace had been issued cyanide masks, and there were no human casualties. But the wildlife was a different story. Pelicans, phaleropes, and sandpipers lay limp, strewn haphazardly around the beach. Even a bald eagle lay stricken, head buried in the sand. And of course, unseen in the brush, the newer forms of ultra rooted, slithered, or crept forth flexing their limblike appendages. Some had a head and four limbs—"mandrakes," the media called them. What next from this puzzling quasispecies?

In other news, the Creep had dropped out of sight again. A White House source put out he was planning some new drive for Antarctica. Still, the vice president's disappearance was surprising so late in the campaign. And President Bud Guzmán had scheduled a special address to the nation for Monday morning, on a new project called "Farmland Security." Timed no doubt to blunt the impact of Unity's convention opening. As for Jenny, the "Mutant speech" meme was still spreading.

To celebrate their win, the Kearns-Clark parents treated the whole team to a barbecue down by the Ohio River, complete with Gandalf-style fireworks. The Kearns-Clarks were a garrulous pair of old-time Quakers who regaled the team with their long-ago adventures in Africa raising goats for Heifer International. No sign of why Ken and Yola had a problem with them. If only Tom could have come; but Jenny kept his window open, and promised to stop by later for dessert. She thought a moment, then blinked the option, "Brainkiss enabled."

Fran squeezed Jenny's arm. "Great start, frog."

Everyone shouted or thumped her on the back, with no specific reference to what she'd done. Ken kept quiet, coping with liveplast pulsing across his chest and several other places.

"Sure you belong here?" Jenny smiled. "I'll scope you, just to check."

He grimaced. "What a shame you and sis got suspended," he muttered. "Why should you waste your nights on plastered bros when there's a game?"

Yola shrugged. "Like Coach said, we can use a couple days to catch up on work. Jenny, there's a public cage up there south of Mount Gilead. We can do fundamentals; keep in shape."

━✦━

When Jenny finally got to the café, the dining room was dark, the chairs put up; it was not the café's regular night for business. The only light was in the kitchen, where Tom sat on a stool waiting with chocolate mousse in a parfait glass.

"Thanks." Jenny enjoyed the treat, despite how full she was. She called up a Paris street in her toybox.

"Congratulations," said Tom.

"Shh," she whispered. "You never know. Rapture's Angels might have their own Anouk."

"But a *Christian*." They shared a good laugh. In his hand Tom held a string of plastic pop beads, which he ran through his fingers. Jenny watched, curious.

"A memento," he said. "The beads were the last thing I put in my pocket before I left home. Amish kids play with them."

"Really." Jenny thought of Wickett Hall with all the famous toys marching around, the rocking horse, the jack-in-the-box, the choo-choo train.

"What was your favorite toy?"

"A magic set," she remembered. "A coin and a card, and a bit of string. And the shell game—the cups and balls. It's amazing how you can make people see one thing when really it's another."

Tom nodded. "Amazing—and scary."

"*Claro.*" Jenny licked her fork. "What was yours?"

He stretched and put his hands behind his head. "A printer carton. A huge one, the kind your all-purpose food-to-furniture printer comes in. My sister brought it home from a Dumpster. It was everything—a house, a car, a spaceship."

Jenny nodded. "Like the kind I kept the ultra in, in our cellar." She wondered whether Tom's sister was still alive. "I didn't think of Jordi for a whole day. Not till I saw Ken out there in the cage."

"Last night I didn't dream of my sister—for two whole nights. In college our eyeballs are just so crammed with everything."

She said with a rush, "So what do you think about Father Clare running for mayor? Should we help him campaign? I was going to ask him, but I missed church today."

"I asked. He said his campaign is run by the Bulls."

They shared a bemused stare.

"The Bulls aren't so bad," said Tom. "Not in the daytime."

She sighed. "I know, I've worked with worse." Any campaign drew a mixed crowd. "Well, thanks for the treat but I have homework."

And the dreaded convention speech Monday afternoon. And plant lab, all mixed up with the business of Mary; weights all crashing down on her shoulders.

"I'll walk you home."

They strolled hand in hand down Buckeye Trail, fireflies winking in the dark, and the clustered lights of Mount Gilead above. "Did you get the molecule of the day?" asked Tom. "It's something aromatic, but I can't sort out the shifts."

"That's one of about a hundred links I've not recovered yet." Meanwhile so many playmates were sending "tips" for her speech that the box nearly crashed again.

The link popped open, as Tom sent it over.

"Iridodial, the insect hormone," she told him. "Those two ketones are distinctive."

As they reached her new cottage, now a single, Jenny's steps slowed. His face looked perfect, every eyelash and strand of hair. Her lips touched his. She held him close, and he felt so good.

Tom pulled back, with a gasp. "We have homework, okay?"

"See you in class."

29

Monday morning, instead of slanball, Jenny was up working on her "speech." Overnight she'd accumulated about a thousand more "tips" from her playmates. Her eyes skimmed them down.

"**Read them my position paper on getting to Jupiter in ten years.**" A well-meaning family friend at NASA.

"**Your first speech, Jenny!**" Her Somers teammate. "*No tengas miedo—* **Show 'em your tusks!**"

"**Do the math!**" From Anouk, now busy tutoring the toymaker's Developmental Arithmetic. "**Please tell these Americans to learn some math!**"

"**Are you saved by the Lord?**" An anonymous ghost. "**Will you be joining your brother in Heaven?**"

She closed all her windows except her parents and teachers, and Tom and Anouk. Anouk was doing better, and closing off would only tempt her. Her box quiet, she kept her eyes open through Aristotle class, and her head down at lunch. This speech would get over, then *nunca más*.

The Unity Party Convention would run for two days, followed immediately by the Centrists. What had once been two full-week conventions had collapsed over the years into less than a week, as each party tried earlier to upstage the other. Given the preordained content of both, Jenny could hardly imagine how they'd ever managed to fill more time.

Jenny's speech was timed for one thirty, in between Anna Carrillo's old high school debate coach and the attorney general of Utah. At one fifteen, Clive appeared in Jenny's toyroom. "They're running just ten minutes behind," Clive told her. "Anna runs a tight ship," he added confidentially, as if she didn't know that. An assistant straightened his collar, and another whispered something in his ear, while two others fussed about his hair. ToyNet could fix everything, but the convention was a big deal for Clive; he'd leave nothing to chance. "I've seen your advance draft, Jenny," he confided, referring to the text the handlers had given her. "It's *chulo*." Trying to sound like a student.

Jenny swallowed. A moment of fright; would she really go through with it? What if she really hurt Anna's chances? Nonsense, she'd be just one of a hundred five-minute speakers, most of them droning attorneys. She straightened and stood an inch taller. Clive adjusted his virtual height to match. Jenny texted, "That's not my speech."

Clive's eyes flew open. "Excuse me? Do I have the latest text?" He streamed her a copy.

It occurred to her, he could cut her off if she spooked him too much. A technical glitch, or whatever. "There was some revision."

"A change? An authorized change?" The word "authorized" had an urgent tone.

"Authorized by me."

Clive nodded. "ToyNews—From our box to yours."

Jenny watched the countdown in her box, and reviewed her text. She timed it out, the letters to scroll one by one for just ten minutes. She barely heard her own name announced. Just in time, she remembered to smile.

"I would like to thank the Unity organizers, especially the party chair, for the invitation to speak on behalf of our party nominee, Anna Carrillo." Black letters marched across the white page, then scrolled slowly up. "I have never done a speech before, because of a condition that I share with many ordinary Americans: I lack the ability to speak in public. So you will have to read my speech in text. At least with the text before you, I can't ever claim it was a slip of the lip.

"Supporting Anna is a pleasure because she will help ordinary Americans. When a pair of socks costs you fifty dollars, ordinary Americans need help. And beyond the price of socks—Anna will start cleaning up this planet, beginning with the Dead Zone." The handlers had crossed out any reference to the Dead Zone, for fear of alienating Southern voters. "In America, the Dead Zone covers part of twenty-one states, and continues to expand. We need to face it: Solarplate is done . . ." Another no-no for the handlers. "We will beam our energy from outer space, where the sun is a hundred-fold more efficient. Of course, the investment will require material sacrifice."

Blinking lights in her box. Would they cut her off?

"Some say that we can escape Earth's problems by moving everyone to spacehabs, like where I live now. Why can't they do the math?" One for Anouk. "In the past century we've built just seven spacehabs, each holding a few thousand people. Where are Earth's billions to go?

"Above all, we need to say that the 'Firmament' is a lie. We need to get past the lies about outer space, and start a new mission for Jupiter. A Jupiter mission will show the world what a great country can do. NASA has the plans . . ." A few points from her friend's position paper.

"No matter how dark the hour, no matter how late the moment of truth, it is better to light a candle than curse the darkness. Just as we chose to bury our carbon in carboxyplast, we can choose now. We can choose to save our water and shrink the Death Belt. We can choose to build ships to Jupiter, a boundless source of fuel."

Everyone would recognize the source of those lines.

"This morning, someone asked me about Jordi. About whether I will see Jordi someday in heaven. Jordi is now outside of time, along with our great-grandmother Rosa and grandfather Joe, and all of our future children. All of them are pulling for us, and for Anna, and for everyone on Earth to save our planet."

She finally dared peek at the pollmeter. The scale read 9.9.

The first call in came from Aunt El. The governor's twin appeared, her model adjusted to show only one head; a way to keep Meg off the record. "Great speech, Mutant." El winked. "Why not speak at *our* convention? Equal time, for your West Coast branch? We need you on our team. Until Jupiter runs low."

Her aunt had barely left the box before her mother called. "An ordinary American—a speaker who texts! Ingenious! Your pollmeter's off the charts."

"Thanks, Mama."

"We'll put you on the list. No more than once a week, I promise."

"But Mama—"

"Don't forget, a week from Thursday: The first presidential debate, in Boulder." Soledad paused for emphasis. "We've placed you in a front-row toyseat, appearing right before the podium. Wear your best suit, and be sure to smile." Soledad nodded as if to herself. "And the following week, guess what—I'll be up to see you!" A ToyDebate meeting, setting up for Frontera's debate. The final one before the election.

"*¡Oye!* See you then."

In Jenny's toybox, Clive's post-convention interview was coming through. "While Rosa's great-granddaughter admirably represents her own views," the party secretary was telling him, "Unity does not reject solarplating. In fact, we endorse sustainable solarplate development and will slow the rate of Death Belt expansion."

Clive nodded. "And does Unity endorse the Ramos position that the Firmament is a lie?"

Jenny held her breath. The pollmeter dipped and vacillated, for such an unmentionable notion to be voiced out loud.

The party secretary, his hair immaculate as Clive's, slightly shifted his head. "As you know, Clive, Unity has a big tent philosophy. We include members of whatever spiritual belief, so long as they support outer space development."

A hollow pit formed in her stomach. Keep smiling, Jenny told herself dully.

+-+

Jenny joined up with Anouk on her way to Reagan Hall to meet the professor about their laughing plants. Overhead, the sausage cloud stretched north, glowing red from the north solar. A group of high school students sailed by, learning to drive the mini-flyers. From the Mound came the roar of motor cars, all the Red Bulls and Ferraris practicing for their Frontera Circuit next Saturday.

"I thought that would be the end of it, but now Mama wants me to do a 'speech' every week."

"Who wouldn't?" Anouk adjusted the diad beneath her scarf. "It was great. Telling Americans to do math—when did you last hear that?"

"But the party gave up on everything," she exclaimed. "Outer space development—how can you support that, when you don't even believe outer space exists?"

Anouk shrugged delicately. "I don't know. Jenny, I do know something else. I'm very near getting to the Creep."

"What? Anouk, you promised."

"I promised not to hack my friends anymore. But your friends—they dared me to do it."

"Look, the Creep is more than just the—the opposition. He's like a black hole, somewhere in the government."

"Precisely," said Anouk. "Don't you wish to know where he's gone; and why? They say he's planning a new operation. A push across the Transantarctic Mountains."

"All the more dangerous."

"As I said, I'm nearly there. What I lack is this certain handshake file, just to see the pattern." She blinked the file type over to Jenny. "Perhaps your father could locate it."

"If it's legal, any teddy could get it for you. If not—go back to Developmental Math."

Candidate Carrillo's window was blinking. "Jenny," said Anna, "I want you to be one of the first to know." One of about a hundred firsts. "My choice for future vice president is Sid Shaak."

"Congratulations." They could only hope most people voted before more scandals came out from Connecticut.

"You know, Jenny, some day it'll be your turn. You can always call on Sid and me."

After the candidate had departed, Jenny was silent. "How can I ever support Shaak?"

"It's a pity," agreed Anouk.

"How do you think such smart people like Anna and Glynnis could make such choices that so lack . . ."

"Wisdom." Anouk gave a delicate shrug. "It's a mystery. We long ago gave up expecting wisdom from *les américains*."

Jenny rolled her eyes. "Don't tell me the French are any better."

"True," she admitted. "*C'est la condition humaine*. What to do?"

A flock of starlings took flight from a naked maple. "*Sturnus vulgaris*." The birds rose and dipped, their mass swelling and flexing like a unified living thing. Like black stars they crossed the light of the north solar. Couldn't humans do better than a flock of birds? Jenny smiled at something. "Two heads. That's what the professor thinks we need."

"Just like her snake?"

"No. Like *Arabidopsis*."

At Reagan Hall, though, the professor was not in the plant lab.

"We're in the basement," Abaynesh called in Jenny's box. "Mind the doors."

The students now had to pass through three sealed doors in order to reach the basement lab, with its incessant whoosh of air. They found the professor with Mary, who was standing on a footstool with her water bottle, leaning over an earth-filled tank. There were now six separate tanks, some filled with water, others with earth. Some ultras were swimming, others growing stalks shaped like celery. All were the same yellow-brown hue, except for one celery shape that had darkened purple. Jenny's hair stood on end. "Are you sure this is . . . safe?"

"The room is sealed, and filtered, with continuous flow of anticyanide." A hiss of air sounded in the background. "So? You look like Abraham watching all the new baramins appear."

"You don't really believe in baramins?"

"Like a hole in the head," exclaimed the professor. "For the post-Flood emergence of 'kinds,' there exists not a shred of evidence on Earth. Zippo. *Nada.*" She looked away, thoughtful. "But the idea of a 'kind' that mutates fast—that's not a bad model for RNA viruses. An RNA virus like hepa Q brings 'hidden' abilities that can be released by mutation. The mutant progeny adapt to different niches in the host." She glanced at the tank of ultraphytes. "From outside Earth, the seed fell in Salt Lake. Who sent it? What was their plan? Could it perhaps make a whole new ecosystem?"

Anouk was inspecting each tank, and counting the eyespots. "Forty-three cells," she concluded. "You let them multiply?"

"Not to worry, their growth is salt limited. So let's see your *terrestrial* results."

Jenny glanced resentfully at Mary, who was getting to study ultra despite her late start at Life 101. Anouk streamed the complete record of their trials with *Arabidopsis sapiens,* the plant with the nervous system. "You see, we got them all to laugh at the inverted light spectrum. And the laugh rate declined, as you'd expect, with adaptation."

The graph marched across Jenny's toybox. Anouk had made it extra fancy, with custom colors and symbols that winked across the grid. Dr. Levi-Montalcini's tumor mouse came over to sniff.

"So you repeated the original already," observed Abaynesh. "Did you devise a new stimulus?"

"Well . . ."

Jenny said, "That's what we wanted to ask you." They had tried but could not find anything else to make the plants laugh. It was tough to imagine what would look funny to a plant.

"Actually," recalled Anouk, "there was one other thing they laughed at." Jenny gave her a look. It wasn't polite to say, with Mary right there.

"Mary helped us," Anouk said.

"Really," said the professor. "Mary, did you hear that? Can you see our data?"

"But," said Jenny, "she can't use—"

Mary's forehead wore a diad.

"I've got her to detect brainstream," the professor explained. "That is, Tovaleh got it to work. Tova downloaded a free brainware called Babynet that makes one window at a time. It shows only text, but Mary can read it."

A crude pixilated window opened. "HELLO." Primary-colored block print letters, like a baby's alphabet. "WE PLAYMATES."

"Guao." So now Mary could use a toybox. Just a window, but still.

Suddenly Mary looked up and came over. "Terrestrial life. That is what we need to study."

"Well, be patient," said the professor, "you've a lot of Life 101 to make up. Mary, why do you think the plants laughed?"

"We are still investigating this question."

"A good question," added Anouk, who was taking notes on the purple celery tower. It looked familiar—Jenny recalled seeing thousands of them, in the ToyNews from Salt Lake. "An inverted photosynthetic spectrum doesn't seem funny to me. But then, I've never understood American humor, let alone that of plants."

Jenny thought of something. "Why not show Mary an inverted *ultra* spectrum?"

Abaynesh tilted her head. "I've heard worse." She brainstreamed to the overhead light source, a panel that covered most of the ceiling. The light dimmed, then turned a dull red.

Mary looked up, and she stepped back, her tie-dyed skirt swishing around her legs. Then she began to laugh. A strange descending laughter that Jenny had never heard before. At last the laughter trailed off.

"Was it all that funny?" asked Abaynesh drily.

"Thank you very much," said Mary in Dean Kwon's voice. "We never realized how funny humans are."

"**Ultra syndrome,**" Jenny texted to Anouk. "**She thinks she's an ultra.**" If Mary were in Jerusalem, she'd be wearing a goat skin.

"Congratulations," observed the professor. "You can see how much there is to learn from plants."

"I thought your ultras were humorless," observed Anouk suspiciously.

Mary said, "We didn't understand. Of course, we have an analogous system." She added, "We can make plants with a much better sense of humor."

Anouk and Jenny exchanged startled looks.

"What did you think?" demanded Abaynesh. "That humans are the only humorous life-form in the universe? To improve the plants' humor, you have all the genetic tools. The gene sorter will make whatever DNA you need."

+·+

Tuesday morning, as expected, Anna announced her running mate. Jenny tried to ignore the news and follow-up calls on her speech, and think about Father Clare's campaign. She and Tom joined the chaplain at the Bulls' table for lunch to draw up plans. It felt odd to be sitting in the dining hall with all the red-shirted *chicos,* their scarlet diads on each forehead, their loose laces all scrambled in a heap beneath their table by the toywall, food scraps still plastered to the ceiling. She hoped none of her teammates noticed.

Fritz Hoffman blinked a sign-up form into everyone's toybox. "The first thing is to raise funds. Everyone here—get your friends and family to chip in a few bucks. We need to buy ads on Toynet Local."

Heads nodded all round. Father Clare nodded too. He seemed content to be educated on the niceties of campaigning.

"Yard signs," Fritz ticked off. "We need to print out yard signs, and get them all over campus. Print out twice as many—the opposition always steals them."

Someone laughed and made a rude noise. Hands went up to volunteer.

"**Mount Gilead,**" texted Jenny.

Fritz looked up vaguely. "Right. I suppose they have a few voters too."

"I suppose they do," agreed Father Clare.

"A speech," exclaimed Fritz, pounding the table. "We need to schedule a speech at the Powwow Ground."

"We could amp it up and reach the whole hab."

A chorus of approvals; everyone liked that. Jenny winced.

"**Message,**" she texted.

"Of course—we need a message of hope and change." Fritz turned to Father Clare. "What's our message?"

"Well, now," said Father Clare. "You're the campaign manager. What kind of message do you think will win?"

"More beer," said someone. Others laughed as if this were an enormously original remark.

Fritz pounded the table. "Grow up, men; if you want more beer, just print it out. We need a winning agenda. Change we can believe in. A new day will dawn for our fair spacehab."

Father Clare nodded. "What needs to change?"

"EMS."

Fritz snapped his fingers. "Of course: medical help. Help for Doc Uddin; she sure needs it."

"Does she ever." Heads nodded, and others murmured around the table. "That Barnside—¡*Oye!* Scary place."

"Space security," added Tom.

"Space security." Fritz looked to Father Clare. "Is that really a problem? I mean, doesn't Homeworld shield us?"

"Remember the blackout last spring, during exam week?" said Father Clare. "From a piece of junk the size of a trash can." President Chase had never mentioned that one. "Within twenty years, the odds of a catastrophic collision are even."

Fritz whistled. "This campaign could mean life or death. With that in mind, who's willing to put in time? Door to door, visit every dorm room, get out the vote."

"Mount Gilead," Jenny texted again.

"Mount Gilead." Fritz looked at Jenny and Tom. "You both are clean-cut kids. You'll look great going door to door in the Gilead."

In Jenny's toybox, the news window flashed urgently. Something important, too important to wait. She blinked to see.

Gar Guzmán hadn't waited till Wednesday to announce the Centrist running mate, as they traditionally did. Instead, he announced his own, just an hour after Sid Shaak. His handlers had timed it to bury the Unity convention and draw momentum for Gold. His choice was California governor Meg Akeda.

30

Tuesday night Jenny was up till all hours, working a heart attack at a homestead and a diabetic shock in a first-year dorm where they slept four to a room in bunk beds. The Barnside was scary, she had to agree. Rain dripped through the ceiling, and power surges reset the instruments. All the while her toybox lit up about the first conjoined person nominated for vice president, and how the governor had run a country-sized state for years without raising the house edge. Jenny thought that since she was banned from practice next morning, at least she could sleep in.

But she woke early anyway, and went out to meet Yola at the public slanball cage. The town cloud ladder was less well maintained than at the college, swaying in the wind, while the distant farms and Scioto Creek swirled above her and below. Halfway up the ladder, her toybox called.

It was Glynnis, Anna's wife, the solarray engineer who'd brought the oatmeal chocolate chip cookies and boiled the ice for the First Lady debate. Now Glynnis looked up at her from a toilet seat in a primary school restroom. "Jenny," she whispered. "Are you alone?"

A sudden gust caught the cloud ladder. The south solar swung crazily, momentarily blinding her. Her stomach heaved. "Um, yes. I'll catch you later—"

"Jenny, this is vital." Glynnis ducked her head out of the stall, then back. "I'm on in five minutes, reading *My Pet Frog* to a kindergarten class. Then an art show in Philly, to snip the ribbon for a Mapplethorpe retrospective; then back to the convention. Listen, Jenny: *How did you know?*"

Jenny swallowed. "My Centrist professor. He's connected somehow."

"More than that. All our intel said the veep would be—well, *nada más*. Now everything's up in the air. They can't replace Meg, that's for sure."

"*Claro.*"

"But what's with the Creep? Is he really done—or is it just a feint? Will he actually come out gunning the Transantarctic? Right before Election Day?"

Jenny shook her head, her eyes tearing in the wind. "I'm sorry, I don't know."

"Please," urged Glynnis. "It's vital. We've got to know how to play this. Do what you can to find out."

✦

That afternoon, she saw Professor Hamilton for her speech practice. Baramins—the model kind of worked for hepa Q, and maybe ultra. Who would have thought? A stopped clock is right twice a day.

"What a magnificent performance," he rhapsodized over her convention appearance. "Ingenious. Heart-stopping. I'll bet they wish they had ten of you."

"Then I'd be worth nothing."

He grinned. "Supply and demand; you know your economics too. Poor Aunt Meg, on the other side." He gave her a wink. "What do you think of that?" Behind him the faces of Meg and El smiled out from the picture as they shook his hand.

Jenny nodded. "Meg has been a fine governor."

"Honorable, and incorruptible," he reminded her. "Family values. Balanced budget for over a decade."

"While expanding the solarplate." There was her aunt's weakness—so smart about the present, but she ignored the ticking bomb that lay ahead. Like the Firmament, she kept her time horizon small.

Hamilton shook his head. "Jenny, Jenny," he mused. "How can any of us ever know what lies ahead? Isn't it hard enough to govern in the present? How many succeed at that? And if you manage well this year, and the next, and the years add up—isn't that what we call wise rule?"

" 'For he that can see ahead with his thought is by nature ruler and master.' "

At this bit of Aristotle, Hamilton's face lit up and he clapped his hands. "Jenny, you are the student to die for. You've hit the nail on the head. If only you were up there yourself on the ticket—which of course someday you will be. Still—" A sly note crept in. "Don't you feel just a bit bad, to leave your own aunt out there without help? Couldn't you give her equal time—just five minutes of convention time on behalf of your aunt?"

"That's the most absurd thing I ever—" She stopped. Her head tilted. "The Centrist convention?"

"Why not?"

"Could I say—that is, text—whatever I want?"

He shrugged. "How could we stop you?"

Her head was spinning. It was utterly crazy. And yet . . . Her eyes narrowed. "Why would I ever do such a thing?"

He shrugged again. "You tell me."

Jenny was silent, her thoughts racing. "What happened to the Creep?"

"You promise? Five minutes?"

"I will text five minutes for Aunt Meg at the Centrist convention."

He nodded. "The vice president has a problem. He won't be seen in public again."

"But— If something happened to the president—"

"Arrangements have been made."

Jenny thought this over. The silence lengthened. "How do I know it's true?"

"I've given my word. I value my reputation."

At the dining hall, Jenny sat with the team but barely heard about the new plays, her mind still working out the notion of this Centrist speech. Could she use it to advantage; make a statement about the Firmament?

"Next Sunday, we host the Beijing Tigers. Last year was at China's spacehab, the Great Wall."

"*Hombre,* their teamwork rocks."

"After that, two away games. Upload your suitcase."

Charlie touched her arm. "Jenny?"

She startled. "Yes, I heard." Ken was still sidelined, and that weekend half the team would be out for Yom Kippur. That Saturday was also the Frontera Circuit; and that night, the Ferrari celebration, Monte Carlo Night at the Mound. A big night for EMS—and then Sunday against Beijing. *Qué desastre.*

At her side, Charlie nodded at a student across the table. "**What happened to him?**"

The sophomore's scalp was nearly bald, his face mottled white, his eyes half closed. "**Ebola, last year.**" The virus printed out easily, in the common toyrooms of the frogs' dorms where they slept six to a room. Strains with no vaccine, hackers scrambled their gene sequence and sent them out. With prompt treatment one survived. If not caught early, the virus liquefied the internal organs. You could end up with brain damage, wasted muscles, and hair loss. Rehab was long and costly.

"Jenny, I've been thinking," Charlie said. "I'd like to train for the squad."

"*¡Excelente!* Check in with Doc Uddin. The training course is intense." She well recalled her course in high school.

"I know, but it's good for premed."

"You can come out on my calls any time."

What would they all think if they knew what she did about the Creep? If it were true. But what exactly had become of him?

After dinner Anouk sidled over. "Remember, *chérie*, you will accompany me to the Monte Carlo Night."

Jenny shook her head. "Sorry, I'll be tied up with the squad."

Mary approached as well, trying to be social. She was always tagging after Jenny or Anouk, in lab or out.

"But Jenny, you promised. Remember, I went with you to the Bulls' pig roast."

She remembered all too well. "I want *nada más* with motor clubs. You can bring Berthe."

"Berthe is staying home."

Surprised, Jenny looked up. "Why?"

"DIRGs are not *chulo*."

"Rafael didn't mind. Why not go with him?"

Anouk tossed her head. Her scarf was particularly cute, golden tree frogs climbing a branch. "This time, I wish to make a different impression. I wish to arrive on my own, with you."

"As your DIRG?"

She drew herself up with dignity. "As my sister."

Jenny sighed. "Okay, I can go for a few minutes." She could use the chance to play her taxes at the Mound. "But you know, Rafael may think I'm your date."

Anouk's eyes flew open. She considered this overlooked possibility. "*Enfin*, so be it. A little jealousy is good for a man; it builds character."

Mary had been listening, her eyes fixed on one, then the other. Her eyes rarely blinked, but Jenny had gotten used to that. "We will come too. We are sisters."

Anouk let out a French expression. "No way she will come. She's not invited."

"Why not? They always want more *chicas*."

Anouk thought this over. "Very well, but she will NOT wear that same old tie-dyed dress. She'll wear what I print out for her."

Jenny asked Mary, "Will you let Anouk print you a dress?"

"Thank you very much," said Dean Kwon's voice.

Jenny eyed Anouk's dress, which matched her scarf, a flowing sheath with one golden frog climbing to the shoulder. "Could you print one for me too?"

Anouk beamed and caught her hand. "With pleasure."

Jenny took Mary's hand as well. "Just call us the sisters *Arabidopsis*."

Wednesday morning after Hamilton's class, Jenny and Tom walked the road out toward the town. "I don't know, Tom." Jenny wore her EMS pin and scanscope, while Tom wore his Homefair toolbelt and hard hat. They both wore power bands on their calves, to donate for charity. They could appeal to the town as contributing citizens. "I just can't talk to all these strangers." She had always worked the back room, tying balloons and writing thank-yous.

"You talk all the time with patients," he reminded her.

"That's different. That's not conversation; it's a medical test. I ask their name; their response shows long-term memory. I ask who's the president; their response shows short-term memory." She half smiled. "The older folks sometimes tell me *I* am." Those who recalled Rosa's term.

"Well, let me do the talking. Your EMS pin will gain respect. Remember, they're used to women who don't talk. Just text and keep your head down."

Indignant, Jenny pulled away. "I will *not* pretend I'm a pauline."

"I didn't mean it that way, I—"

"You think I'm a pauline like Leora," she insisted. "You and everyone else."

"Not at all. It's just that—" He swallowed and tried to explain. "Some paulines are actually more like you. More than you might think."

For practice, they stopped first at Sherri-Lyn's place. The amyloid cottage was owned by an established family, who generously let the new colonist and her children stay in their sitting room until their Homefair house was done.

"You're in luck," Sherri-Lyn told them, "I'm just heading out for my shift at Lazza's. Hey, Jenny, we've missed you."

"Thanks. How's the build?"

Sherri-Lyn wiped her hands on her overalls. "Down to the punch list. Right, Tom?"

"You bet. Say, we're here supporting Father Clare for mayor. Any questions?"

Jenny said, "I've got a flyer I can stream to you."

"No need. You've got my vote for sure."

"Thanks." Tom asked, "What about your host family?"

She hesitated a split second. "Sure, you know Sarah; she delivers the meals with Leora."

Jenny recognized Sarah from her one day at the Homefair build. Sarah came over leading a mini-horse with a child astride. She wore riding boots and jeans, her hair capped.

"Good morning," said Tom. "That baked ham was a great lunch last Saturday."

"You're welcome."

"We're here supporting Father Clare for mayor. Any questions?"

Sarah looked uncertainly at Tom, then Jenny.

"I can stream you a flyer."

"Yes, thanks."

"Father Clare supports more medical help, and space security. Did you know Homeworld Security cut back their coverage?"

Sarah turned to her child, and patted the horse on the rump. "The Lord will provide these things, if we honor creation."

They stopped by two more families before winding up in the town square by the courthouse, amyloid red brick with a square clock tower, shaded by a naked oak tree. The courthouse was where they all had to go to vote. Jenny eyed the edifice curiously. "Why on Earth would everyone have to hike to one place just to vote?" They all had a toybox.

Tom shrugged. "This isn't Earth."

Jenny half smiled. "It's 'Ohio.'" Ohio was notorious for its political idiosyncrasies, and for the absurd amount of special treatment it got as the ultimate swing state. "But is it fair to the students away on break? Aren't they disenfranchised? There ought to be a court challenge."

Tom said, "That's so English." "English" was what he called the non-Amish. "Students can vote; they just need to get their return flight a few hours early."

The tower clock read half past noon, and the pigeons crowded so thick

Jenny had to shove them aside with her foot. She walked past the Smythe Power Bank, where colonists lined up to connect their bands and bank their energy. She looked up at Lazza's. The town diner looked larger than she remembered. At least two floors of amyloid had been erected behind, dwarfing the original storefront. A window popped up: *"Lazza Hotel and Conference Center welcomes America's candidates."* The diner was preparing for Frontera's presidential debate.

Inside the diner, the tables were full, so she and Tom sat on stools at the bar. Jenny eyed the antlered deer head. "Not sure how much good we're doing."

"It can't hurt," said Tom. "With so few votes, even one could make a difference."

"That's true even for the whole country." The last two presidents had turned on less than a hundred votes. How could that be? It seemed improbable statistically. "But here, Father Clare could reach every voter himself. Why doesn't he?"

"He wants us students to do everything," said Tom. "I wonder if that's why he ran."

A loud cough at Jenny's ear. Leora had taken the seat next to her. It was Wednesday, the day the mayor's widow came.

Jenny exchanged a look with Tom.

"Excuse me." Tom got up and headed for the restroom.

"Campaigning?"

Leora didn't miss much, Jenny realized. "We're informing voters about Father Clare. Father Clare supports medical help, and hab security. Preventing disasters, like the flood."

Leora adjusted the diad beneath her bonnet. "You know both men well."

That was true, Jenny realized. Had Hamilton bragged about his Ramos Kennedy student? "One is my professor, the other my pastor."

"Which is the better man? The better Christian?"

Jenny's throat constricted. This was not at all what she was prepared to answer. "We're campaigning on issues. Father Clare's plan will make our community safer."

"Plans are made to be broken. The better man must win." Leora turned and looked her in the eye. "You know them both. Which is the better man?"

Her pulse raced. All is fair in war and politics. "Hamilton had this." She streamed the image of the Z token she'd seen on the professor's desk.

31

Jenny's convention appearance for her aunt was scheduled for Thursday noon, before Life lab. She felt less nervous than she expected; it was just five minutes, after all.

At the sight of her, Clive swallowed and flexed his hands. "Isn't there some mistake?"

"I'm on the schedule."

"The schedule keeps changing. It's full of errors." He added helpfully, "This is the Centrist convention."

The convention chair came over to shake her hand, holding a bunch of gold balloons, a big grin on his face.

The full impact hit Clive. "Hairstyle twenty-six," he called out. "And get me the commentators. We'll need a full instant analysis." Then she was on. "ToyNews—From our box to yours."

Jenny took a deep breath. **"I'm here to congratulate my Aunt Meg and Aunt El, on Meg's selection as candidate for vice president. If you traveled all the stars of the Milky Way, you couldn't find better aunts anywhere. Meg and El are the ones I can always count on in a pinch. Meg runs the great state of California, which funds research on how ultraphytes move their genes into pile worms."** The governor probably didn't realize that, Jenny thought with a smile. **"If only she saw our future as part of the universe, she'd be the greatest. I sure wish she were on our side. If she were, she'd have my vote."**

Jenny had to rush to catch Life lab. Rushing was a mistake, for she took the wrong corridor in the postmodern maze of Reagan Hall, ending up somehow in Physical Science.

A physics professor, Zhi-Li Zhang, an egg-shaped man with scant hair, looked up from his bench. "Can I show you our museum?" He waved her over insistently. "An analog device: a broadband radiowave communicator." He twisted a screwlike dial; the machine emitted pops and squeals. "An ancient eyeglass laser projector, straight onto your retina—the first ever made, fifty years old. An Amymax amyloid printer, resolution point-five centimeters, no color; eighty years old . . ." On the wall an old poster of Hari Seldon, the fictional psycho predictor; every campaign had their own "Seldon" now. "The first brainstream device, a game of Pong. Look, Pong!" The physicist stared. A bright white bar moved slowly up and down a black screen.

"Um, thanks, but . . ." Another crazy professor. "Could you please just show me to Life lab?"

"Certainly. A right, then a left, then bear right to the end of the hall."

The other students had already started. The lab was about an "RNA switch," a bit of roller-coaster twisted RNA that could open a DNA helix and change how its gene was read. It could turn on genes to make neurons grow in a certain direction, to activate the laugh module. The RNAs were printed out by a device a thousand times more precise than the printer in Jenny's sitting room. Solutions of RNA were suspended in bulbs with long tubes that hung down. The tubes attached to a delivery device, like a miniature scanscope for the *Arabidopsis* plant. The device delivered the RNA into the plant neurons.

"Now the RNA switch responds to a 'semiochemical.' A chemical signal." Abaynesh squirted an atomizer near the plant. The plant shook with laughter.

Anouk asked, "Does the semiochemical make the plant laugh even though nothing is funny?"

The professor shook her head. "The RNA switch acts as an amplifier. It amplifies something the plant already detects as funny." No sign of what that could be, unless it had to do with Mary, who kept near the professor. Mary's one makeshift window appeared in Jenny's box. "PARTNERS."

Jenny sighed resignedly. "Yes, we are lab partners."

"What use is this semiochemical?" asked another student, a diehard premed. "What else can plants do besides laugh?"

A light blinked in Jenny's box. It was her mother's window. Jenny blinked to wait. She would have to answer after class.

Another student was asking how the cells were selected, and how the neurons fit together. This was explained in the paper by Ng and Howell, who Jenny had visited in San Francisco in the toyroom. She never understood more than a fraction of what went on in this introductory lab.

Her mother's light blinked faster, urgent. Jenny frowned. It must be urgent indeed to interrupt her class. She stepped out into the hall.

As soon as Soledad appeared in her window, she let out a breath. "Jenny, what have you done? Are you *totalmente loca*?"

"What is it, Mama? I'm in the middle of class."

"You went to the Centrist convention and endorsed the Gold ticket!"

"I did not. I just congratulated your cousin."

Soledad rolled her eyes. "What were you thinking? Look."

Clive popped up, his hairstyle modified for post-event commentary. "To recap, the big news of the convention is that Jenny Ramos Kennedy showed up for the Gold ticket, to vote for her aunt the California governor—"

"But I said no such thing. I talked about the universe, and about ultra-phytes."

"I explained to you, *hija mia*, that what you say makes no difference. A convention is all about symbolism. You showed up—it was the only unscripted event all week."

"But what I said is all there in text."

"Text? Who reads that?"

"How could he report the exact opposite of—"

"Because now you're *adulta*, understand?" Soledad glared, her voice falling to a whisper. "There are unwritten rules for children. But for adults, anything goes. All you can do is hold it over their head, to refuse to talk next time. But then, besides Clive who else is there?"

Clive was Toynet, and Toynet was everywhere. Toynet reported first; and they made sure all independents got the news a few seconds later. It was Clive here, Clive there, and virtual Clive for the local news.

"Who put you up to this?" her mother demanded. "It was Dylan, wasn't it; his Teddy class."

"No, Mama, absolutely not."

"He will hear about this. Well, keep your head down and let the news cycle out. Just remember: Keep out of trouble, from now till Election Day."

Dylan was in his toyroom with Senior Staff, facing no end of grim news. Orin Crawford shifted his weight around the oak desk in his spliced slice of office. "Rapture's put in a bid for the Mound," he growled. "They want to buy us out—a branch campus."

Rapture's Holyland was five times the size of the Mound, hugely popular, second only to Towers. They'd had their eye on heathen Frontera for the past year. "We're a private college," Dylan assured Orin. "And the Shawnee will never sell."

"Private," said Orin, "but are we solvent? Our insurance rate's quadrupled," he added. "Thanks to Homeworld Security's cutback."

That rate would eat up half Frontera's student fees. "I'll fix it with Homeworld," Dylan promised. Since Gil wouldn't, he was working down the list of Board members.

Nora Kwon had two students on the ropes. "Nick Petherbridge," she told him. "Third violation." Dylan's favorite assistant, a model taxplayer, pillar of Doc Uddin's squad. And, like so many medics, a chronic abuser of the scanscope.

"Do his parents know?"

"We informed them under FERPA."

Dylan sighed. "Third time you're out." He ached for Nick, a great kid ruined by a habit.

"And then," Nora added, "there's Mary Dyer." The salt-drinking Long Beach refugee with ultra syndrome. "She has no parents to contact. She's just not going to make it, not in the regular way. She's barely hanging on in two courses, Life and Politics."

"Interesting." Helen drummed her fingers. "Those aren't easy courses."

Dylan asked Nora, "Is there a . . . nonregular way?"

"Sharon wants to keep Mary half-time in class, and half-time on her research."

It was unlike Sharon to support a failing student. Dylan exchanged a look with Helen. He knew what she was thinking. If the arrangement kept them both out of trouble, why not.

Only Luis Herrera Smith brought good news. "Applications are up twenty percent," the admissions director reported from his recruiting trip in Kathmandu. Behind him rose the Trans Himalayas, brown-gray mountain slopes topped with some of the world's few remaining snowcaps.

"Congratulations on your op-ed," called Zari at her desk, handing one of her teddies a Phaistos disk. Luis had outdone himself in *The New York Times*, arguing for acceptance of DIRGs and mentals as applicants on the same basis as human beings. Innate "humanness" is immeasurable, Luis argued; thus, all that counts is ability, whether human or not. The piece, cleverly designed to be half serious and highly provocative, had scored a full-length interview with Clive, plus the attention of parents and students everywhere.

In Dylan's toybox Soledad's window lit up. He'd have to take it later.

"Quade, what's the state of the hab?"

Quade appeared in overalls and power bands, out at some building project. "We put out salt traps for stray ultra," he said. "In various locations of all the major ecotypes: stream, forest, underground, solar end—"

"And did you catch anything?"

"Only the salt-loving student." One guess who that would be. "Meanwhile, the Flood preparedness program is getting under way."

"*¿Perdón?*" Dylan took a closer look at whatever it was Quade was building. A crude platform with crossed planks of carboxyplast.

"In the event of substratum overflow," the ecoengineer explained, "the human population can escape on lifeboats built by the Homefair volunteers. But where will all the animals go?"

"Outstanding," muttered Dylan beneath his breath.

"The elephants, the deer, the cattle." Quade ticked off the minis. "With only a few feet of water, we just need a raft and a ramp for the beasts to climb up. Then we can ferry them to higher ground at the north solar."

"Quade, wherever would we store such a contraption? The chance of a so-called flood is negligible. It's just not our brand."

Nora was nodding in sympathy. "Just another structure to avoid getting vandalized."

"An 'attractive nuisance,'" agreed Orin. "Another thing to raise our insurance rate."

"Actually . . ." Luis put one hiking boot in front of the other, as he peered into Quade's spliced section for a better look. "The ark—that *is* our brand. Isn't Frontera the ark for an endangered Earth?"

Dylan's pulse shot up, and he saw others tense.

"The ark of education," Luis intoned. "We could theme a whole brochure."

As soon as he got out, Dylan blinked Soledad's window. "*¿Qué pasa?* Quite a convention."

"Don't tell me about the convention." Soledad glowered, as enraged as he could remember seeing her. "What have you done to my daughter?"

He lifted his hands. "*¡Oye!* What's wrong?"

"That *loco* appearance with the opposition. You put her up to this, I know you. You and your Teddy."

"What's Teddy got to do with it? Teddy would have joined Unity, you know that—"

"All your liberal arts *tontería*." Soledad's Wall Street side came out at times. "Values relativism. Consider all sides, no matter how stupid."

"Soli, students get their own ideas. They need to think things through for themselves."

Her eyes narrowed and she jabbed a finger at him. "I know my daughter. I know someone put her up to this."

Dylan bit his tongue. Hamilton was known for "turning" liberal students; a sociology major switched to Aristotle, or a Peace Corps volunteer suddenly joined the CIA. But no one could put a finger on him. All's fair in the war of ideas. And no matter how controversial, Dylan had to protect his faculty. "Soli, maybe you're right. Maybe Teddy led her astray. Look, I'll have a talk with her."

Soledad breathed, still glowering at him.

"Did you know she's campaigning for Clare, for mayor?" he recalled. "With the student Unity Club, canvassing Mount Gilead."

"Indeed. Well, get your house in order. The presidential debate will be here before you know it. I'll be up next week with ToyDebate."

"With DIRGs again?" ToyDebate's DIRGS had combed the hab all last summer, evaluating the proposed presidential debate site. But now, after mosquitoes, and ultra, DIRGs were just not the Frontera brand.

"What do you think, with both candidates and their entourage coming up next month?"

Then it clicked. "What about our space protection? Did you know Homeworld cut us down to ninety-six?"

Soledad was highly math literate. "That's a death sentence."

"Exactly. What will your candidates think of that?"

"We'll fix it. The triple-A standard, ninety-nine point nine nine percent. Through Election Day. After that—" She shook her head. "It's a death sentence for us all, if we lose this election. Don't let my daughter forget it."

That evening, Dylan sank into the black suede couch and picked an apple from the bowl. "If I were a betting man, which I am, I'd give a whole lot better odds for our hab." He took another apple and offered it to Clare.

Clare took the apple. "So? To whom do we owe our good fortune?"

"Soledad will get our security raised." He took a bite and munched.

Nothing cleared the head of a day's troubles like the juice of a fresh apple. "For the candidates, of course."

"Of course."

Dylan chewed thoughtfully. "You know, you could put this out for your own campaign. Your accomplishment for the hab."

"Not a chance."

"Why not?"

"Because I had nothing to do with it."

Dylan nodded with satisfaction. "You're so hot when you're pure."

Clare punched him in the arm.

"So how's it going?" Elephants hadn't come up in the last Senior Staff; a good sign, the students were buckling down to work.

Clare chewed thoughtfully. "Two more lifeboats."

Dylan groaned. "Okay, so you won that one. Save the animals. Bring on the ark." Overhead, the Sistine ceiling cycled into the Flood. The Flood was one of Michelangelo's most complex scenes, with the most intense emotions, yet also the most problematic artistically. The doomed victims climbing ashore looked more like they were riding an escalator than clambering up a bank. And the "ark" was a nondescript square box, with a dove in the window while human victims tried to raise a ladder. "At least make sure it looks like one. Michelangelo drew only one thing really well, and it wasn't shipping."

Suddenly a window blew open half his toybox. A burst of light, a bleached-out view of a gigantic figure, like God in some Biblical toyworld. The apple fell from Dylan's hand. Actually, there was just an outsized man in dark glasses, hands clasped upon a gigantic desk. Behind him, nothing; a plain, unmarked room, its very emptiness signaling menace.

"Dylan?" Clare tapped his arm, but he barely noticed.

"President Chase." The anonymous man spoke in a flat monotone. "It has come to our attention that someone from your college has attempted unauthorized entry to the vice presidential toyspace."

"Yes," said Dylan, clearing his throat. "That is, yes, if that is the case, we must certainly—"

"This will be your first and final warning."

"Of course. We will put a stop to any further unauthorized access attempts."

Clare's jaw tightened. "She must have slipped," he guessed. "We thought she was doing so well."

32

Jenny tried to reach Clive, but all she got was an android assistant, a Toynet construct.

"What is your news event, Ms. Ramos Kennedy?"

"I did *not* come out for the Centrist ticket. You must place a correction."

"Your convention speeches are no longer news," the assistant told her. "They are history."

"But you got it wrong. Correct the record."

"You could make a new speech, and we'd cover it, but your support for Unity would hardly be worth covering."

Frustrated, she browsed through the independent reporters who got perhaps a hundredth the audience of ToyNews. HuriaNews, out of Minneapolis; a one-person show, a reporter-announcer who did her own hair. A woman Jenny didn't know; had never met.

For a moment she froze. Looking aside, she counted to ten, and tried to remember the brain exercises she'd done with Hamilton. "I want to give you a story," Jenny said carefully. "To set the record straight."

The HuriaNews reporter, Lane Mfumo, listened sympathetically. "Look, I'd love to do a story on Jenny Kennedy any day." Her lip curved. "Of course, HuriaNews won't get the coverage worth your time."

"It's better than nothing. If you help me, I'll help you build audience."

Mfumo frowned dubiously. "Warmed-over convention rhetoric. Was there anything you said with a hook?" She scanned Jenny's short speech. "What's this about ultraphytes moving genes into pile worms?"

"I just tossed that out, for people to think about." As if they wanted to think.

"Is it really true?" The reporter paused in thought. "Ultraphytes putting genes into worms. Does that mean they can transform Earth creatures into ultraphytes?"

Jenny thought this over. "I guess you could say that. The worms would be part ultra. That's not new; it's in the literature, from Semerena's lab."

"Maybe, but it's the first I've heard it put that way. Interesting. Why don't you give me a piece on ultra-worms? You can use the chance to set your record straight."

✦✦

Friday morning she was back at slanball, prepping for Sunday's game hosting Beijing. She browsed for her piece on HuriaNews. It came up, exactly what she'd told Mfumo, about number hundred thousand down the headline list.

That afternoon she worked with Mary on the plants in her cottage greenhouse. Their homework was to make the plant laughter respond to an RNA switch detecting an airborne semiochemical. The students had to inoculate different RNA switches into different seedlings. Where was Anouk, Jenny wondered; the *parisienne* was normally punctual.

In her toybox Anouk's window opened. "Sorry I'll be late. I'm in trouble," she explained. "I got caught tapping you-know-who."

Jenny rolled her eyes. "Just stop already. You know it's no good."

"I won't get caught again. Jenny—this means life or death for your American election. If only people knew the truth . . ." A lot of good that would do.

Mary held up the vial of RNA switch. The pale violet tube had been printed out by Professor Abaynesh's machine. "RNA switch for *Arabidopsis sapiens*. Turned on by jasmonate." Jasmonate was a common plant semiochemical; some kinds were used for pest control. If the RNA switch worked, a whiff of jasmonate would "turn on" the plant laughter.

Jenny took out the plant injector, a flexible tube that fitted to the RNA vial. "Here, we need to inject twenty of these plants." Twenty replicates of the scrawny little mustard plants; she felt tired of them already. "And then another twenty for controls." If only she could do orchids instead. Mary did not seem to mind all the replicates. A good lab partner, she worked alongside Jenny, dutifully injecting all the plants.

At last the seedlings were done. The accelerated strain would grow up in a week. She stretched her back, then pulled up one leg and the other, loosening her stiff calves.

"Twenty more seedlings."

Jenny frowned at Mary. "Really? What for?"

"Reverse control."

"Reverse control? What does that mean?"

"Experiments need a reverse control."

Jenny blinked her window for Abaynesh to ask what her *compañera loca* was getting at. But the professor did not respond. It was late afternoon; she was probably picking up Tova for dinner. Jenny shrugged. "Be my guest," she told Mary, and put out twenty extra pots.

✦✦

Before dinner Jenny stopped at the Café de la Paix to help Tom slice carrots. She had to have Friday dinner with her team, but she had a free moment now, and would again later after closing. Tom in his white coat and *toque* was carving turnips into roses. *"Guao,"* said Jenny, "you could carve anything."

He placed one in her hand. "Did you see Semerena on ToyNews?"

"Really?" Annoyed at Clive, she'd quit browsing ToyNews. She blinked for the morning clip. There was Clive, spliced next to Swiss-born chemist Wolf Semerena, who taught down the hall from Abaynesh. Long sandy hair in a ponytail, hunched forward slightly, in a "Devil's Tramping Ground" T-shirt from his stint at North Carolina.

"Dr. Semerena," Clive was asking ingratiatingly. Hairstyle twelve, she guessed, the one for "We've discovered something." Clive asked, "Can you describe for us your new finding on ultra?" A finding buried in the research literature for two years.

"Sofort," agreed the professor. "The ultraphyte gene sequence into the genome reading frame of numerous coding sequences of *Neanthes succinea* becomes integrated." His Swiss-accented southern English was intelligible with effort. "Of course, the sequence integration requires RNA conversion to DNA by an ultra-encoded ribonucleic acid transfer-integrase."

Clive nodded intelligently. "In other words, ultraphytes can turn Earth creatures into ultra?"

Jenny looked at Tom. "That's what HuriaNews said." No credit for the source.

Tom smiled. "It's nice for Semerena. A plug for his research."

"Claro. I'm looking forward to his class next term."

"So, you'll be back for dessert?"

"Unless EMS gets busy." Jenny was first on call, the one night she didn't have to get up early. "Then Saturday you've got Homefair, and I've got optional practice with Yola." The team would be short, with Ken and the Pezarkars out for Yom Kippur. "It's always something."

Tom grinned. "That's what we're here for. At least I'll see you for dinner Saturday."

Jenny winced. "Sorry, I promised Anouk I'd go with her to Monte Carlo Night. Instead of her DIRG."

His face fell. He pulled back, about to close into himself. "Never mind. Of course, you need your First Lady."

Dios mío, he's jealous, she thought. "It's not like that." Anouk was *chula* all right; the sort of First Lady her handlers would pick, minus the mental baggage. "Anouk is my sister. We even have to take Mary."

He looked up. "Mary Dyer? Is that wise?"

"What do you mean?"

"Mary . . . doesn't always follow what's going on."

"We'll look out for her. I'll bring my own drink; and Mary drinks only salt. Look, I'll just stay long enough to play my taxes. Then I'll come back to the café for dessert."

Saturday afternoon was *un lío* with all the motor cars roaring around the track at the Frontera Circuit. The circuit ringed the northern cap, beyond the Mound, just below Lake Erie. The track was dry and dusty, as the rain had been turned off for the past week; something about the fall harvest. Jenny missed the daily afternoon rainbows.

Four visiting clubs from Paris, Rio, Santa Monica, and Mare Crisium brought their Renaults, BMWs, and Toyotas, the low-slung cars gunning their motors to make as deep a roar as they could. Frontera's lead drivers were Fritz Hoffman in his padded Red Bull suit, and Rafael in sleek black. They waved to a screaming crowd of lace-dragging students, neon-feathered tourists, and what looked to be the entire male population of Mount Gilead.

"What a track—none of those tiresome chicanes."

"Feh—no test of a real driver."

"Nothing but raw speed."

"At half a g—watch your spin."

The track rose up into the curve of the cap, about three hundred meters off radius; not quite half a g, but you felt the difference.

Rafael drove up into pole position, based on Ferrari's winning season the year before. Soon all the cars zoomed by, careening around the curves, especially those unaccustomed to low g. All went well until the inevitable first crackup, a BMW spun out of control.

Jenny and the medibot converged on the scene; Charlie tagged along, his first run as a trainee. Fumes of melted amyloid choked her. "**Mask up**," she warned.

The window frame had crumpled; no way the door would open. Breathing through her mask, Jenny eyed the door. Point, point, she selected, then blinked the virtual "jaws of life." The amyloid picked up her brainstream, melting through the lines from point to point. The crumpled door separated like a jigsaw piece. She began to lift; it came up an inch, then Charlie added his weight.

"What's your name?" No response from the driver. He was breathing, though the blood pooled around him. Jenny gave a quick glance at Charlie, to see how he took it. Charlie looked *bien*. She went ahead and scoped the driver. "Charlie, can you get his legs out?" At length they extricated the driver, flew off with the medibot, and introduced him to the amenities of the Barnside.

She and Charlie had scarcely returned to the track when another car skidded into the lake. After the third crackup, Frank Lazza finally took over. Jenny returned to her cottage exhausted, and fell asleep in an instant.

She was awakened by a call from Anouk. "Rafael won again!" Anouk was flushed with excitement. "You should have seen—he beat the Brazilian by half a car length. Are you ready for the Mound?"

Jenny blinked the Babynet window for Mary. She and Mary soon arrived at Anouk's cottage for the great fashion debut. For her own outfit, Anouk had outdone herself in a dress that fell from her shoulder like a waterfall. It covered all her body, from neck to ankle, but the fabric flexed with every curve. Her silken scarf flowed around her hair, then over her shoulder and down to her waist. The scarf's color shifted continuously, timed through a rainbow of greens, pinks, and golds.

Anouk pointed to Jenny's feet. "*Enfin*, off with those horrid laced things."

Jenny felt disoriented, the scenes of mangled amyloid still spinning through her head. But things changed as she let Anouk slide silver ballet flats onto her feet. Then a sheath of silver enveloped her, with orchids parading up to her shoulder, a never-ending line of unique cultivars. A silvery scarf that made her look bundled up for winter; yet the fabric was so thin, it felt like nothing, like being draped in sheer light. In the toyroom Jenny watched as her silvery form turned slowly around. She smiled. "Mama should see this."

For Mary, Anouk had done a white sheath with sunflowers, a wholesome country-girl look. With all else covered, from feet to hood, Mary's face shone.

"*Merveilleuse*," breathed Anouk. "She looks . . ."

A timeless face. Almost Monroe.

"You're quite prepared?"

"Of course." Jenny had her drink and her scanscope in her purse.

Outside, Rafael drew up silently in his car, polished like a mirror. The three dresses glinted in its sheen.

"Congratulations," Jenny told him.

Rafael stood as straight as possible and bowed from the waist. "A close finish, but we honored Frontera. And now, the honor of three enchanting ladies."

Mary tripped on her dress, but Jenny helped her up and into the car. Anouk sat up front and chattered away in French with Rafael. The car glided effortlessly up Buckeye Trail, steam puffing out the exhaust. There at the north end glittered the entrance to the Mound, pyrotechnic red, blue, and green. Attendants handed a glowing feather to each guest.

"**Entering Mound Security zone. Toynet worldwide access closed. What happens at the Mound, stays at the Mound.**"

Jenny's windows all abruptly shuttered, save for Mary and Anouk, and the Mound security and game stations. Casinos always discouraged outside distractions. The Mound was entirely underground, no windows, and every tenth person would be plainclothes. Overhead pounded the hooves of flying horses, their Shawnee riders calling to battle. Below, Ferrari brothers strutted in their black suits and XX earrings, as did their black-suited guests from their brother clubs at other schools. Many Begonias had come, along with unfamiliar *chicas* from the other schools, most in moonholes and midriffs. But heads turned for the three scarved ladies. New windows popped up, begging acquaintance. Like magic, suited young gentlemen approached with punch and margaritas.

Enrico, from Hamilton's class, offered a glass. "Perrier," he assured her.

Jenny smiled, accepting the drink. She casually set it down, replacing it with the vial from her purse, which morphed into a glass. She held the new glass covered by her hand, a trick long practiced in high school.

"Your speech was *estupendo*," Enrico told her. "I sure wish your aunt were at the top of the ticket."

That would have been tough, all right. But at this point, Aunt Meg was lucky enough to be the country's first conjoined running mate. More than luck, of course, knowing her aunt.

"Aristotle is *chulo*, don't you think?" Enrico added. "Even the 'History of Animals,' about sponges and all. 'With animals a change of action follows a change of circumstance, and a change of character follows a change of action.' I never knew that, how hens could behave like cocks and so on."

Jenny nodded. "All politics is a field of animal behavior."

"Do you think so? I'd like to take a Life class sometime."

She scanned the betting stations. The blackjack table, with the cards laid out in a pie wedge. Anouk's eyes gleamed, and she headed for the table, trailing Rafael behind her. Jenny took Mary by the hand.

"Looking for something?" asked Enrico.

"Roulette."

Enrico nodded. "The purest game of all. Nothing clever; it's all between you and Providence." He steered her to the table, a crowded spot. The wheel itself was obscured by all the guests leaning over and laughing at where the ball came to rest.

As the wheel came to a halt, Jenny eyed a number. The window came up in her box, and she blinked to brainstream her bet.

Behind the table, the croupier looked up. "May I help you?"

She looked him in the eye. "I placed my bet." Fifty thousand dollars, her "optional" quarterly play.

"*Momento.*" The dealer stepped behind and brought forward the manager, a short dark-haired man with an obsequious air.

"No trouble, no trouble, Ms. Ramos Kennedy," murmured the manager. "You may place your bet."

The crowd fell silent. Some of their faces showed they'd never seen a bet of this size, whereas others smirked as if to say this was nothing new to them. The wheel turned, faster, its numbers spinning out of sight. The ball rolled the other way, gradually slowing, until the numbers passed one by one. The ball fell at last, just one slot past the number Jenny had picked. The crowd gasped.

"So close, so close," observed the manager admiringly. "You're welcome again any time, Ms. Ramos Kennedy."

Jenny shrugged. Her tax was played, done till the next quarter. She moved on, Mary in tow, ignoring the other suits. She wandered back toward the blackjack table, wondering how soon it would be polite to leave.

At the blackjack table, Anouk and Rafael were no longer there. Of course, Anouk would not have stayed long with the low rollers. The higher stakes would be played in a more discreet location. Jenny blinked Anouk's window.

"**Here I am, this way.**" A red pathway stretched ahead of her toybox.

"Mary, this way." Jenny followed the path where it turned out into a quiet corridor. The Shawnee were gone, the ceiling dark. The pathway turned at a side door. The door was ajar, with light streaming out.

As she pushed the door in, Jenny saw three suited *chicos* at a pool table. She suddenly wondered how she knew that the generic message had actually come from Anouk.

+++

Jenny found herself lying on the floor. Her eyes felt like lead as she forced her lids open. Her dress was torn down to her waist; how had that happened? She could not remember where she was, nor how she'd got there. Catching the pool table, she pulled herself up. Where was everyone? Why were all the windows gone in her toybox?

Mary leaned back against the table, the hood draping from her tilted head. In her arms she held the suited body of a *chico*, his head hanging limp.

At the sight Jenny scrambled up and dragged herself over to look. The unconscious victim was still breathing, rapid shallow breaths. His skin was unnaturally pink. *Mangled amyloid . . . get him out of the car.* Jenny shook herself. This wasn't the track; she was indoors. Where?

"Humans are dying," observed Mary.

"*Dios mío*, what happened?"

"Our stress response."

"Lay him on the floor, *por favor.*" Where was her EMS button, and all the rest of her windows? Jenny grabbed her purse from the floor and pulled out her scanscope.

The student's face was pink, his neck flushed. Blood trickled from his scalp where he must have hit something as he fell. The blood was bright scarlet, the opposite of cyanosis. So it wasn't nitrate poisoning. Yet the *chico* could barely breathe.

On a hunch, Jenny took the cross from around her neck. She snapped it open and took out the cyanide antidote she always carried, like the day before college when the ultra got the squirrel. She pressed the vial to his neck.

"Humans are beautiful," Mary added. "And poisonous."

The door opened, and two DIRGs came in. Mound Security. How on earth had she got to the Mound?

33

Dylan sat in his office, not the place he'd hoped to be on a Sunday morning, with the southern light just a glimmer. He'd spent most of Saturday on a campaign retreat with major donors, then read tenure dossiers on postvirtualist Shakespeare and premillenarian theology. His hoped-for cozy evening with Clare had instead been spent visiting crash patients at the Barnside and chemical assault victims from the Mound, and reassuring all their anxious parents on Earth. Soli's daughter, a week before Soli brought up the debate advance team; *qué lío*. Nonetheless, by morning he'd had the advantage of several hours' sleep, unlike the two hollow-eyed Ferrari brothers who now faced him.

He'd spent breakfast reviewing the voluminous security report that followed the drug-and-cyanide incident Saturday night. Such incidents were unfortunately less rare than one could wish. In fact, much of this case felt like déjà vu from the year before. It always recalled the painful memory of his own mishap in high school, the time he'd entered the wrong kind of bar and ended up unable to walk for a week. It was the one thing that could make him wonder, just for a moment, whether he'd really done the right thing founding yet another institution with vain aspirations of civilizing the young.

The cyanide, though, was a new twist. Mound Security would release nothing without a court order; "What happens at the Mound, stays at the Mound." Who had used the cyanide; how and why? Not this year's "thing," Dylan hoped. At least with alcohol, the squad had time to get there. One couldn't always count on one's rape victim being a first responder. In any event, college security had spent the night grilling various persons of interest, while Nora had compiled a background list of potentially related incidents since term began. Now the two club leaders in their black suits, president Rob LaSalle and pledge educator Rafael Marcaydo Acuña, faced the heavy hitter.

Dylan smiled. "Good morning, gentlemen."

Rob said, "Dr. Chase, we truly regret this whole thing happened. Fortunately, no one was hurt. Everything's under control—believe me, this won't happen again." Behind him, Rafael nodded solemnly.

"Glad to hear all that," said Dylan. "But please, fill me in on exactly what happened—this rape and cyanide business, the whole story."

Rob's eyes flew open. "Nothing actually happened to the *chicas*. We know for sure."

The medical report had not been released. Yet these guys knew the whole story. "So who else was there?"

Two determined pairs of lips were sealed.

Dylan tapped his finger on the desk. "A witness placed two other gentlemen in the room."

"That *chica* is *totalmente loca*, everyone knows."

Rafael looked up in alarm. "What Rob means is, there were so many people about; Mary was confused. It's the first time she's been to a big affair." He gave Dylan an earnest look. "I brought her myself; I should have looked after her better."

"And your other guest, with the memory blackout."

Rafael looked genuinely miserable.

Rob sat up straight. "Look, Dr. Chase, with all due respect, you don't understand about these *chicas*. They come out dressed to kill; those three, you should have seen them, with the clothes like painted on. They drop wads of cash; fifty grand on one number, what's up with that? They drink too much, and some of the bros get overexcited, they drink too. Stuff happens. Then in the morning, the *chicas* try to blame us—"

Rafael was trying frantically to get a word in. "Sure, like Rob says, stuff happens. But we know these are high-class *chicas*. We're sorry they got caught up in—"

"Excuse me," said Dylan, "I'd like to hear more, Rob, about what I don't understand about *chicas*."

"That amnesia drug," Rob went on. "That Ramos *chica*—she's a med tech. She had a scanscope in her purse. Those techs scope themselves, they all get in trouble."

Dylan looked him in the eye. The club president didn't blink. What could one possibly say to this humanoid?

"As for cyanide, that was *not* our doing. Why on earth would we do that?"

"Why, indeed." On this point, Dylan knew that Nora was inclined to agree; the cyanide came from elsewhere. But still, the truth was unclear. "Your club has some unfortunate history. There was that snuff toyworld for your rush party."

Rob waved a hand. "That was an old recording, something *chulo* for our nonalcoholic event. Nothing about cyanide."

"A serious error in judgment," Rafael added quickly. "For which we accepted our sanction, and counseling, and it will never happen again."

"Glad to hear it," said Dylan. "Unfortunately the . . . cyanide takes the current incident to a higher level. Attempted murder can't be handled by us alone; it goes to Judge Baynor in Mount Gilead." He paused to let that sink in. "It would be extremely helpful to provide more of the story." They wouldn't, of course. Nobody would tell on those other two bros.

Rob spread his hands. "On behalf of the club, I accept full responsibility. Any sanction should apply to us all." A clever move; one could hardly expel the club's entire membership.

"Well then," said Dylan. "From the college point of view, this serious incident requires loss of this year's pledge class."

The two looked relieved. Of course, they'd keep their pledge ties underground for the year.

"Furthermore, this incident demonstrates the need for us all to better understand the viewpoint of *chicas*. You will undertake six weeks of sensitivity training, under twenty-four-hour Monroe surveillance. Since your club takes full responsibility for the incident, we will expect all of you to undertake this training."

"Monroe? A mental in the head to make us think like *chicas*?" Rob was aghast. "Why would you want us all to have *that*?" With a sudden thought he gave the president a very ugly look.

"Thank you, Dr. Chase," said Rafael quickly. "What an opportunity. I'm sure we can all benefit from learning more about the kind of high-class *chicas* at college today."

Jenny had slept fitfully; she kept waking up in a panic, wondering where she was. Being hurt by fellow students was bad enough. Then the security interviews, and the humiliating medical test. Turning into a statistic.

She rose early and ran the shower, over and over, as if she could clean herself out.

In her toybox, the Marilyn face floated like a balloon. Marilyn pursed her lips. "Jenny, remember—it's not about you. Your assailants will face the judge. You're still you."

Jenny did not feel at all like herself. She felt like a used rag. She still could not remember where she'd spent the evening nor who had done what to her. Worst of all, she no longer trusted Anouk. She had closed Anouk's window, and Rafael's, and those of every other member of the Ferrari club. Then for good measure, she closed the rest of them, all the students, and all the dumb administrators who kept asking questions. They were all connected—she trusted no one at this place anymore.

"The shower," Marilyn persisted, out of the void of inner space. "It's run for an hour."

Jenny's fingers were soaked and wrinkled. Still she said nothing.

"Aren't you going to church? Father Clare needs his flowers."

"I'm getting out," Jenny said abruptly. "I'm going to my aunts'."

"There," said Marilyn. "That would serve everyone right. Frontera—they all let you down."

"*Sí, verdad.*"

Marilyn's face drifted off, then loomed closer. "You didn't want a DIRG."

"Why should I need a DIRG? What good is a place like Frontera, if I need a DIRG?"

"That's more like it," Marilyn agreed. "DIRG or no, you're not the one to blame. So why should you be the one to leave?"

"Why should I care?"

"What was the real reason you didn't want a DIRG?"

Jenny said nothing.

"You wanted to find out what it's like to be a real, ordinary person. Ordinary people don't have DIRGs. And now and then, they get screwed."

Jenny frowned and turned away, toward the shower wall. But of course, Marilyn was still there.

"Most people feel like they get screwed by politicians."

"What?"

"Average people—that's how they feel, all the time."

"About me? I want to throw out bad politicians."

"How can you stand up for people, if you can't stand up for yourself?"

Jenny closed her eyes and ran her hands again through her streaming hair.

"Set an example," urged Marilyn. "Show them how it's done."

Jenny shook her head, the water spinning out. "I don't know how it's done. I just don't want to ever face those *chusma* again."

"You have to press charges."

"But they're still here—I'll have to see them every day." They could be anyone, anywhere.

"Practice," urged Marilyn. "Practice what to say when you see them, anyone who disrespects you. Repeat after me: 'Scram.' 'Beat it.' 'Get lost.'"

Jenny half smiled. "Get lost."

Out of the shower, she got herself to church just in time to set her arrangement of white phalaenopsis at the communion table. If only Tom could be here; but he was busy serving brunch to Orin Crawford's investment partners. The familiar church service brought her a respite. But as the service closed her eyes flew open. Suddenly she could barely recall the hour gone by. Was she losing it again?

Father Clare came over and laid a hand on her arm. "Jenny, how are you?"

"I'm okay," she insisted. "Just . . . fine."

"Say, I could use more help on my campaign. Could you stop by my office in the morning?"

"All right." She hurried home to get some extra sleep before the game with Beijing.

Her mother called again. "Jenny," Soledad sighed. "So dreadful. And you all alone there."

Her father appeared in Iroquoia, speaking around his pipe. "**Only the Salt Beings cause harm to women.**"

"Don't worry about a thing," Soledad assured her. "Our staff will handle everything." A window opened for the family lawyer.

"**Alone among Salt Beings, without your brother.**" Her father's Iroquois words curled sonorously around his pipe. "**Brother-sister, the most sacred bond.**"

"I know, Dad." She bit her lip. "The Condoling Council—I'll be there." During October break, she'd promised she would play Iroquoia.

"**We must undertake a Mourning War.**"

Her eyes widened. "The Council is enough." No war for her, even in a toyworld.

"**We need a Mourning War. To replace your brother.**"

"Only if the Chief Woman rules," reminded Soledad. "Jenny, we should have known better. You simply must print out your DIRG."

"I won't."

"You don't understand, *hijita*. Real life isn't Iroquoia. You think DIRGs are for children; but DIRGs are for adults. You are the daughter of two presidential families. Your aunt is the governor of California. There will always be criminals that try to take advantage of such a person."

"But I don't want a DIRG."

"You'll live with it, like the rest of us."

"Frontera is my last chance without."

Soledad watched her for a while without speaking. At last she shook her head. "We'll talk again soon, when I come up with ToyDebate. By the way, that club that abused you; Ferrari, they're called?"

"*Sí.*"

"Security will pay them extra attention."

Jenny slept through lunch but managed to print out a quick amyloid sandwich that she finished on her way up the cloud ladder, crumbs floating down. Coach said nothing at first, but as the others spread out for drill, he took her aside. "You should sue the pants off them."

She smiled. "Thanks, Coach."

"It's not just you. Every year they assault frogs. It's their tradition. Someone has to put a stop to it."

Yola agreed. "They can't get away with this. Right, Ken?"

The bros would face the judge in Mount Gilead, Dean Kwon had said. A hearing; she'd have to relive the whole stupid thing.

Ken said, "It's an insult to the whole team." Still recovering from his Melbourne injuries, Ken limped out into the cage despite Doc Uddin's disapproval.

Coach clapped his hands. "We're all walking wounded this week," he called. "Let's get together. Focus."

Fran and David zigzagged across, their timing a bit off. Everyone seemed distracted this week, a long night's study here, a quick trip home there. Only Yola still hustled for every catch, and managed to steal a few. Jenny rotated in and slanned one for Ken, but still the Bears lost to Beijing by ten points.

After the game, Jenny dragged herself home. Her toybox lit up with student chatter, much of it Bulls crowing over their rivals' punishment.

"The Ferraris—Did you hear?"

"Monroe in the head, every one!"

"Next year they'll drive PINK cars! ROTFL!"

"And wear skirts to our Halloween House. That LaSalle is quite a *meringue!*"

Jenny pulled the diad off her forehead. Stillness; the breeze on her cheek, the oriole in the naked maple, the long axial cloud swelling to shower. Sometimes it felt good just to breathe.

At her cottage she found Anouk sitting in the porch swing, like Mary used to. Beside the porch waited Berthe, back in service. Anouk jumped up to meet her. "Jenny, I'm so sorry—you have to talk to me. Please!"

Jenny looked away. The porch, the maple; it all looked like yesterday. Except everything was changed.

"We're sisters, remember? We're lab partners."

Jenny shook her head. "Not anymore."

"Jenny! I didn't do it; my trust was abused."

"Then who did?"

Anouk hesitated. "What does it matter—they all got punished."

"I still have to pass by all those *chusma*, not knowing which one pulled down my dress. I want nothing to do with them, especially Rafael."

"Rafael is heartbroken. And now he has a Monroe in his head, twenty-four hours a day, just like you."

Jenny rolled her eyes. *"¡Qué lata!"* As if that would bring back her lost memory.

Anouk took a deep breath. *"Écoute,* Jenny. You must *not* let the bad ones win. That's what they try to do: Split us up, so we all depend on them."

"I can't depend on you."

Anouk caught her arm. "Look, it was these two." Two windows popped up: F. Scott Moreby, and Owen John Longford III. Ferrari seniors. "Their toyboxes will have the trace; I told the dean. They'll get expelled."

Jenny regarded the two suited *chicos*, like worms appearing within an apple. Two seniors she'd seen around but barely knew. Students like all the rest, yet predators.

Anouk's voice dropped. "I should never have gone without Berthe. I should have known better."

Jenny sighed. Overhead the trees rolled up into the fields dotted with mini-cows and combines, and little amyloid homes with lollipop driveways. "You shouldn't need Berthe here. Frontera should be a—a community." Their last refuge, before the "real world," the DIRGs' life.

"The only 'community' I trust is the laboratory. You can't cheat science—it always comes out." Anouk stood up from the swing. "How are the laughing plants?"

Upstairs in Jenny's greenhouse, alongside her returned orchids, the plants with the RNA switches were growing fine. "I test them each day, but they all laugh the same."

"*Enfin*, let's try again today."

Jenny shined the humorous light spectrum, then Anouk squirted the plants with jasmonate, the signal to turn on the RNA switch. After testing all sixty plants, Anouk summed the results.

"The RNA switch plants 'laughed' for twice as long as the controls."

"*¡Oye!*" This was so exciting, for a moment Jenny forgot all her mishaps; the assault, the lost game, and her ever mounting pile of homework.

"But the third set didn't laugh at all." Anouk was puzzled.

"Mary's 'reverse control.' You were out, remember?"

"I see. What exactly is this 'reverse control'?"

Jenny frowned, not wishing to admit she didn't know. She muttered, "There are all sorts of controls."

"We have to ask the professor. . . ."

In Jenny's toybox, Levi-Montalcini's tumor mouse crawled up onto a window, then sniffed over the edge. Levi-Montalcini's sim had said she could visit the toyworld again. Curious, Jenny blinked at the mouse.

A window opened to reveal Dr. Rita Levi-Montalcini, the neurobiologist who'd looked at everything from dead babies to chicken tumors and finally reached the Italian Senate. Levi-Montalcini's enormous expressive eyes smiled at her. A Toynet construct, but a very good one; she looked more alive than many a real person. "Have you brought me another hen's egg? From a hen that ran with the rooster?"

Jenny smiled, remembering the toyworld. "Sorry, but I do have a question. I'm sure you know all this stuff."

"You may try. My century of life was long, but did not quite reach into yours."

Suddenly Jenny wanted to ask something else: Why had the famous neuro research doctor become a senator at age ninety-two? But she caught herself. "What is a 'reverse control'?"

The Roman eyes gleamed. "Controls. You know I love controls."

Jenny glanced uncertainly at Anouk, then back to the window in her toybox.

"There are many kinds of controls," Levi-Montalcini continued. "Positive controls confirm that you can detect a positive result. And negative controls confirm that without your key ingredient, there is no result."

"Yes," said Jenny, "we have both of those for our plants. But what would be a reverse control?"

"A reverse control can be a DNA sequence that reads backwards. The backwards sequence should show no effect."

"No laughter," said Anouk. "That sounds like a negative control. A reverse control is different."

Levi-Montalcini nodded slowly. "I recommend you inspect your plants with care. Remember this."

Before Jenny's eyes appeared a virtual beaker covered with gauze.

"Hold it tight."

Jenny held the beaker.

Levi-Montalcini raised a gloved hand. She held out a snake. The snake bared its fangs and hissed. With a fluid motion, the doctor thrust the snake at the beaker. The fangs tore into the gauze and shot streams of venom into the beaker, where the liquid collected, clear and deadly.

"Venom was my control, remember? It turned out to be full of nerve growth factor—ten times as much as the mouse tumor. So you see, the control may be more important than the experiment." She tossed the snake into a tank. "Now if you'll excuse me, I have an important vote coming up. A vote on the future of Italian science."

After Levi-Montalcini vanished, Jenny shared a doubtful glance with Anouk. "Could this 'reverse control' be dangerous?"

Anouk shrugged. "Italians love drama. Our plants did nothing."

"I don't know. I'll bring one back to Abaynesh tomorrow, and see if she knows what Mary did to it."

At suppertime, as Jenny reached the dining hall, a Ferrari senior blocked the doorway. Owen John Longford III, one of the two Anouk had fingered.

Jenny stopped, uncertain.

The suit leaned into the door frame, arms crossed. He wasn't quite her height, but his face looked ugly. "Nothing happened to you. You don't have to rat to the judge."

Out of habit Jenny glanced over her shoulder. Back home, there would always be a family DIRG to expel intruders. But not here, where she was "safe." Disgusted, she started to turn away. She could print the same food at her cottage.

"Jenny." Marilyn popped up in her toybox, batting her long eyelashes. "Remember, Jenny, what we said."

Jenny took a deep breath, and made herself stand up straighter. Looking slightly aside, she told the suit, "Get lost."

For a long moment the Ferrari stood there, then at last he moved aside, just enough. He spat on the ground as she passed.

34

Monday morning, Jenny had waffles with strawberries at the café. Tom in his chef's white jacket sat at the table, arms crossed. "Who did it?"

"Two seniors." She was getting tired of the whole thing; if only it would just go away. But she'd testify all right at the amyloid courthouse, whenever the judge put it on the docket. The court was on recess while they all harvested their corn and soy.

"I need to know," said Tom. "So I can deck them."

Jenny blinked in surprise. "You would?" That sure felt good.

"Where I come from, that's how it's done."

"I thought Amish were peaceful."

"Boys aren't Amish till they get confirmed."

Those Ferraris deserved it. And so did all those Firmament people, who lied even to their own children. An hour of memory lost is one thing—a lifetime of banned knowledge, think of it.

"ToyNews—From our box to yours." Clive was back, hovering above the Pacific coast, blue-brown waters washing up white beaches. Governor Akeda had the National Guard dumping acaricide all along the coast, to wipe out pile worms. All because the worms had a few ultra genes. Jenny shook her head. Now that Aunt Meg was the running mate, being California's first sensible governor wasn't enough. She had to act tough on ultra.

"It's too bad about the pile worms," Tom said. "Professor Semerena is pretty upset."

"I wonder what other animals have got infected with ultra genes. And what plants."

✦

Since Politics wasn't till ten, Jenny had time to stop by the chaplain as promised. Instead of her orchid, she took with her one of Mary's reverse-control plants, to show Abaynesh after class. The topmost leaves of the scrawny plant tickled her chin as she walked down Buckeye Trail.

In her toybox, Clive recapped the latest on the pile worm eradication. Her normally sensible Aunt Meg had made a great show of force, even driving a tank offshore. The sight of the tank forced a giggle to the back of her throat. Poisoning pile worms off the Pacific coast, while all forms of ultra crawled the countryside out of control—the absurdity was overwhelming. Jenny started to laugh. She tried to stop, but as soon as she caught her breath, the absurdity struck her again. It felt so good to laugh, like a spring cleaning for the soul.

At the chaplain's door she paused to catch her breath. She went in, set down the plant, and immediately went to the puzzle to place a piece, a red shard contributing to what looked like a giant tomato.

"I'm so glad you're here." Father Clare sat at his desk with the dog-eared book, the Virgin Mary cradling her Son behind him. "How are things with my campaign? Should I give another speech?" Hamilton had just done a speech before First Firmament Church, surrounded by farmers and Ferrari brothers. He'd announced the new increase in space protection, as if the deed were his own.

"A speech would be good," Jenny said. "We can feed all the brainstream from local toyboxes into a pollmeter. Then as you speak, you watch the pollmeter, and use that to pick your next talking point."

The chaplain nodded politely. Pollmeters were out of his league, Jenny guessed.

"I ran your voter analysis," she added. "Based on surveys and registration patterns, you'll win the campus vote two to one." Hamilton was a popular professor, but so was the chaplain; and the faculty and staff favored him. "But in Mount Gilead, you'll lose by the same margin."

"I see. It's really a science, isn't it."

"Not enough of one." The big campaigns ran pollmeters, toyworld town meetings, and hundreds of electoral simulations; and still, one off-remark from a First Lady could lose it all.

"So we really need to turn out the students."

"But it's the students' long weekend, and we have to vote here."

Father Clare nodded. "It's hard to believe that's constitutional. Maybe we should look into the law."

"Good idea, I'll check into that." Pre-election legal challenges were part of the game, especially in Ohio.

He leaned forward on the desk, hands clasped. "Jenny, how are you? Can I help?"

"I'm fine." She was sick of talking about it.

"It's tough, isn't it; being up here at Frontera, alone."

She lifted her chin. "I've done well. Keeping my grades up."

"You always did."

"I'm not cutting myself."

"That's good."

"I haven't 'visited' Jordi in a long while."

He nodded. "Jordi can manage without you now."

She hadn't thought of it that way. No more boosting his slan, no more help with math. No, Jordi no longer needed her. Now others did. But once you began down that road—all the others in the universe who might need you, the whole planet expecting Ramos Kennedys to save them—*Dios mío*, it was all too much. And this chaplain expecting her to run his campaign for mayor. She looked him in the eye. "How about you, Father? Are you okay?"

He leaned back and clasped his hands behind his neck. "Guess I deserved that." He thought it over. "I'm doing well, all things considered. My Renaissance students have started some lovely frescos."

"Claro." She had to get Tom to show her his. "What I really wonder is—" She took a deep breath. "How can you stand to be Christian?" Her pulse raced. Like a bubbling pot, it had just boiled over. She half expected Mary's statue to look up.

He nodded slightly, as if unsurprised. "I can't not be Christian," he said. "Does that make sense?"

"But look at everything people do in the name of Christ. Lying to children about the age of the Earth, and the span of the stars. Leading our planet to death."

"I could say that not all Christians do that," the chaplain reflected. "And not only Christians. But that would be no answer." He sat up and took the dog-eared ancient book off his desk. Its cover was blackened, moldy in appearance, with an end torn off. "This is a replica of the *Codex Anaxagoras*, the sole surviving work of a pre-Socratic philosopher. Anaxagoras was the first to define a concept of mind, as an organizing principle of the universe." The book fell open. The vellum inside was full of faded medieval script. "But what became of his work? Most of the pre-Socratics are lost to history. This codex was saved because a medieval cleric took the parchment to reuse for writing prayers. He washed out the original, wrote his prayers over, then left the prayer book in a monastery. But the washing was incomplete. Centuries later, scientists used X-rays and ultraviolet to reveal the original."

The book snapped shut. Father Clare put it aside, then leaned forward on his desk, hands clasped before him. "That's what most preaching is—mine, and everyone else's. We preserve the word of God by scribbling prayers over something infinitely more valuable. It's up to you to find the original."

Jenny had to rush to class, potted plant in one arm and Aristotle in the other. All the students sat around the ornate oval table, while Hamilton paced as usual. Mary sat at the far end, with her usual vacant look. A playmate button lit up from Enrico, pleading to restore his window. Ignoring him, Jenny hurried to find her place in the book.

"Now, Aristotle finds important difficulties with Plato's idea of common property, in particular the idea of owning women and children in common." Hamilton turned to face the table. "What difficulties does Aristotle raise?"

Enrico said, "If you don't know your true father, it's hard to avoid incest."

Claro, thought Jenny with a yawn.

"Enrico," observed Hamilton as if intensely interested in this new thought. "You've truly hit upon a key point. Avoiding incest is a pillar of civilization, don't we agree?" He looked around the table.

"Friendship is watered down," observed Ricky Tsien, reading from the text: " 'Like wine mixed with water.' "

Hamilton's eyes widened. "Friendship, Ricky. Where would we be without friendship? If all are owned by all, how can one have a special friend?"

Someone giggled. It was Priscilla Cho.

"Other problems?" continued the professor. "What other problems does Aristotle raise with Plato's utopian ideal?" In Hamilton's class, utopias were invariably bad, whereas dystopias were a necessary compromise with human nature.

Priscilla giggled again, louder. Hamilton paced in the other direction, but Priscilla raised her hand. "Aristotle says—" She could scarcely contain herself. "That keeping away from someone else's woman is a noble deed, and that owning women in common deprives us of this virtue."

At that, Enrico chuckled, then was still.

Ricky burst out laughing. "That's really good." Another student next to Jenny laughed, then another nearby.

"Yes, yes," observed Hamilton. "Any other . . . issues raised?"

"It says here," Ricky began, "that when the Spartans came home from war, they listened to Lycurgus; but when Lycurgus told women to obey the laws, they resisted, and so he gave up."

Priscilla threw back her head laughing, and there was general laughter around the table. Even Jenny couldn't help it; the picture of all the women being ungovernable, while their soldier men did as they were told, was too precious.

"And here," added Priscilla, "Aristotle says that in warring nations, all warriors are conspicuously obsessed with sexual relations—either with men or with women!" She could barely get the last word out, and collapsed under the table. Hamilton was left trying to speak. The only student not laughing was Mary.

"REVERSE CONTROL WORKED."

Jenny's eyes flew open at Mary's message. She quit laughing. She stared at Mary, then at the plant on the table, surrounded by laughing students. Her heart beat so fast she thought it would burst. Scooping up the plant and her book, she left the table and ran from the room. She ran all the way to Reagan Hall, to Abaynesh's office.

"Professor!" She stopped to catch her breath. "Professor, this plant— Mary did something, and—"

Professor Abaynesh was feeding headless mice to her two-headed snakes, their tanks all stacked on the far wall. "Diad off, please."

Jenny pulled off her diad, to avoid alerting the Toynet animal activists. By the desk, Tova sat on the floor with the blacksnake, Meg-El. At Jenny's entrance, Tova got up and ran across to her, a crayon drawing in one hand, a book in the other. The book, *The Diary of Anne Frank*, fell from Tova's hand so she could point professorially at her drawing. She craned her neck up at Jenny. "Kudzu now grows in Yukon," she hyperventilated. "Kudzu makes long purple flowers with a pleasant sweet smell."

"Enough, Tovaleh," said her mother. "Go play with Meg-El." She turned to Jenny questioningly.

Jenny swallowed. "What is a 'reverse control'?"

The professor took the plant from her and snipped a piece for the analyzer. "I told Mary not to do it already," she muttered. "Students never listen."

"What is it?"

"The plant expresses a human semiochemical," Abaynesh explained, still watching the analyzer. "One of several discovered in the last decade. They bind receptors deep inside your nose." She turned to Jenny. "Did you ever know someone who invariably makes people laugh, and no one can quite say why?"

"Sure." Mimi, Rosa's first lady, was known for making everyone laugh. It was part of her charm.

"It's genetic; they express a high level of laughter-enhancing semiochemical. Now, Mary sees you and Anouk as part of the experiment. So when you applied jasmonate to the plants, to make them laugh harder, Mary made the reverse. She made the RNA switch turn on the human pheromone, cloned on a plasmid. To make you humans laugh."

"But—" Jenny's thoughts spun. "We only laughed in Hamilton's class. And he didn't laugh."

"It's not laughing gas; it doesn't make you laugh at nothing. It only amplifies what you find funny already."

Jenny shook her head. "Well, it's *not* funny." In fact, it was like what those Ferraris had done to her—a chemical altering her brain, without consent.

"Certainly not. In fact, it's illegal." Abaynesh frowned at the plant. "Premeds. All they want to work on is humans. They want me to spend class dissecting a cadaver."

"Professor, Mary is no ordinary premed."

"True." The professor gave her a hard stare. "Are you?"

"Me? I keep up four classes and don't nearly kill someone."

"The rape gas could have killed you. Luckily you got just a whiff before the bros fled. Mary saved your life."

"With cyanide? She has ultra syndrome."

The professor threw up her hands. "What shall I do with her? She has no other home on Earth. And now I've said too much already."

Twenty illegal plants in Jenny's greenhouse. For sure, Mary's health was none of her business, but here she'd got Jenny in trouble again. The *compañera* from hell.

"I made a mistake," the professor admitted. "I should never have sent those plants home with you. Bring them all back, and we'll set you up with lab space, where I have the proper permits. The air is filtered, so any semiochemicals won't affect you."

A key code opened in Jenny's toybox.

"Laboratory access," the professor added. "You can get in anywhere, any time of day or night."

Jenny's eyes widened. "Access to your lab? That's a big responsibility."

"All the research students have access. It's important, especially when the power fails and I can't get here in time to check."

She thought this through. "I don't want to be here alone."

"Of course not; bring your partner. By the way, how did your experiment work?"

"The experimental plants laughed significantly more than the negative control." It hardly seemed important now.

"So you're done with that exercise, the test that's been done a hundred times. That was just practice. Now you're ready for a project that's never been done before. The wisdom circuit. Can we construct a plant whose nervous system guides it to do the right thing?" Abaynesh blinked rapidly, downloading papers for Jenny to read.

The wisdom plant, Jenny recalled, the plant with all the flower heads. Two heads might be wiser than one, although not for snakes. For her aunts, maybe.

Then she thought of something. "Professor? Is there a . . . 'reverse control' for wisdom?"

"None that I know of," said Abaynesh in a low voice. "More's the pity."

At supper, Jenny barely followed the banter amongst her teammates as she tried to read her homework in her toybox while dutifully consuming her amyloid. Teddy Roosevelt had just established the Census Bureau and bid for a canal in Panama. The class went well—Uncle Dylan truly was a first-rate professor. By contrast, her toyHarvard class dragged. Cuba had just been invaded by Columbus.

"**We built another lifeboat today.**" Charlie smiled from across the table. Jenny smiled back. "**Thanks.**"

"We'll build the *sukkah* Wednesday," announced Ken. "Be there with your space suits down south at the circuit, at four o'clock sharp."

"*¡Oye!*" cried goalie Xiang Jones. "Wouldn't miss it."

"Way to go," said Iris Ortega. "We get to shake the whatchamacallit."

Fran Pezarkar held up a bunch of palm fronds plus what looked like a large wrinkled lemon. "*Lulav* and *etrog*." "*Citrus medica*, citron," added Jenny's taxon window.

Yola jogged Jenny's arm. "Dwork, are you awake?"

"I heard everything you said," she insisted.

"You know about Sukkot?"

"Of course." Grandma Rosa and Mimi had celebrated the harvest festival.

"They build this hut called a *sukkah* outdoors, beneath the stars. Out of tree branches and symbolic fruits."

"So Ken and Coach will be busy again." And Fran and David, the Jews from Mumbai. But why would Yola be interested?

"Aren't you listening? *The stars.* You have to see the stars through the branches—with nothing in between. Get it?"

Jenny thought. "You mean . . . outside the spacehab?"

"Up on the polar cap," Ken explained. "The only place where we won't fly off the rotating hab."

Yola nodded. "We all go out for a look. It's not every day you walk in space to see the stars."

35

Wednesday morning, Jenny met Tom after politics to go canvassing in Mount Gilead. Holding hands, they swung their arms as they headed out Raccoon Run alongside the creek, alone except for a mother teddy bear trotting across with her cub. Far ahead, the down-pointing First Firmament steeple grew and rotated up. Tom wore his Homefair hard hat and nail pockets, and Jenny carried her scanscope. She noticed what looked like a burn on his arm. "Did you have an accident?"

"Not in Homefair," he told her. "Art class. Got some wet lime on my arm, and it burned."

"That's too bad. How is your fresco?"

"I finally got the paint to stay," said Tom said, "without running down the wall."

She squeezed his hand. "I'm sure it's *chulo*. When can I see it?"

"The others are much better."

"ToyNews—From our box to yours." Clive in the window, with his hair back to his everyday style ten. "All eyes and ears await tomorrow night's first presidential debate, on foreign affairs. Candidates Anna Carrillo and Gar Guzmán square off directly for the first time."

Now, *por último,* having won the primary, Anna could come out strong and promise to save the world. Here at Frontera, Father Clare would do the same. Jenny swung Tom's hand happily. "You know what Father Clare said? He said that preachers preserve the word of God by scribbling prayers over something infinitely more valuable."

Tom took a breath. "Really." He let out a long sigh. "That sure helps."

"What do you mean?"

He smiled as if watching something far off, beyond the hab. "They used to drive me out to service on Sunday mornings, in a windowless wagon. The horse clopping ahead; I still dream of the sound. The service was in somebody's home, not a church. Benches and chairs all around a living room. The sermon, and the hymns." He nodded. "I still miss the hymns."

By the road, the creek foamed, worse than usual, thought Jenny. "Father Clare should give a speech on pollution, don't you think?"

"Good idea."

Jenny smiled; she could only feel cheerful, holding Tom's hand. "Are you going out this afternoon to build the *sukkah*?" She hadn't space-walked since sophomore year, with Jordi.

"I don't know. I don't have a space suit."

Jenny started to offer him one, but thought better of it. "How's Sherri-Lyn's house?"

"The punch list's nearly done. The housewarming's next Saturday. You're invited."

"Thanks." She tilted her head. "Would you like to see more magic?"

"Sure thing. Cups and balls?"

Jenny shook her head. "Coin and nails. You got some?"

Tom fished three nails out of his pocket, then dug deeper for a ten-dollar dime. Jenny produced a round box with holes. "Put the coin inside." She capped it with the cover. "Now the nails."

Each nail poked straight through the box, all the way out the other side. The solid coin was inside; it must have been pierced.

"*Guao.* The coin must be amyloid."

"Your own coin?" At his look, Jenny laughed.

Tom fingered the nail tips, then pulled them out one by one, finally opening the box to retrieve his dime. "How do you do these things?"

She shrugged. "A mystery, but it's only 'magic.'" Life in a clouded mirror.

"No, really, how did you?"

Jenny pulled him closer. "For a kiss?"

He hadn't yet sent her a brainkiss. He looked her in the eye. "A real one."

She cupped his head in her hands and kissed. He held her in his arms, a long satisfying time.

At Lazza's, amid the noonday crowd, there were only two seats at the bar, next to Leora. As if she'd saved them, Jenny thought. Jenny sat up as usual, she and Tom towering over the power-banded colonists. Above loomed the fourteen-point buck's head with its gloomy glass-eyed stare.

"How is your campaign?" whispered Leora.

"Not bad." Jenny ordered her usual chicken sandwich. "Today we're space-walking. Outside the hab."

"For repairs?"

Jenny shook her head. "To build a *sukkah*. For the Jewish holiday. You have to see the stars." She thought of something. "Have you ever been . . . outside the hab?"

"Often, with my late husband. To inspect for repairs."

Jenny blinked in surprise.

"But I've never seen a Jewish holiday. That would be interesting."

"Well . . ." She exchanged a look with Tom. "You could come. I'm sure Coach—that is, Rabbi Porat wouldn't mind."

About fifty students gathered at the track with their space suits. Besides the slanball team, many first-years were there, curious about the "outside." Already halfway up the cap, the grav was half a g. Fran and David skipped around easily, carrying various fruits and branches. Priscilla tripped but recovered herself in slow motion. Enrico was struggling with his suit, which had inflated too soon. With a start, Jenny saw Leora Smythe dragging an old much-used suit, her skirt replaced by overalls.

"Welcome, *uzhpizin*, that is, 'guests,' to our Sukkot tradition. Welcome all who would help us build the *sukkah*, a hut to worship God in the wilderness." Rabbi Porat wore a dark business suit and a fringed prayer shawl. Other than that, he was brisk as usual, like getting up to practice. "Mind your step."

In the ground a crack opened, and a door slid slowly over. Below was a ladder, down to a dimly lit flight of stairs. A crude maintenance tunnel. Everyone had to climb single file, first down into the substratum, then up the curving stairway. Jenny felt her weight fall away. In her toybox a map showed her progress, curving inward toward the cap at the axis of the rotating hab. As she reached about tenth a g, the stairs gave way to a pair of rails which she climbed hand over hand, like she would inside the space lift. Down, up, or down; which was which? A pungent smell; someone had emptied their stomach. Not so great for everyone else.

"Watch the hole."

The hole appeared at her feet, up-or-down. Jenny crouched, pushing her suit first through the hole. A bit too fast; she launched herself after it to catch up. The weightless corridor opened out into a hemispherical room. *"Northern Cap Station,"* read her toybox.

Doc Uddin and Frank Lazza were already there waiting, checking out all the suits. Jenny placed her feet into the two leg holes. The amyloid climbed up her legs, and she felt her hair stand on end, as if she were being swallowed by a snake. She waited for Doc Uddin's inspection before closing her head-gear. Sound cut out, all but the hiss of her own breathing.

"Which way is up?"

"How do I move—I'm a statue."

"Can't breathe!"

Dios mío. The doctor hurried off to check someone who'd closed their suit too soon. Fifty newbies heading out to space; this was worse than Home-fair.

Jenny flexed her muscles, adjusting the actuators until she could move. *Jordi*—she kept seeing him everywhere. Anyone in a space suit could be Jordi. They had trained together for a month before his great "To Jupiter" speech, at the lunar station, the same one that had launched the fatal Mars mission. Most Unity strategists had advised against it. But Soledad had sided with the proponent. Jordi's speech had gone over surprisingly well. Something about the sight of young *chicos* headed for space still moved the heart of post-Kessler America. That strategist had taken over Jordi's schedule, building his image for the next two years, culminating in Battery Park.

Ken floated past her head, carrying a bunch of tree branches. He really seemed into all the rites, although the rabbi still wouldn't convert him. Fran and David, Illyrian twins, looked indistinguishable in their suits except for their toybox labels. Fran held up the bundle of palms and willows. All the suited students now floated around the station, tagged with names in her toybox. The one tagged "Charlie" waved at her in slow motion.

"Last call before the airlock." Rabbi Porat's voice pinged through her toybox. "If you're feeling queasy, now's your chance to turn back. This is about observance, not martyrdom."

A student pulled off his suit and floated back to the tunnel. After a moment, two others followed.

Within Jenny's suit the low pressure sign came on, as air was pumped out of the chamber. One by one, the suited students headed up-or-down into the next lock. Jenny followed the lightguides. In her toybox, the map showed her at the very end of the pole. Frontera, the medicine capsule.

At last Jenny's arms pulled back the exit rim. She felt as if she were emerging from a pool. The hab was a black object, blocking the sun from behind. Above, all was black except for the stars. Points of light glowed, like a million lighted cities of vast unknown countries on the opposite side of a universal hab.

A flash. It seemed distant, though there was no way to tell. Homeworld's laser had caught a stray, she guessed. Out of the corner of her eye, a tiny flash at the hab's surface, then another. Tiny particles vaporized, too small to be worth catching; though at ten times bullet speed, they might pierce a suit. She swallowed hard.

Straightening out, Jenny stood against the black surface and blinked to engage her surface grippers. Beside her a light came on, illuminating the surface from which they emerged. Deep purple, the microbes swam in the depths. The salt-loving microbes absorbed blue, green, and red, reflecting only the purple-to-ultra range.

At the observation platform, the contours of four poles jutting outward. "Upward," she mentally corrected. The poles were meant to be the frame, like the Homefair house. Ken floated over, attaching a pole crosswise to a vertical pole, while David Pezarkar attached the other end. Now the "hut" had its first window.

As Jenny watched, she frowned. Something invisible was pulling at Ken, tugging him away and around. Then she remembered. The entire hab was rotating, once a minute. The stars, the entire sparkling blackness, turning forever, around an axis pointing out from the hab across the universe, thirteen billion light-years and counting.

"Help!!"

A space suit was spiraling away, out of control. Heart pounding, Jenny repressed the impulse to blink off her grippers and launch herself after the hapless student. Seconds passed, each one an eternity. At last the student bounced off the barely visible net of anthrax line that enclosed the whole visitor area. The student slowly drifted backward. David headed out to help him return.

As they returned, Jenny noticed the dark Frontera surface had brightened all over, a dim purple glow. Over the past minute, the hab had rotated toward the sun, exposing its microbes to photosynthesize. And the Earth could be seen, just behind the southern cap, beneath the *hijab* of stars. Father Clare—what a backdrop, she thought. This was the place for him to speak, to explain to the town why he was running for mayor.

In her toybox Rabbi Porat began. "We build the *sukkah*," he explained, "to commemorate the biblical Israelites wandering in the desert for forty years. For them, the desert was their outer space. Their place of visions. Their highest frontier." He raised his arm toward the pole frame. "They had only crude dwellings, made of plant fibers, which in the desert were scarce. The scant roof barely covered the hut, and cracks between the branches revealed the sky."

"*Lulav* and *etrog*." The suited Fran held up a handful of palms, myrtle, and willows. Her other hand held up a large greenish-yellow citron; desiccated by the space vacuum, it was wrinkled as a walnut.

"The commemoration became a harvest festival, for which we thank the Lord by shaking the Four Species of fruits . . ."

The great square of Pegasus. Jenny caught sight of it, ahead. Farther up, the W of Cassiopeia, and the bright star Vega, marching around. The sweet white wisp of the Milky Way. Out of the corner of her eye came a flash; her eye winced. Whatever it was vaporized with a comet-like trail, presumably lased by Homeworld Security.

At her left, the suited Leora listened intently to the rabbi. Then she turned to Jenny.

"The stars," Jenny texted Leora. "**What do you think of the stars? Millions of light-years away?**" How could anyone who walked out in space think the whole world revolved around Earth?

Leora's eyes peered out from the face plate, which reflected Jenny's helmet. "**Our pastor says that now that Earth is doomed, God's universe rotates around Frontera. Frontera is the ark to be saved from the Flood.**"

Jenny stared back. Her lips parted but no words came out. Within her suit her hands shook. Her eyes stared back in unconcealed horror.

"What does your pastor say?" asked Leora.

Jenny swallowed twice.

"Blessed are you, Lord, our God. . . ." Rabbi Porat's voice came through, reciting the Sukkot blessing. "Sovereign of the universe, who has sanctified us with His commandments, and commanded us to dwell in the *sukkah*. Amein."

Jenny remembered something. She blinked to text Leora; it came out garbled at first, needing to start over twice. "**Father Clare says that all preachers preserve the word of God by scribbling prayers over something infinitely more valuable.**"

$+$

36

As always on Thursday morning, Jenny rushed home from slanball to catch Life at seven. But her toyroom opened more slowly than usual. Inside, the branches of the tree house were clothed with kudzu. Surprised, then homesick, Jenny watched the fuzzy green leaves swell and grow. The virtual leaves budded and unfolded, extending across the branches, climbing up even over the eight virtual doors.

But her nostalgia soon turned to annoyance. The "kudzu" crowded out everything; it literally buried the doors of the toyroom tree house. Time itself seemed to slow to a crawl, as the kudzu smothered all.

"*Hombre,* what is this green stuff?"

"Not that Convolvula again?"

"LOL, *tonto,* it's a ghost."

Her toybox filled with frantic chatter. Not just her own toyroom, but the whole college seemed infected. The windows all ground to a halt, all except for Mary's Babynet window. "HELLO."

From Toy Land, a flickering glimpse of toymaker Valadkhani with her apron full of Phaistos disks. "**Attention: Local Toynet shut down. All classes suspended until further notice.**"

Jenny took off her diad and left her cottage. Outside, diad-less students streamed from all directions, laughing and tossing bits of worn amyloid. With classes suspended, there was nothing particular to do. A group of them cornered an elephant in a ring, laughing as the panicked creature tossed back and forth until it at last ran out from under their arms.

By lunchtime, the virtual kudzu was cleared out, with a conspicuous lack of explanation. Anouk claimed to know the cause. "A certain overeducated offspring," she observed with satisfaction. "One with a propensity for invasives."

Jenny's eyes widened. "*No puede ser.*"

That afternoon, they met Abaynesh in the lab to set up their plants with the wisdom circuit. The "real" research. "How is your DNA toyworld, with the baobab?" Jenny asked politely. "Did it get restored okay?"

The professor looked away, embarrassed. Behind the row of *Arabidopsis sapiens,* Anouk hid her smile. Mary looked oblivious as usual.

"Tovaleh needs a special school," muttered Abaynesh. "Never mind. The question is: Which of Ng and Howell's combinatorial circuits makes a plant to be wise? That is, two plants to be wise about each other."

Each pot actually contained two seedlings, Jenny saw. The two seedlings had one of Ng and Howell's combinations of connected neurons; a different combination for every twin pair. The potted twins stretched in vast rows, far longer than twenty, she realized with some apprehension. Anouk and Mary strolled down the rows, their heads alone visible above like moons. In the class window read Frontera's motto, *Sophias philai paromen.*

"So . . ." Jenny swallowed, trying not to sound stupid. "How can two plants be 'wise'?"

Abaynesh lifted a tube and squirted the nearest pair of twins, brushing their tips thoughtfully. "We spray them with the scent of insect larvae; the kind that could chew up their leaves. Then they need to communicate with semio-chemicals. Each plant emits a different insect repellent. If their neuron circuit exhibits wisdom, then what do you think?" She glared suddenly at Anouk. Not glaring, really, Jenny knew by now; just an intense gaze.

"Together, the two plants ward off insects better than either could alone." Anouk stroked the flower heads. "So the wise course is to share their potting space, instead of crowding each other out. It's called the prisoners' dilemma," she added in her bored I-know-the-math tone.

The professor nodded. "So how many different circuit connections do we have to test? Jenny?"

Jenny swallowed, remembering all the combinations that spewed out from Ng and Howell's lab in Seattle. "About . . . thirty-six hundred?"

"Yes, well, but most of those were barely above background. I suggest you start with the top thirty-six and—" She stopped and stared at the ground. Stooping, she scooped up what looked like a long worm with about a hundred legs. "*Wolf!*" Abaynesh blinked like mad at her toybox. "Quit yodeling already, and get yourself up here."

Within a minute, Wolf Semerena strolled into the lab. Tall, with a runner's lean muscles and a slightly hunched back, his sandals clacked on the waterproof floor. "*Was ist los?*"

She dangled the worm in his face. "I told you, *no* invertebrates up here. Downstairs with ultra."

"Certainly, *sofort*." The biochemist smiled cheerfully, extending his palm for the intruder.

Jenny watched curiously. "Is that a pile worm?"

"I'm afraid so," Semerena admitted. "It must have crawled out when the worms I transferred." Semerena popped the hundred-legged worm into a jar, and put the jar in the pocket of his cutoff jeans beneath the "Devil's Tramping Ground" T-shirt. "Until the day before yesterday, no one cares about my little saltwater friends. Then suddenly, Homeworld Security shows up in the box, and says, 'Your worms are ultra now.'" He shrugged. "Fortunately, Sharon an ultra permit has."

"So we keep them downstairs," said Abaynesh. "With the real ultra. *Not* up here. You know how my plants feel about invertebrates." She sounded genuinely ill.

"Hah." Semerena pointed a finger. "Just wait till the ultra starts putting their genes into ver-te-brates." He emphasized each syllable.

Jenny's hair stood on end.

Professor Abaynesh considered this. "Maybe we shouldn't wait. Maybe we should test and see."

"It's been tested," said Semerena. "Ultra genes in vertebrates? No one ever finds."

"There's always a first time. Come." She turned and marched out. Back at her office, she faced the wall of snakes. "Diads off, everyone."

The wall parted down the middle, and the snake tanks swung inward to either side. Behind the snake tanks stood cages of frogs, rats, and chickens. "Let's sample from each," Abaynesh advised Semerena. "Take them downstairs with the ultraphytes. Then test their DNA every now and then, to see what's happened."

"Um." Jenny swallowed. "Let's see what Mary's up to." She and Anouk slipped back to the rows of potted twins, which Mary was eying reflectively.

"We might as well start our experiment," Anouk sighed. "We have all these plants to spray with insect juice. Then sample each plant for semiochemicals, to see if they shared information, showing wisdom." Her eyes scanned the protocol.

Mary looked up. "For humans, what is wisdom?"

Jenny rolled her eyes. "Not this again."

"She learned what laughter was, remember." Anouk added out loud, "Wisdom is . . . when people act wise," she finished lamely. "When they make the best choice. In truth, wisdom is hard to find in Frontera."

"Father Clare is wise," Jenny said. "Father Clare always knows the right thing."

"Yes, Father Clare," said Anouk. "And also the toymaker, Zari Valadh-kani. A Twelver, but she always prays wisely." She looked at Mary. "Does that answer your question?"

"Yes," Mary agreed. "Father Clare is positive control. Where is negative control?"

"Negative control?" Jenny frowned thoughtfully. "You mean, zero wisdom?"

Anouk laughed. "Total foolishness—*mon Dieu*. Look all around you."

"Those motor clubs," agreed Jenny.

Mary asked, "Motor clubs have zero wisdom?"

"Not quite zero," remembered Anouk. "My Rafael, he treats me wisely."

"And the Bulls do some good things," Jenny recalled. "They encourage voters."

"There's your Politics class."

"Yes, they always say foolish things. Except for Priscilla, and sometimes Enrico." It was surprisingly hard to think of anything or anyone in Frontera who never had a wise moment.

That evening was the first presidential candidates' debate in Boulder. At supper, the Red Bulls had their table near the toywall, plates full of red jello to sling at the opponent. Ferraris wore suits and ties, ostentatious *adultos*. On the side, the nonpartisan Begonias raised a large tablet to score points.

"Can you believe next month they'll be *here*?"

"Breathing our air."

"Eating our amyloid jello?"

"*Tonto*, their DIRGs won't let them eat our jello."

"We can throw it right at them, LOL."

The first debate was the culmination of months of planning by Soledad and her Centrist codirector of ToyDebate. Thanks to Jenny's convention treachery, she was bumped from the event; no front-row toyseat, no need to wear her best suit and smile. Just sit back with her teammates and Mary, biting her knuckles, hoping Anna made no mistakes. The polls were neck and neck as usual, and the candidates fine-tuned their messages by the minute.

The toywall came alive with the Mound preview show. Head-feathered

Shawnee warriors offered viewers odds on how many times Antarctica got mentioned, on whether *plátanos* came up, and whether a candidate stumbled across the stage.

Mary was watching the toywall, but she would see nothing because Babynet did only text. Jenny blinked through Babynet: "I WILL TELL YOU WHAT THEY SAY."

At last Clive came out, with truly big hair, the most stylish she had ever seen. Then the two candidates strode out, each to their own podium. Applause from the Boulder audience, in a stage before a twilight backdrop of the Rockies. Applause and jeers from the Frontera students.

"Our first debate," announced Clive, "focuses on foreign affairs." Clive preened and turned his head, showing his coif to best advantage. "The first question is for you, Governor Guzmán."

Gar Guzmán, in his gray suit, winked at the audience and spread his infectious grin.

"Governor, tell us what you'll do about the most pressing foreign issue facing our country: protecting our Antarctic farmland."

Jenny closed her eyes, though it only blocked out her fellow students; the diad mercilessly streamed the debate into her brain. "Our farmland" indeed.

The Cuban governor's eyes widened, and he nodded at the audience, his look assuring them at once how weighty the question was, and yet how he was totally on top of it. "First, let me say how important farmland is for America—as American as bighorn sheep or Wisconsin cheddar."

A few chuckles at that; the Golds were pushing hard for Wisconsin this year. Jenny guessed that her parents might end up voting there.

"Of course the Antarctic Treaty System ensures in the interests of all humankind that Antarctica shall continue forever to be used exclusively for peaceful purposes. That is why our peacekeeping forces are stationed at the Transantarctic Mountains, to protect our West Antarctic wheat fields—the breadbasket of the free world."

At the mention of "peacekeeping forces," red jello appeared splattered across the toywall. The Begonia scoreboard, however, flashed a ten, presumably for the impact on the public brainstream.

Meanwhile, the Boulder audience applauded politely, and Clive nodded importantly. "Governor Carrillo, your response: What will you do about the most pressing issue facing our country: protecting our Antarctic farmland?"

The Utah governor began. "First, in a bipartisan spirit, I must agree with my fellow governor that I'm fond of Wisconsin cheddar—and very, very concerned for the bighorn sheep. I'm also concerned about the blue spruce, the columbine, the lark bunting, and the greenback cutthroat trout."

Extended applause from the studio audience. All these wild flora and fauna were dear to the heart of Coloradans, yet barely survived in the wild.

"I'm concerned about more than farmland; about the entire Earth as home and food source for all human, animal, and plant members of the divine natural world. And we have to do something about that. We must use our human powers to preserve this planet, the one world we have, of whose stewardship we've been entrusted. Before it's too late."

A promising start; Anna had even got the word "divine" in there before Gar did. Jenny let out a breath. But the Begonia scoreboard listed only five points. Something was missing.

"So of course," continued Anna, "our peacekeeping forces must remain stationed at the Transantarctic Mountains, to maintain our enlightened stewardship of West Antarctica."

Jenny closed her eyes again. Farming Antarctica was the worst distraction from solving Earth's problems. No sun from April through September, and the sparse coastal wheat crop required extensive fertilization and irrigation of the arid land. Plus ongoing "peacekeeper incidents" with opponent forces.

"Governor Guzmán," Clive pursued, "Governor Carrillo just now brought up the role of the 'divine.' What do you see as the role of the divine in our stewardship of Earth?"

Guzmán nodded sagely. "I know in my heart that the divine will above the Firmament ordains the fate of our Earth. And that fate is not far from coming. The end time is not far off. Yet it's not too late to repent of our worldly ways. Restore family values—that will save America. When the Flood comes (as our scientists keep telling us it will), those of us who've followed divine rule will be saved."

Silence fell in the dining hall. Flood and salvation were nothing new, but to hear a future president predict it as policy gave pause for thought.

"And Governor Carrillo," said Clive. "Do you share your opponent's view? What is the role of the divine in our stewardship of Earth?"

Here was Anna's chance to tell the truth: that God created the entire universe, in all its vast size, and found it good; that humans had to find their place on Earth, and take care of it; that we must clean up our mess in space, and set our sights on Jupiter.

Anna said, "The Unity coalition embraces a big tent philosophy. We embrace citizens of all beliefs regarding the Firmament, all who share our fundamental principles of government serving the people. Divine wisdom calls different people in different ways to serve our country."

"WISDOM," texted Mary in Babynet. "IS THIS HUMAN WIS-DOM?"

"ZERO WISDOM," Jenny replied. "NO WISDOM HERE."

37

The first call Dylan found in his toybox Monday morning was Gil Wickett. Gil's window fairly vibrated with distress as the round-faced Toynet trillionaire glared anxiously out at him. "Dillie, what's going on? It's there in the code. Your staff have been using a—a competitor."

"Excuse me, Gil?"

"A competing system." Behind him a rattle and a whistle, as the toy train chugged around the amyloid mountain. Tiny lights blinked red and yellow at the road crossing.

Dylan flashed his "let's have fun" smile. "Sorry, Gil, it's been a long weekend." Red Bull alums from Frontera's first graduating class were back to fish the Ohio, sky-bike the cloud, and drop wads of cash at the Mound. And boost endowment for the campaign. "You know I'm not up on those toy details like you are. But my staff is the best—the finest staff at any college in the world. I'll get right on it with them. Did you ever solve Zari's last Phaistos disk? Of course you did; right away I'm sure."

Gil paused as if avoiding a smile. "Of course I solved that trifle. Tell her to send me another—a hard one this time." Then he frowned again. "You know I can't stand . . . a competing system. It destabilizes transmission."

"Destabilize—goodness, Gil, we can't have that. You know we value stability above all else." The ghosts in the current system were bad enough—the latest one from Sharon's five-year-old took down the whole college for a morning. And just when the Ebola died down, a new flu outbreak sprang from the printers.

As soon as he'd got Gil taken care of, Dylan blinked for Zari. The toymaker appeared in the midst of her Monday morning staff meeting. All the teddies sat around on their nap rugs, each with a glass of milk and a chocolate cupcake.

"Good morning, Zari. How's the system doing? Is last week's . . . instability under control?"

Zari nodded. "*No problema*. We took care of the culprit."

"Glad to hear it," he said with relief.

"In fact, she's right here." Zari nodded in the direction of an intense curly-haired five-year-old sucking her thumb on a nap rug. "The youngest we've hired."

"'Hired'?" The perpetrator of the kudzu ghost throughout the college.

"For a special job, not everyday service," Zari assured him. "She's testing the new Babynet system. A few Babynet hubs in the net could enormously stabilize transmission."

"I see." These children, this generation, born with brainstream in their heads. *Childhood's End*, it gave him the creeps. "I don't suppose this 'Babynet' might be considered a . . . competing system?"

"Competing with Toynet? No way. Not today, anyhow. Tomorrow, who knows?" The toymaker grinned, her brow lifting. "Tova's nearly the age Gil was when he first set up Toynet. Maybe she'll build her own network some day, and found a college on Jupiter."

Dylan forced a smile. "Well, we can take the competition. Could you spare a moment to send Gil another Phaistos? *Le mucho gustaba* your last one."

The ToyDebate planning group gathered in Dylan's toy-half conference room; half of them there in the flesh, the rest out on Toynet. Soledad, in her dark purple suit, whispered something to her cochair Jeremiah Stone, in a gray suit with a gold bowtie. The pair got along famously, considering each thought the other was Satan. At left the Secret Service director, with Sigourney Weaver's trademark chin, scanned her toybox ceaselessly. Dylan thought back to Teddy Roosevelt, the first American president to experience Secret Service protection; Teddy's own bodyguard, "Big Bill," had died in a trolley crash, the first officer to die while protecting the president. Two centuries had brought much change, but the vigilance of the Secret Service remained the same. The director sat flanked by her two Weaver-type DIRGs, standard for civilian crowd control, the gentle ruthless look.

"The powwow ground," Soli was saying. "And the faculty processing in their robes—we love it, don't we, Jermy."

Jeremiah nodded sagely. "Great show, great view. As good as outdoors—first 'outdoor' debate ever."

"And great symbolism."

"The Mound below," he agreed. "All those taxplayers, the foundation of government."

"However sinful." Soli couldn't resist.

"However wasteful," he needled back. "Play and spend."

"Yes, yes," interposed Dylan hurriedly. "The powwow ground will be *chulo*; don't you agree, Bobby?"

Next to the Weaver DIRGs, Bobby Foxtail Forrester smiled. "No trouble, no trouble. We'll cooperate in every way." The Shawnee would be in on everything, as would Mount Gilead, represented by Judge Baynor until the mayoral election. Judge Baynor had a barrel chest and the largest size power bands Dylan had ever seen. The judge cleared his throat and nodded curtly; he wanted out of here to get the last of his soybeans in. Quade had turned off the rain to get the bean moisture down.

The head Weaver looked up, still scanning her box. Her blue neck ring turned green, with a variant star design, as did the neck rings of both DIRGs at her side. The rings, and their box windows, would change style at coded intervals. "The powwow ground is way too open. Projectiles could come from anywhere, overhead in the hab. We'll need a bell jar enclosing the stage."

The bell jar was standard, ever since a candidate got bumped off at a primary debate the year Rosa won. Above the table projected a model of the grassy powwow ground, with a stage covered by a nearly invisible "jar" of transparent amyloid. It looked like one of those domes that now enclosed desert cities; Congress had just passed a bill to build one for D.C. The stage contained models of the two candidates at their podiums, with a model Clive. Clive of course was here at this meeting, not physically, but spliced in the toyroom alongside several other ToyDebate staff.

Jeremiah stroked his chin. "Could the jar rise from outside the ground, cupping the whole audience? Kind of like the Firmament."

"That too," said the Weaver. "Both layers of protection are warranted. Plus we need trigger barricades all around."

Dylan nodded. "I assume your DIRGs will get to work on this."

"They have already."

"There will be no . . . disruption of classes?"

"Our Weavers are discreet. Please note our special concerns." A long list scrolled through, everything from poison dart frogs to the plutonium source in Reagan Hall's physical science lab.

"A very small radiation source," Dylan assured her. "For teaching purposes."

"Nonetheless, one disruption there could render your hab unfit for life."
A cheery thought.

"Any criminal element?" asked Soli. "That incident last weekend?"

Dylan's heart took a plunge. Of all people, why those *chusma* had to pick
Jenny. "The college has addressed the incident, and charges have been filed."
The courthouse would get to it in December, when a sprinkling of snow for
Christmas marked a brief respite before the winter planting. But Nora would
deal with the perps well before then.

Jeremiah pursed his lips. "I'd say the college staff and students need
checking out, like everyone else."

"Minimally intrusive," the head Weaver assured him.

"There are privacy rules," ventured Dylan. "The college is bound by
FERPA."

"So are we." She blinked over to his box a hundred-odd pages of regulations.

Dylan turned to the codirectors. "How are we set for accommodations?
Your candidates' special needs?"

From his spliced slice of toyroom Clive spoke. "We need accommodations for all our service personnel, including my style crew."

"The town has that covered, don't we, Judge?"

Judge Baynor gave a satisfied smile. "Frank's printed out a four-star
hotel."

"My style crew requires a separate block of rooms, plus a special menu."
Clive's staff had listed twice the requirements of the two candidates combined.

At each dorm and residence, a Weaver-class DIRG emerged from the printer,
just like Jenny's mental had tried to do. Forewarned by Dean Kwon, the students went about their business as the DIRGs discreetly scoured the campus,
looking politely into every dorm room.

"What if they find someone's stash?"

"What if they find a facehugger? ROTFLMAO."

"They'll find ultra for sure."

For some reason, the Weavers took all day going through Ferrari house,
politely emptying every drawer and cataloguing the minutest items. "Did you
hear—those DIRGs recorded everything they found," Anouk told Jenny.

"Even the stains on their underwear." She added primly, "Of course, if those *chicos* used proper hygiene and avoided impure behaviors, they wouldn't have stains."

Jenny looked up, toward the woodland curving out past Mount Gilead. A wisp of smoke floating downward into the cloud. "*Dios mío,* what's that?"

Off the Buckeye Trail, a city-trained Weaver had stumbled upon a bear's den. The mother bear got strafed by a helibot sent to cover the DIRG. The DIRG got discreetly hauled off, leaving a mess for the ecoengineer. Elephant Man took home the orphaned cub to bottle feed.

Meanwhile, Jenny had other concerns, specifically her mother. She'd reserved a special table at Café de la Paix for her mother plus the Kearns-Clark twins, the most presentable of her friends. And she finally got Tom to show her his painting from Father Clare's art class, eager to add that to the list of her *novio*'s talents.

The student paintings were all lined up on the fresco wall in the art building. The wall had a peculiar damp smell. "Wet plaster," Tom told her. "You have to paint on wet plaster, made from lime, calcium hydroxide. The alkali reacts with carbon dioxide from the air, and it traps the colors." Each student had done one panel on the wall. Some had picked Renaissance themes, like Giotto's saints, while others looked more like Diego Rivera's workers. "If it dries out, you have to plaster and start over."

"*Guao.*" Jenny thought it sounded like a lot more trouble than digital paint. "So which one is yours?"

Tom seemed to hesitate. "It's there," he said evasively.

A shape of a willowy female with long dark hair, pink pigment for her shirt, black pants, kneeling on the grass. Her hand held the head of a *chico* lying down in an awkward position, perhaps injured. A large guy, with football shoulders. Jenny peered at the faces, which were hard to make out. Then she stepped back. Warmth crept up her neck. "It feels so long ago." The opening night on the powwow ground. Charlie had stepped into the bear's den, and Tom had lent her his rolled-up shirt. Swallowing hard, she dared not look at him.

Tom's hand pointed to a dark smudge at right. "That was supposed to be the bear, running off. I'll plaster it over."

"It's lovely." She smiled, remembering. "You should take your shirt off again."

+–+

At the Café de la Paix, the table for four was set with an elegant white cloth and spotless silver. A print of a Paris street on the wall. All as her mother could wish, Jenny thought.

Yola said, "Hope your trip went well, Ms. Kennedy."

Soledad waved her hand expressively. "Space was cleared for our flight, thank goodness. But for how much longer, I don't know." She shook her head. "Your scenery is beautiful. The birds; the sparkling river; the brook trout."

A preappetizer arrived, a single Périgord truffle upon a crostine, lozenge-shaped like the spacehab. Jenny admired the presentation, simple but elegant. Ken ate his truffle, carefully reserving the crostine so as not to chew the murdered wheat.

Soledad pressed Yola's arm. "Congratulations to your parents, for the new library. Such a generous gift."

"Thanks," said Yola. "Our dad just goes nuts about Frontera." Ken only frowned; he would not say a word about his dad.

"I share your father's passion. Frontera's lovely; George and I have reserved our own spot of land here."

Yola was taken aback.

"Just for vacations," said Jenny hurriedly.

"Everyone can't live out here," muttered Yola. A sensitive topic; they heard too much from the First Firmament folks.

"Of course not," Jenny's mother agreed. "We need to get beyond that notion. That is why this election is so important. Your college has been so hospitable, taking the trouble to host the final debate. I hope the students are signing up voters."

Ken said, "We don't vote, but sure, the Bulls are signing people up."

Jenny tensed in every muscle. She cast about for a change of subject.

"You don't vote?" Her mother's fork stilled, suspended in air.

"The candidates are all so corrupt," Yola explained. "Ken and I decided years ago that voting for any of them would violate our principles."

Ken nodded. "That Sid Shaak, for instance. Who'd vote for him?"

Jenny said, "Ken is phenomenal at defense. You should have seen him at Towers." Their first away game, against NYU, last weekend.

"*Asombroso*," exclaimed Yola. "We were twelve points down against NYU; a grudge match for them, after we whipped them last year."

"We even had a player out the second half," Ken recalled eagerly. "He got sick at the halftime show." The towers collapsing; Jenny had seen it any number of times, but the first time could be unnerving.

Yola popped a cage diagram into everyone's toybox. "Fran had the ball, but the NYU guard had her covered. So Ken set a screen. The guard plowed straight into him; how they didn't get a foul, I don't know."

Ken shook his head. "The ref hates us."

"But Ken slips out and takes a pass. What a slan! Jenny was right there too." Yola winked.

After the game, the NYU coach had sent Jenny a secret offer to sign her with a pro team. She doubted Play Twenty-nine could stay secret much longer. But then, it wouldn't—next week was their own grudge match, at Rapture.

Her mother was nodding, between forkfuls of Tom's special, the rack of lamb *persillade* with extra herbs to make up for the lack of salt. "George and I loved the game. Jordi would have been proud." She caught Jenny's hand. "I'm glad you got out to Towers. A break from your studies. Did you get to play the toyworld?"

"No, too much to study."

"We've got a hundred toyworlds here." Ken enjoyed his spirulina soufflé—how Tom got it to rise, Jenny could not guess.

"Well, Jenny, you'll enjoy Iroquoia over October break."

Yola looked up. "Iroquoia? I've heard of it."

Soledad nodded proudly. "George is the original sachem. We've scheduled a Condoling Council."

"Fantastic! What do you think, Kennie-boy?"

Ken's eyes lit up. "Could we play?"

Soledad pursed her lips. "A level-ten authentic preindustrial society. No voting."

"No way," exclaimed Jenny. "You guys *don't* want to play."

"She thinks we can't handle it," said Yola.

"We're in," said Ken.

"But Mama—"

"You're in," her mother agreed. "Check your box for your summons. I suggest you bone up on Kanienkehaka."

For dessert Tom brought a *gateau au chocolat* with dark *ganache*, decorated with white chocolate stars of the Great Bear and Little Dipper and surrounding northern stars.

"Perfect," exclaimed her mother. "My dear, you eat so well here."

"Tom," called Jenny before he could leave. She caught his hand. "Tom is my special friend," she said in a rush. "He paints beautiful frescos. And he always gets the daily molecule."

"A-triple-plus in chemistry," agreed Yola. "He's a dwork, just like Jenny."

"Impressive," said her mother. "Dylan's scholarship program certainly draws talent."

✦

Jenny walked arm in arm with her mother, up Buckeye Trail. The lights of Mount Gilead were like stars, an occasional peeper called, although fewer since the rain was off.

"Now *hijita*," her mother began. "I want you to know I understand all this—this youthful rebellion."

"Mama, it's not that."

"All this flirting with the opposition, and not voting."

"That's not me. Look, I've knocked on dozens of doors for Father Clare."

"I know," sighed her mother, "you were always good for the locals." She stopped. "I just don't want you to flip like your aunts. Promise me you won't."

"Of course not. How could I? The stupid firmament."

Soledad hesitated. "We always have to compromise. If a few more vote for us, who cares what they think of the night sky. They still admire NASA, *¿entiendes?*"

Jenny turned away.

"I know it's hard to get excited about Anna. She's no Kennedy." *Claro.* "But she'll do the best for now. There's Glynnis; you understand her, the solarray engineer. She'll get her chance too."

Silence. As if ten thousand klicks separated them both.

"Your Tom. He's a good *chico*."

Jenny turned quickly. There was an edge to her mother's voice, something unsaid.

"I just feel for you so. I only want the best."

"What do you mean?"

"He lacks an entire chromosome." No male-X, just the old degenerate Y. "All those singleton genes, with no backup. You can't know what that means. And his first fifteen years without preventive care." Soledad shook her head. "You know how it felt, losing your brother young. You'd lose this one too, by my age."

38

Jenny's latest assignment on Aristotle addressed the Best Government, in which citizens led the best life. The best kind of human beings (the Greeks) governed the best cities; while the Northerners were ungovernable, and the Asians were enslaved. The best governors required education, particularly in the arts of music and drawing.

"ToyNews—From our box to yours." World news, a welcome break from ancient philosophy. "Our Antarctic peacekeeping forces encountered heavy resistance today in their defense of Ellsworth Land. The regional commander is confident of protecting our crops of wheat, lichen, and bryophytes . . . On the home front, new forms of ultraphyte are invading our cities, some larger than Florida pythons. Twenty deaths today from cyanide poisoning. The new biotypes go undetected by Homeworld Security. And the latest on the presidential race; the two tickets still splitting the pollmeter down the middle—"

At practice, Coach was getting tenser by the day. The Whitcomb Angels at Rapture; the team they had to beat. "The Angels are the toughest team in our division. Above all, they are sure they're right—they've got God's will behind them. Ever since the Flood." The center for baraminology. Coach jabbed a finger at Yola. "But they're wrong."

"Course they're wrong," said Yola. "We've got our secret weapon."

Jenny didn't look at Ken. After this Sunday, the truth would be out.

Coach looked around at the players. "So what's the one thing you *all* need to do this week? For your brainstream?"

Jenny knew, she had to close her EMS window. But she remembered the nitrate baby, and Donna Matousek's husband, and the student near-deaths every Wednesday.

Before Wednesday Politics, Jenny stopped by to see the chaplain. The reddish region in the puzzle seemed to be filling out, with a brown shade along its curve, where Jenny had placed her first piece. An apple? A bit of green leaf would do.

"I've looked into the local voter regulations." Jenny leaned forward in her seat and streamed the document to Father Clare. "Frontera is classified as a county; and the county rule is, everyone must go to the courthouse to vote, between seven in the morning and seven at night."

Father Clare nodded. "That's how it's always been."

"But then it says everyone has to record their vote in ink, in a bound paper book." Kind of like Aristotle's codex. "They even specify the ink—something called uranyl acetate. Isn't that weird?"

Father Clare grinned. "Sounds weird to me."

"But—" She stopped. "Isn't this unconstitutional?"

"Not really. The parties still have public primaries; there's the Iowa caucus, where you not only have to declare your choice, you have to gather with like-minded electors at one side of the room."

"But that's party business. This is the federal election."

"The local mayoral election," he corrected. "Though it works the same in November. It's an old American tradition. Colonial Virginia had public voting; the sheriff called each voter up to state their choice."

"That's in here too. If the vote gets challenged, they call in the DIRGs to make everyone state their choice." Jenny frowned suspiciously. "Don't you know all this? Don't you vote every year?"

"I vote," he admitted. "I just never tried to change the rules."

"And nobody else does either?" If she did, Jenny thought, she'd be called a carpetbagger.

"Go check the rolls, and see who votes. It's all in that book, in the courthouse."

Jenny thought she'd take a look. But just as she left for class, there came a call from Anouk. "Jenny, can you sub for me this afternoon, for Developmental? Just this once, _chérie?_" Anouk's face in the window looked flushed, preoccupied. "Something important I must attend to."

"Substitute? For your tutoring?"

"It's just arithmetic. You can handle it."

Toymaker Valadkhani's class, which satisfied the general math requirement, was held in Toy Land, in the big toy-half conference room. The class was for students with documented limits to their math ability, usually associated with a known gene, although others could talk their way in. The room filled with fifty students, each of whom got a mat to sit on the floor, plus a box of smartsand.

Up front with her jumpsuit full of pockets, the toymaker pointed to giant numerals in the toywall. "Today, we learn negative numbers." With a shovel she scooped a hill of smartsand from a large sandbox. The scooped sand turned red. She dumped the red scoop on the surface, a little red hillock. "Here I have one scoop of sand. Plus One. Say that."

Everyone said "Plus One." Jenny noticed several students she knew, including Suze Gruman-Iberia, as well as Rafael. Suze's face had a bored look, like she was just here for the easy A-triple-plus. Rafael looked rather uncomfortable, and not just at seeing Jenny, who hadn't spoken to him since Monte Carlo Night.

"Now, let's look at the hole we left behind." There was a hole in the sand, the same size as the red hillock she'd removed. "But the hole is not sand—it's where one scoop got removed. *Minus* One. Suppose we add two scoops of Plus One to a *Minus* One. What do we see?"

The students got busy scooping sand. Next, they were adding three to minus five, and subtracting nine from seven. A student texted Jenny to check her work. Pretty soon, her box filled with texted questions.

Rafael still looked lost. Jenny wandered over, casually. "*¿Qué pasa?*"

"This is not for me," he said.

"Why not? Don't you have to figure your car speed?"

"The toybox does that." Rafael scooped a shovel full of sand, then put it back in the hole. "Zero is zero. How can something come of nothing?"

"Suppose you owe a debt; isn't that a negative number?"

He shuddered. "Usury. Negative numbers are not in the Bible."

Jenny thought this over. "We're out in a spacehab. Try doing off-world arithmetic."

After class there was still no word from Anouk. The northern light had gone red.

"ToyNews—From our box to yours." Clive had a twist in his hair, the kind for a juicy scandal. "The FBI has opened an investigation into business partners of vice presidential nominee Sid Shaak, charged with financing an underage pornography toyworld including zoophily . . ."

Amid all her blinking windows, one had gone unnoticed. But Jenny saw it now. It was Mary's Babynet text window. "HELP ANOUK."

That was odd. Why, Mary? "WHAT IS WRONG?"

"HELP ANOUK."

Anouk's own window would not respond. Her coordinates were gone— she was nowhere to be found in the hab. Jenny called Security and Toy Land. Anouk was not in her cottage, nor her toyroom, nor any of the science labs.

Yet she had to be somewhere. She could not access Toynet, but she still had her Babynet link to Mary.

From the Babynet connection, Valadkhani gradually short-listed the coordinates to a little-used toyroom on the third floor of the art building. The toyroom was somehow stuck closed. When they finally got the toyroom open, there lay Anouk, huddled on the floor with her head in her hands, in a state of shock.

Anouk went off to the Barnside, away for several hours. Upon her release, she begged Jenny to spend the night with her.

"So *horrible*, you cannot imagine," she exclaimed, while Jenny sat cross-legged on the little Noah's Ark sumak amid the Mandelbrot chairs. "I can't remember a *thing*."

"Tell me about it," muttered Jenny.

"All I know is, I was getting so close—and when I tried to check it out at the source, they tricked me. Somehow they got me to go to that toyroom, and then—" She shuddered. "I didn't know they could zap your mind long distance."

Jenny shook her head. "You of all people should know better. What do you think? Where brainstream goes out, it can go in."

"But I don't *know*. What if they *dishonored* me?" With a shudder she wrapped her arms around herself.

"They didn't steal your honor; they just borrowed it."

Anouk clutched Jenny's arm. "I do recall one thing. I wrote something here, on the sumak, where they couldn't erase it." She pulled up the edge of the carpet, beneath the flowered border. In black ink was some Arabic script. "What I wrote says, 'Ultra at Naval Observatory.'"

"Naval Observatory? The residence of the vice president."

"The Creep has ultra syndrome. Like Mary," Anouk explained. "Security finds ultras at his residence—and his West Wing office. They even found one under the Teddy Roosevelt desk."

"*¡No puede ser!*"

"Is it so surprising? When one is so obsessed with attacking a thing—"

"But not the West Wing!"

"Come on, Jenny, you know presidents can do anything; they sneak *chicas* half their age into the Oval Office. Your own great-grandfather sneaked elephants."

Jenny put her hands to her ears.

"Sorry. But look, this is why Guzmán finally dumped the Creep, *n'est-ce pas*? Won't your candidate like to know?"

39

So the Earth's foremost superpower was run behind the scenes by an ultra nut like Mary, with hands that crept away like cells that might take off on their own. And look at his likely replacements. The vice presidential debate was on Thursday in Wisconsin. The candidates would probably stick this year; it was unlikely that the Creep could oust the governor of California. Still, Jenny thought, never underestimate him.

"Senator Shaak," Clive asked, "do you believe the electorate will support a candidate under investigation for child pornography?"

Shaak had the dark suit, the Kennedy haircut, and the smile down pat. "Clive, as you know, public officials are always the target of insinuations and mudslinging, as well as nuisance lawsuits. The point is what we do in office. The last time Unity was in power, we passed the toughest child protection act in our nation's history." Rosa, again, another thing she'd got done her first year in office.

"And Governor Akeda," Clive asked in turn. "Do you believe the electorate will support a candidate who can't keep ultra off our shores?"

Aunt Meg smiled, and Aunt El kept decorously quiet. "As you know, Clive, ultraphytes have now spread through all fifty states, and to countries on all continents. But of course, that's no excuse for us to give up. I've activated my state's National Guard to protect our homeland and drive ultra into the sea."

Not much new from either would-be vice president. It was especially depressing to hear her aunt reduced to platitudes. Jenny wished she'd spent the time on her homework about the colonial Spanish massacres in Cuba.

The next day, curious, she checked what HuriaNews made of the debate. Since her interview about the ultraphytes, she'd found that Lane Mfumo often had a different take. To her surprise, HuriaNews actually reported some parts of the debate that Jenny had missed on ToyNet. An audience member had asked the candidates about voter fraud; about reports that ToyVote could be penetrated. "A study showed that ToyVote tallies of votes could be intercepted, decoded, and altered without detection."

To that, Shaak had said, "Unity has always demanded a physical record of every vote. Unfortunately, the current administration abolished the physical vote requirement, and not all states maintain it. Carrillo's first act as president will be to reinstate the requirement of a physical record for every vote."

Aunt Meg, of course, had a different view. "To preserve our freedom, we must stop voter fraud. Why, in some of our polling places, in the old days"—before Centrists won three terms—"security was so lax even an ultra could come in and vote." Laughter from the audience. "But then ToyVote instituted a multiple redundant system of checks. They make absolutely sure that only qualified American citizens can vote, and vote only once."

The argument was an old one. Perhaps signing a book in uranyl acetate had some advantages. But why had the entire exchange gone missing in ToyNews? Clive's office did not respond to her call, but Mfumo did.

"ToyNews has a new policy," Mfumo told her. "Their policy is they will report no stories on voter fraud within the six months preceding an election."

"What? Why not?"

"To avoid being manipulated into undermining confidence in the election results. That's what they say."

It was true that months of challenges ate into the term of many elected officials. "But still, that's censorship."

"Self-censorship. HuriaNews offers a different view." For those who listened. "Say, Jenny, have you got anything more on ultra? Your last interview played well."

She was helping set the tables for Tom's Friday night crowd at the café; Uncle Dylan had a Board committee meeting. "What do you think, Tom," she asked. "What do you think of having to go in and record your vote in public?"

Tom brought out the pitchers of fresh flowers. "That should decrease turnout."

"That's how they did it in colonial Virginia."

"Back then only a few white landowners voted." He adjusted a salad fork here, a butter plate there.

"*Imagine*. The Creep has ultra syndrome." Jenny shook her head. "Anouk says I should tell Glynnis. But Sid is no better—he's just been charged with running child porn. Everyone knew that already; how could they have picked such a person?"

"Beats me. How are your orchids?"

"*Muy bien*. Well, this is the last week for Father Clare's campaign. After the Rapture game, I can spend afternoons knocking on the last few doors—"

Tom crossed his arms and slammed his elbows on the table. "What's got into you? Is that all it is—election this, election that?"

She stopped short. "What do you mean?"

"I thought you were into chemistry. You haven't mentioned the daily molecule all week."

"Oh, right." There was always another one.

"Like, the one I posted?"

"I see. I'm sorry." Her face went hot. *Qué lío,* what a thing to miss. "Well, this is just till November, then it's done." For this year.

"It feels like forever to me." Tom looked away. It had been a while since he looked like that, one of his moods; she'd forgotten. Finally he looked back. "What did your mother say about me?"

Her eyelids fluttered. "What do you mean?"

"I just want to know. She was here; she saw me. What did she say?"

"Nothing much."

"She must have said something. What?"

Her hands uneasily gripped the tablecloth. "She said you were very nice."

"What else?"

"She said you would live half as long as—" She broke off.

Tom said nothing. He exhaled thoughtfully. "That's okay. After I'm gone someday, you can marry a First Lady. And run for president, like your great-grandmother."

Her lips parted, but she could think of nothing to say. Before she could think, Tom had turned and strode back to the kitchen. The door slammed behind him.

Jenny rushed to the door but it would not open. "Tom!" She pounded the door with her palms. "Tom, open up! It's not true, it's not—"

In her toybox, Tom's window went blank.

Jenny was devastated. She spent the night waking and crying, then drifting into troubled sleep. The next morning she could not get out of bed. Yola called at last, frantic over her missing the required optional practice. "Jenny, what on earth's wrong?"

"Feeling sick," she muttered.

"Well, for heaven's sake get better. You're our secret weapon."

Jenny half smiled. "I know."

"Get plenty of sleep, remember."

She lay on her back, watching the blank ceiling. The depth of loss swept over her again. At last she blinked for the mental.

The Monroe smiled as usual, her eyelids fluttering. "Jenny, you've been doing *so* well."

"How can I get him back?"

Monroe pointed an exquisite finger. "That's for *you* to find out. First, love is always a puzzle. But you can work it out." Her words trailed off in song. "I'm through with love . . . I'll never fall again . . . For I must love you or no one . . ."

Squeezing her eyes shut, Jenny turned over and back to oblivion.

The next time she roused, it was an EMS call for a grandmother on a farm near the Ohio River. Out the farmhouse window in the afternoon light chorused peepers, while Jenny stroked the woman's hand and let Charlie take the scanscope readings. Afterward she checked the readings to make sure. "Good job," she told him.

Charlie beamed. "Hey, maybe I'll amount to something."

"Sure you will. You and Tom were great knights, remember. Saved the day."

He chuckled. "I'll be a knight again, at the castle."

The Castle Cockaigne; the great Feast of Fools, the Kearns-Clark twins had promised at midseason. Wednesday next week, just before October Break. Jenny looked forward to it; she'd even looked into her costume. She'd planned on going with Tom. The thought of Tom nearly brought tears again, but she bit her lip and squeezed shut her eyes.

Once the patient was stabilized at the Barnside, Jenny walked home with Charlie. "What's got into Tom?" Charlie and Tom were best friends, she knew. "Why won't he answer? He even did that painting—"

"I've seen it."

"Then what's he mad about?"

Charlie shook his head. "He thinks he's not good enough for you."

Jenny rolled her eyes. "Like a soap toyworld. Look, I'm the judge of that. He will come back, won't he?"

"Jenny, I'm sure he'll come back." Charlie added in a low voice, "And if he doesn't, there's other guys."

She patted his arm. "Thanks, Charlie, you're a good friend." Still, she felt hollow inside.

Then suddenly angry. What right did Tom have to make her feel like this—after making up to her for weeks. How could a random-born *chico* just flip a switch like that? That no-good Y chromosome.

After checking all her wisdom plants in Reagan Hall, completing Roosevelt's plans to build a canal in Nicaragua or Panama, and reviewing Coach's report on the Angels team, Jenny got to bed early enough. Deep into sleep, she was woken once again. To her surprise, it was Yola.

"No EMS—I turned it off," she objected sleepily. What was Yola doing this late Saturday, with the shuttle to Rapture leaving early Sunday?

Yola looked distracted. "I can't get him down, and Dean Kwon can't either. Can you try?"

A Bulls sophomore was stuck atop the cloud ladder, eyes glazed, with a "lost in the toyworld" look. His name was Fritz, one of the dozen Fritzes she knew. He yelled unsteadily, "I'm going to ju-ump!"

By the time Jenny got there, Travis Tharp and three other maintenance men, plus half the Bulls club members, were gathered around the ladder, staring up. Dean Kwon gave Jenny a look. "He's got relationship issues."

"Why me?" insisted Jenny.

"You're the better talker," said Yola. "I can't talk at him; I'm too mad."

"Why not his bros?"

"They tried already. He just climbed higher."

"Can't the medibot get him?"

"They're afraid he'll jump."

Jenny searched the name and opened a window. A freckle-faced guy, kind of pale, with eyes unfocused. She blinked for the old talk-them-down script; it had been a few years. "Hey, Fritz, *amigo*. I'm coming up for a chat, okay?"

"Go away."

"Okay, *amigo*, but first can I hear your story? Please? Just the two of us, okay?"

No response. One foot after another, Jenny climbed, shivering in the nighttime breeze. Out in the dark called an owl, a long echoing call, the kind of owl that feasted on peepers. Climbing the cloud ladder at night, with a medibot hovering ominously near, was not where she'd ever planned to be.

"Go on," encouraged Yola. "He's let no one else that close."

At last she neared the rung of his feet. His arms cradled the ladder like a *novia*. "She's gone," he whimpered, voice slurred. "She won't come back."

"Hey, I know how you feel." Jenny opened the scanscope; if he let her snap it round his ankle, he would sober right up. "Hey, *amigo*, may I just fix your foot, *¿por favor?*"

Waiting it out, he finally came to and was coaxed to climb down. In the corner of her box, Jenny checked the time. Three A.M.—just ten hours till jump ball at Rapture.

40

Jenny got out Sunday morning with four hours' sleep; just soon enough to scarf down some amyloid from her printer and catch the shuttle below. Her head throbbed, but her toybox woke her up when she started to nod. As she filed onto the anthrax lift with her teammates, she avoided looking at Coach at all. Slumping into a seat, she strapped herself down and willed herself asleep again.

The next thing she knew, Fran was nudging her awake. Nearing the Rapture spacehab, Coach gave their final prep talk on the opposition.

He jabbed a finger at the virtual cage hovering in the aisle. "Here's their center, Number Seven." A player appeared, like a finger doll. A young man with snub-nosed face and straight blond hair precisely cropped beneath his slancap.

Yola murmured, "Immaculate Conception."

Jenny frowned, and Ken elbowed Yola in the rib. They could see Coach was in no mood for jokes.

"Number Seven has the highest scoring percentage. Yola, you keep on him."

"Right, Coach."

"Downside for Number Seven: To keep his percentage high, he stays down in the cap zone; never tries for a three-pointer." Coach jabbed again. Another player, broader shoulders, legs a bit splayed. "Fran, you've got Number Twenty-one. He's their outside shooter."

"You bet, Coach."

Down the list of players, until at last the goalie, Number 13. "Number Thirteen didn't give up one goal in his last three games."

Charlie raised a tentative hand. "This sounds dumb, I know, but, like, where are their *chicas*?" Division rules mandated an even ratio on the team.

Coach nodded. "As some of you recall from last year, Whitcomb maintains the largest roster allowed, including women. But they never field them."

"Paulines all," explained Yola. "You'll see them on the bench."

Charlie's face scrunched, as if trying to grapple with a tough problem. "I know I'm just dense, but where I come from the uber-Christians are, like, 'chivalrous' to women. How do they cope with women players?"

Coach pursed his lips, weighing his choice of words.

Fran and Yola smirked at each other. "We're just pagans," said Fran. "We don't count."

At that Coach frowned. "Enough already. Tough players deserve our respect, no matter what. But believe me, expect no chivalry."

Kendall let out a breath. "Believe me, we won't."

"Goalie Thirteen," reminded Coach. "He deflects every shot, no matter how fast. How to get past this guy." His fingers drummed on the clipboard. "Our only chance is surprise."

Everyone looked at Jenny.

Yola reflected. "I don't know, Coach. When they find out . . ."

"No chivalry doesn't begin to describe it," finished Kendall.

"I'll do it," said Jenny. "For the team."

Rapture was a more recent spacehab, built twenty years after Frontera. Twice as large, with a double-thick hull, it had solved substratum overflow and other engineering problems that dogged the older spacehab. As Jenny came up from their entry, her eyes winced in the unaccustomed summer-level light. Twice as bright as the Frontera daylight she'd grown used to, it consumed ten times the power. At the far end of the hab, the casino complex was built as a scale model of ancient Jerusalem, from the Pool of Siloam to the Golden Gate, with the temple arising on the original hill. The Holyland Hotel and Worship Center.

"Holy smoke," muttered Charlie.

Grinning, Yola punched him in the side. "Wait till you see their cheerleaders."

The cloud ladder would take forever, Jenny thought. But in fact, there was a motorized amyloid stairway to heaven. In two minutes they were up in the clouds, looking out upon the gleaming rooftops of Jerusalem. The clouds pulsed in artful patterns of white and gold, like the edge of God's robe.

An enormous crowd was gathering all around the cage. It was the usual regulation size, but the audience tube was set farther out to accommodate a greater number of seats. Nearly every seat was full; an astonishing home turnout. To her relief Jenny located the small brave contingent from Frontera with a Great Bear banner. The Kearns-Clark dad wore a bear suit. As Frontera's team arrived, he stood up on his seat and growled.

Trumpets blared and echoed from the distant farmlands. As the fanfare soared, angels began to arise from the cloud. Gigantic robed forms, white with gold-edged wings, the virtual spectacle grew till it nearly filled the hab. *"Angels from the realms of glory, wing your flight o'er all the earth. . . ."* Their song pounded in Jenny's ears.

"**Cheerleaders**," texted Yola.

The Bears this time wore purple with white stars. The Angels, half again as many as Bears, came out in white trimmed with gold, and their three coaches wore white suit and tie. Women players sat on the bench, bonnets over their slancaps. A priest led the team in a prayer circle.

"Hey Ken," texted Charlie, "won't **Coach give us a blessing?**"

"He won't," returned Ken. "**Separation of church and game.**"

"We're sunk," groaned Charlie in Jenny's ear.

The national anthem; the hovering choir sang it beautifully. Everyone paused to listen. For a moment, Jenny had a prickly feeling that the audience, team, and angels were all part of one something.

At long last Yola faced off with Number 7. The sudden hush took her breath away. Even the heavenly host was still.

The game got off to a good start. Fran and Yola zigzagged all the way down the cage and got in some fancy passes, and David got a straight shot to the goal. David had practiced shooting like crazy all week, and his hard work paid off.

Except the ball did not go in. A straight fast shot that would have been a sure thing in their past two games veered off at nearly a right angle. Just before Number 13, the ball had turned and bounced around the cage, picked up by an Angel who headed back and scored. The crowd erupted in cheers, the loudest crowd Jenny had ever heard.

After another two misses, Coach called time-out.

"Coach, what do we do?" demanded Ken. "That guy's an animal."

"Listen," Coach said. "We've learned two things. First: No easy shot will get past Number Thirteen. Second: Their defense is lazy, figuring why bother. Once we do penetrate, we'll make good."

"Send in Jenny."

"Too soon," said Coach. "Jenny's shot would do no better; and they'd have time to adjust. For now, just hammer them the best you can. Tire them out."

The rest of the half was grueling. Jenny went in for a few minutes, just to zigzag and get the feel of the cage. But her teammates got nowhere slanning, and there were laughs and catcalls whenever they tried. They wound up twenty to zero.

As the halftime bell sounded, Jenny slumped to her feet, tired and disoriented, just wishing she were home. But somehow there was a change in the air. The audience members strained from their seats, looking this way and that, exchanging short questions.

Then it happened. Two-thirds of the audience simply vanished. Where individuals had occupied seats, there were left purses, drink containers, shoes. But the people were gone. The remaining audience cheered and raised their arms. "Praise the Lord!"

"Rapture," texted Yola. "See, the audience wasn't really that big."

Above the distant Jerusalem rose a great light and the figure of the holy destroyer. Bolts of lightning streaked from the clouds. A bolt hit the temple with a blinding flash. The temple cracked asunder, the sound reverberating the length of the hab.

As the thunderclaps faded away, Coach tapped Jenny on the shoulder. "You know what you've got to do."

Jenny's lip twisted. "Yeah, I know."

✦

As Jenny entered the cage, the score was twenty to zero, the crowd clapping cheerfully, expecting a rout. Staying near the midline, she crouched low, trying to look smaller than she was. Her Angel guard gave her a disdainful look, wondering why she held back instead of helping her poor teammates defend their goal. Finally he left, and helped score another goal.

As the goal was scored, and the ball turned over, the Angels sent in a new goalie; a first-year, obviously to give him a bit of experience against this hopeless team. Yola saw too, and she shot the ball to Jenny. The Angels were falling back, when Jenny slanned. For a moment everything else vanished; then she poured all her mental energy into moving that ball all the way down the cage, as fast as it could go. She closed her eyes, then hurriedly she opened them. The ball was nowhere in the cage.

"Five points for the Bears." The score for a goal from the midline.

The crowd hushed. Only the Frontera contingent leapt to their feet, cheering in their bear suits. The Kearns-Clark dad let out an amplified grizzly roar.

Disoriented, the Angel defenders pulled back, one of them heading toward Jenny. In their confusion, they lost the ball to David, who sent it back to her. The guard tried to intercept; but from six feet away from him, Jenny slanned again, all the way down the cage. Another five points.

Goalie 13 was sent back in, but the Angels seemed to have lost their playbook. They double-teamed Jenny and Yola, leaving Fran and David clear to hammer the goal at close range. Points started to creep up.

Outside the cage, the monumental Angel cheerleaders moved in with their song, as if to provide moral reinforcement. "*Ye who sang cre-A-tion's story . . .*"

Jenny's two guards did not look happy. They crisscrossed in front of her. "Whore of Babylon," muttered one, passing behind her. As he passed behind, her leg felt a blow. The leg exploded in pain.

The pain was unimaginable. Her leg dragged as if hanging by a thread.

"Jenny? Are you all right?"

In her toybox her medic sign was blinking and beeping. But if she gave up injured, they'd have gotten rid of her. She blinked to disable the medic.

Out of the corner of her eye she saw Coach yelling at the ref, practically shouting down the guy's throat.

"Coach Porat," came the announcer. "Suspended for the rest of the game."

"Keep going," texted Yola. **"I'll call the plays."**

Overwhelmed by pain, Jenny barely knew what was going on, but she could still zigzag across the cage with her arms plus her one good leg. The points were gaining, particularly Fran's and David's side shots, which seemed to unnerve goalie 13. She was just aware enough to deflect a distant pass to Ken, and he swiped it in. At some point she lost track of time, and then faded out.

"Jenny? Jenny, can you hear me? Who's the president?"

Jenny's eyes flew open with alarm. Not me, she tried to shout, but it was like one of those dreams where you can't open your mouth. She found herself lying outside, not even remembering how she'd got back down to ground. Coach was there, and the trainer was plasting her leg. Doc Uddin was berating Coach. "How dare you keep a student in the game with a tibia fracture."

"Did we win?" Jenny whispered.

The trainer nodded.

41

The great win gave rise to effusive congratulations and celebrations, tempered only by the return to practice Tuesday morning. But the practice week would be cut short Thursday, as students rushed to finish their exams before October break.

In Jenny's toybox appeared the long-anticipated invitation:

> King Mark and Queen Berengaria of the Maple Realm
> Proclaim
> THE FEAST OF FOOLS
> You and Your Guest are Summoned to Castle Cockaigne
> Entertainment required
> *Morias philai paromen*

"Morias," according to Toynet, was Greek for "folly." Anouk, seated in Jenny's porch swing, read the invitation enviously. " 'Friends of folly, we are here,' " she translated. "The castle—it sounds *merveilleux*."

"You may come with me," offered Jenny. "If you provide entertainment."

"That I can do indeed," said Anouk with an air of satisfaction. "Thanks so much, *chérie*. And of course, Berthe will assist."

Jenny shrugged. "She'll blend right in with the amyloid help."

"I'll assist with your costume. You'll need a persona." And entertainment, Jenny reminded herself.

She remembered Tom, with a fresh well of pain. Tom didn't even appear to her in Life class, now that he'd closed his window. But he would be at the feast; Ken and Yola had hired him for the food. Remembering, she chose her "medieval" name, Lúthien Tinúviel.

Wednesday night, she and Anouk arrived in good time at the castle. As they came across the drawbridge, a pair of amyloid trumpeters blew a fanfare. "Princess Lúthien Tinúviel. Accompanied by la Reine Zazzua."

Jenny crept through the portal, taking care to avoid tripping on her long kirtle. She held up the meter-length pointed sleeves of the mantle, a navy blue cloak that parted dramatically down the front. After fixing her hair several ways, she had finally let it hang straight and loose, fairy princess style, with a tiny half-crown in front. Anouk, as Reine Zazzua, had her hair bound in a red turban studded with pearls, and wore a gold-trimmed white fur coat down to her toes. The coat flowed out in all directions, as if covering a full petticoat beneath.

The great hall was lined with amyloid torches, their knobs simulating a ruddy glow. Amyloid dwarves went to and fro, carrying dishes and pots. At the far end, a high balcony held musicians playing lutes and viols. The slan-ball team members and their guests were arriving, in various outlandish garb. Charlie, in chain mail, had invited Priscilla, in a Greek tunic; her window proclaimed "Hypatia of Alexandria."

"The Countess Mandragora!"

Jenny winced at this joke on Mary, however well meant. Her *compañera* was there, all right, in her usual tie-dyed dress. The only one who'd come as herself.

A goose waddled past her feet; Jenny startled. The goose raised its wings and hurried, followed by a small pig, a carving knife in its snout. Amyloid, she hoped, as the floor filled with strutting edible animals. Medieval nobles were partial to meat.

Upon a dais beneath the musicians sat the reigning monarchs. "Hear ye, nobles and guests fair." King Mark was actually Yola. The King wore a huge jeweled crown, and a fluorescent blue robe with gold maple leaf decorations flowed down across the floor. "He" raised a glittering scepter. "Welcome, all, to the Maple Realm. Find your places and let the feast begin."

"And remember your entertainments." Ken was Queen Berengaria, his russet gown cinched tight at the waist, a velvet headpiece draped beneath his crown. "We expect to be entertained. If it's too dramatic, we delicate ladies may faint." He appeared to relish the prospect. Like Jordi, Jenny recalled with a sudden pang. Jordi as "Lady J," at that last private megabuck fundraiser, before the waves took Fire Island. She smiled, quickly wiping her eyes.

Besides the students, Coach and Professor Abaynesh were there with Tova. The mop-headed girl gazed all around, her eyes wide. Not missing a thing—Jenny wondered if a child really belonged at this event.

The long table was already filled with baskets of fruit and cheeses. At each place sat an enormous wine jug with a fretwork of figurines and holes in between. Charlie picked up his jug to drink, but the wine flowed out through the holes. "What's this?"

Jenny smiled. "It's a puzzle jug. My 'entertainment.'" She'd pulled that one from her magic repertoire. "If you can't figure out how to drink from it, you've probably drunk too much."

"¡Oye! I've drunk *nothing* for weeks."

Anouk looked away. "Water, please," she asked a dwarf. Around the table, there were spills and lots of laughter.

Priscilla poked at her jug, one hole after another. Finally, she covered one spout and drank from the other. "See?"

The dwarves set out tureens of soup. A delicate cream soup, the sort Tom always made, Jenny thought wistfully. The soup was followed by individual stuffed quails.

The trumpets played a flourish. King Mark pounded "his" scepter. "And now, for our next entertainment: Knights of the Maple Realm."

Charlie and David came out to the side, where the dwarves shooed the geese and pigs out of the way. In the clearing the two knights raised their swords. The swords clanged, and each took quite a beating. When David lost his footing and landed on his back, Queen Berengaria called a halt. Both knights approached the queen to receive a laurel wreath.

"HUMOR?" texted Mary.

"ENTERTAINING," Jenny sent back.

"Next," announced the King, "la Reine Zazzua."

Anouk stepped forward with great dignity. The cloak fell away, revealing a full ballet skirt of white tulle down to her ankles. She launched into a ballet number, "Archimedes spiral." As she danced, her red turban whirled. Virtual numbers streamed down around her, the radial series that generated the famous spiral spinning out to infinity.

"WISDOM?" texted Mary.

"WISE. ENTERTAINING."

Next to entertain came the Philosopher Queen. Priscilla stepped forward, putting on an enormous donkey head. "Kind gentles, I present a discourse upon the question of Best Government. I argue the case for Government by Ass."

Appreciative laughter around the table.

"Let us argue for the Rule of Ass," nodded the donkey head, "rather than the Rule of Man. Firstly, those who think it better to be ruled by Man argue that the Man will deliberate more nobly when it comes to particulars. But experience shows that even an Ass can judge particulars better than a certain Man."

More laughter. It was no secret who that Man might be.

"Furthermore, the Ass need not in fact be better at deciding particulars, since the multitude could be better than he is and less corruptible. But beware lest the Ass will hand things over to his children. If the Ass's children succeed him (and behave as some heirs have done) they will ruin everything. . . ."

By the end, Priscilla could barely be heard, there was so much laughter all round; Jenny had to wipe the tears from her face.

Queen Berengaria tossed a bouquet of flowers. "Gentle Ass," cried the Queen, "you *must* come before us to kiss our hand."

"HUMOROUS AND WISE," Jenny texted Mary.

The King banged his scepter. "And now," he announced, "we present: Pope Innocent and Lady Godiva."

Laughter swept the table, with pointed comments. "Innocent of what?" texted someone, followed by increasingly ribald answers. Jenny frowned, eying innocent Tova. She hoped the party guests screened their text to the windows of students.

Lady Godiva entered, riding a small Gilead horse. Virtual hair cascaded to the floor, decorously covering her supposed lack of clothes. "Gentles!" she cried. "Let us save the poor from taxes!" Like the poster for the Mound.

Pope Innocent followed, his pointed mitre bobbing above his scarlet robes. The robes swayed as he took a long step forward. "Save Earth from disaster—Burn all the witches!" Suddenly the Pope pulled apart his robes to reveal the exaggerated virtual form of a flasher. The hall erupted in screams of laughter, while Godiva cartwheeled off her horse, revealing equally exaggerated female charms.

"What, ho!" Queen Berengaria banged her staff on the floor. "I'll not have this impudence at our family-friendly feast."

"Family friendly." King Mark extended his scepter. There erupted a blast of light. The virtual body parts disappeared, revealing two slanball sophomores in tights. There were sighs of disappointment.

"Only students saw it, anyhow," muttered Charlie.

Jenny was not so sure. She doubted any toy-view escaped Tova.

From the balcony above, the trumpets blared. Below, four dwarves came out bearing a tray with an enormous mound of gilt pastry, shaped with ruffles and florets. The tray was set down upon the long table. A knife stuck in the center. From the crack emerged two dozen tiny birds flying in all directions. Amyloid, Jenny hoped. Medievals knew nothing of hygiene.

"Hark, minions!" King Mark rose from the throne, holding aloft his scepter. "Where is our Master Cook? Bring him hither."

The dwarves rushed out. Two of them returned, dragging a bewildered Tom between them. Tom wore his usual white toque and jacket.

"Behold the creator of this feast—Master Cook René Verdon de Pouzaugues."

Everyone rose to their feet, and the applause echoed through the hall.

"But—but my soufflé," Tom stammered. "It's burning."

The King waved "his" hand, and Tom hurried out. "And for our final act . . ."

Curious, Jenny blinked up Tom's chosen name. "René Verdon" had been the master chef of the original Kennedy White House. She took a deep breath, and for a moment heard nothing more.

The final act consisted of Fran Pezarkar done up as a mock DIRG with a giant Weaver head, battling a great bear. Fran's aim with the anachronistic laser was outrageously poor, sizzling a flagstone here or there while the bear reared menacingly around the gathered company. At last the bear made a rush for the Queen.

"What, ho! Save me!" The Queen threw up "her" arms and collapsed with dramatic abandon.

Just in time, the Weaver-headed Fran aimed her laser right at the bear's head. The grim beast collapsed, rolling neatly on its back.

"Great Bear," cried the King. "Arise, and show thy true self!"

The bear's head came off, and out of the costume crawled none other than the ecoengineer, Quade Vincenzo. At this surprise appearance of the students' favorite administrator, the crowd erupted in applause and clamor.

"Elephant man! Bring on the elephants!"

"Encore, encore! Bring on the poison frogs!"

"Ultraphyte! Let's set the bear against ultra! See who wins!"

Charlie nodded. "Hey, that's a good one. Ultra against the bear. We'll bet on which wins—and no house edge!"

The crowd stamped their feet. "Ultra and the bear—ultra and the bear!"

Suddenly there were gasps. Along the floor snaked a long, sallow shape with the regular eyespot cells of an ultraphyte. A few students got up and drew away. Jenny cried out, then clapped her mouth. It was amyloid . . . wasn't it?

"Mary!" Professor Abaynesh called above the din. *"Get back to the lab!"*

Mary was nowhere to be seen. The ultra glided easily along the floor, finding its way amongst the geese and piglets, slinking out at last toward the drawbridge.

┿

In the morning the ecoengineer's snoopers were seen swarming around the castle and the moat, but no news was heard. That afternoon at the lab, Jenny and Anouk were sampling their wisdom plants. In each pot the twin seedlings had matured. Jenny had set up the test the weekend before, spreading caterpillar semiochemicals onto one member of the pair. Now she and Anouk were sampling the leaves for any response from their neurons. Would the plants wisely cooperate to defeat insects? Meanwhile her toybox filled with unanswered interview requests, and her mother's reminder of Iroquoia. And so much back homework to do over "vacation." Her other classes were going well, but her Life grade was still only A. She had to get that up somehow. Other students had already transferred out.

Anouk stopped to stretch, patting her scarf. "Last night," she demanded suddenly. "What Mary made. Was it?"

Jenny was embarrassed. "I don't know. It sure looked real. The light was dim, and we'd all been drinking."

Anouk drew herself up in third position. "I was not drinking, and *I* saw it."

"So? What did you see?"

She hesitated. "It looked just like the other ultras. The ones in your cottage."

"Mary's cottage," Jenny emphasized. Would she never shake her connection with that *compañera*? "*Vaya*, the college admitted her with all her problems. The admissions director says he'd admit even DIRGs. She's half amyloid herself; so, she's made an amyloid ultra."

Anouk just tilted her high-bridged nose.

"You think it was real? Not just amyloid, like the dwarves?"

Anouk's hand drooped upon the lab bench. "If it was real," she reflected, "I suppose they'll have to melt the whole castle."

Desastre. And much good it would do. Would the college end up melting down the whole hab?

"How could they admit her?" Jenny wondered aloud.

"They had to," observed Anouk succinctly. "You and Mary were the last two they took, to fill the class."

Jenny didn't ask how she knew, but glared. "You must have been the third."

"Precisely. I would *never* have come here, if I weren't banned from Earth."

Three broken toys, admitted to meet the college budget. *Dios mío,* why didn't the college just take DIRGs? "You know," Jenny reflected, "if scientists could ever make amyloid detailed enough . . . it wouldn't matter, would it? I mean, we're all made of protein, right? It would be the same as real. Someday, even amyloid people."

"Not any time soon," said Anouk. "Not in *this* lab."

"What do you mean? Is something wrong with our experiment?" After all the work they'd put in—Jenny's heart squeezed.

Anouk let out a breath and clasped her hands upon the bench. "I've been reading back, all the professor's papers from the last twenty years."

"I know, I have to catch up."

"Do you realize, that the professor has accomplished nothing significant on 'wisdom' since Ng and Howell?"

Jenny fingered the sprayer. "She found other things. The find-your-mortarboard plant, and the praying plant. *Asombroso*—even Howell thought so." Howell had sounded jealous, like he thought Abaynesh would get the Nobel.

"But never wisdom plants. Over and over again, students have assayed different combinations of genes, testing different neural networks for 'wisdom.' Still nothing."

Jenny considered this. "It's not like your MIT stuff, coding a new ghost every month. Plant development takes a while. The laughing plants; they worked."

"Laughter is a simple reflex. Even rats can laugh. But 'wisdom'—every religion in the world tries to solve that one. Do you think science will succeed?"

Another cart full of seedlings entered the lab room, accompanied by Mary Dyer. The two students startled at seeing her, but Mary took no notice. The enigmatic *compañera* approached at leisure, ignoring the two pairs of eyes that bored into her. Jenny had questions she scarcely dared think of, let alone ask aloud. Observing the pots on the cart, she swallowed. "Mary, what are those?"

Mary brought the cart over, and started arranging the pots in a row. "Reverse control."

Jenny exchanged a long look with Anouk. Then Anouk turned to Mary. "Mary, *chérie*," she said. "There is no such thing as a reverse control for wisdom." No one knew a wisdom semiochemical for humans.

Mary set the last of her twenty potted seedlings alongside the experimental plants. "There is now."

42

An ultra in the castle, and a wisdom control. Was it all real, or just more student follies? So much went spinning through her head that Jenny actually could not get herself to sleep, no matter how early she got to bed. Thank goodness for October break, she thought Friday afternoon as she took the space lift down and caught the heli to Westchester.

It was her first return to Somers since August. Looking out from the helicopter, the kudzu forest seemed a different color, faded yellow. At her home, all the leaves were drooped and shriveled, hanging from a tangled network of bleached vines.

"No rain since August." Soledad held her hand, and they strolled down to the Somers intersection, just like the old days, the drone overhead and the white-faced DIRGs inconspicuously behind. "The reservoir is so low, you can see the foundations of the old flooded homes." The reservoir was New York City's water supply.

"The kudzu always comes back." Jenny stepped around a dead skunk covered with ants. There were other dead animals, a squirrel and a python overcome by the heat.

"Even kudzu won't come back, once we become the Sahara." Her mother squeezed her hand. "The hurricane may bring some rain up the coast."

A reverse control for wisdom, Jenny wondered again. What if you really could make humans do the wise thing, like the way you could make them laugh?

"But where you are," her mother added, "there are maples and coneflowers."

"And peepers in the Indian grass. And bears and elephants." Ahead rose the old redbrick Elephant Hotel, its front cleared of kudzu. The old trees where she used to play hide-and-seek with Jordi had long ago dried out. Old Bet atop the pillar, her metallic surface mottled as if with the residue of ancient floods; the old circus elephant looked squat and stolid, compared to the little live ones with their donkey tails. Across the street stood the white-painted gazebo, where Jordi always waited. Yet now it all felt small, like a doll's house, the things of childhood left behind.

"The pollmeter is closing in," her mother added. "Much closer than last time." Last time they'd lost by two electoral votes. "Holding the final debate at Frontera could just make the difference for Ohio." Soledad paused thoughtfully. "If Ohio looks good, we might vote in Wisconsin. Our cottage in the Dells, *recuerdas*."

Back at the house, her father sat in an icosahedral toyroom with twenty spliced doors. His two wristwatches stretched on his arm, and his two Illyrian ties hung loose from his neck. "Could you use some change?" A stack of ten-dollar coins stood between two fingers. In a moment, they all fanned out, one balanced upon each fingertip. A flip of the wrist, and they vanished.

"*Chulo*." Jenny patted his knee and kissed his cheek. In some ways, he was still the boy that had peeped out from beneath his father's desk in the Oval Office. "My friends liked that one too. How's Toynet?"

"Eighty-six percent functional. Just now, when you asked."

Her eyes scanned the triangular doors. One was draped with virtual bunting, red-white-blue. "Is ToyVote sorted out this year?"

"The committee of a hundred gets together."

"So many. What do they talk about?"

"Change of residence times. Most states say noon on Election Day, but some say six in the morning, or seven that evening. Time zone effects. Electronic time delays; what constitutes a late vote."

She grinned. "You should see our mayoral election. We all go to a courthouse and sign in a book."

"The Iroquois meet in a longhouse, in winter. In summer, the councils meet outdoors." The women's council, and the men's council. "The meeting takes many days."

And it was almost time to play. "It can't take days this time, Dad," she warned. "I have to get back tomorrow, to check my plants." Experimental plants, and their controls.

++

In the old second-floor toyroom, Jenny put up her arms to activate. It had been so long, she had to dig out her window into Iroquoia, which had receded behind a thousand windows she hadn't used for two months. Through the doorway shone a forest of pines, a dark green mass of branches above a ground thick with pale dry fallen needles. Not a kudzu in sight; like Mohawk country would have looked in the nineteenth century. She took a deep breath and stepped in.

The toyworld applied her fringed deerskin skirt and tunic, moccasins beneath leggings up to the knee. "Sunflower Spirit" was her name, an herbalist. From her neck hung a pouch of dried plants, meadow-rue for nosebleed, wood nettle for loneliness. Ahead lay a clearing around a fire, blankets spread on the needles for other seated women of the council. About thirty women, most toy-construct. Those actually playing today had their names highlighted. The Chief Woman, Green Snake, turned and lifted her corn pounder. *"Onenh wegniserade. . . ."*

Hurriedly Jenny switched on the translation. English text hovered below the names. She'd given up on the language years ago; the toyworld would convert as they played.

"Now, you startle me by your coming, Sunflower Spirit." The Chief Woman, played by a Toynet coworker of her father's, addressed her before the Council. "Think how many obstacles you must have overcome to travel so far, from your trials among the Salt Beings. Wild beasts have lain in ambush; trees could have fallen upon you; the floods could have drowned you; the deadly Rotting Face disease could have destroyed you. And along the way, you passed former habitations of our forebears; their ghostly footprints must have distressed you." The preindustrial Iroquois used to leave their homes every few years to set up new villages on more fertile land. Sort of what the Centrists thought they could do, leave Earth behind. "With all that, we give thanks that you have safely arrived."

It would have been a tough journey, all right, back in those days; a thirty-mile hike through the trees might have been riskier than thirty thousand klicks from a spacehab. Other women of the Council raised their corn pounders and echoed their thanks, weaving notes into their shell-bead recorders. Amongst them Jenny saw her mother, "Bean Planter."

"Yet you come in good time," the Chief Woman continued, "to share our deliberation of the weighty matter brought before us. Your Bear Clan has lost too many sons and daughters of late to the Rotting Face disease." The smallpox that wiped out entire villages. "Your own brother Handsome River was among them. Before we could condole for him properly, the Men's Council asked us to approve a Mourning War."

At the edge of the gathering, two of the "women" in skirts were men. These men were Speakers the women appointed to hear and report their deliberations to the Men's Council. The skirted men drew forward and listened intently, their shell-bead recorders weaving symbols in white and blue.

"Um—" Jenny knew she wasn't to speak yet, but she preferred to head off the war talk. "After surviving so many, um, obstacles to get here I really feel ready for the Condoling Council for my brother." The Condoling Council would last all day, with many colorful speeches and some not-so-bad poetry.

"You will speak in good time, my daughter. Since the time you last sojourned among us, the Women's Council did call for a Mourning War upon the Salt Beings, those creatures who place unhealthy salt upon all their food." The Europeans had been scorned for eating salt, just like ultra was today. A lot of good it had done. "The Mourning War has been waged and won, and prisoners taken. Now, we must decide how to have the prisoners: To feast, or to replace our lost offspring?"

New players, the standard routine. At least, Jenny hoped so; she really didn't feel like playing cannibal today.

Her mother, "Bean Planter," raised her corn pounder. "How can I feel at ease with my son's place empty? Surely we need to adopt new offspring."

Other clanswomen spoke in support of adoption. The agreement seemed general within the group. A rapid decision; such deliberations could go on for days or weeks, to get everyone to agree. Iroquoia, like Castle Cockaigne, did not necessarily follow a strict script.

"It is agreed," spoke the Chief Woman. "We shall prepare the prisoners for adoption. *Hiro kone.*"

At the perimeter, the men in skirts jumped up with their corn pounders, eager to relay the women's decision to the Men's Council. Jenny "Sunflower Spirit" got up and followed, as did her mother and two other women. They in turn would get to hear the men respond.

The Men's Council sat in another clearing amid the pine needles. They all wore trousers, feathered hair clips, and nose rings. The Chief Man was Jenny's father, George Ramos, "Spreader of Data." He spoke the pipe-friendly Iroquois language while virtual smoke curled above his head. As Chief Man, George puffed on his pipe in utter solemnity, but Jenny knew how he enjoyed himself. Imaginary though it was, Iroquoia was the place her father felt at home; the world he loved as his own. For a moment Jenny wondered: How many others were like that, today? How many people got through their daily life in the real world, living for those few cherished moments of their fantasy?

A male Speaker from the Women's Council waved his corn pounder and excitedly reported all that had transpired, checking the blue and white pattern of his shell-bead recorder. Several men had to speak, each getting his turn to smoke the pipe. "Remember our need for meat. Our hunting has been unlucky. We could consume these prisoners and acquire their courage."

"The Women's Council chooses adoption," responded "Chief Man" George. "Adoption fills gaps in our family. Family is the heart of all life. Without family, our people are like dust on the Earth; empty footprints and dissipated smoke from pipes long cooled."

Jenny's eyes filled; she brushed them hurriedly.

"*Onenh,* let us test the mettle of our prisoners for joining our family. Let the gauntlet begin. *Hiro kone.*"

Now all the men and women got up and began ordering about excitedly. The men went off to fetch the prisoners, while the women arranged the gauntlet. Bean Planter especially got into it, Jenny noticed. Even children appeared to join the gauntlet, though at Level Ten they could only be constructs. Bean Planter looked back over her shoulder at Jenny. "Come on, Sunflower Spirit," she urged her daughter. "You can join the fun with your new siblings. No voting."

Jenny's jaw fell. "Wait—no—" Of course, that's who those new prisoners would be. "No, *wait,* I said! The—the spirit forces are out of balance; the ceremonies have been neglected. Call it off! *Hiro kone!*"

None of the other players took notice. Jenny tried to reach them in her windows, but there was no response. Helpless, she hung back and watched the gauntlet form, the two lines of women and construct children with sticks and knives to beat and stab the prisoners. At Level Ten, they would feel the pain.

There was cheering and shouting as the prisoners were delivered at the other end. She could just make them out, Ken and Yola with their faces painted red; black would have meant torture and feast. But the adoption gauntlet was bad enough. The shouts went on, and a cheer went up for a particularly sharp blow. Jenny could no longer see her friends amid the torturers, but she marked their progress down the line. At last they appeared, smeared with blood and dirt, virtual fingernails pulled. Their faces registered shock, but they had managed to hold themselves together.

"They didn't cry once," observed the male Speaker admiringly.

"Welcome, offspring of the Salt Beings," said Bean Planter. "You have now become our own offspring of the Bear Clan. Welcome to No Voting Land, Iroquoia."

✦

Unlike most students, who'd be gone till Tuesday, Jenny headed back up to Frontera to record the wisdom plants. That was it with experiments; you had to keep them going. The college was a ghost town. Buckeye Trail was deserted, and the Ohioana closed for business.

She had barely returned, when EMS was blinking already. A new Ebola strain had struck Huron dorm again, sent by malicious "salt beings" through the printer. The colonial volunteers were overstretched; even Frank Lazza was consumed with setting up his hotel. Fortunately most of the dorm residents were home, but like Jenny, a few always stayed, "dworks" catching up on work, or those who could not afford the trip home. One who'd stayed was Tom.

With the medibot, she combed Huron for sick students, suiting up each for quarantine and scooting them to the Barnside. Huron housed frogs six to a room, in two banks of three, adjoined to a shared toyroom. The rooms were so narrow the medibot could scarcely fit inside. The beds were like turned-up shoe box tops, barely long enough for someone of average height. When she reached Tom's room, her skin crawled. "Tom?" She could barely get her voice to work. She climbed one ladder, her isolation suit twisting around her legs. The third bunk was empty. On the other side, she climbed the other ladder. There was Tom, feverish and breathing unevenly, red swollen spots appearing on his face and arms.

"Antivirals ready," called the medibot.

Jenny's head broke out in a sweat beneath her hood, and her gloved hand shook so she could scarcely fit the scanscope. But she had to get the antiviral injected, and get him and three other victims out to the Barnside.

43

Over the weekend, Jenny camped out at the Barnside, hovering over the patients and checking out their signals to adjust the antiviral. All were isolated beneath an amyloid bell jar. Tom was barely conscious, and Jenny did not try to speak to him. Enveloped in her safety suit she felt like a monster. Doc Uddin had to push out an extra room for the patients; to save on amyloid, she lowered the ceiling. This made it hard for Jenny to stand straight. "You're too tall for a colonist," joked the doctor.

"Do I really need the suit?" Jenny asked. "I don't get Ebola; I've got HIV."

"Human improvement vector protects you from casual exposure, but here we take no chances." The doctor opened a new box of meds.

"Are those the regenerators?" After the antivirals got rid of the virus, in the next twenty-four hours, the body cells had to be repaired right away. Unlike an ultraphyte, a human body contained trillions of cells, of which billions had been blown by the virus; a billion holes poked in the blood vessels. Microscopic regenerators could plug them all, and rebuild the tissues—if added in time.

Doc Uddin shook her head. "No word from the supplier." A hurricane was churning through the Carolinas, and the country's medical service was preoccupied. "We may have to try Shanghai. It'll blow my budget for the year."

"Why can't we stop these epidemics?"

"It's not our problem; it's Toynet." Doc Uddin stuck another scanscope onto the recharger. That reminded Jenny to hand over the power bands she had worn in Mount Gilead. Every bit of juice was a few dollars more for those who couldn't pay.

"Why can't Toynet be filtered? With antivirals?"

"It's like monoculture. There's only one Toynet; it's grown like kudzu for the past decade. You grew up with it, the direct brainstream plug-in. Tova was born with it. Those born with it, their brains expand in ways we don't yet understand. But there's only one code. If anyone anywhere in the world subverts it, it spans the globe within minutes."

Her eyes widened. "You mean, other Tovas in other places . . ."

"Kudzu is the least of it." She adjusted the window that enclosed one of the worse-off patients to breathe oxygen and epithelial stabilizers. "Always the children get there first. In the early twentieth century, children could not even keyboard. But once they learned, they invented everything."

The twentieth century. That came after the shell-bead recorders, and before the networks. Jenny thought back to first grade. "I remember *gafas*, eyeglass windows—we all wore them." Lasers onto the retina; she'd seen one in the physics museum. It felt odd to think of, a part of her childhood gathering dust in a glass case.

"The first *gafas* were for cartoon worlds. A convenient babysitter. Then they were everywhere; at your age, I loved my *gafas*. But now it's Toynet—it exploded overnight, and it's all one thing." She shrugged, and shoved a wisp of blond hair back into her braid. "Hey, that's Zari's problem; I've got my plate full."

So Jenny stayed on to help the nurse, keeping an eye on Tom and the other patients. In her toybox she caught up on the Northern Securities Case, the decision for which Roosevelt had compared Justice Holmes to a banana. The Northern Securities company had combined three crosscountry railroads, despite a law prohibiting any combination "in restraint of trade among the several states." A good thing Roosevelt never lived to see Toynet straddle the world's countries, moon, and satellites.

As she sat in her suit at Tom's bedside, Yola's window lit up. Yola greeted her from the Tasmanian coast, where she went shark watching with her hunky *novio* from Melbourne. "We saw a Great White—the real thing, no toyworld. *Hiro kone!*"

Jenny smiled and caught her up on the Ebola epidemic. A while later Ken appeared on a beach in Eilat, resting up with his *novia* on army leave. The beach was refrigerated beneath an amyloid bubble against the hundred-fifty-degree heat. "Say, I found this thousand-year-old menorah in the Old City. Just in time for Festival of Lights."

"Um, did you get a permit?"

His *novia* punched him in the arm. "I told him it was a knock-off."

There was the mayoral race, the last weekend before the Tuesday special election. Time for "get out the vote." Jenny hadn't heard much lately from

Fritz Hoffman or the other Bulls campaigners; they'd had their share of work to catch up. Still, she had the list of registered voters, annotated where contacts had been made. She started blinking down the list, reminding them to vote at the courthouse. The Mount Gilead contacts went fast; those she'd met with Tom seemed likely to vote. Then she started blinking students.

"My cousin's getting married. I'll vote online. No? Why not?"

"My mom reserved my return shuttle months ago, before we knew."

"I have no Wednesday class, I'm coming back then."

"There's a vote Tuesday? For what?"

Exasperated, Jenny wondered what had happened. Didn't they hear all the candidates, including Father Clare's last speech from out in space? Didn't the Bulls canvass the dorms? Finally she reached Fritz Hoffman, the Bulls' pledge educator and campaign director, out at Suzuka Circuit for the Japanese Grand Prix. "Look," he said, "I'll get back if I can, but it's *totalmente loco* to have to vote in some amyloid shack in a spacehab."

Suddenly she remembered Tom, in the bell jar. She looked over at him, breathing calmly, still covered in red spots. She blinked Doc Uddin, out on call. "When will the students get out of quarantine?"

"Goodness, a week at least. They'll have to do classes by Toynet; they can use our toyroom."

She looked over again through the amyloid at Tom. He breathed easily, his face no longer contorted with pain. Swollen, but saved from rotting. Jenny opened her mouth, then closed it and swallowed twice. "Tom?" She spoke up a bit louder. "Can you hear me?"

Tom's head turned on the pillow. Then he nodded.

Jenny nodded back. "Do you . . . need anything?"

Tom's lips opened as he tried to talk. "Water."

Jenny pushed her suited arm into the amyloid. Recognizing her, the amyloid molded in, allowing her hand to reach the water line and pull it up by Tom's face.

Tom drank from the tube, his throat moving as he swallowed. Then his mouth opened, but he could not speak. He swallowed and tried again. "Will I . . . live?"

"Of course you'll live. The doctor told you." The pain he must be feeling, blood vessels leaking throughout the body. "You'll be feeling a lot better tomorrow, as the antivirals kick in. But you have to stay in quarantine for the week."

"Can I get out to vote?"

His window was back. Jenny felt a rush of good; it was wonderful to connect again. Then she felt sad, remembering. **"I don't know, but I'll find out."**

She found the courthouse window and blinked a message: What did they do for a voter in quarantine?

"The pie with flying birds was *chulo,*" Jenny told him.

"Thanks. So were the puzzle jugs."

Suddenly, half her windows disappeared. All her Earth windows, gone.

Outside, the light dimmed throughout the hab. Another brownout. A notice read that Frontera's supplemental power from Earth had been redirected to fight the hurricane that devastated the Atlantic coast. Maryland's Chesapeake seawall might not hold.

There was no word from the courthouse, and the hab stayed dim through Sunday. Jenny joined the EMS crew flipping backup switches, powering down elevators and printer nodes, and posting signage for potable water. Then, left alone with her orchids, Jenny found herself wondering. Like, how could Earth just commandeer Frontera's power; and what if they didn't give it back? And what was in Mary's mysterious reverse control plants for wisdom, the shoots just starting to sprout leaves?

With the power partly down, she checked the lab twice a day now, making sure the backup generator kept running when the professor had to be out. Most times, though, Abaynesh was there.

"Mary thinks she knows a semiochemical for human wisdom." In the Reagan basement, Abaynesh's voice rose above the hiss of ventilation. The ultraphyte quasispecies continued to grow, their tanks now surrounded by those of rats and chickens. "A combination of chemicals, in fact. Her sense of smell is finer than ours."

"The omniprosthesis?" Omniprosthetics could be designed for special abilities.

"If Mary's right, it suggests a different approach to our research. But we'd need human subjects. I don't have a permit."

Whereas she did have a permit for ultra. "Have the ultraphytes done anything to the rats and chickens?"

"Not that I can tell," said the professor. "But they seem to notice the animals. Those kept in an adjacent tank develop creeping forms; whereas those next to a plant develop stalks."

Jenny looked. She saw a mixture of stalks and creeping forms in both tanks.

"Statistically different, anyway."

Mary had gone upstairs to the plant lab to study Earth creatures. "The castle," blurted Jenny. "What happened there?"

Abaynesh shrugged. "I can't tell you. I ran an inventory here that night, and none of mine were missing."

Jenny tried to reach Uncle Dylan about the quarantined voters. But his window was blocked. He must be dealing with the brownout, or an important donor. Jenny's eye fell upon Leora's window. She blinked to ask for help.

"We've never had a voter in quarantine." Leora seemed more comfortable with her private window than in public. "What could we do about it?"

"Record the person's vote online."

"So it wouldn't go in the book?"

"You could still put it in the book. But really, votes ought to be secret."

Jenny stared hard, wondering how the pauline would take that. Beneath her bonnet Leora stared back, with a look as if she had something else on her mind. "You can ask Judge Baynor." She added, "Let me know what you find out."

Unlike Leora, Judge Baynor had not opened his window. The only way to ask the judge at present was to find him out in the soy field. By the time she got there it was Monday afternoon. The hab was still dim, and the temperature had fallen; Jenny shivered in her sweater. The combine was churning, kicking up dust so she coughed.

"So your client admits to tipping a cow into the stream?" As the judge drove his combine, he appeared to be conducting a virtual court session. "A mini-cow, sure, correct the record. So he tipped the mini-cow in broad daylight? Out in an open field? Where anyone across the hab can see?" The judge braked and the combine hissed quiet. "Are you telling me your client is a total idiot?"

A long pause while the judge listened to his toybox. Jenny wondered if she'd have to come back later.

The judge wiped his brow and replaced his power band with a new one to fill. "Well, I believe in giving a total idiot a second chance. Guilty as charged, sentence suspended." He turned to Jenny. "I've read your complaint. If you can make it to the courthouse door, and sign your name, you can vote. That's the law."

"But—" His abrupt response confused her. "What if you get sick?"

The judge shook his head. "Illness knows no party. In the long run, it evens out, doesn't it? Don't mean to be unkind, but with so many tourists and all, we make sure only genuine local residents vote for our mayor."

"So it's different in November?" President, senator, rep and state rep, everything down to morality officer.

"In November, it's just the same."

Something creaked within the combine machinery. Beyond it the rows of stubble swept up into the sky. "Who makes the law?"

"The town council. Your Mr. Vincenzo sits on it."

"When does the council meet?"

"Next January."

On the road back, Jenny blinked for her family lawyer.

"The Board of Election has to help," the lawyer said. "The state provides a client rights advocate. They must bring the ballot to your bedside if necessary."

"It's not a ballot. It's a book with special ink."

The lawyer's eyebrows rose. "An open book? File a complaint with the state."

"The state of Ohio?" That would scarcely win points with the locals. How many of the sick students even wanted to vote? Would Tom want to press the case, or would he get upset again? Jenny thought she'd see how things went, and plan for November.

The lights came up Monday afternoon. Dylan sighed with relief. Only 20 percent of their power came from Earth. Frontera was nearly there, just one step from independence. Their main generator was a massive solarray, the kind Glynnis had helped design: An orbiting complex of solar collectors distributed over a thousand cubic kilometers. There were always one or two knocked out at any time, but they were self-regenerating; and no piece of space debris was big enough to knock out the whole. The prototype of a system that could stabilize Earth's entire power grid. Of course, building another one would take decades, with an added point on the house edge.

In Dylan's box, four backlogged windows blinked red. The first red he took was from the frog about his seminar grade; always students first. "Certainly, I understand," Dylan said with his most winning smile to the *chico* taking a break from the green at St. Andrews. "An understandable oversight in your essay, confusing the two presidents."

"That's what I thought, Professor. The coach posts our grade averages— Xiang has A-triple-plus. You know I can't get into law school without A-triple-plus."

"Well, I wouldn't be too sure of that, but I know how you feel."

"And besides, it was my *novia*'s birthday the week before; I had to go visit her at UCLA."

"I understand your oversight," Dylan empathized. "After all, Teddy and Franklin were, shall we say, of the same blood; fifth cousins, in an inbred community. Almost clonal, by today's standards."

"Exactly what I was thinking."

"Both statesmen played larger-than-life roles in world politics. And Teddy, like cousin Franklin, pursued social justice through government regulation. The Square Deal led to the New Deal. Forest Conservation, then Soil Conservation. The bully pulpit, and the fireside chat. Republican, and Democrat." Those twentieth-century purples really stood for something.

"Exactly," exclaimed the young man in his polo shirt. "I knew you'd take care of my grade."

"You can be sure I'll continue to give the matter my utmost consideration. And let's see your next essay, okay?"

Next red: Nora. "The Ebola students are recovering, but their meds have blown my budget for the year."

Dylan shook his head. "We can't go on having Ebola outbreaks twice a semester."

"Not my department," she pointed out. "Hepa-Q, yes, that's our bailiwick. But Ebola is Zari's department."

Zari's desk spliced in as she assisted a teddy with a wooden Chinese puzzle. She hastily put down the puzzle with one leg still extending. "Dylan, we've reached the limit: These outbreaks are going up exponentially."

"So what's our answer?"

"Babynet," she said succinctly. "Not the whole system; just the core receiving stations. With Babynet in the mix, no Toynet-based viruses can get through. And a host of other things."

Dylan drummed his fingers. "Gil won't like it."

"It won't hurt him, he'll still be the biggest trillionaire. Isn't it time Gil grew up?"

Zari's impatience was rare; she must really have reached her limit. "Very well," he sighed.

"Thanks a bunch, Zari," added Nora, with considerably more feeling. "Dylan, just so you know, I confronted the two bros from the Monte Carlo incident and convinced them to withdraw from the college."

"Excellent." The culprits would be gone; no more court case.

"On the other hand, just so you know, the Kearns-Clark monthly payment bounced."

Dylan gulped. "Not again." Two years since the last time; he'd hoped the family had straightened out.

Third red: Helen. "Two faculty are out," the dean of the faculty told him. "The Brain Arts prof came down with Ebola, probably incubated from here. She's at Columbia, out for a week. Clare can fill in."

"Very well."

"And Sharon canceled class for a week. Said she 'needs to think.'"

Canceled class—to think? Think about what, if not teaching? Students first—that above all was Frontera's brand.

"Students complained," added Helen. Complained at the Life prof's absence—there was a change. "For now, I set them up with toyHarvard, if that's okay with you."

"Good thinking. If it goes beyond a week—"

"It won't," Helen assured him. "I do think this colleague merits an extra evaluation this year."

"My thoughts exactly," said Dylan. Helen always had things in hand.

At last, the ecoengineer. Quade spliced in from his south station by the river, with the bear cub on a leash. A bad example; Dylan would have a word with him, but not now. "We've completed a thorough analysis of the castle and moat."

"And?"

"Some of our chemicals registered positive." Quade paused. "I'd give a thirty percent chance the ultra was real."

The two men stared each other down. Thirty percent. Should they melt the castle or not? And if ultra had been there, where else by now?

"You know why South America has so few ultraphytes?" Quade asked.

"Why?"

"Army ants. Army ants love ultra—swarm over 'em, can't get enough."

Dylan absorbed this. Then his eyes flew open. "*Ni hablar*. No wolves, no bats, and no army ants." No ultra either. Unless they were here to stay.

Out of the corner of his eye he spotted a contact he'd missed. Jenny's window, with no urgent flag. Still, he shouldn't have missed a student.

44

Jenny headed out Raccoon Run to vote, along with Priscilla. Anouk accompanied them; although she could not vote, she looked forward to any opportunity to feel superior to *les americains*. Already she wrinkled her nose at the mud clinging to her ballet flats. Jenny and Priscilla wore hiking boots to town. A mosquito landed on her arm; Jenny slapped it, and blinked a complaint to the ecoengineer.

"Homefair just raised a frame for our next house," Priscilla told her.

"Muy bien." Priscilla had become quite a carpenter, no more falls from the roof. "Who's the homeowner?"

"Leora's sister. Leora comes from, like, a large family."

Exasperated, Anouk yanked off her shoe and knocked off some of the mud.

"Come on," muttered Jenny, "France has farms."

"You bet," agreed Priscilla. "Where else do they grow all that café stuff?"

Anouk said, "Our agricultural science is the most advanced in the world."

Priscilla sent Jenny some text, which she diplomatically ignored.

At the courthouse, the flock of pigeons cooed and scattered as the three students climbed the steps. Inside waited half a dozen colonists in power bands, plus a croupier from the Mound. The croupier waved at Anouk. *"Bonjour, mademoiselle.* We hope to see you again soon."

The pollworkers were Leora and Frank. One for each party; that would be standard. Before them on the desk rested a book, about the shape of Jenny's Aristotle book, only larger.

As the man at the head of the line approached, the book was opened to the spot with his name. The man bent over and wrote something in the book, in a bright yellow dye.

"What's that?" asked Priscilla curiously.

"Uranyl acetate. A microscopy stain." Jenny recalled uneasily that her handwriting was out of practice. She opened a window for a quick review.

Priscilla wrinkled her nose. "It sounds disgusting."

At last Jenny's turn came. "Jennifer Ramos Kennedy."

Frank opened the book, but could not find it at first amongst the Ks. "Ramos," Jenny corrected.

Beside the book, Jenny saw an instrument with fluctuating numbers. A radiation dosimeter. Her eyes widened. There by the book was a pen with a bottle of uranyl acetate. A salt of uranium. Her jaw dropped. "Is that . . . radioactive?"

"It's depleted," Frank assured her. But the dosimeter still registered.

Jenny looked back at her friends.

"No way," exclaimed Priscilla. "Like, my family is cancer prone."

"Why?" Jenny asked Frank.

"Security," he explained. "No one can go in with any old ink and change the votes. We monitor the activity of each signature."

"Unbelievable," muttered Anouk, probably blinking away to all her Parisian playmates. "*Enfin,* the exposure is not so bad, if you calculate. Just be quick about it."

"Don't you have gloves?" Jenny asked.

"Sorry," Frank apologized. "It goes so quick. Just keep your hands clean."

Leora nodded, her eyes downcast. "**Gloves are a good idea. We should keep up with the times.**"

Holding her breath, Jenny picked up the pen. She carefully traced out the outline of her name. "So where is the ballot?"

"Just write the candidate's full name next to yours."

Right there in front of everyone, on the line with all the others. Her face burned. Quickly, she scribbled Father Clare's first name, though the *C* looked just like the *l*. More carefully she drew the big *F* for his surname. She dropped the pen and wiped her hands on her pants.

Priscilla shook her head. "I can't even write, much less use that pen. What if I make a smudge, and the radioactivity gets all over?"

"Could a witness help you?" suggested Frank.

"Allow me," said Anouk. Holding Priscilla's hand, she completed her name smartly.

Stepping aside, Jenny was already blinking her lawyer's window. No way would she put up with this in November, no matter what the town thought.

—✦—

The Toynet Local announced Hamilton's win. The windows were full of congratulations for the new mayor, the first college professor to run Mount Gilead. The inaugural celebration was announced for Lazza's new hotel ballroom.

In the morning, Jenny stopped by Father Clare to condole.

"Don't feel too bad," he told her.

"But scarcely any students voted," she blurted. "After all our canvassing." The Bulls had gone around with their sheets and slogans; then they hadn't bothered to vote.

"October Break has a Pied Piper effect," Father Clare observed. "But you know, considering the voters were mostly colonists, it came out much closer than your analysis. Your canvassing must have done some good."

"That's true." Fifty-one to forty-nine, not two to one. She would let Tom know he'd made a difference. "Well, November will be different; everyone will vote. Won't they? What was it like in oh-four?"

The chaplain hesitated. "Maybe this year will be different, after the debate."

"*Claro*, that will be an inspiration. But—why should students vote here, when they have to trudge into town and sign in radioactive ink? They could vote for president in Wisconsin."

"If they own a home there."

Jenny reddened. The price of socks; she had to remember.

"I guess that's why Ohio stays the way it is," he added. "Voters flee."

"Not this year." Her chin lifted. "We're filing a complaint."

The chaplain grinned. "God doesn't take sides, but I wish you luck."

Jenny started compiling her list for the lawyer: the courthouse location, the radioactive ink, above all the open ballot. Now that her terrestrial windows were back, she reviewed the lengthy form at the Ohio Secretary of State.

A window blinked for her; it was Uncle Dylan. "Jenny, I missed your call. Is everything all right? All your connections back?"

"The students couldn't vote." She sent him her list.

"Goodness—why didn't you tell me? Of course, you did try. Well, don't you worry." He smiled. "We have to work this out for November. And I'm sure we can, now that we have a professor for mayor." Mayor indeed; she'd have to see.

Meanwhile, on her Life professor's window she had found the following note: "Class canceled. Busy thinking." Wondering what this cryptic message meant, Jenny stopped by the lab.

Outside Reagan Hall stood a group of students carrying signs.

PROFS TORTURE PLANTS.

SAVE PLANTS FROM ALIEN DNA.

NO FRANKENPLANTS.

Pictures showed imaginary plants sprouting ultraphytes. A leaflet texted how the Life professors were putting ultra genes into helpless animals and plants with neurons. Next to the picketers stood an outsized clay-colored urn full of soil, with a student crouching on the soil holding a tormented flowerhead. The crouching student was Kendall.

Jenny looked down at her teammate and smiled. "*Hola*. How was the beach?"

Ken looked grim as death. "What goes on in that lab—you can't imagine." No Yola around, Jenny noticed. Yola was a Life major who needed to get her grades up to graduate.

She found Abaynesh in her office, sitting upon her desk, beneath which Meg-El lay curled up asleep. The professor sat, chin in hand, thinking. Around the professor sat pots of her representative plants: the laughing plant, the praying plant, the find-my-mortarboard plant. Jenny cleared her throat. "I'm here to check our experiment." She added, "Are you okay?"

"*Claro.*"

Jenny nodded. "Did you see . . . outside?"

"Somebody left their diad on."

It had never occurred to her whether plants with neurons could feel pain. Nor how the pile worms and chickens might feel about getting recombined with ultra. For that matter, how did the ultraphytes feel? "Is that why you canceled class?"

"Of course not. I told you, I'm thinking. My NIH is up for renewal." Her arm swept the air. "What do you think pays for all this?"

Jenny nodded slowly.

"My students can take a break; they're weeks ahead of the Harvard class." The professor's eyes blinked furiously, as if recording a sudden thought. "I need a new direction. Some other way to make a wisdom circuit. Vertebrates and vascular plants are both overdeveloped, fossilized patterns. Ultraphytes have a more adaptable different kind of nervous system, with entire circuits contained within a single cell."

The next morning, after Hamilton's class, he called her aside. "Jenny, thanks so much for raising these important points about our voter process. In the future," he added ingratiatingly, "I hope you'll bring them directly to the mayor."

Jenny listened warily. Her professor had just spent the hour explaining Aristotle's conclusion that democracy was a perversion of good government. "Democracy" meant rule by the impoverished, who always try to rob the well-off.

"What a pleasure to see a student take such an active interest in the community," Hamilton added. "Of course, we must see to the needs of ill voters. The town secretary will bring ballots to the Barnside. And overall— the ballot will now be secret." He smiled as if he'd accomplished this himself. "The first secret ballot in the history of Frontera."

"That's nice." Jenny knew better than to say too much before consulting her lawyer. "Can we vote online? Without that radioactive ink?"

A moment's hesitation. "Those details are under consideration." By the council that wouldn't meet till January.

Her lawyer, when she checked, had a different view. "They're trying to head you off," the lawyer said. "Go ahead and file."

She filed the complaint, with signatures from Priscilla and Tom.

45

By Saturday morning Tom was up and out of quarantine. The blotches on his skin were fading, though he still moved stiffly. The other students had left the Barnside already, but Tom seemed in no hurry to leave.

"You can go now," Jenny assured him. "Just check in daily for the regenerators." The regenerators would take weeks to build his muscles back.

Tom pulled a chair up to the bed, like a desk. "Doc said I could stay a while, until they need the bed. My dorm, with six in a room—I never could study there."

Jenny stared, and her pulse raced. All week she'd been asking her mental the same question, but the Monroe just went on singing old torch songs. Jenny nearly called her doctor in Somers, half convinced the mental had gone bad. "Why don't you come live in my sitting room?" She sat on the hospital bed and caught his arms. "You can have your own room, all nice and quiet. Use my own toyroom, instead of the common one that gets all the viruses."

Tom shuddered beneath her hands. She realized then how weak he still was, like a hurricane had gone through inside him. But she felt just a bit ruthless. That painting; he had put everything into it. "Tom, you care for me. What's wrong? Why do you get so upset?"

He breathed but could not speak.

"Everybody needs a little time away," she said. "After all that we've been through . . . Why can't we get back together?"

"I can never go back. I left them all. The ones I cared for as much as you."

Her eyes closed, then opened. "You didn't leave them. They left you. They put you outside to die. I would never do that."

"All right," he said at last. "I'll try."

✦

The rest of the weekend went by like floating on a cloud. Jenny reshaped her cottage, carving a private bedroom out of the amyloid. She left Tom alone to study and get his strength back. But just knowing he was there while she plowed through her Cuba midterm made everything a different world. They went together to supper, breakfast, and church.

The next week, ominous texts began appearing about the Kearns-Clarks.

"Ken and Yola—They have to leave school."

"The castle; I heard it's coming down."

"Ultra again?"

"No, something about bills."

Yola's window was closed, and there was no response at the castle. But at suppertime, Fran called an urgent team meeting.

In a private room at the Ohioana, the teammates crowded around the table, eating quietly. Coach was there, and everyone was subdued.

"It's true," said Yola. "We're wiped out. I had given my cousin a safety account, enough for me to get by, but Ken has nothing."

Ken looked devastated, and did not eat at all.

Fran pressed Yola's arm. "You're sure? Didn't your mother take steps?"

"She tried, but it's all connected. He even went through our trust funds." Yola shook her head. "We thought Dad had got over it. But after our game at Rapture, those guys lured him back to play. 'Experience the Holy Land.' He lost everything."

Charlie exclaimed, "But how could—I mean, Quakers don't—"

"It's a disease, like cancer."

"Stupid," exclaimed Ken. "As stupid as voting."

"Well, who else was stupid?" said Yola irritably. "We all should have . . . done something."

Coach said, "There's nothing you could have done. We always have about twenty students and faculty in rehab. The state foots the bill."

"We don't need rehab," said Ken. "We need to quit and start over, on our own."

Yola shook her head. "Ken, we don't need to quit school. I told you, the Lazzas will take us in." The EMS squad was always thankful for Yola. "And my account will get us through our final term."

"Get you through."

"Get *us* through." She looked around, as if appealing to the team.

Xiang said, "She's right, Ken. The team needs you. You can't just quit on us."

"What's the use? My grades won't get me anywhere, anyhow."

"We never cared about grades," admitted Yola. "We always did . . . other things."

"Good things," added Jenny. "The Flood demo, that was good."

"And the mosquito benefit." Charlie grinned in recollection. "That was *chulo*. Hey, who knows what will need you next? Maybe an ultra benefit."

No one seemed amused. Yola pushed the gravy with her fork, as if not seeing the table.

"So what will you do, Ken?" Jenny asked.

Ken shrugged. "I'll go live with my *novia* and join the IDF."

Yola looked up sharply. "The Israeli army? You? You can't even cut a potato."

"There's always latrines. I can kill germs."

From the walls the six-point mini-buck heads stared.

Coach shrugged. "Less work for me. I was planning your exam for conversion."

ToyNews was now inundated with electioneering, especially second-guessing the final debate at Frontera. The near-equal poll results from Betty and Glynnis back in August had continued, after bouncing around some, but once again the race was "too close to call." The kind of race Clive liked best. In the toybox, student windows were framed in purple or gold; purple outnumbered gold two to one. The town, though, would be the opposite story. Meanwhile, the Weaver DIRGs were back, along with others looking less friendly, inspecting every inch of the debate site for the following week. DIRGs all over—why had Jenny ever bothered to leave home?

In Mount Gilead, the new mayor's first act was to inventory all energy supplies throughout the hab, those storing the motion energy harvested by the colonists' power bands. This project led to a revelation.

"It seems," announced Hamilton on ToyNews Local, "that the core energy reserves of the Smythe Power Bank have yet to be found."

The Smythe Bank had been run by the previous mayor, Leora's late husband. Everyone stored their harvested energy there, either donating to the town or logging for future use. The energy was stored in compact cylindrical cells. Where else could the cells have been placed?

Everyone in Mount Gilead had an opinion, but most of all, attention focused on Leora. In Jenny's toybox, Leora appeared being interviewed for ToyNews Local. Her face looked grimmer than usual, but she kept her eyes downcast.

"Mrs. Smythe," asked the interviewer, "can you offer any clues as to where your husband kept the energy stores from the Smythe Bank?"

"My late husband said that the right mayor would find the stores." After this cryptic pronouncement, Leora looked up and stared directly from the window. Her face showed a brief, twisted look of defiance that Jenny had never seen. Then it was gone, her eyes again downcast.

Mystified, Jenny blinked for Sherri-Lyn. Sherri-Lyn appeared in her bright new home, her two children running around the sitting room. "Isn't it beautiful? Thanks so much for your help."

Jenny smiled. "I did little—it was Tom and Priscilla. Do you know any more; *qué pasa* with the bank?"

Sherri-Lyn's eyes widened. "Nobody knows." Her voice sank to a whisper. "Can you believe it—in all the hab, they can't find the reserve?"

"But—does Leora really not know?"

She shrugged dramatically. "That's the least of it. Did you see the book in the courthouse?"

Jenny shuddered. "Briefly."

"Did you see how she voted?"

"For Father Clare? *No puede ser.*"

"*Puede ser* all right."

Whatever might have changed Leora's mind, Jenny was not about to say. "All right, but what does she mean, the 'right mayor'? Hamilton's elected now, and the votes are there in the book." Much as Jenny hated to admit it, that much was fair. Even the quarantined voters would not have changed the result. "After it's done and certified, that's it. That's democracy."

"If you ask me, people up here talk a lot about democracy, but they don't always know what it means."

Thursday afternoon in the lab, a week to go before the debate. The various wisdom plants all stretched their spoon-shaped leaves to the light. Jenny and Anouk took readings on the shape of their neurons, and compared their competitive growth. It was repetitive work, especially when no positive difference showed up. Mary took readings too, although she seemed more interested in the "reverse control." Jenny found herself thinking about Leora's odd behavior, and Hamilton's election, and the Life professor canceling class instead of pacing her own work the way students were taught to do. They all could sure use some wisdom around here.

Anouk stopped to stretch her back, as she often did for her health. She watched Mary reflectively. "So, Mary. How is your reverse control?"

Mary looked at her quizzically.

"Well? Does it work?"

"We cannot tell. Too much ventilation."

Instead of rolling her eyes at Mary, as she usually would, Anouk kept on staring. As if waiting for the proverbial shoe to drop.

Jenny smiled uncertainly. "We have no permit to test humans."

"So? Why should that stop us?"

"Look what happened to you," Jenny warned. "Do you want to get in that much trouble again?"

"No, but you do."

"Me? What do you mean?"

Anouk leaned her arms on the bench, her scarf brushing the leaves of the nearest plant. "The fate of Earth, remember? That's what's at stake—you're always telling me. Yet the candidates and voters are all so foolish. Don't we all need some wisdom?"

"Not this way. No clinical trials—who knows, it could cause cancer."

"Where would we be if Pasteur and Koch thought like that? Koch tested anthrax in his sitting room."

"Anouk, you're crazy. This is no disease here; it's just—"

"Isn't folly a disease?"

Human folly. *Morias philai paromen.* Poor Ken and Yola, losing their castle and all. Closing her eyes, Jenny shook her head. "How would we even know if it worked?"

"How will you know, if you don't try?"

Her eyes narrowed. "Why don't *you* try."

"Aside from Life, all my classes are toyMIT."

Jenny's jaw dropped. "Try it on *my class?*"

"Why not? You're always complaining about Political Ideas."

Democracy just for the poor. Coincidence perhaps, but that class had been a joke ever since the day she unwittingly brought the laughing-gas plant. But these so-called wisdom plants—there was no sign of any result. Jenny shrugged. "So I'll bring another plant to class."

✦+

Friday, Political Ideas had a test, so the "experiment" would have to wait. The slanball team spent Saturday morning helping the Kearns-Clark twins clear out their castle. The wine collection Tom took on consignment for the café, to earn the twins a bit of cash. There were tapestries, toiletries, a few bits of jewelry, surprisingly little that wasn't printout.

"*No importa,*" muttered Yola heroically. "The castle plan's all online. We can visit there any time."

Jenny felt a bit sad for the dwarves, then chided herself for being silly. She looked wistfully up the winding staircase with the trip step. "Could we just . . . go up to the lookout?"

Ken bounded up around the stairway, two stairs at a time. Jenny and the teammates followed more slowly.

At the battlement, the breeze lifted her hair. From the lookout where the Jackson Square tribute band had played, you could see the whole college: south Buckeye Trail to Harding Hall and Reagan with the colored beans, and the Arts dome where Tom did his fresco, all the way to the river where the newly arrived frogs had gone peeping. Then back, north past the frog halls, and the stylish upperclass amyloids; and all the way out to the Mound. Jenny shuddered to think how many players had gone bust like the twins' dad. Craning her neck, above were the tiny square homes of Mount Gilead, amyloid except for a dozen Homefair homes. She could almost pluck the church steeple pointing down.

That afternoon, Tharp came with his crew to melt the amyloid. Such a large structure was not to be collapsed at random, lest the material ooze out and mess up other buildings. Ken and Yola made themselves absent, but a large crowd had collected, particularly Red Bulls and Ferraris to hoot and jeer. Recalling Leora's interest, Jenny had told her; and sure enough she came by, her youngest boy in hand. Jenny looked furtively at Leora, face hidden beneath her bonnet. She was wondering at the past week's abrupt transformation of the mayor's revered widow into a woman of scandal. The colonists owned precious little, and nothing could incense them so much as the apparent theft of their precious energy stores.

At Tharp's brainstream, the battlement melted down, first one corner, then the rest, collapsing into the keep. A loud cheer went up from the motor clubs.

"How can someone just let a sick person play?" Charlie shook his head. "There ought to be a law."

"There are laws." President Ramos, Jenny's grandfather, had set up the taxplayer system. The law forbade anyone to play who'd lost more than half their net worth. But the law applied only on Earth. "Off-world casinos are the loophole."

He frowned. "What was there before taxplaying, anyhow? How did the government run?"

"They just took your money. Like tithing."

"Well, that's no good. At least at roulette, you got a chance."

One of the drum towers sagged and crumpled. Jenny felt her scalp crawl, reminded of Twin Towers. The tower opposite melted down next. After all the towers, the crenellations slumped into the outer walls. At the very last, nothing was left but a smooth square of amyloid, ready for the next well-off tenant. Jenny stared in vain for a sign that the castle had ever stood there.

Her eye caught a glimpse of something unmelted, sticking up from the amyloid slag. She crept over for a closer look. A puzzle jug, one of those she'd designed and printed herself outside the castle program.

Jenny looked around; no one else seemed to notice. So she reached down to grasp the jug, intending to keep it as a memento. But the jug was stuck fast in the congealed amyloid. *Morias philai paromen*.

46

After Monday morning practice, Jenny stopped at Reagan Hall to "borrow" a pot of reverse control. On her way to Political Ideas, ToyNews reported the new antiterror offensive across the Transantarctic, timed of course to remind the electorate that Centrists were tough on terror. Meanwhile, new details emerged on Sid Shaak's child pornworld empire. Jenny blinked it off. Her toybox filled with debate news—which celebs were coming, where to get tickets. Clive's entourage was already filling up Lazza's hotel; the Begonias went to town following up a rumor that his style staff was freelancing.

Soledad blinked Jenny about tickets. "I can promise you eight seats in the front row," she said. "We have to be fair; both sides get the same number. Then there's the press, and the notables."

"Thanks, eight will do." Herself and Tom, Anouk and Rafael, Charlie and Priscilla. Ken and Yola wouldn't come—Ken had posted a picture of Satan saying, "Why pick the *lesser* of two evils?" But Fran and David would appreciate seats.

"*Bien,*" said her mother. "All purple?"

"All but one." Rafael, despite Anouk's promise to convert him.

"I'll make sure Jermy's side includes one of ours."

At class, Jenny set her potted plant upon the inlaid table, in the middle rather than right next to her. Mary was there as usual, with her hands creeping over the table—hopefully she'd keep quiet, or only say something uninterpretable. Jenny's hands shook with nerves. When Enrico glanced in her direction, she jumped. Calm down, she told herself. By now, he and Ricky and the rest were accustomed to her carrying one plant or another, so no one took notice. Anyhow, she told herself, the plant's a dud. At least Anouk would be silenced.

The class began as usual, with Hamilton pacing, reprising Aristotle's view of various governments, especially kingships and tyrannies. Today was about change—how a government might be destroyed, or not. Amazing how such a hair-raising topic could be made so dry.

The professor turned to face the class, leaning his hands on the table. "So what is the most important way for any government to preserve itself—to prevent change?"

Priscilla raised her hand. She did not wait for permission, as she knew by now Hamilton would never call on her. "Look, Aristotle says that tyrannies are the shortest-lived of all governments. So, duh, if you want to preserve your government, don't be a tyrant."

The class was still. Where Hamilton stood, his head leaned near the plant. In fact, all the heads leaned slightly, close together; as if, Jenny thought, they were all flowerheads of one communal organism. Don't be a tyrant. She found herself thinking: What did that really mean? Despite their short lives, why did the world have so many tyrants and tyrannies? And what did it really take not to be one?

Hamilton was still watching Priscilla, or something beyond Priscilla, Jenny could not tell which. "You know," he said slowly at last, "there are other philosophers besides Aristotle. One said, 'He who has done you the most wrong, you must call your greatest teacher.'" He paused reflectively. "The one in this class who does Aristotle the most wrong is Priscilla." He nodded in her direction. "So, Priscilla—you will lead the rest of the class." With that, he sat down expectantly.

Priscilla stared. "Me?" She looked around, as if there might be some other Priscilla. But the other students were all watching her. "It's true, I detest Aristotle," she admitted. "Aristotle doesn't care about people, unless they're rulers. Right up front, he compares women and slaves as different tools for work. And the barbarians, too, are slaves. Then, 'In every household, the eldest is king.' Duh, what if Grandpa has Alzheimer's?

"Anyhow, for the rest of the book, all that counts is whoever rules. Like a chocolate sampler: Which one should I pick to be, a good king, or a tyrant, or an oligarch? Would I pick our Constitution if it were a chocolate in a box? Like, I dunno. But that's what we've got, see?"

She waved a hand. "Democracy is where all the barbarians get to vote—even if the ballot's radioactive. And the poor vote like they might be rich someday. And the slaves don't bother." She stared meaningfully around the table. "Find me that in Aristotle."

All around the table, the students looked at Priscilla. Then they looked at the professor, who was still listening. Then they looked around at each other.

Enrico reflected, "You know, Aristotle wrote other books besides *Politics*. For extra credit, I've been reading *History of the Animals*. 'We must not recoil with childish aversion from examination of the humblest animals.' Amazing, don't you think? Here, Aristotle speaks of hens and cocks, even sponges. 'Every realm of nature is marvelous.' He sounds like the Sierra Club. How could he care so much for sponges, yet not for lowly human beings?"

Priscilla leaned back, as if saying, "Don't ask me."

Beneath the table shoes scraped on the floor. A couple of students actually took up their books and turned the pages, looking for a passage.

Ricky said, "You know, I wonder what Aristotle really even meant by 'slave' or 'animal.' These words were used over two thousand years ago. Today, don't we know that humans are animals? Maybe Aristotle cares about slaves and animals, even though he doesn't think them human. Even though they don't vote."

Priscilla's eyes widened. "Two thousand years." She leaned forward, as if struggling with something in her head. "I wonder what people will think of our politics today, two thousand years from now. Will they ask how we treated animals? Or even ultraphytes?"

Scary, thought Jenny. What if ultra were nature's rulers, two thousand years from now—or sooner?

"Maybe," said Enrico, "we need to take the things Aristotle gets right, and sift them from the rest. I mean, we're not children that have to accept as true all the things we're told."

"Maybe we can't help but act like Aristotle's rulers. So we ought to know how to rule." Priscilla was shaking her head. "Two thousand years from now—I can't imagine what they'll think. I hope they think we were like children beginning to see."

"When I was a child, I thought like a child, I reasoned like a child . . ."

"And when I became a man," said Hamilton quietly, "I gave up childish ways. For now we see in a mirror dimly. If this book is a dim mirror, at least it's that." He nodded. "Think of that, during Thursday's debate."

The students got up and dispersed for their next class. Only Mary and Jenny remained. Jenny sat still, transfixed.

Hamilton looked straight at her, past the plant. "The class went well today, I thought. I learned something. What did you think?"

Jenny swallowed but said nothing.

"THE REVERSE CONTROL. DID IT WORK?"

Suddenly she wondered: Does wisdom always mean well? Could a person bent on destroying the world find a wise way to do it? What if Satan became wise?

"Excuse me." She scooped up the plant and hurried out.

+-+

Out on Buckeye Trail and throughout the hab, the Weaver DIRGs were now a familiar sight, like an insect infestation out of control. Jenny's toybox over-loaded with window requests; she had to clear it out and restart everything. All this while running to the Life lab to return the plant, before the professor noticed; then running as fast as she could to Anouk.

In Anouk's sitting room, Jenny flopped down onto the sumak and caught her breath. Anouk shifted from one collapsing Mandelbrot to another. "So? Significant difference?"

"*Estupendo.*" Jenny told her how the class went. "But what does it mean? What's really going on? Is it wisdom or hallucination?"

"It's your class. What do you think?"

Jenny didn't know what to think. "What if it fries the brain? Or causes cancer?"

"You can't get cancer, you have HIV. We students have all the latest pro-tections and sensors, *n'est-ce pas?*"

"We have to find out what the plant really does—what semiochemicals does it make?" She was having second thoughts about the Politics class. "Maybe it was just a fluke. Maybe the class was just better than usual."

"Of course, a single trial means nothing. You must try your other class too."

Jenny looked up. "Abaynesh? No way. Besides, Tuesday's not in lab; we're all in our toyrooms, so it won't work."

"Mary shares her toyroom," Anouk pointed out. "She lets Mary get away with anything."

Jenny raised her hands. "You talk to Mary—I'm out of it."

"Very well, I shall." Anouk blinked. "Someone is looking for you—it's Tom."

At Anouk's door waited Tom, looking agitated. "Your window is gone. Are you okay?"

"Oh, I'm sorry." She'd forgotten his window, when she cleared out her box. "I had to restart them all, and I missed."

They collapsed in each other's arms.

┼┼

That evening at the cottage, Tom seemed more like his old self. He sat with Jenny in her old sitting room, where he'd be staying now. They kissed and held each other forever. Jenny put a hand beneath his shirt. "Why don't you take it off again?"

"You want me *ignudo,* is that it?"

She smiled. "Yes, just like the Sistine ceiling."

The shirt came off. The blotches remained on his skin, and his arm moved stiffly. Jenny held him close, trying to be careful. Soon they were just skin and skin together. Tom felt her with his hand and brought her to climax.

"What about you, did you get enough?" Jenny gasped.

"For now." Tom leaned back on his hands, barely visible in the nocturnal glimmer. "Best be careful. You don't want my genes."

Jenny brushed his cheek. "My parents didn't want each other's genes. That's why they picked our relatives. Known successful combinations."

Tom stared. "That's weird. I mean, it's not natural."

"The Iroquois didn't care about genes. They kidnapped their enemies and married them."

He thought this over. "I suppose it went the other way too. Colonials went and married a squaw."

"*Gantowisa,*" she corrected. For some reason she thought of Mary Dyer. She wondered what kind of genes Mary had.

47

The next day, the ruling on Jenny's complaint came down. The complaint was supported in full. All voters should have the choice of a brainstreamed ballot through ToyVote.

But Hamilton, on behalf of the town, accepted only the provisions he'd agreed to before. The rest—the radioactive ink in the courthouse—was appealed to the state supreme court. ToyNews Local played a comment from Judge Baynor: "We'll have no carpetbaggers voting in our town." So much for wisdom.

In the meantime, there was Life class in the toyroom, which she now shared with Tom. In the background of the professor, the old baobab tree grew. Abaynesh, true to form, picked up her lecture as if nothing had been missed in her absence. Two more students had transferred to toyHarvard. The last exam had seen no grade above A, and the remaining faces looked grim.

"Today, we begin a new unit." Abaynesh stood in her toyroom with Mary, who was holding a plant. "So far we have focused on DNA and RNA, the most ancient information molecules of life. Now we deal with a more modern life molecule: protein."

As the professor went on, Jenny could imagine hearts sinking in the other spliced toyrooms. Charlie and the rest had a stoic determination. They could only be recalling DNA as the helical slide, RNA as the roller coaster, and now protein—What could it be? Nothing good, that was for sure. Only Anouk, the curve breaker, looked serene.

"Proteins are Johnny-come-lately in evolution, a mere three-point-seven billion years old. One can imagine a cell without protein, but not a cell without RNA. Nevertheless, proteins form essential parts of all cells today, so we're going to—" The professor stopped. For the first time she looked around, at each student in their spliced toyroom. Beside her stood Mary, with her usual expression and tie-dyed shift. The plant in Mary's hands held up its little spoon leaves. "You know what?" began the professor. "You all look terrified."

The students at first said nothing. Of course, the plant was not in their toyrooms, so they would not feel its influence. And perhaps the professor was just being unpredictable as usual.

Charlie let out a laugh. "Sure, I'm terrified. Ever since the beginning. But, hey, I'll put up with it." Like Ken, a good sport, he'd always take it on the chin.

Abaynesh listened thoughtfully. "When people are terrified, it's hard for them to learn." She thought again. "When I was a child, I was terrified by anything larger than myself. Children feel comfortable with toys they can handle, toys their own size. And adults learning something new are like children." Then she started blinking like crazy into her toybox.

Within each student's toyroom, a model protein appeared. A model about the same size as a student, containing about twenty amino-acid building blocks.

"You all care to know this, or else you would have left by now. Figure out for yourself how each building block works; ask, and it will tell you. And if not, ask the class."

Jenny looked at Tom. Then together, they looked at the protein, with its blue and red atoms, and gold for occasional sulfur. She touched one sulfur atom.

"I am methionine," said the amino acid. "I always start the protein. What kind of atoms do I have?"

The proteins talked, and the students asked questions. They continued thus till the end of the period.

"DID REVERSE CONTROL WORK?"

Jenny met Father Clare in his office. "I have to know something very important." Her hands flexed in agitation, like Mary's hands. "If you could make someone wise, would it be right? I mean, what if an evil person became wise? What if, say, they wanted to blow up Earth; would they become wise enough not to do it, or would they just learn a wiser way to do it?"

The chaplain listened considerately. "Jenny, by this time of year, students become convinced that all they've experienced has cosmic impact—"

"Can't you just tell me? I mean, just to think about."

His face shifted, and he rubbed his forehead. "You're right, I shouldn't have said that. Of course—everything you learn *does* have cosmic impact. That's why you're here, to learn the key things. The heart of the universe."

"Claro."

"What if an evildoer became wise? Would the person cease evil? Or is the evildoer a subtler part of God's plan?" Father Clare shook his head. "And I have to tell you—in truth, I don't know. I don't know, because so much of God's plan is incomprehensible to me. Unknowable now." The puzzle in the mirror. "God's folly is wiser than our wisdom."

Jenny looked down, disappointed.

"I'll say one thing." The chaplain's voice intensified. "If destroying Earth is wisdom, I'm a fool."

In Anouk's sitting room, Jenny sat on the sumak, her diad off, her mental banished by Anouk's bit of code. Anouk sat on a Mandelbrot chair, Berthe nowhere in sight. Tom tried to sit on the floor in a Mandelbrot valley, until a cushion arose to push him aside.

"We can't take long," Jenny warned. "I'm in good with Marilyn right now; I don't want to risk a setback."

"Risk," repeated Anouk. "I'll tell you about risk. The time has come to risk everything."

"Sure; let's tell the professor. She can put it in her grant, with clinical trials—"

"I mean everything. *Tout le monde.* Two days from now."

The debate. Jenny's eyes widened. She shared a look with Tom.

"You're crazy," Tom exclaimed. "You're in enough trouble. Keep Jenny out of this."

"You've said for weeks the fate of the Earth is at stake," Anouk reminded her. "Yet whoever wins is consumed by folly. It's lose-lose right now, isn't it?"

"It always is," Jenny sighed. "We always say the Earth is at stake, every election."

"Well this time, it *really* is," said Anouk. "The ice is boiling. I've seen the numbers."

"So what's the use? Even if Americans—"

"Everyone follows America. Why do you think we give your presidents Nobel Prizes, just for stumbling in the right direction?" Anouk nodded. "You can do it, Jenny. You can wise them up."

"But—" Tom was getting upset. "These semiochemicals; you can't know what they're really doing, or even how long it lasts." The laughing plants, they'd got tired and stopped.

"Every response adapts," said Anouk. "So what? A little wisdom is better than zero."

Jenny caught Tom's hand. "It's impossible anyhow," she told Anouk. "The candidates' security—you've seen all the DIRGs."

"But your mother runs the show. Won't she let you in . . . inside the bell jar?"

Jenny's mother appeared in her window, conferring with the Centrist codirector.

"The seats," said Jenny. "We've still got the eight?"

"*Claro.*"

The Centrist assured her, "And our side's included another purple. Fair is fair."

Jenny hesitated. "The front row gets under the bell jar, right?"

The two heads shook in unison. "Sorry," her mother told her.

"Nobody gets inside that bell jar," the Centrist agreed. "Not with the candidates."

"Security is firm," said Soledad. "Just the two candidates, and Clive. But you'll be right up front; you'll see everything." A model appeared in her toybox: the stage on the Mound, and the positions of the three podiums, with the seats around in a semicircle.

Disappointed, Jenny also felt relieved.

Then she froze. Staring at the model, she recalled the stage right there atop the Mound, on the first day she arrived back in August. The teddies fussing around the podium to get everything right. "Um—" She took a breath. "The stage. It looks so plain without . . . decorations." Coneflowers and Indian grass, they'd had around the podium. "Could I provide flowers?"

"Floral decor?" Soledad turned to the Centrist. "What do you think? A touch of class, no?"

He frowned. "Not usually done. It would have to be professional."

"But I do flowers every week," Jenny said, "for the sanctuary."

"Oh, well then." He nodded. "Flowers blessed by the Lord."

48

Jenny and her friends joined the crowd of visitors, feathered tourists, news media in big hair, DIRGs, and professors in academic gowns heading north up Buckeye Trail. Above sailed dozens of medibots and security skybikers, one of whom had already crashed in the unfamiliar grav. In the naked maples, the foliage had yellowed, preparing to fall. Students wore fewer moonholes and more sweaters. They brain-juggled balls of amyloid in loops of eight. From behind, the south solar was starting to dim, while ahead the north solar brightened; the brightest time of day. The space between trees burst with blue heather and yellow coneflowers. The peepers had dwindled, although Jenny stepped around one squashed underfoot. As she passed the Reagan Hall of Science sprouting its jelly beans, she recalled the first time she'd looked up her professor's plant in Toynet. *"Arabidopsis thaliana,* var. *sapiens,"* at the Levi-Montalcini Brain Research Institute. **"Modified to form human neurons. Model system for nerve function and development."**

The deer had dwindled, thanks to the ecoengineer's hormone treatments, but the elephants were hopeless. A whole family of the minis ambled across the trail. They bunched up and pulled each other's ears, until a DIRG did something that made them squeal. Their trunks blared like toy trumpets, as they hurried indignantly into the woods.

"All debate attenders must present tickets and submit to full body scan." The announcement texted amid a hundred others.

"Jenny?" From Professor Abaynesh. **"Have you seen Mary?"**

Jenny had not, and she fervently hoped her *compañera* would spend the day elsewhere, drinking her saltwater. She gripped Tom's hand tight, and also Anouk's. Rafael walked slightly ahead, playing the owl again, with a touch of his former superior air. "We'll see which questions they select. I put in a question on reform of children's education." Students and community members had sent in questions. "Remember, though," Rafael added, "it's just a sideshow. The real action happens next." He meant, once the parties had counted their polls, if they'd fallen behind, they would quickly switch out the running mate and hope for a bounce. Centrists had put in the Creep three times, and it worked for them. But this time, Aunt Meg could not be replaced. Unity had tried a switch once, with less success; they would not try again.

The crowd jostled, pressing in and up climbing the Mound toward the stage. "Watch your step," texted Dean Kwon as everyone approached the risers surrounding the powwow ground. "Visitors, remember: You lose weight as you rise." Below ground, amid the buried maze of halls patrolled by Shawnee warriors, the taxplayers toiled without ceasing at blackjack, roulette, and slots.

Clearing her box, Jenny zoomed to center stage. Light from the south solar glinted on the upper curve of the bell jar. At the sight, Jenny's hands squeezed those of her friends. Beneath the bell jar were three podiums. Around the base of each were arranged purple coneflowers and Indian grass. And the little spoon leaves, she could just barely make out. The pots were well watered and artfully placed.

The seats took forever to fill, while everyone got through security. The candidates' entourage, including Glynnis and Betty, had their roped-off section. Jenny stared pensively into the bell jar, at the plant decorations she had placed. Then she looked a little closer, and zoomed her box.

Something had changed. Originally she had placed the *Arabidopsis* plants only before Anna's podium, artfully hidden amongst the Indian grass. But someone had redone the arrangement. The little round leaves were now distributed evenly amongst the three places.

"Anouk! They moved the plants all around. *Desastre—*"

"Shh, we're all watched."

She had planned to influence the Unity candidate more than the rest; but someone had redistributed the plants. Everything had to be equal, even the decorations. If only she had brought some blank plants that didn't make the semiochemicals. The one experiment where she'd forgot the control.

At two o'clock, the drums began. The eagle-feathered Shawnee elders led the way in, a quaint touch requested by Soledad and her Centrist counterpart. "All feathers are cultured; no animals were harmed to conduct this ceremony." Elders carried the American flag, the Ohio state flag, then the eagle staff with its proudly hooked beak. "Veterans of the Antarctic Defense." Black and white feathers fanned out from their backs, swaying in the breeze. The elders planted their flags before the stage.

"Our first Americans." Clive in her toybox provided running commentary. "Proud of their traditions, and proud to serve our country. And likewise, coming up, the college faculty with their frontier traditions . . ."

Dean Helen Tejedor carried the frontier ax, leading the faculty in their black robes to take their seats in the section reserved.

The bell jar on the stage remained empty, as President Chase came up to the side. Jenny could imagine how Uncle Dylan would feel, at his big moment at last.

"Welcome friends and visitors. Welcome Gar Guzmán, governor of Cuba; and Anna Carrillo, governor of Utah. Welcome to our moderator, Clive Rusanov of ToyNews. We welcome you all to our beloved habitat, our outpost on the highest frontier." A dramatic pause. "Frontera, the world's first permanent and self-sustaining space habitat, is a radical venture in the project of human civilization. Some would call our spacehab a refuge from Earth. But remember—no matter how perfect our habitat, it remains truly a *frontera*; a frontier in outer space, just as Frontera College is a frontier in humankind's search for knowledge. What better place to debate the future leadership of our country?"

Far above, the second "firmament" of amyloid was growing upward all around, the edges contracting inward. At last the second bell jar was complete.

"If democracy," continued President Chase, "is the highest calling of our country, and of all the free peoples of Earth, as we believe it is; and if Frontera College is one of the world's finest institutions of free inquiry, as we know it is; and if the entire community of our college and spacehab are the wisest and most industrious we know, then we are most grateful for the truly unprecedented honor of hosting this final presidential debate."

The stage floor opened. Up rose the two candidates and their moderator. The applause echoed throughout the hab. Clive had a new hairstyle; Jenny was certain she'd not seen quite this wave before. The candidates smiled and shook hands; it was obvious that Anna's face had a few wrinkles, compared to Gar's boyish grin. They took their place behind the podiums with their Ohio floral decorations, including the little spoon-shaped leaves.

"ToyNews—From our box to yours." Clive proceeded to summarize the rules of debate. "Our previous two debates focused on foreign and domestic affairs. Tonight's final debate focuses on our president's most weighty responsibility: the morality of our nation." A reverent pause. "Our questions," he reminded the audience, "were selected from a list of thousands submitted from across the country, based on our collective brainstream response. The result of the coin toss is that Governor Carrillo goes first, and Governor Guzmán has the last word."

Another pause. Somewhere in the distance called a barred owl, "Oo-oo-oo *oo-aw*."

"First question. Our country faces a grave threat to our existence—our very existence as a nation, a people. That threat is moral decline. At every turn, we find our citizens drawing more public largesse from games of chance, denying the Firmament, and sinking deeper into animal relations. These forms of moral decline harm our economy, disrespect our Creator, and debase our humanity. How will you as president turn our country around?"

Jenny tried to sink into her chair.

At her podium, Anna of course showed no lack of confidence. This was precisely the kind of question her trainers had drilled her on for weeks. "Clive, I'm so glad you asked that question. Exactly what Glynnis and I ask ourselves every morning, when we get up and hear the birds singing—the few that remain on Earth, unlike this pristine spacehab. What to do about moral America? The morality of a country that turns aside from our shrinking farmlands? That turns a deaf ear to the songbird?" She nodded meaningfully. "Unity is on record: We will pitch in and literally turn the tide of the rising seas. We will be good stewards of Earth, as our Creator commanded.

"As for public largess: Unity is on the record of denying any house edge increase for any taxplayer program. Our 'smart start' plan will improve public health, increase home ownership, and send more children to college—all achieved through smart fiscal management, with no impact on the public game.

"We don't try for the kind of brainstream control that some of our opponents do. We maintain a 'big tent' philosophy: If your world has a Firmament, we can still work together. Together we can still support NASA, that great American institution, to resume humanity's quest for the heavens—in outer space, and inner spirit."

Anna's response clocked in precisely to the number of seconds allotted. The pollmeter rose hopefully. NASA—people worshiped the Firmament, yet they still thrilled to the sight of a spaceship tilting into it.

"Governor Guzmán, your turn," observed Clive. "What is your plan, to turn around America's moral decline?"

The Cuban governor gave his best avuncular smile, the kind of smile Jenny knew well from her own extended family. "Clive, with due respect I must say I don't wake up and listen to birds, or any other pagan creature that might tempt animal desires. First thing when we wake up, Betty and I pray to our Creator. Pray to overcome that day's temptations, and all temptations of the days to come." The governor nodded meaningfully. "As for public lar-gesse, well, as we say where I come from, ¡No me digas! It was Unity, and its twenty-first-century forerunners, that drove our country into debt." The line drew applause. Not that the past decade had restored a dime.

"Now as to these signs of earthly distress—the famines, the rising seas—all of these point to God's wrath. And His judgment on people that make their living off the most vile practices, such as those sponsored by my opponent's running mate." More applause.

"God's wrath cannot be stayed; but we can prepare for His coming. Like Noah, we can build arks for the righteous. Space habitats like this one. Here at Frontera, can anyone doubt that the original Garden looked just like this? Depend on it, the Guzmán administration will build the spacehabs to trans-port the righteous above the Earth's destruction, in the coming time of Tribulation."

The deep voice echoed back from the northern cap, the hills of Lake Erie.

"Governor Carrillo," called Clive. "Your response?"

At her podium Anna hesitated. Or rather, she waited, as if watching something beyond the audience. "You know, Clive," she began slowly. "I've been thinking. In fact, I'd like the audience to spend half my response time thinking about your question."

In the audience eyes blinked and exchanged furtive glances. Feet scraped on the grass. A flock of sparrows rose from a nearby maple. Something scam-pered across Jenny's foot; she startled. Only a blue-tailed skink.

"Something about the atmosphere of this frontier college habitat," Anna observed, "must have clarified my thinking. I'm thinking: Why should any thoughtful person have faith in my candidacy, with a running mate whose live-lihood harms American families? No matter what the calculation, whatever good we've done, how can people believe we will be good stewards of Earth? Whatever the great plans of our party, they only sound like a clanging gong or cymbal."

A breeze lifted the grass. From humans there was not a sound. Clive, too, watched as if mesmerized. Then he caught himself. "Excuse me. Governor, your time is up. Governor Guzmán, your . . . response?"

Gar's mouth was rolled up like a window blind, as if it were determined not to open that day. "There is truth in what you say." He hesitated. "And you know, something about this frontier air has made me wonder a few other things. Like, if games of chance are against the Word on Earth, then how can they be *muy bien* out in orbit?" He paused at this novel thought. "And another thing. If relations with animals really are harmful to the soul on Earth, then how come they're not just as harmful to my Christian brothers on their vacations on the moon?"

Jenny's jaw dropped. Feeling faint, she realized she'd been holding her breath, and let it out with a rush.

Anna came out from behind the podium and faced the audience. "Gar is right. And another thing we might think about together is the Firmament. The reason this 'Firmament' is wrong has nothing to do with science. Even if the 'Firmament' could be consistent with an honest understanding of the heavens—it would be wrong. It's a belief totally self-centered. How can we teach children that the entire universe revolves around our own selfish existence? When God so clearly expects us to grow beyond what we are now."

From his podium Gar came forward too. "God does expect us to grow beyond; beyond even the Firmament. And that's what has me wondering. Calculating, in fact. How many people are to be saved? How many spacehabs do we need to build, for all the righteous people of Earth, and their children? When I was a child, I thought like a child. I tried to learn the math, but I never quite got it. How can anyone be president who can't do the math?"

Anna nodded. "That's right, Gar. And how can anyone accomplish anything as president while trying to agree with everyone? When I was a child, I thought like a child. I never learned to make hard choices."

"When I was a child, I reasoned as a child. When I became a man, I gave up childish things."

"It's all a puzzle, but I'm beginning to see."

Clive came around in front of his podium and joined the two candidates up front. "You know, something about the air of this high frontier college has got me thinking outside the box today. In fact, I just realized that it's more important for the people of this country to listen to the candidates than admire my hair." He nodded at the enormity of this revelation. "So if I may suggest—"

The hab went black. Not just dark, like the usual Frontera brownout. Jenny's toybox went blank. Gasps and shouts in the audience. No one knew what had happened. After an interminable moment, emergency lights came on in the trees around the hill, shedding isolated pools of light at intervals. Not a window in her box, but by now Jenny well knew the EMS drill: Activate backup lights, check the sewage pumps, shut down the elevator—

"A trick," hissed Anouk. "*No* accident. Someone shut us down."

Shut down a presidential debate? There were always dirty tricks on both sides, but endangering a spacehab—*diable*.

"Remain seated." From a DIRG somewhere amid the peepers, a voice called. "Audience remain in your seats."

A rush of voices swelled through the audience. Colored feathers appeared in the trees: red, blue, and green, the Mound's emergency system. The DIRGs sprouted searchlights that swept around the audience, and then upward, lighting up the forest across the hab.

Anouk squeezed Jenny's hand. "We lost more than our Earth-based support this time—much more. Accident, this was not." Accident indeed. But who stood to gain from election folly?

Tom's head wheeled around. "Could it flood?"

Jenny thought quickly. "Only if the pumps went out."

"We've made lifeboats," Tom said, "but not yet enough."

Charlie leaned over. "About fifty, I think. Father Clare would know."

Within the bell jar the emergency light remained, but no sound emerged, although the three performers could be seen conferring intently. At one point, Clive drew out a ten-dollar dime and flipped it in the air. The two candidates peered at the result.

"Calm, everyone," came Uncle Dylan's voice, hypnotic in its reassurance, just like when the bear had interrupted convocation. "If we pursue a true frontier, as indeed we do—what's a frontier without a few power-downs. Those of us who live and work here are used to it. There is no danger, but the security of our candidates requires that we suspend our event. In the spirit of our great nation, I ask that we all do our utmost to cooperate, enabling our secure departure from the powwow ground; and for visitors, orderly departure from Frontera. We wish that your stay could have been less brief . . ."

The candidates had already descended into the Mound. Already people in the aisle seats were rising as directed, the DIRGs escorting them out.

"Wait!" Jenny shot up from her seat. "I have to tell her—"

A hand gripped her shoulder. One of the Weavers, kind but firm. The star lapel turned orange. The broad chin said, "Wait your turn, dear."

Jenny's toybox was empty; she felt blind without it. Her head darted this way and that. "Glynnis!" she shouted. "It's me, Jenny—listen—"

"Quiet, please. Stay here."

She gave up; she would have to wait till ToyNet came back.

Suddenly the Weaver shifted position, and several others moved over.

Jenny caught a glimpse of Glynnis, arguing with her escort. Finally the candidate First Lady got within earshot.

"Glynnis? I can explain—"

"You'd better," said Glynnis. "What were they smoking?"

Jenny gulped. "Um—" She looked back at the stage, just visible in the gloom. "The little spoon leaves."

Glynnis stared. "Got it."

Away from the powwow ground, Jenny hurried south on Buckeye Trail, the yellow night lights on. "I need to check the lab, in case Abaynesh can't," she told her friends. "The plants, the snakes, and the ultra room."

"The pile worms too?" asked Tom.

"Of course, they're all in the basement with the ultra."

Tom nodded. "I need to check the lifeboats; make sure they're out clear of amyloid. After watching that castle . . ."

Abruptly some windows returned. "Local service only," announced Valadhkani from Toy Land.

Anouk nodded. "We'll stay in touch. I must check my Mandelbrot cottage; the mechanism is so delicate."

"And our cars," Rafael added. "They're delicate too. If the power surged—" For a moment Rafael and Jenny locked stares. Whatever did he make of what had transpired?

She looked back at Tom. With one last squeeze of his hand, she turned and hurried off to the lab.

Reagan Hall looked the same as usual. "Professor?" No response from her window. Within the building, all the lights were on in the right places. The generator must be working; for how long, Jenny had no idea. The hidden two-headed snakes looked fine. The plant lab was fine, except for the missing reverse controls. Jenny's scalp prickled; what would Abaynesh do when she found out? She had hoped to fetch them back after the debate, but now everything was mixed up.

In the basement, the pile worms were fine; when she tapped their tank, they slithered away. The chickens clucked, barely audible above the ventilator hiss. The tanks of ultra beneath looked the same as usual, except for the one in the middle. A large snake-form ultraphyte undulated beneath the ultraviolet light source. It looked a lot bigger than she remembered. Surprising, as she knew the professor limited their growth with salt.

Suddenly she remembered something. "Where is Mary?" She realized no one had seen Mary all day. She looked around the large tank. "Mary, are you here?"

A scrap of cloth lay on the floor. A piece of clothing; Mary's old tie-dyed shift. *Dios mío*—had the ultraphyte—

Jenny screamed. She blinked all the windows she could: Abaynesh, her friends, Father Clare. *"Mary Dyer! The ultra ate her!"* She sprinted to the door. The first of three containment doors opened, then closed behind her.

As she ran upstairs, she ran straight into Professor Abaynesh. "Stay out," Jenny gasped.

The professor put down her academic gown from the powwow ground. "Ultras are not carnivores. They use ultrasynthesis."

"But—she's *gone* straight out of her dress." Like the Rapture. Jenny blinked for her mental. "Did you see it? Didn't you?"

In Jenny's window Marilyn pursed her lips. "We saw a dress on the floor. We saw several dangerous captive ultraphytes. I must say, I'm not certain you're the one here that needs a mental."

Jenny avoided relaying the last bit. "My mental saw it too."

The professor clicked open the door, then the next one. She led the way into the room.

There stood Mary, in her dress. Her hands crept up and down her sides, as usual. As if nothing happened. *But from where?*

Mary asked, "Where did the light go?"

"We lost power," Abaynesh told her. "The whole hab. The hab needs more energy."

"Where did *you* go?" demanded Jenny.

"We're sorry you were scared," Mary said in Dean Kwon's voice. "If you could make cyanide, you would feel better."

The big tank was empty. "But it was full."

"Well," said the professor, "keep quiet about it. Imagine what they'll do to her."

Jenny backed away until her hands pressed the wall. "You're . . . a . . . ."

"We are ultraphyte," Mary said. "We study humans. We stayed home, like you said."

"You did," agreed the professor. "I'm sorry, the game is up. I kept you as long as I could."

"You *knew* she was an ultraphyte?" said Jenny.

"What else could I do? You left her in my lab," the professor reminded her. "What would the world do to her? What they did to Anne Frank?"

"We don't eat humans," Mary added. "We just borrow their DNA."

The door burst open. Anouk rushed in, followed by Tom and Father Clare. Anouk gave a critical look. "She looks fine to me."

"She's a mandrake."

Anouk's eyes widened. Her chin nodded ever so slightly, as if a final calculation fell into place.

"What?" exclaimed Tom. "Are *both* you two *chicas* insane?"

"Father Clare," began Jenny, keeping her eye on Mary, "those people with the syndrome who think they're John the Baptist. What if one of them actually were? How would you know?"

Father Clare glanced uncertainly at her, then at the professor, who stood there in stony silence, her arms crossed.

"My mental saw it too, okay?"

He sighed to himself. "That will make this week's third mental gone bad."

"If you don't believe me, and you don't believe my mental, what do you believe in?"

Father Clare straightened himself and turned to Mary. "Mary, tell us who you are, and why you came here."

"We are scouts," Mary said. "To learn to live like natives."

To live like humans—by "borrowing" their DNA? By becoming part human? *Dios mío y todos los santos.* "Show us what you really are."

The hands. Jenny's pulse raced. **"Anouk, grab her hand."**

From behind, Anouk grabbed Mary's left hand. Jenny lunged forward to grab the right. "Your hand, Mary. Give it to me."

Mary did not resist; she never did. "Be careful. This is stressful."

The air vents hissed; Jenny hoped they were good. Holding her breath, she yanked Mary's hand with all her strength.

The hand came off. The cell congealed into a blob, which Jenny hurriedly dropped on the floor. She let out her breath, and touched the cross at her neck.

The former hand crawled away rapidly, climbing up the tank in search of salt. Meanwhile, the rest of Mary collapsed into a snake form, stunned.

The larger form trembled for another minute, then pinched off another "hand." Now restored to an odd cell number, the body began to reform. A ghastly approximation of Mary's head rose from the floor. "Humans . . . are . . . beautiful . . . but poisonous . . ." Her opposite end was re-forming a snake, starting to creep purposefully along the floor. The head started to collapse. The snake end found the edge of a floor drain. It shaped itself into a thin file and started to flow through.

Professor Abaynesh sprang forward. "Come back—you'll get trapped down there!"

From outside sounded an alarm.

"Damn—they broke the seal. It met all Homeworld specifications."

49

That night Dylan met with his staff. The terrestrial visitors from the cut-off debate had all returned safely home, and the ToyNet connection was getting restored. The coincidence with the debate troubled Zari. The DIRGs were tight-lipped, but Dylan wanted answers. He filed a terror report. It was about time Homeworld gave the struggling spacehab better protection.

Whatever the cause, this time, the cutoff had damaged the transponder and fried half the network—more than any brownout before. Zari had to order parts from Earth. In the meantime, another blow like that, and the backup might not kick in.

As power was restored, so was news of the bizarre turn in the presidential campaign. The two candidates had suspended their campaigns and retreated in seclusion; with what end, no one could say. The election was twelve days off.

But none of that had anything to do with the dilemma the college now faced. The kind of crisis that was the true test of a college president.

Orin wore his most skeptical look. "Are we really sure what happened? Amyloid can play all sorts of tricks."

"The readings are clear," Quade assured him. "The laboratory recorded the whole transformation. The quasispecies development is fascinating. . . ."

Poor Clare, to have witnessed such a horrible thing; a "student" he'd worked with. And the students present, even Jenny; they'd all need counseling. Nora looked grim; she'd spent weeks trying to train an ultra to act like a human being.

"What if there've been other cases?" wondered Helen. "Those 'mandrakes.' "

"She used Babynet," pointed out Zari. "Text only, but still. That means she had some kind of human-like brainstream coming out. How could a 'mandrake' imitate that?"

The staff pondered this.

Dylan added, "The omniprosthesis institute who claimed responsibility for her does not return calls." The one with ties to the vice president.

"I've suspended all classes in Reagan," Helen added.

"And the laboratory?"

Quade said, "Homeworld DIRGs cleaned out the basement lab and posted guard around Reagan Hall. But the ultraphytes are out in the hab. For that matter, they were before."

"But *how?*" demanded Dylan. "Look, a DIRG is one thing—" How they'd laughed at Amherst. "But how could our college have admitted an ultraphyte?"

Everyone turned to the admissions director. Recruiting in South Africa, Luis stood out in his spliced wedge atop Table Mountain, an island whose cliffs dramatically overlooked Cape Town. The beach was a surfers' paradise, especially in winter when the temperature was habitable.

Luis tossed his wind-blown hair back above his sunglasses. "It's not in our questionnaire."

Orin was incredulous. "You mean, you don't ask if they're *human?*"

"We can't even ask if they're alcoholic or schizophrenic. They have to self-disclose."

"Well, what did you think? Didn't you even wonder?"

Luis hesitated. His eyes beneath his glasses could not be read. "I did wonder."

"You *wondered* if she was human?"

"Look," said Nora, "there are lots of students I wonder about, every day. Especially after Amherst. This could turn into a witch-hunt."

Dylan nodded thoughtfully. "*Ahora,* what do we do now? A student disappears, and the hab is full of ultra. Do we send everyone home, close the college, and clean out the hab?"

Orin snorted. "Show me a home free of ultra."

Helen added, "Mount Gilead and the Mound would have a say."

"What, then? Do we tell the world our student turned into an ultraphyte and vanished?" Lurking somewhere, down in the salty substratum.

The staff flexed their fingers.

"You can't tell the world about Mary," Nora exclaimed. "FERPA regulation."

A window blinked in Dylan's box. Someone from Homeworld expected him in the toyroom, *ahora.*

+-+

The dark glasses and the gray suit faced Dylan again, out of some undisclosed Homeworld location. Dylan's hair stood on end; he rarely felt claustrophobic, but alone in a toyroom with Homeworld was not somewhere he wished to be.

"The cause of your disruption is clear," spoke the mouth beneath the dark glasses. "A momentary transit of an Antarctic space drone crossed the path of your solarray power beam."

Dylan stared. "An Antarctic drone? Isn't that rather . . . far off course?"

The speaker went on as if he had not heard. "So your power goes out again, and your student goes ultra." The dark glasses didn't sound particularly surprised. "Such signs of instability have not escaped our attention."

Dylan clenched his teeth. "Our toymaker has good evidence the shutoff was deliberate. There must be an investigation."

"Terror, you say. And alien invasion? All in one day?" The head slowly shook. "On top of that, the debate was sabotaged by an illegal substance. From your students."

Illegal substance? The frontier air? *Dios,* thought Dylan, another bombshell. But the vague phrase tripped his suspicion. "If that's true, we'll take appropriate measures," he parried. "And we reported a new kind of ultra threat: Ultra can mimic a person."

The glasses said, "This was an isolated incident. It won't happen again. And it's classified."

Dylan's thoughts whirled. "Won't happen again? How do you know that?"

"It won't happen outside your unstable habitat. I can tell you, Homeworld is concerned about your whole management—the town, the taxplayer site, and the college. We may shut you down any day now. A buyout is on the table; we advise you to cooperate."

The Centrists wanted Rapture to buy out Frontera, the last heathen-owned spacehab. But where did Mary fit in? The ultra-*chica* who came recommended by the vice president's own doctors? Dylan's head spun; he had to break through somehow. "We can't just keep quiet about Mary." He took a breath. "People are concerned. They want to know."

A line appeared in the forehead above the glasses. "No one needs to know."

"Her aunt does." Dylan swallowed. "Mary texted her aunt every day. Her aunt wants to know where she's gone." Dylan stared down the glasses as hard as he could, the pulse throbbing in his ears. He was bad at lying, a trait that had ruled out for him many occupations outside academia.

The seconds ticked by. Dylan saw a shift in the jaw, an expression that reminded him of someone, the Ferrari club president after the incident at the Mound. At last the glasses said, "You are mistaken."

Dylan thought he'd gone too far out on a limb to stop now. "Mary's aunt wants to know some other things," he said quietly. "She wants to know why there is ultra at the White House."

The toyroom burst into white, and Dylan lost consciousness.

He awoke to find Zari and Eppie Uddin looking down at him, the doctor's scanscope clamped on his arm.

"Dylan," called Zari, "do you remember?"

His head ached like the devil. "I remember enough," he said, wincing as speech made his head worse.

"I cut the connection just in time," Zari told him. "Before they did what happened to Anouk."

"Nothing else from them? No other message?"

Zari exchanged a look with her wife. "I think we got the message."

Eppie stuck a line into the scanscope on his arm, and Dylan's head began to ease. "Ultra in the White House," he mused. "How can it be?"

She looked up with a shrug. "Back when there were Arab terrorists, their cousins sold oil in the White House."

The world's greatest democracy, the pride of Teddy Roosevelt, had come down to this. With Homeworld against them, what could Frontera do? Could they get by till the election? Dylan raised himself upright. "We need to make sure Mary has an 'aunt.' Someone down on Earth . . . needs to know everything that happened here."

50

At supper Friday, Ken and Yola silently spooned their amyloid. Yola had skipped practice to study for an exam. Tom had closed the café for another weekend; he was rattled and exhausted, and still getting his energy back. Jenny knew how badly he needed the money. She'd purchased some of the Kearns-Clarks' vintage wines, on which Tom would get the commission and Ken and Yola would get the rest. Anouk sat with her usual ballet posture, no sign of strain that she shared the terrible secret of the *compañera*. She'd managed to drag Rafael away from his motor club table. His eyes sleepless, Rafael had that lost-in-a-toyworld look.

Jenny looked around at the amyloid forks picking up amyloid food. "So, um." She swallowed a forkful. "Any thoughts on the debate?"

Yola's fork paused in mid-air. She glanced at Ken. Ken kept on eating. He'd agreed to stay at Frontera, at Lazza's with Yola, but kept to himself. "They said," Yola began, "something about 'the air of Frontera.' The candidates said."

Jenny quickly looked at her plate. Then she looked at Rafael. "What did you think?"

Rafael's face struggled with itself, trying to look owlish. "*Tonterías,*" he said at last. "That woman said what everyone knows already—the Unity 'big tent' will take in anyone, even child molesters. Whereas Guzmán forgot himself and destroyed the Centrist vision."

Yola's eyebrows rose. "What vision is that?"

"The spacehabs change everything." He sounded agitated. "Look, the Bible doesn't say anything about what you do on a spacehab. Off-world casinos, zooparks, whatever. Why did he have to disrespect that?"

"So the Bible only applies to Earth?"

"Yes. I mean, no." Rafael appealed to Anouk. "You play the numbers too."

"I break rules," Anouk admitted. "But I know what the rules are."

Rafael took a breath. "What's wrong with solarplate anyway? Why does it have to be off-world like a casino? Does that make sense?"

"It's all in the numbers," Anouk patiently explained. "Solar energy comes to Earth; but most of it reflects out. The difference between in-flow and out—the negative number—that sets our Earth's temperature. If the Earth traps too much more of the sunlight—as in solarplate—it overheats."

He blinked several times as if seeking one of his lost windows. "What about windfarms?" Marcaydo Windfarms.

"Windfarms just capture heat that's here already. But it will never be enough for a hungry world."

Yola looked away. "I felt sorry for both candidates," she said. "It's like, they each woke up and saw what a jerk they are, in front of the whole world."

"Don't feel sorry," grumbled Ken. "Like drunks that sleep it off, they'll forget soon enough."

✦

That weekend Reagan Hall swarmed with DIRGs and Homeworld drones, the kind Jenny had called down at her home in Somers, to hunt ultra. Still, her experimental plants had to get checked. Showing up at the lab, she found Anouk and Tom waiting outside facing a Weaver DIRG. Tom had his pile worms to check too. "What's going on?"

"Only humans allowed," said the Weaver in her firm contralto.

"That's us," Jenny affirmed.

"Prove it."

Jenny shared a look with Tom. Anouk gave a delicate shrug, as if to say, "These *americains*, they cannot even tell what's human."

Jenny blinked for Dean Kwon. The dean looked at her with haggard, sleepless eyes, the look of a refugee who'd escaped untold horrors. "I told you, class is canceled. What do you want in that lab?"

"But we have to check our experiment. You can't stop science!"

Kwon's look turned suspicious. "Only a mandrake would go in there."

"But—" In consternation, Jenny looked back at her friends. "You know who we are."

"Do I? You were her *compañera* . . ." The dean looked more suspicious than ever.

"Look—let the DIRG scope us and see."

Dean Kwon considered this, and the other students agreed to be screened. The DIRG got out her scanscope, similar to Jenny's, only more advanced. "Very well," Kwon grimly concluded. "You're *adultos*. Enter at your own risk."

✦

Inside Reagan Hall, they found the laboratory transformed. The original basement was sealed off; its door could not even be found. The plant lab was moved aside, and smaller, the flats crowded into shelves beneath doubled-up light banks. Abaynesh was there with Semerena, feeding headless mice to the snakes behind the professor's office.

"The plants." Jenny felt guilty about the missing ones, which the candidates had kept. "We came to check on our experiment."

Abaynesh shrugged. "Yes, well, you can go ahead with the plants upstairs. The basement creatures were not so lucky."

"What do you mean?"

Semerena's shoulders were more hunched than usual. "With the ultra they are gone." He hid his face.

"You mean they . . ."

"Cleaned out," observed Abaynesh succinctly. "By Homeworld Security. As the saying goes, 'straight to the gas.' "

The whole contents of the ultra basement. Besides the ultras, they'd burned all the rats and chickens too. Jenny felt sick. The three students stared without speaking.

"Apparently Mary's ultra cells had learned to dissolve the amyloid drain." Abaynesh looked at Semerena. "We think they got those genes from the pile worms."

Semerena nodded. "It's true, the pile worms have that pathway. But our new polychlorinated amyloid should stop them. The annihilation was unnecessary."

Jenny watched the two-headed snakes coiled in their tanks, and the remaining rats and chickens in the professor's hideaway. The lucky terrestrial survivors. "So the ultraphytes acquired pile worm genes? Not the other way round?"

"Both ways," said Semerena. "On the pile worms first, the ultra practiced."

Abaynesh put back the snake she was feeding. She wiped her palms on her jeans and adjusted the sleeve of her designer shirt. "The quasispecies begins with a seed. Wherever the seed falls, it sprouts and makes offspring. The offspring evolve into forms compatible with the host world. They mutate fast, and the most successful forms survive."

That had gone on for years. "But didn't something change?" Jenny thought of the biofilm that appeared in Great Salt Lake.

"Some forms of ultra learned about native life by copying their genes into native organisms. Then the more advanced forms acquired host sequences encoding host traits."

"That started in the biofilm?"

"From that biofilm, the quasispecies has evolved faster. Instead of just random mutations, the cells take up Earth creature DNA and copy it to their RNA, acquiring useful traits. It makes sense: If you find yourself in a new environment, copy the successful traits of the natives." Abaynesh paused. "But some of them must have started earlier. Before Mary. How did that happen? Why are there no intermediate forms, half-human things?"

Mary. How many human genes did she have? What was she after all?

Tom asked, "What about the pile worms? Could they . . . evolve to be ultraphytes?"

"Unlikely," said the professor. "Worms don't do the genetic engineering. Who really cares about pile worms?"

In a cage, one of the snakes started to fight between its two heads. The little jaws lunged out, each trying to consume the other.

"*You* ask her," Anouk insisted.

Jenny took a breath. "What was Mary?"

"Mary was a community," said Abaynesh. "A whole research lab of ultras, trying to be a human."

Anouk said, "To find out about us?"

"They did a pretty good job."

"But why us? Are there others on Earth?"

"There's always a first time. Frontera is a small, closed environment. Only a few people to worry about. A good model system."

Jenny thought about the Creep. "Washington is also a small, closed place. You can sit alone in a room, seeing only who you want to see."

"I knew it," exclaimed Anouk. "The Creep is ultra too!"

The two professors exchanged a look, as if they'd had a long argument. "So it could be," said Semerena. "Many Europeans would agree."

Abaynesh shook her head. "The Creep had a long history as an Idaho senator. Like other uber conservatives, he was hiding a tendency. I think he really does have ultra syndrome."

"Mary didn't just happen," argued Semerena. "The Creep instructed doctors to make a mandrake. As a defense experiment. That is always the excuse to make biological weapons: to devise a defense. That is government logic."

"That's why the government made weapons-grade anthrax," agreed Abaynesh. "To test defenses."

Jenny bit her lip. "Mary never seemed like a biological weapon. Just a mixed-up *compañera*." Similar to a normal human, yet not quite. An Illyrian human.

"That is why I hid her," said Abaynesh. "Sometimes you have to do what is right. We had long conversations. But now?" The professor shrugged. "Who knows what ultra's next move will be."

Tom caught Jenny's hand. "What if Mary's cells are dangerous? Could they destroy the hab?"

The professor looked him in the eye. "There are worse dangers to the hab. That power-out was too convenient."

Jenny's scalp prickled. This kind of politics she was not prepared for. "What about the wisdom plants?" she wondered suddenly. "Did Homeworld destroy them?"

Abaynesh gave her a long hard look. She didn't say if those reverse controls had ultra genes. "Some of the plants were gone already," she pointed out. "Perhaps the rest of that group will disappear." She inclined her head toward the back of the lab. "The guard on the west side doesn't function very well. I think it printed out wrong."

Jenny and Tom sat in her second-floor greenhouse, watching the two *Arabidopsis* plants placed inconspicuously amongst her prize-winning Blood Star, the vanillas, and the giant purple vandas. "I don't feel any wiser, do you?"

Tom held her closer. "I don't know how I should feel. Maybe my nasopharynx lacks wisdom receptors."

That was what had scared her, when she first brought the plant to Hamilton's class. All she felt was overwhelming questions.

"But it feels okay," added Tom. "Like, I don't know now, but someday I'm sure I will."

"ToyNews—From our box to yours." A new announcer appeared, with a special news bulletin. Jenny looked closer. It was Clive after all. His head was shaved, as round as an egg. "We bring you live coverage from the Carrillo campaign headquarters."

In the purple-lined window, Anna Carrillo and Gar Guzmán appeared together. They each held what the text labeled as a "souvenir native plant" from Frontera. The spoon-leafed plants looked well watered.

"Good evening, my fellow Americans," said Anna. "My campaign has a special announcement to make. Following prayerful consideration, my running mate Sid Shaak has decided to step down, in order to take care of pressing family matters." She paused. "In selecting a replacement, I took seriously my promise to maintain a bipartisan spirit in government. And during our recent debate, in the clear frontier air of Frontera, I came to appreciate the fact that a difference of a tenth of a percent in poll numbers has no existential meaning. I realized that I agree with my fellow governor of Cuba in so many things—in our love of Wisconsin cheddar, our concern for the bighorn sheep, and above all, our devotion to the welfare of our country."

Gar nodded thoughtfully. "During our debate, I came to realize how much I agreed with my fellow governor of Utah. And so I brought back to my fellow party members the need to discuss a bipartisan effort. Regrettably, my party thought differently. And so, that is how I became available for a different position."

"Of course," Anna went on, "the Unity party has long experience with a 'big tent' philosophy. We merged two parties before, and we could do it again. We are by nature bipartisan. So we welcomed Gar as the new running mate for the Unity ticket."

Gar beamed, with his avuncular smile. "This is actually a great opportunity for me. Away from the pressing needs of running a state, I can go back to study mathematics, and its applications to large, complex societies. With eight years of math under my belt, I'll be in great shape for my turn at running the world's most powerful nation."

As the world's audience was absorbing these words, the bald-headed Clive returned. "The candidates and their entourage agree that something about the frontier air of Frontera inspired this remarkable turn of events. In the meantime, the Unity party announces their response."

There appeared Aunt Meg and El—and next to them, the former senator from Idaho, now the longest serving vice president in history.

"Good evening, my fellow Americans." Meg sounded like the authoritative California governor she was, the kind who solved budget problems and drove out ultra with tanks. "As you know, the Centrist party has just experienced a change of leadership. But as always, Centrists manage change in a way that promotes stability—the most important thing for any government.

"When we learned that our candidate no longer professed the ideals and principles of our party, our course became clear. The Centrist national committee selected me, as the next highest primary vote recipient; after all, less than one percentage point separated us. Following this logical selection, I asked the current vice president to continue in his position." She smiled with the triumph of this logic. "So you see, my fellow Americans, the choice is clear: Continue stable, competent government, with us—or risk a change, with candidates whose flaws and mercurial allegiances became all too evident in the clear frontier air."

The last-minute shakeup had everyone's head spinning. Stepping out on an errand, Jenny was so confused she stumbled over her shoelaces, forgetting to watch the pebbles on Buckeye Trail. Anna and Gar . . . Aunt Meg and the Creep. How could Aunt Meg have picked him? Even Hamilton knew the Creep had to go.

Upon her return, three elephants were up on her porch again, their trunks probing at the window. Jenny tried to shoo them off as usual, but the third one had to be dragged by its donkey tail, squealing. At that very moment, her aunts' windows opened.

"*¡Hola!* Jenny Ramos Kennedy!" Aunt Meg with her smile of triumph.

Aunt El's head shook. "Tsk, tsk, *sobrina*. Molesting the minis again."

"Hi, Aunt Meg, Aunt El," Jenny replied with a resigned sigh.

"We still treasure your endorsement," Meg reminded her. "And your promise to vote for us—now that you can."

"Blood is thicker than politics," El reminded her.

Jenny bit her lip. If only she could print out a wisdom plant for her aunts. Not yet—maybe through Babynet, someday. "Look, Aunt Meg, I know you mean well, but—" Where to begin? "Tanks just won't do against ultra. Believe me, I know."

Meg nodded briskly, as if sealing a deal. "Our ultra program needs a director. You're hired."

"You won that prize," reminded El. "And since then—my goodness, Homeworld must have found something to blast in your lab."

Jenny took a breath. "The Creep. He has ultra syndrome."

El glanced sideways at the head that shared her shoulders. "What did I tell you—"

"Shut up, El." Meg's curt retort was a surprise.

El looked hurt, then recovered her smile. "We've got plans for our dear vice president, haven't we, sis. The day after election. A very, very secure undisclosed location."

Meg relaxed. "Can't take you anywhere, El," she concluded in her old way. "As for you, *sobrina*—see you on Election Day."

51

The convulsion in the campaign landscape rippled out in many directions. While the campaigns tried frantically to reposition themselves and recalibrate the pollmeters, a new media industry grew up overnight: the quest for Frontera's air. How had the "frontier air" caused the candidates' epiphany?

From every public printer on campus, a bald-headed Clive emerged to investigate. The Clive printouts roamed the college for news, leaving no remote lead unexplored. One, of course, stopped by the college president's office.

"President Chase," the amyloid construct began. "Your college motto is 'Friends of wisdom, we are here.'"

Dylan smiled his most ingratiating smile. "*Sophias philai paromen.* Wisdom is the highest frontier."

"And some say that wisdom breathes in the very air of Frontera."

"I certainly hope so, Clive."

"And it was your air that wised up our two candidates. Can you tell us, what is it that's so special about your frontier air?"

Dylan's smile creased with just a hint of nerves. It would have helped immeasurably if in fact he had the faintest notion of what had happened to those two candidates; but since he had none, he could only respond in a way that placed the college in the best possible light. "As you know, Clive, our habitat circulates pristine air at all times. Combustion of all kinds is prohibited throughout the hab." Except for the Mound, which maintained its own circulation.

"Pristine air," repeated Clive. "No brain-altering particulates."

"And the proportion of gases," Dylan recalled with inspiration. "Oxygen, nitrogen, carbon dioxide—the proportions are not those of Earth today, but were set by our ecoengineer Quade Vincenzo at precisely those of three centuries ago, before global change. When Thomas Jefferson first wrote the Declaration."

Clive's eyes widened. "The air of the Founding Fathers. No wonder."

Dylan nodded, hoping that would suffice.

"I suppose," Clive went on, "your water supply, your Ohio River, is equally pristine."

"Of course we filter all the college water."

"So your water requires filtration?" Clive had the newshound's instinct for irony. "What is the hab's water quality?"

"Quade will help you out on that one. Of course," Dylan was quick to add, "the college is responsible only for our own water. Mount Gilead is . . . an agricultural community." The local produce did not meet college standards; that was why the students were fed regulation amyloid.

"We're printing out at the courthouse, as we speak. By the way, the mayor-elect is one of your faculty, correct? Can you help us locate him?"

"Of course, as soon as possible." Dylan hadn't seen Hamilton since the debate. Even Helen had no clue.

"And for local color, I understand the debate stage was decorated with native Frontera plants, including the intriguing 'wisdom plants' bred here in your own college laboratory."

Dylan's heart sank. "The Reagan Hall of Science, yes. Unfortunately off-limits for interview. Ultra cleanout."

"Ah, indeed," observed Clive, reveling in the irony. "Even the wise spacehab cannot escape the war on ultra."

"Claro," admitted Dylan miserably.

"Not to worry; as printouts we're okay with the risk. The Reagan Hall of Science—first science lab built in a spacehab. You raised the funds for it, didn't you?"

Suddenly Dylan's guard was up. "That was ten years ago, yes." He'd gone to Washington to pick up a congressman for a trip to the Lunar Circuit; the *casinadie* who ran the subcommittee on naming buildings for presidents.

"A nice bit for our academia window. We'll have someone follow up."

Dylan's heart took another plunge. The last thing he wanted, on top of all else, was to resurrect the details of just how he'd spent that Washington trip ten years before.

The Clive printouts scoured the college interviewing every "friend of wisdom" they could find, for their clues to wisdom, or better yet folly. Quade Vincenzo at length, every incident ever recorded with the bears, the poison frogs, and the infamous elephants. They even dug up the time he'd spread an illegal insecticide to eliminate gypsy moth. "I have an inchworm phobia," he told Clive. Then Orin Crawford was asked about the time he spent endowment to build the frogs' dorm. And Luis Herrera-Smith admitted accepting students who'd avoided math since kindergarten. And Dean Helen Tejedor was asked how those faculty junkets to conferences in the Caribbean were financed out of student fees. Most interesting of all, Nora Kwon had to explain how Frontera handled student social follies, which were as frequent as at any earthly college. Records showed that every year for the past ten years—including just that month—certain motor club members had been eased out to avoid assault charges.

The students too faced relentless scrutiny. Their voting record—one percent in the mayoral election, barely ten percent for the last presidential. The Begonias' gardener sold a story on the entertainment he'd provided them. The twins whose father had lost the family fortune at Rapture. The daughter of the Euro minister, a polymath and compulsive hacker. The Amish mutant who'd left his family. Overnight the entire community was spread under the same microscope where Jenny had found herself since the day she was born. In fact, she seemed to be the only one the Clives ignored, since they already had her whole life on file.

One did pop his bald head in her cottage door to ask about the stage decorations.

"The, um, wisdom plants," Jenny admitted vaguely, looking aside. "Ask Professor Abaynesh—they're her research."

The printout Clive braved ultra contamination to investigate Reagan Hall. He gave Abaynesh a full-length interview.

"My students and I have studied plant wisdom for the past decade." The Life professor waved her arm dramatically above the rows of plants, now arranged to take up maximum view in the window. "Five hundred and eighty-four different wisdom circuits, at last count."

"And how exactly do these wisdom plants work?"

"Each pot has two different plants, with slightly different neuron circuits. Illyrian pairs, you might say. Each has to agree wisely to cooperate with the other against caterpillars."

"Astonishing," observed the printout. "Isn't that like what our candidates learned to do?"

The professor shrugged. "I'd be delighted to share the seeds with any colleague."

Jenny zoomed her window on the plant rows, and blinked for the labels. All were the neural combinations that had scored marginal results over the years. Mary's reverse controls were nowhere to be seen. Aside from the two in Jenny's own greenhouse.

At supper, Jenny asked Yola, "What do you think now?"

The pollmeters were all over the map, completely upended. Some states swung away, others came into play.

Yola looked up. She chewed her amyloid thoughtfully. "Okay, you win. I'm voting."

Ken looked up at her, incredulous. "For what?"

"For the team," she said. "Look, we're kind of responsible, see? We made this happen."

Charlie agreed. "The whole world's eyes are on us now. We have to set the example." His eyes widened. "Think of it—Our votes at Frontera could swing the entire election."

52

Clare burst into the study. Dylan looked up from his grading. *"¿Qué pasa?"*

"Hamilton's gone, all right," Clare told him. "Along with all the inventoried power stores."

Hamilton's backstory, too, had been unearthed by the Clives. There was quite another life to that professor, much of it on the moon. Debts to pay off in Mare Crisium, at some of those ungodly establishments that had revolved around Dylan's car as it fell. Mare Crisium had its own take on rehab— exempt from Earth standards.

"Running the college is enough for me," Dylan sighed. What a hornet's nest that town was.

"Dylan, we have to send the students home."

"What do you mean?"

"Homeworld gave you warning, didn't they? They're determined to shut us down."

Clare had been on edge ever since Mary collapsed; who could blame him. "Clare, I know you had a terrible shock—"

"This is *not* about me. It's about getting our students home safe." Clare had never looked so agitated. "'The air of Frontera'—Do you imagine the Centrists will let us off? Someone at Homeworld will do us in."

"You can't know that. The whole world is watching us now. How can we just up and leave?"

Clare leaned his arms on the desk. "The students; and all the children of Gilead. They have their individual lives ahead of them."

"Are they any safer below?" The forests gone in smoke, the desert wasteland. "Didn't they come here for the frontier?"

To that Clare said nothing. He stormed out the door. Dylan followed Clare's window as he left, heading out to the Homefair shop. The students were hammering carboxyplast into lifeboats, crude boxy things like Michelangelo's.

The next day Dylan hiked into Mount Gilead for an emergency session of the town council, of which he was a member ex officio. Clare wasn't speaking, but at least he'd left his window open. Orin reported in his window. "Sorry how that old history came out," Orin gruffly apologized. "You recall, back in the day, our survival mentality."

"No problema," Dylan assured him. "We needed a frogs dorm; our donors understood."

Then there was Nora, about all those quick expulsions. "It never occurred to me," the dean of students reflected, "what we really were doing."

"We did our best," Dylan told her. "The evidence was always fuzzy, the lawyers expensive."

"But over the years, we let go all those student rapists to prey on others elsewhere. Like the old Vatican with their priests."

The town too had not passed unscathed. One of the Clives unearthed that busybody social worker's survey of mini-animal abuse by colonial farm boys. Thirty-nine percent admitted experimenting.

The pigeon-thronged courthouse was draped in red, white, and blue bunting for the election a week off. Inside, at the council, the morality officer, Judge Baynor, presided in his robes, along with Frank Lazza and two other well-muscled farmers. "The mayor has his reasons, I'm sure." The judge looked around the councilors as if defying a response.

Beneath the table, boots shifted position, and a power band squeaked. Frank drummed his fingers. "A lot of us want to know where those stores went." The ones Hamilton had tallied, then disappeared with.

Another farmer nodded agreement. "We wear them bands day and night, all for a bit of extra juice at home. Where'd it all go?"

"I said, Phil has his reasons." The judge's voice rose.

"Sure, we know his 'reasons.' "

Another farmer laughed. "A guy's gotta do it somewhere."

The judge sat up straighter. He pounded the table with his hand. "I will not hear our community disparaged by outsiders. Doing the devil's work. Spreading dissent among the faithful."

The testosterone level was palpable. "Excuse me," Dylan interposed, "I believe the motion on the floor is to appoint a temporary mayor."

No one spoke. Judge Baynor reluctantly nodded.

"Given the frequency of power-outs this year," Dylan said, "would it not make sense to pick a mayor who knows the hab mechanics well? Someone who can fix a broken tile and keep things running?"

The judge said nothing.

"The widow Smythe," muttered a farmer.

"Leora knows the hab inside and out," agreed Frank.

"Well then," said the judge, "you better get those *other* missing stores from her."

Dylan avoided pointing out that had the Smythe Bank reserves appeared sooner, they too might have vanished with the errant professor-mayor. He had made some delicate inquiries of his own. Leora had some knowledge of Hamilton's debts in Mare Crisium.

In Hamilton's absence, Jenny now had a substitute politics course from toy-Harvard. The class was a total bore. On her own, she leafed the pages of Aristotle, finding she actually missed Political Ideas. At least Priscilla or Enrico would come up with some novel remark. But Life class was on a new track with interactive models, like a Nobel prize kindergarten. And her Life lab had metastasized into the real world.

On the way back from Wednesday class, Tom's window was blinking. He appeared at the Homefair shop with Charlie and Priscilla, and the Pezarkar twins. "We've just completed the lifeboats for the frog and sophomore dorms." He sent her a long brainkiss.

Jenny closed her eyes and enjoyed it. She sent one back.

The rest of her windows revealed a tectonic shift in allegiance. Among students, purple-lined windows now outnumbered golds ten to one. But her town contacts had shifted the other way. Even Frank Lazza, with all his EMS calls, had gone gold—that hurt to see.

"ToyNews Local. The town council announces the appointment of an interim mayor, Leora Smythe. In other news, the missing reserve units of the Smythe Power Bank have turned up. A custodian discovered them in the attic of First Firmament Church, stacked neatly beneath the Easter service."

Leora was the mayor—an intriguing turn in the town soap opera. Jenny blinked her congratulations.

The new mayor shortly returned her call. "Jenny, the town is working on our new voting system."

"I see." Jenny's lawyer's appeal had been denied by the state court, and the Supreme Court turned down the case. Apparently off-world communities had wide latitude to specify any form of ballot that preserved privacy, even radioactive ink. So the uranyl acetate stayed, though there would have to be a secret ballot.

"What do you think of this ballot form?" Leora blinked it over. The new form looked clear enough, a list of candidates with boxes to check. The few local seats—morality officer, sewage director, town council reps—were uncontested, and the rest were based in Ohio thirty-six thousand klicks away. No senator was up that year. Carrillo-Guzmán versus Akeda-Creep; to see it in print startled her. It was truly for real.

"The ballot looks good to me." She'd write in Father Clare for morality officer.

Leora hesitated. "We need to get more students voting."

Jenny raised an eyebrow. "You think so?" There was a change.

"The students are really citizens of our town. They bus tables at Lazza's, assist the one-room schoolteacher, and run EMS." Which ToyNews report might she be quoting? "The town thinks it might help to have student poll-workers processing voters at the courthouse. Could you perhaps serve as a poll judge?"

Guao. "Sure, I could do that."

"We'll need a second student," Leora reminded her. "Someone from the other party."

Jenny searched her windows; there were so few Golds left. "Rafael Marcaydo."

As she approached her cottage, someone was sitting in the porch swing. Like Mary before—Jenny's hair stood on end.

The visitor wasn't Mary. It was Lane Mfumo, from HuriaNews. The reporter waited patiently, pumping the floor with her foot. Her cornrows swept up in a spiral, like Abaynesh's style. "It's me, all right," Mfumo assured her. "In the flesh."

Jenny took a breath, and tried to collect her thoughts. "You're not print-out?"

"I rode the anthrax up. My spent ticket." She blinked it over.

Jenny pulled out her scanscope. Mfumo held out her arm, and the scope clicked. The readings scrolled down, a standard blood workup. "Okay," Jenny said. "Nice to meet you."

"Look, Jenny, I know there's a story here—and you've got it." Mfumo rose from the swing. "Why won't you let it out? Don't you want the world to know the truth? How everything could change for the better?"

That was precisely what Jenny had asked herself, since the debate. But all her life since the cradle, Jenny knew only one thing for sure about the media: Never trust them. "Suppose the wrong side wins." If Centrists found out, she'd end up in prison, or the blue room.

Mfumo nodded. "I understand. But this is the big story. The frontier air—the wised-up future leaders of the free world—the fate of the Earth. I've got my job to do," she warned. "I'll keep digging."

Jenny looked away, her gaze sweeping the hundreds of windows in her toybox. Then she froze. There amongst the windows was the Babynet window. The one Mary had used. Yet Mary was gone. Wasn't she?

53

Jenny's mother called every day now with poll updates. The states were swinging wild in all directions, and the operatives were in a frenzy to pull them back. Invariably Soledad was blinking away the whole time, multitasking one campaign director or another. But Sunday night she was all business. "Jenny—I hear alarming things about Frontera."

"Really, Mama?" Jenny crossed her mental fingers.

"We know what happened—and the other side doesn't like it. Your hab is breaking down—it could fall apart any day now."

Jenny said nothing. The power-out was a bad sign. But she couldn't just give up and leave.

"Jenny, I want you home right away. You can take an early Thanksgiving break, and complete your papers on Toynet."

"Mama," Jenny said, "science doesn't work that way. I have to check my plants."

"Print out helpers." Soledad added starkly, "If the hab goes, your science goes anyway."

"And besides, I have to vote."

"What—you haven't voted yet? Just vote in Wisconsin, on your way down the anthrax."

"But—our community. They made me a poll judge." Why was it so important, Jenny wondered herself. For Father Clare? For Leora? "Look, Mama—the whole world is watching us now, on the highest frontier. Will they say the Ramos Kennedys cut and run?"

Soledad stood back. Her brow furrowed as she thought for a long time. "Very well," she said slowly. "Your father and I will come up Monday and stay again at that Lazza's. We'll see firsthand how it goes. We'll see if Ramos Kennedys cut and run."

Dios mío, thought Jenny.

Jenny met Anouk in her Mandelbrot room, which Anouk swore was the se-curest place on campus. "Do you still see Mary's window?" ventured Jenny. "Is it there in your box?"

"But of course, *chérie*."

"But—how can that be?" Only a diad on someone's forehead out there could generate a window in active toyboxes.

"I asked Zari."

"You *told* her? But Anouk—"

"Jenny," she sighed, "the toymaker always knows all the secrets."

Like Jenny's father, it was true. "But how could this be?"

Anouk shrugged dramatically.

"But Mary . . . she dissolved and went down the drain." Like an octopus through a crack. "What became of her diad?"

Anouk raised an eyebrow.

"No way," Jenny said. "I'm the one in trouble now. You go ask the pro-fessor."

Anouk blinked for Abaynesh. "Professor, can you tell us—we were just wondering. What became of Mary's diad? Was it found, before the cleanout?"

The professor appeared in her window. "Maybe," she observed. "And maybe not."

Jenny shook with apprehension. She felt an impulse to pull off her own diad, contaminated as it was with the mystery window.

"Perhaps Tovaleh is playing tricks again," Abaynesh suggested.

"Oh, of course," Jenny breathed.

"So listen up, you two: If you ever read anything there, either of you, let me know immediately. Okay?"

Jenny closed her eyes, but the windows remained. She felt trapped in a toyworld she couldn't escape. But this toyworld was bigger than herself, big-ger even than Frontera. There was no "out" to escape to.

Yet, no matter how scary, a little knowledge is a dangerous thing. Over the weekend, as she plowed through her Teddy paper and her Cuba reading, Jenny's eye kept straying to the empty Babynet window. At last, without really deciding to, she blinked. "MARY?"

Her stomach did a somersault, but nothing happened. No response.

Every now and then, she typed something else.

"HUMOR?"

"WISDOM?"

"SALT?"

Sunday night was a long, hard slog to finish her Teddy paper. Back then, interstate commerce involved companies running choo-choo trains, like the one that chugged around the top of Wickett Hall. A holding company tried to control all the trains, from one state to the next, all across the country. That made sense—people loved one big system, plain and simple, to get from one shore to the other. But the plain and simple system snuffed out competitors. No Huria trains, only amyloid Clives. But was that so bad? Judge Oliver Wendell Holmes didn't think so. It wasn't enough to agree with Teddy; Uncle Dylan expected an argument, in her own words. "The forms of combination have been metamorphosed into new shapes . . ." Her eyes defocused.

In the morning, as Jenny negotiated the Weavers into Reagan Hall, her steps slowed at the door of physics professor Zhi-Li Zhang. Catching her eye, the egg-shaped man eagerly waved her over. "Look at my latest acquisition!"

Amid the angular brass instruments full of toothed gear wheels stood a square mirror upon a wooden tripod. The mirror was mounted to pivot up and down.

"A heliograph," Zhang exclaimed. "U.S. army, from 1886. Used in the battle to capture Apache chief Geronimo."

Jenny puzzled over the instrument. "What did it do?"

"It reflected sunlight, blinking up and down to send Morse code. It could reach an army camp fifty klicks away."

Those clever Salt Beings. "So anyone with a mirror could 'spread data.' "

"If the sun were shining." Zhang grinned. "But then, people invented this." He held up a disk sliced from a bundle of metal bars. "A chunk of the first transatlantic telegraph cable."

"Transatlantic? Strung above the ocean?"

"Below," he corrected. "In the deep."

"Guao." Talking along a wire, amongst the deep-sea fishes; that was hard to imagine. "So then, was the cable a monopoly, like the railroad?"

"The voice phone was a monopoly, for a while, until there were satellites. Then the Internet, the first full network. And then Gafanet." The gafas on everyone's eyes.

"And now Toynet."

"Toynet, the first brainstream," concluded Zhang.

"Toynet is all one grid. What's wrong with that? I mean, isn't it efficient to have all one system?"

The professor hesitated. "Sure, it's efficient. Of course, like the helio-graph, all the infrastructure starts with the government."

"So the government reads all our brainstream?"

"They could. To find ultra, remember; everytime you see an ultra, they want to know. The Alien Intelligence Act."

Her scalp prickled; she never liked to think of that. "Can they see how everyone votes?"

"Not if you shut your windows. But users forget." Zhang shrugged his shoulders. "What does it matter? Voting for president is just tradition."

"What do you mean?"

The professor glanced up at the Seldon poster, the psychohistorian under a bell jar. "Today, anyone with a pollmeter is a Seldon. Any candidate can predict the vote, and calibrate one's response."

"It didn't work for me."

"The mayor's race? Your candidate didn't use a pollmeter," he reminded her. "For the past five presidential races, the number of votes was a statistical tie." President Ramos, then the four Centrists who followed. "The difference lay within the range of counting error."

She hadn't thought of it that way. All her life, the vote had been close, and there were riots for months afterward. "Well, this year it's different. Every-thing got shaken up—a candidate even switched parties, just days before the vote. Who can predict now?" New York and Kentucky were suddenly swing states, while Michigan and Maryland had swung off the map.

Professor Zhang grinned. "We'll see."

Jenny's eye glimpsed the Babynet window. The window was no longer empty. "SALT. LIGHT."

For a moment she stopped breathing. She stood transfixed.

"Something wrong?"

She shook herself. "Excuse me." She hurried on to the plant lab.

Anouk was there, inserting the assay probes and tallying responses. Jenny asked, "Where would Mary find both salt and light?"

Anouk thought a moment. "The purple microbes, out in the shell."

The purple microbes, the ones that swam through the saltwater shell of Frontera. The ones that drank sunlight to help power the hab.

✦

The night before Election Day, Dylan came home late from an exhaustive faculty meeting. Frog seminars, Antarctic studies, the orating still swam through his skull. In the end, he'd pulled off what he hoped for: the frog seminars. But Quade's news was more worrisome. The hab's control circuits had sustained damage from two recent power-outs; next time, a backup switch might fail. And in the phototrophic zone, the purple bugs that pumped amyloid and yielded a quarter of the hab's power showed some kind of contaminant. A brownish muck was spreading, something resistant to the usual antibiotics. If Quade didn't find a cure, they'd have to tell Mount Gilead to expect a deep-freeze winter while they tossed in chlorine and restarted the culture. The Mound wouldn't mind, they'd put up a ski slope. But the colonists—that would do wonders for town-gown.

Yet none of that was his main worry just now.

Clare looked better rested than usual, and more attentive. He'd actually come home for dinner instead of building lifeboats till all hours with barely a word to say. Clare sat on the couch next to him, reading Aquinas. "What is it, sweet?" He clasped Dylan's hand. "Tough faculty meeting?"

Dylan held Clare's hand tight, the way he used to back at college, a senior still fearful the frog would run off with some well-built guy who hadn't already lost a liver. Above sailed Michaelangelo's *Last Judgment*, Christ separating the saved from the damned.

"The frog seminars," Clare asked. "Did it finally pass?"

Dylan smiled, still looking away. "It passed. With an unconscionable amendment on staffing. Orin blew a coronary."

Clare stroked Dylan's arm. "I knew you'd set your heart on frog seminars."

"Don't you know it." As a senior, he'd talked a professor into letting him audit a frog seminar on early American religion just so he could see Clare every day. After class the two of them had lovely walks along the river.

"I guess I'm the only guy who ever got seduced through Jonathan Edwards's sermons."

"'Corruption of the heart of man is boundless in its fury.'" With a laugh, Dylan finally dared to face him. "Guess I've been burning in brimstone again."

"So, what?"

He took a breath. "The Clives finally dug up something."

"Well?"

"It was ten years ago, for God's sake—my one slip. I was in Washington making the big ask for the Ronald Reagan building."

"I remember," said Clare.

"It was stupid. I was jet-lagged, and a bit rattled; we'd blown a tire on the Lunar Circuit." Clinched the deal, though; to this day, the congressman bragged of it, as if he'd driven the car himself. "Afterward, I lost my head and made a fool of myself. With some guy I met in the hotel gym."

Clare thought a moment, then nodded. "I guessed as much."

"You guessed? You never said anything."

"Why let you confess? You burned in your own brimstone."

Dylan sighed. "I was miserable. I always wanted to be clean with you." The last thing he wanted to be was some aging guy who couldn't keep his pants on. "It never happened again."

"I know, sweet. You've always been good to me."

"How those printouts dug it up after all these years—"

"In Washington everything gets dug up. Just forget it." Clare fell back on the couch, suddenly short. He looked away as if preoccupied.

Dylan studied his face. "So what did they get on you?"

The chaplain crossed his arms. "Telling you won't help."

"What could you possibly do that I couldn't forgive?" More curious by the minute, Dylan pressed his shoulder, but Clare pulled away. "Except maybe donate to Williams. You didn't, did you?"

"Oh, hush."

They sat in silence. How God set them in slippery places, sang the Psalmist.

"You'll hear soon enough," observed Clare at last. "My photos, after high school. They're up on Toynet."

"Photos? Of you?"

"My final summer, I needed to complete my tuition payment."

"But your scholarship—"

"There's always the work contribution, as you well know. I modeled for two weekends. The first was with clothes. They promised anonymity but—"

"Photos? Goodness, Clare, where *are* they?"

"Will you shut your toybox and *listen?*"

"Of course, dear." Clare exposed, back in high school; the thought was overpowering. "Look, anyone would understand; you were a scholarship boy, you needed the money."

Clare shook his head. "I didn't *need* the money; I could have spent the summer caddying ten hours a day. Instead I worked two weekends, then spent the summer reading Aquinas."

Dylan glanced overhead at a passing *ignudo*. "The Church fathers thought well enough of the male form."

Clare started to get up from the couch. "If you won't listen, I'm going to bed."

"I'm listening, Clare; really I am. Please."

"Don't you see—I spend all my days counseling students *not* to sell themselves. What will they think of me, when they see myself out there?" Clare shook his head. "A hooker sells himself for a price. These students— they sell their health for nothing. For laughs at the motor club."

Dylan winced at that, but kept quiet.

"How can I ever look them in the eye again?"

They sat on together in silence. Slowly Dylan shook his head. "You know, Clare, this is why I can never believe like you do. One narrow way to heaven, and a million ways to hell. A God who truly loved His children would not set them in a minefield."

Clare caught his arm, just like he used to that year, after class. "Dylan, you've got it all wrong. There's a million ways to heaven. A mother raising four children; a toymaker connecting half a planet; even, God knows, a college president serving young billionaires."

"You don't say." Dylan smiled ironically.

"There's only one way to hell."

"Which one?"

"Separation. Turning away God's grace. Refusing to be forgiven. That's the only hell there is, Dylan."

54

Before the south solar dawned Tuesday, the courthouse pigeons cooed and huffed into the air a few feet, disturbed by the sleepless Clives. Lane Mfumo leaned against a pillar blinking at her toybox. As Jenny arrived, Mfumo stood and extended a hand. "Jenny Ramos Kennedy. We have a date in your greenhouse."

Jenny looked her in the eye. "After the race is called."

Rafael was there already, nodding and bowing like the experienced owl. "A fine day for voting."

A line of students had formed already, many bleary-eyed from staying up all night with excitement. This was Frontera's day. "Hope they've practiced their handwriting."

"Not to worry." Rafael nodded at Anouk.

Anouk beamed, extending her hand *allongé*. "I cannot vote here, but I shall offer my services."

Inside, the amyloid floor had been cleaned till it shone. There was a long desk with the registry, this time with the addition of a large antique polycarbonate jug. The cap of the jug had a slot for ballots. The ballots were sheets of crude carboxy paper, with the form Leora had sent Jenny before. And of course, the bottle of radioactive yellow ink.

At the desk were two voter stations, one for Jenny and Rafael, the other for Leora and Frank, who went about fixing signs and regulation markings. Frank's toybox window had gone gold; but Leora's had gone purple. Go figure. At any rate, no other campaign hints were allowed, just voters with their ballots.

Rafael went immediately to the desk and started working through the regulations, as trained. Jenny took a step, then looked around. "Where are the other desks?"

Frank turned from the wall, where he had posted the sample ballot. "We blinked the county board of election, back on Earth, to set up more desks, but it was denied."

"What do you mean?" Eight hundred students, plus about the same number of colonial adults and employees from the college and the Mound. If each voter took five minutes, and there were two desks . . . "Did they do the math?"

"They said we had to base our preparations on previous turnout," Frank explained. "Even the town never turned out more than twenty percent."

Jenny blinked for a window outside. The line in the early light included farmers and women in bonnets, some with children in hand. "Get the Ohio secretary of state."

Frank looked at Leora.

"I will," said the mayor.

Two lines of voters snaked into the hall, down to the two desks. The first, a farmer who delivered potatoes to Lazza's, blinked his ID to Jenny and gave his name to Rafael. Rafael had to leaf through pages of the Aristotle-like book. After a time that seemed to last the age of the universe, he found the name and checked it off. Then the man moved to Jenny's side to get his ballot. He picked up the pen full of yellow ink. The ink spattered as he pressed too hard; the radiation meter went off scale. Jenny winced. After he was done, the ballot went in the slot of the polycarbonate jar. There were already several more people waiting.

Jenny texted Leora, "Are there more pens?"

"We're waiting to hear."

The voters moved through faster, as Rafael and Jenny got the hang of the system. The students were not thrilled about the ink. Probed for health incessantly since the cradle, some could not believe they actually had to touch something radioactive. A Begonia held the pen at arm's length, her left hand holding her nose. The students though at least let Anouk guide their writing. Seeing this, some of the colonists let her help too, and the line moved faster. It was not perfectly anonymous, but at least the ballots went into a jar.

In the window appeared Jenny's mother, and her father "Spreader of Data," toy-clothed in his feathers and leggings. They appeared to be standing outside the courthouse amid the pigeons. "*Hola*, Jenny!" called Soledad. "What century are we in?"

"Century zero," Jenny texted back. Then to her dad, "How is the vote back on Earth?"

From where he stood, George would be processing the data stream, along with his fellow toymakers in the fifty-two states, all day until the last vote came in. And he'd continue for the next two years of court challenge, if the last three elections were any guide.

"One hundred thousand sixty-two hundred votes, twenty-three law-suits, and four appeals so far."

Jenny reached across the table to the arm of an elderly woman shaking from Parkinson's. A shame they didn't fix that here.

George Spreader of Data was finger-weaving his bead recorder. "Two days plus eighteen and a half hours."

"What's that?"

"The time we will need to stay here, until you finish."

Jenny texted Leora, "Did you reach the secretary of state?"

"Our request is down to number seventy-one."

Soledad had turned away, busy in her toybox, while George puffed on his pipe. "Democracy among the Salt Beings." He spoke now in sonorous *Kanien'kéha*, his words flowing around the pipe, converted to English text. "What the Salt Beings know of democracy they learned from the People of the Longhouse. . . ."

"Tom!" At last Tom would get his chance to vote. With his Amish training he swiftly penned the candidate names.

Jenny caught Tom's arm. "How is it out there in the line?"

"It's hard on some folks, all the standing."

A blink at her box. At eight in the morning, it looked like half the hab was standing out there. "Maybe you could pump some amyloid for chairs?"

"The Iroquois League of Six Nations taught the Salt Beings the value of uniting states. They taught separation of powers amongst the chief, senate, and people to the Founding Fathers at their Great Council Fire of Philadelphia."

Jenny replied, "The Iroquois didn't teach voting." She refilled the pen. The level of ink in the bottle had dipped noticeably. She craned her neck to take a look at Leora's bottle. Leora's level had dipped less, probably because without a handwriting assistant fewer voters were processed.

Tom came back with two chairs in each hand. That meant four of about a hundred people waiting inside could have a seat. Most had sat on the floor by now; students brainstreamed a floatball back and forth, while farmers played cards. A woman in a bonnet with two small children got up and started to leave. Jenny's eyes followed her out the door. "Tom—maybe you could help them write at Leora's table?"

"The People of the Longhouse never engaged in the bitter practice of voting. . . ."

A drop of yellow on the table; Jenny tried to wipe up the radioactive stuff. "Leora, have you heard yet?"

". . . so their deliberations took many days. The Salt Beings with their voting decided much faster."

Leora replied, "The secretary of state now lists us at eighty-seven."

Eighty-seven; *Dios mío*, that was worse than the hour before. Were there more complaints, all over Ohio?

"But today, the Salt Beings face an even more bitter practice. The pollmeter splits the vote ever closer. It is the end of voting as we know it."

Rafael whispered, "I cannot find this gentleman's name." Orin Crawford stood there, looking grim.

Jenny leaned over to check the book. She found Crawford's surname, interchanged with his given name.

Spreader of Data added, "One might as well flip a coin."

Suddenly she wondered: Professor Zhang had said the difference always lay within counting error. So how did ToyVote ever declare a winner?

"Jenny!" In the window her mother looked scandalized. "For goodness' sake, what is going on in there? This *tontería* is inexcusable."

"Mama, there's nothing we can do. The state won't get back to us."

Name after name, each ballot was sealed and confirmed with the radiation meter, then dropped in the slot. She could hear each ballot land on the paper below; the jug held quite a pile. From the north window, the afternoon light grew; Jenny winced as it shone in her eyes. Anouk stretched her arm and massaged her palm, but did not complain. Hours passed, yet the line outside only grew longer, as voters arrived faster than the early ones left.

"What about my class?"

"I'm missing practice. Coach will kill me."

"My paper is due."

An announcement came from President Chase. "All students in the voter line are hereby excused from classes and sports. If our students are true pioneers, in Teddy Roosevelt's understanding of the term (and we know that they are), then indeed they are frontier democrats, in instinct and principle; and their right to vote must not be denied." At this announcement the students cheered.

Near the door, people got up and started moving around, some sort of commotion. Students got up and farmers stepped aside. In strode Soledad, trailed by three printout Clives. "As a concerned citizen," Soledad loudly announced, "I demand an explanation. Everyone knows that long lines are designed to keep genetic inferiors from voting."

"Mama!" Jenny whispered. "Keep your voice down."

Soledad repeated louder, with deeper sarcasm, to the Clives: "Everyone knows that long lines keep genetic inferiors from voting."

Jenny put her head down while her mother stalked out, the Clives in her wake. The colonists ignored the incident, but students grew sullen. Students had little experience of being oppressed, and they were uncertain how to handle it. There were dire mutterings and ugly glares at Frank and Leora.

After about ten minutes, a couple of courthouse workers appeared, carrying a table and a poll book. A second table and poll book soon followed.

"We heard from the state," texted Leora.

Jenny sighed with relief, although even with two more tables the line might still last another day. "What about ink? The ink is getting low." Her bottle was down to a thin yellow residue. Perhaps they could dilute it.

"Judge Baynor approved regular ink."

But the students would have none of it. "It won't count if it's not radioactive," one shouted. "It's a trick—they won't count the ballot." One student thrust his thumb in the ink and shoved his hand in Leora's face. "You can't say I didn't vote."

Most of the colonists moved over to the new tables, while most of the students stuck with the uranyl acetate. Meanwhile, new voters were arriving from their work in the fields all day, and students after dinner. The poll closing hour approached, with hundreds of people still in line.

Jenny took a break behind the tables with a sandwich from Leora's hamper. She blinked for news. Despite the late shakeup, the pollmeter showed a tight race all over the country. Apparently the week had been enough time for the parties to soak up the electoral brainstream and recalibrate their campaigns. Zhang must be right, Jenny thought. If even two candidates seeing the light could not break the cycle, voting was a broken system; outdated as a heliograph. But what could they do about it?

"ToyNews—From our box to yours." Clive appeared, back to his old hairstyle. Jenny's heart sank. "An exciting Election Day—as vigorous as we've ever seen. Poll traffic is more than twice the volume four years ago." He nodded smartly, the old Clive Rusanov in charge. "All across the country, votes are pouring into ToyVote in record numbers. What a horse race—too close to call." His voice began to slow. "And everything . . . is running smoothly. ToyVote is in . . . control . . . reporting . . . fewer problems than. . . ." Clive stopped. He stared directly at the audience without speaking.

Suddenly Jenny noticed her father's window was gone. "Mom?" she called. "Where's Dad?" George always multitasked hundreds of windows at once, including his daughter. There must be real trouble at work, if he'd had to close her out. Or had something happened to him—had the stress got him down? His Aspie nature could take just so much.

At ToyNews, Clive put his hand to his head and grasped his hair. With one swift motion he pulled the hair off. "In truth," the bald Clive spoke rapidly, ignoring the hairpiece at his feet, "there is chaos at ToyVote nodes across the country. Some nodes are overloaded, others have shut down. Hundreds of complaints were filed in Ohio alone, and in states from Cuba to California . . ."

From behind Clive, two Weaver DIRGs approached. Each broad-jawed DIRG had a motherly tough-love look, like that of a matron handling a tantrum on a kindergarten playground.

". . . while in Washington the riots have begun, not even waiting for the outcome—"

The DIRGs each grasped Clive by an arm.

"Clive Rusanov, reporting from somewhere in custody—"

The window closed.

Jenny looked up. At the table, Rafael calmly processed voters, with the efficiency of long practice. Anouk and Tom helped handwriters. The other tables looked the same.

"Jenny?" Charlie appeared, outside somewhere in the line, in the dark, where the pigeons had tucked their bills under wing. "How are we doing? Do you think Frontera will tip the election?"

It was now a rational, orderly process, the way voting ought to be. Unlike the madness on Earth. And utterly obsolete.

Jenny blinked HuriaNews. **"What's going on?"**

"I don't know," replied Mfumo. **"All I have is rumors. I tried to head Earthside, but the lift is stalled."**

Jenny froze. She swallowed hard. **"The lift isn't running? No one can get out?"**

"They say the anthrax is sporulating."

That made no sense. She tried Tusker-12 and her other Earth friends. All their windows were frozen. Frontera was cut off, she realized. One tiny capsule suspended amongst the stars. Cut off from Earth.

At three in the morning, her toybox went blank. A collective gasp. Everyone in the room had lost their box. Just a roomful of people, nothing more.

Leora conferred quickly with Frank. Then Frank stood and cupped his hands. "Quiet in here," he called. "Everyone be quiet. We're working on a fix."

The lights dimmed. All went out except the one backup light.

Frank barked, "Quiet," again, as people rustled and muttered. Meanwhile, Leora got up and went to the window. She put her head out, surveying the landscape.

Jenny joined Leora at the window. "What is it?" Outside, stark backup lights spotted the landscape with pools of light amid darkness. This was no brownout; this was black, darker than the darkest night.

But Leora wasn't looking. She was listening. Jenny listened too, but heard nothing except the call of an owl.

Leora came back and spoke a word to Frank. Then she climbed onto the table.

"As mayor of Mount Gilead, I am calling a flood drill." She emphasized the word "drill." "The drill we've practiced Sundays after service. We all walk out, straight to Buckeye Trail. No stopping, and no running: Just walk out. At Buckeye Trail, head north—and keep going."

Voices rose again; Frank banged on the table. "Order in the courthouse. Listen to the mayor."

Jenny's mother and father: Where were they?

"Remember," Leora called again, "head straight to Buckeye Trail. Then north all the way. *Do not leave the trail.*" She took a breath. "To keep us in order, remember, we will sing. 'Nearer, my God, to thee, nearer to thee . . .' "

The colonists took up the song, evidently one they knew well. It made a good walking song. Farmers marched out, and mothers marched out with children. The students didn't know the drill or the song, but they fell under the calming influence of those who did.

"Jenny!" called Rafael. "All the students—the frogs back in the dorm. They won't know what to do."

"There's Elephant Man, and Dean Kwon, and—"

"They can't all get north in time." Tom took a breath. "We have to get out the lifeboats."

55

Jenny found herself hurrying down Raccoon Run, disoriented, barely able to think after nearly a whole day awake. She stumbled in the darkness that came in between the pools of light. She dodged a stalled DIRG; without Toynet, they were useless. Now she could hear something in the hab, a distinct rumbling sound that she'd never heard before. Had the pumps failed? A deep, grating sound. Her foot stumbled again, and her leg collapsed. Was the substratum cracking?

Anouk caught her hand. "*Écoute,* Jenny. I know how you feel about floods—but you must stay calm."

The plants. All her orchids, and the wisdom plants. That was it; she had to save the plants. At Buckeye Trail, Jenny turned south.

"Jenny!" Anouk yanked her arm. "What is wrong with you? You heard the mayor."

"I have to get my plants."

"You're crazy. We can't carry plants."

"Some of them."

"*Merde.*"

"The wisdom plants, remember?"

A bullhorn called, "Buckeye Trail, head north. Buckeye Trail." Dean Kwon raced by, and other staff. Students and professors, all heading north.

Jenny barely noticed. She had to reach her cottage.

When she got there, everything was dark. She fumbled in the darkness trying to collect several pots in her arm.

"Madness," Anouk insisted. "You can grow more plants. Let's get out of here."

From outside, a gush and a roar. In the distance water fountained up from the ground, pouring in all directions. Above, across the hab, another jet of water fountained downward, then up, pouring over the farms. A whiff of microbial stew.

Jenny handed Anouk a wisdom plant. "We'll put these in the boat." Outside the cottage, she pulled at Tom's lifeboat leaning at the wall.

Anouk tugged the boat down. "There, leave your dumb plants; the boat will float. Let's run for the trail, before it's too late."

Jenny arranged the last of her plants in the boat: Vandas, vanillas, Blood Star. And the two wisdom plants. But others were left upstairs; there was no more room. She started to cry.

At her feet the water rushed over, icy cold. The rush of water filled her ears now.

"*Merde*, it's too late." Anouk jumped into the boat and savagely shoved the plants back. "Get in here, you crazy person."

Jenny lifted her leg and stumbled into the boat. None too soon, as the water rose around it. A foul odor arose from all the photosynthetic microbes, like the smell of a beer-soaked carpet the morning after.

The boat heaved, and Jenny slid across, banging into the side. A couple of the pots fell out. She stretched her arms, desperately trying to hold on to the rest.

Anouk let out further exclamations in French. She took hold of an oar, but the boat kept rocking. "Keep your head *down*!" She shoved Jenny down to the floorboards. "Just hope we stay afloat—"

The boat grabbed Jenny and took off on its own. A current was flowing, where, she had no idea. Screams, and cries for help. Someone out in the water, waist deep, raised their arms and called out. But Anouk could not yet control the boat, which still lurched and rocked in the current.

As the boat drifted away from buildings, Anouk's oars dodged the trees. The current slowed. The fountains gradually subsided into the water. Water was everywhere, water above upon the farmlands, its distant wavelets reflecting pools of light from the backup beams. There were cries for help, chilling in the distance. I didn't help them, thought Jenny. First responder.

Anouk got out the oars and started rowing. "Look there."

Along Buckeye Trail, survivors from the courthouse were still walking north, in about a foot of water. The trail was somehow "higher," apparently following a ridge that stretched the length of the hab.

"Let's get over there. I don't trust this boat." Anouk started rowing over toward the trail.

They had nearly reached the trail, when the boat slammed into a tree. Jenny slid out, holding just one of the wisdom plants. She gasped at the chill.

"Come on!" Anouk grabbed her arm and pulled her, wading slowly, to join those walking north.

✦

Before the water came, Dylan knew what had to be done. Quade had got out one briefing before the cutoff. This time, the fried system had failed, and the pumps shut down. The unthinkable had happened; and they had to get the students out to safe ground. The college staff divided up amongst the dorms and faculty residences, systematically calling out the students. Once they reached the trail, above the solid rib of the hab, they'd be okay.

Dylan knew that time was short; but he also knew there would be students in those dorms that didn't hear the call. Entering Huron, he hurried down the hall, yelling and banging on doors. A frog was fast asleep on the couch in a lounge; Dylan pulled him up and shoved him toward the door. Another was curled up on a bed, frozen with panic; the loss of Toynet could do that to some. Still another, disoriented in the dark, couldn't find her way out.

As he got through the third floor, his foot sunk and half stuck. The amyloid was melting. He raced out the hall and down the stairs, his feet sticking and sinking. At the doorway, he nearly got out, but his shoes completely stuck. He slid his feet out; but then his left foot stuck in the amyloid.

Dylan reached up to the door frame, and he just managed to hold on. Unlike the upperclass residences, the frog dorms had a frame of carboxyplast. He held on, and managed to keep his other foot up, without getting stuck. But he was trapped, as the dark water rose icily around him.

56

The powwow ground was covered with colonists, children, professors, students. The toymaker and the doctor huddled with their whimpering teddies. Students were crying, or staring, or asleep beneath blankets handed out by workers from the Mound. The darkness, amid all the blank toyboxes, could be felt almost like a solid weight.

From the distance came the high-pitched groan of a bear. Then a lowing of cattle. Exhausted beyond imagining, Jenny propped herself up on an elbow and peered out upon the flooded fields.

In a pool of light at the foot of the Mound, where the water lapped the new shore, Quade's square-cut ark floated into view. The carboxyplast platform was crowded with miserable teddy bears, mini-deer, mini-cows, and some of the most dejected elephants she had ever seen. The ecoengineer, along with Fritz Hoffman and a couple of other Bulls, had to shove the animals out onto dry land, which the creatures no longer seemed to trust. Then a deer bolted, and the rest began to scramble off on their own. Fritz started unloading cages: the cages from Reagan Hall, that held the Life professor's chickens, rats, and two-headed snakes.

"*Jenny!*" Soledad found her. She caught Jenny and held her so tight she could barely breathe.

Jenny gasped. "Where's Dad?"

"Your father is here—he had a fit when he first got cut off, but now he's fine. He's helping Zari restore the system. As for the rest of the world—"

Jenny's eyes closed, and she finally fell asleep.

Still caught in the congealed amyloid of Huron, Dylan sculled the water with his arms and tried to stay awake. The foul-tasting microbial soup had leveled off, but he had to keep moving to keep his head above water. And his limbs were numbing by the minute. At least his caught leg no longer hurt. With his right hand, he caught the side of the door frame again, but could not keep holding on. He had to keep his mouth out of the water. But he found himself nodding; if once his chin slipped, he'd lack the strength to cough his throat clear. His head swarmed with visions; the bright green lawns of Westchester, the redbrick halls of Harvard Yard, the hair-raising turns of the Dubai Autodrome. The chapel where Clare had delivered his first sermon. *That saving grace that is in the hearts of the saints* . . . Jonathan Edwards would have the last laugh.

"Dylan? Is that you?" Someone was calling him, from a long way off. From the world he was leaving.

"Just reach up." Out of the darkness an arm reached downward, with a hand outstretched, like God at the Creation. *"Dylan!"* With a voice like Clare's. Dylan smiled to himself, and his eyes closed. He'd always known God would sound like Clare.

"Dylan, *wake up.* Just reach out, *please.* I can't reach any farther."

His eyes opened. There was Clare upon the ledge above, braced against the carboxyplast, his arm with its hammer-honed muscles reaching down. "Dylan, can you hear me?"

Dylan's lips moved, but no sound came out.

"Dylan, do you remember our first time, years ago? That night, remember? We'll do that again—at Lila's Beach. Lila's Beach, you hear?"

The thought of Clare on the beach struck a spark in the mortal world. His circulation quickened. All his effort went into lifting that arm. He couldn't even feel it, but somehow the arm lifted out of the water. Clare grasped his hand and pulled. A bolt of pain up his leg, as if his foot were torn off. After an eternity he slipped free and was hoisted up where he sank into the waiting lifeboat.

57

When Jenny awoke, the hab was still dark. The black roll of water lay throughout the hab, making a muddy shoreline around the cap just below the powwow ground. Treetops stuck out, spreading jagged shadows across the pools of emergency light.

But her toybox filled with Babynet text. The toymaker and her teddies had managed to get Babynet up.

"BANDAID, ANYONE?"

"CHARLIE? HAS ANYONE SEEN HIM?"

"WHEN DOES HOMEWORLD GET HERE?"

"DID WE WIN?"

All messages were local; there was still nothing from Earth. Wolfing down amyloid from the Mound, Jenny looked up at her mother. "How long has it been? Why aren't they coming?"

"A day and a half—we don't know." Soledad's voice was grim. "Homeworld should be here by now, as well as FEMA."

From the shore rose excited cries. Reesie Tsien and Suze Gruman-Iberia were hauling up a huge jug they'd found drifting in the water. "The votes!" she exclaimed, cradling the radioactive jug. "All the ballots—they're here. They'll count!" The most verifiable votes in the whole election.

"EMS NEEDED." From Doc Uddin. "ALL EMS VOLUNTEERS REPORT TO THE MOUND."

Feeling somewhat restored, Jenny roused herself. The wisdom plant was still there with her, not entirely wilted. Furtively she gave it half her water ration.

At the Mound entrance, the lights were all out to save power. But inside, the lights were on, enough to see the games. Maybe she could sneak her plant in there. Frank and Judge Baynor were at the gate, along with Yola and other EMS. Doc Uddin explained the Mound's medical system that they'd rigged up, a surgical cart Babynet-linked to a scanscope. The scanscope data had to be read from a flat box on the cart. Inconvenient, but it worked.

Jenny trundled a cart down the hill, checking out various students sick from the foul water, bruised children, and elders suffering hypothermia. And damaged limbs; Uncle Dylan's foot had lost a toe and half the skin, but the amyloid bandage held without infection so far.

"I'm sorry, Jenny," he told her. "I promised your mother we'd take care of you."

Jenny shrugged. "We are here." Except Charlie, the thought nagged at her. Charlie was one of four students unaccounted for, along with two colonists.

"And then you had to face all this, after your brother."

She looked off in the distance. She actually hadn't thought of Jordi. She'd thought only of her plants. Crazy, maybe, but it kept her sane.

Dylan strained his arm, trying to sit up. "I should have sent the students home," he said. "We knew the cutoff had fried the network. Zari had to order parts. In the meantime, we knew the hab couldn't withstand another blow."

Jenny shook her head. "We didn't cut and run."

"Ten years as president," he reflected. "I hung on too long. I should give someone else a chance to do better."

She half smiled. "You'd regret it—like Teddy did."

"I could go back to being a professor."

"You're a great professor," she told him sincerely. He was her only professor who didn't need the plant.

"And you've become a wise *gantowisa*."

"JENNY—COME HERE IMMEDIATELY," her mother texted. What could it be?

On the bank with Soledad, there was George—the first Jenny had seen of her father. She hugged him close.

"Jenny," whispered her mother, "your father is about to go out. Outside the hab."

Zari Valadhkani stood there in spacewalker's overalls, along with Leora, and Coach Porat. All were experienced spacewalkers.

"Your father and Zari think they can pick up a Toynet signal. To find out why no help has come. And what's going on . . . on Earth."

Jenny shuddered. "So what can I do?"

"Go out with your father. In case he needs help. *¿Entiendes?*"

✦

Outside the cap, the stars shone, and the moon was a sharp sickle. The hab's surface looked browner than before; yet it yielded power, more than expected, Quade Vincenzo had said. The brown contaminant absorbed ultraviolet, a range of wavelengths missed by the purple microbes, and it transferred extra electrons to the electrodes. Quade didn't have to say what that contaminant might be.

On the platform where Coach and the Pezarkars had built the *sukkah*, the spacewalkers now rigged up a Toynet node and tried to get up a signal. George Ramos was not accustomed to spacewalking; he'd spent most of his life in his den in Somers. Now he hung out there with the others, with a nudge from Jenny now and then when he forgot to hold on. All around reeled the stars. A bright explosion as a bit of Kessler debris flicked the brown surface of the hab.

"ToyNews. From our box to yours." The window appeared, with Clive like his old self, full of hair.

A huge sense of relief—Jenny had never welcomed a toy window so much. Not that the news was much help; more casualties in Antarctica, more flooded islands in the Pacific, and more confusing numbers from Election Day. There was still no presidential winner, though the popular vote margin favored Carrillo/Guzmán by half a percent, the widest margin in two decades. With all the lawsuits and riots, had nobody noticed *el desastre* out in space?

"Still no word from Frontera," announced Clive at last. "The power-out prone spacehab, with all their friends of wisdom, still lacks contact with Earth." The last phrase held an ironic tone. Jenny frowned; it didn't sound right. "We have this message for Earth from Frontera College president Chase."

A message from Uncle Dylan? Who was resting injured below at the Mound?

The supposed president Chase appeared, his usual jaunty self. "Not to worry, all is under control. The outer link will shortly be restored. If our beloved space habitat is the frontier (as it certainly is), and our students are the great pioneers that we know them to be, we can manage nicely on our own for the time being, and will soon be back in touch."

Around the rig, the spacewalkers froze—Leora, Coach, Zari, all receiving this in their heads.

"LIES LIES LIES." Her father's space suit began to flail its arms and legs. "ALL LIES—SALT BEINGS ALWAYS LIE. TEDDY LIED TO THE IROQUOIS—"

Coach grabbed George's suit from behind, and tried to pull him toward the airlock.

"DAD, CALM DOWN. IT'S ALL A MISTAKE, DAD."

They got him back inside and into the pressured chamber. George's head burst out of the suit. "What Dylan said—it's all lies. Teddy lied when he said, 'The Ohio Valley belonged to the Americans by right of conquest and of armed possession.' Teddy called the people of the longhouse 'wild and squalid warriors.' His men threw Iroquois children into the fire—"

"Dad, *stop*. This is not real. It's not—*appropriate*."

George subsided, his eyelids fluttering. "Not real? Not appropriate?"

Jenny swallowed hard. "Just be appropriate. We need . . . appropriate now."

Coach demanded, "How can we get out a message?"

Zari shook her head. "We're still waiting on parts for our main transmitter."

Jenny thought furiously. "A heliograph—reflecting the sun?"

"To where? Who'll see the faint signal?" The toymaker snapped her fingers. "The laser. Zhang keeps it on second-floor Reagan—it should be okay. We'll point it at the moon."

58

Jenny brought her father back to rest with her mother. "I'm sorry," he said simply.

"You did your best. You reached Toynet." Her teeth chattered, and she drew the blanket closer. The ToyNews clip had shocked her as much as her dad. Uncle Dylan, and Clive as well; no doubt both were faked. If news could be faked like that, what else could one ever believe on Toynet? She sure hoped the laser worked—and that somebody cared enough to come. They had to come before the Mound's power gave out, and the hab froze.

"The vote is too close," her father told her. "This time, I wonder how they'll decide."

She regarded him curiously. "How do they usually decide?"

"We look at the numbers," George said simply. "Some are hard to define. Where the signal volume is high, we see traces of lost data. We try to reconstruct it. Or we estimate." He added, "That is why long ago I called Dylan for help."

"Uncle Dylan? Why?"

"For advice on what was right," George said. "Dylan always said he had the finest faculty, the best scholars anywhere. So I asked him for a politics expert to help out."

Jenny's eyes widened. "Not . . . Hamilton?"

"An award-winning professor. The wisest in the land, Dylan said." George nodded. "Phil always helped us. ToyVote loved him. He helped us decide the fairest, the best way to reconstruct the vote."

Jenny put her head in her hands. No wonder the Guzmáns always won.

Up the bank trudged Tom, his steps weary. He sat down beside Jenny. "We found another student." He'd been rowing out with Father Clare to pick up stranded survivors.

"Charlie?"

He shook his head. "A *chica* trapped in a tree."

"Does she need care for exposure?"

"Yola is treating her."

After Tom left, Jenny turned to her mother. "Mama, I love Tom. And I don't care about his genes. Just like you didn't care about Dad's."

Soledad took her hand. "Jenny, there is something you should know. In case—I don't know how all this will end." She took a breath. "The real reason we made you as we did. Your father and I so loved Grandma Rosa, that we longed to see her again in you. And we were never, ever disappointed."

Fritz Hoffman trudged up the hill. Like most of the survivors, he still wore what he had from two days before, in his case further soiled by hauling animals from the ark. "Jenny? Is there anything you can do for hurt elephants?"

Jenny tried not to inhale. "Did you ask the town vet?"

"He's only tending the livestock." Fritz shook his head. "The elephants can't take the cold. And some of them got really banged up."

Reluctantly she followed Fritz out behind the Mound, where the ecoengineer had put up a fence to keep the animals more or less separate from human survivors. The less traumatized of the elephants had already got out, and were poking amongst the people for a handout. But several injured creatures lay beyond the fence, their bodies limp as if clinging to life.

"This one." Fritz patted the back of an elephant that still managed to stand, barely, on three legs. "His foot looks bad. I was really fond of Dumpy. He was like our mascot."

Jenny warily watched Dumpy swaying on his feet. The animal let Fritz hold up his injured leg for Jenny to inspect. "The foot pad looks infected," she said. "I doubt Doc Uddin will give you antibiotics. The Life profs might. I'll check the Mound."

Inside the Mound, the ceiling was dark and lights were dimmed to conserve power, but you could still see the slots. "It's a pleasure, Ms. Ramos Kennedy," said Bobby Foxtail Forrester, rubbing his hands. "Free drinks at roulette." Taxplayers continued in the windowless hall, surreally unconcerned by the catastrophe outside.

"Thanks," she told the manager. "I just need bandages and veterinary antibiotics."

"No trouble, no trouble at all."

Beyond the gaming stations, the guest rooms were filled with students and colonists. Anouk was holding a review session for the upcoming exam in Developmental Math. Professors' families doubled up in the more private rooms. In the back, Doc Uddin was holed up with the Mound's medical staff. Jenny picked up some bandage amyloid, and some hints on antibiotic dosage from Semerena. On the way back, she paused to check the small private room she'd reserved to keep her wisdom plant under a light.

Outside at the fence, Fritz held up the leg of the injured elephant, and Jenny managed to scour out its foot. The calm of the injured animal surprised her, as she knew the scouring could not feel good; a child treated thus would be screaming. She gave it a shot of antibiotics, and a blob of amyloid for the foot to sink into. The bandage congealed around the foot; it was the best she could do.

Fritz grinned. "*Guao,* just like Saint Francis."

As she rose, massaging her back, which was sore from stooping, she couldn't help notice other elephants as well as bears showing gashes or limping on damaged paws. So she took the drugs and amyloid and did what she could. With a well-practiced gesture, Fritz tossed a blanket over a teddy bear and held it down groaning in protest, while Jenny cleaned the wounds and slapped amyloid.

Without warning, the south solar came on. After days of dark, the light was blinding.

Jenny squeezed her eyes shut and fell to her knees in the mud. A collective gasp rose, and then cheers, all around. As her eyes adjusted, she could see at last down the muddy cylinder of the hab all the way to the Ohio River, where there shone just a hint of a rainbow. At mid-cylinder, out of the water poked the rectangular foundations of Wickett Hall and academic buildings, the First Firmament Church, and the few Homefair homes build of carb. No matter; at last the hab was getting fixed.

"DID THE TOYMAKER RESTORE POWER?"

"DID HELP ARRIVE?"

"SOME BIG *CASINADIE* SHOWED UP AT THE CAP."

Ignoring the rumors, she went on plasting bears and elephants. At the Mound entrance, a commotion erupted as workers scurried out on some sudden errand up the hill. Jenny paid no mind, until she heard a familiar voice.

"Goodness me."

She looked up, covered in mud and animal hair. "*Hola,* Aunt Meg and Aunt El."

Aunt Meg and El stood there, surrounded by Secret Service DIRGs with orange neck rings, campaign aides, and obsequious Mound croupiers. "My goodness," said Meg.

"I'm just, um, tending the wounded."

Just then, Lane Mfumo showed up with a hand camera. That woman had a nose for news all right.

Meg's gaze swept the hab. *"Qué lío."*

El added, "Like the Rose Bowl, the day after New Year's."

"Of course, the brave frontier needed no help." Meg wrinkled her nose. "I smell a powerful odor."

"An odor of mendacity," added El.

Jenny wiped her hands on her pants. "Look, could I just clean up first? I'll tell you everything."

"You'd better," agreed Meg. "Someone's got a lot of explaining to do."

They met in Jenny's small back room, where her plant was well lit and the walls hopefully secure. What happens at the Mound, stays at the Mound.

"Look, Jenny, you'd better say quick just what happened here," demanded Aunt Meg. "And why someone at Homeworld would want to take out your hab."

Jenny watered the plant, but her arm shook and it dripped all over. "How should I know? Maybe Hamilton knew." He'd known about the Creep—and when to clear out.

"We're sorry about Hamilton," said Meg. "He was supposed to look after you."

"And help you see the light," added El. "Like we did."

"We didn't know he had a problem."

"Lunar debts," added El, "and worse—"

"Enough, El. Jenny, you know what I'm asking. What is the frontier air?"

Jenny took a breath. "First of all, my *compañera* was an ultraphyte."

Aunt Meg rolled her eyes. "I come here and pull your chestnuts out, amid the campaign and the recount—and you give me an old roommate story?"

"Meg," said El, "I told you—"

"Shut up, El."

"No, I will *not* shut up." El glared at the head next to her. "All the time now, it's 'Shut up, El,' or 'El, shut up.' Who do you think you are? Ever since you accepted as running mate, you've forgotten whose head shares your shoulders. I've caught you in your toybox, cruising those 'head removal' toysites. As if I'm just a—a tumor to get rid of. You think I don't know what goes on."

Throughout this tirade, Meg kept quiet, while Jenny watched. At last, when El had done, Meg and Jenny exchanged reflective stares. "Okay, Jenny," said Meg at last. "Tell us about your *compañera.*"

Jenny picked up the plant, her old habit to stay calm. "They told us Mary was an omniprosthete. Like the Creep. Fixed up by his doctors." She gulped. "Mary drank salt all the time. Then, after the debate, the first power-out, she turned into an ultra and—"

"She did what?"

"Went down the drain."

El exclaimed, "No wonder. The ultra reverted to single cells, throughout the hab; you can see it from outside, in the color of the shell. Homeworld panicked—they had to get rid of it." She shook her head. "But Frontera—we had no idea they'd sent the mandrake here."

"Who sent the mandrake?" asked Jenny. "Why?"

"That's classified. What did it do?" Meg demanded. "Did it ever hurt you?"

"Never," said Jenny. "But she let out cyanide under stress."

"Just a minute, Jenny. If you please," Meg added pointedly to El. "Jenny, you're leaving something out. The candidates."

"Yeah, that debate," agreed El. "What happened?"

Jenny held up the plant. "Take a look. A really close look."

"The souvenir." Meg's hand took the pot, and El's hand held the other side. They stared curiously, for a long while. "So this is it," said Meg at last. "The 'frontier air.'"

"*Claro,*" agreed Jenny. "Be careful. The ultraphyte made this plant for our intro lab project, and it's not been tested."

"Your intro lab project. You talent prize winners are altogether too dangerous." Meg added, "Well, I can see we have a problem."

"Do we ever," agreed El.

"A problem with our running mate."

"But not the problem you think," El told Jenny. "Who cares if he has ultra syndrome. Ultras, elephants, interns—whatever."

"The problem is," said Meg, "what to do with a vice president who designs a weapons-grade mandrake, only to test it out on an unsuspecting spacehab and practice defense against it."

El nodded. "I won't say I told you so, because I can see how dumb it is to needle the head that shares your shoulders. But yes, we have a problem."

Claro, Jenny thought with a sigh.

"Especially," added Meg, "when our conjoined body is subject to all sorts of ailments the public never hears about."

"Lung infections," offered El.

"Could take us out any day."

"Just like that."

Meg observed, "Our lieutenant governor's the best, though." That was true, unlike other states where the governor and lieutenant governor were not on speaking terms. Meg's eyes narrowed thoughtfully. "There's still the recount."

"But recounts always favor Unity," said El. "I wonder why. Maybe your dad knows."

"What!" exclaimed Jenny.

Meg observed, "The Founding Fathers never heard of a recount. Maybe for good reason. Look, we know voting is done. Obsolete."

"Outmoded as a telegraph," agreed El. "Might as well flip a coin. It would be a lot cheaper."

"But what's to replace it?" Meg asked. "Did your ultra ever say?"

Jenny shook her head. "They do no better."

Meg looked at the plant. "This 'souvenir.' How long does its effect last?"

"I don't know." Jenny thought back to her reading. "If it's like other stimuli, the response will adapt—maybe even swing the other way." It sure did for Hamilton. But different people might react differently.

The two heads looked at each other. "So we'll do the Nixon thing," said Meg. "Let it be, for the good of the country. Let the Kennedy babes have their bottle."

"And we'll have *mucho* fun watching Gar and Anna try to get along in the White House, for the next four years." Holding up the plant, Meg and El turned to leave.

The last wisdom plant was leaving with them. Jenny's mouth fell open to protest. Then she clapped her hand over it. Fair was fair.

At the door, the governor paused. "Thanks a bunch, Jenny. *Hasta la vista.*"

"Four years from now," added El.

59

The microwave link from their solar station was restored, after a huge chunk of Kessler trash had somehow blocked the entire beam. Somehow—there was a big question. At Homeworld, nobody was talking; the kind of nobody-talking that meant plenty of lawyers buzzing. For once the Creep had reached too far. Meanwhile, Toynet was restored, with printout restricted until power was fully up. In Washington, President Bud congratulated FEMA for "doing a heck of a job" on the relief effort.

In the hab, as Quade got the pumps back working, the muddy soup began to recede. Piles of debris remained on the hillside, pressed together in unpredictable clumps: broken scraps of carboxyplast, a Chinese puzzle half assembled, a student's Aristotle, a drawer from Orin's real oak desk, and a surprising number of jigsaw pieces from the chaplain's office. From Mount Gilead came a pigeon, flapping awkwardly with a wisp of Indian grass in its beak. The pigeon settled and pecked at the flotsam.

"Jenny?" In her toybox Tom appeared in the boat with Father Clare. "We've found Charlie."

"Charlie!" She rushed down the hill to meet the boat, careful to keep to the boardwalk laid down upon the treacherous mud, where anyone could sink to their waist.

The boat got as far as it could, until it lodged in the mud. As Jenny arrived, she became aware of several things simultaneously: that Tom and Father Clare looked very solemn; that no one was rushing off for help; and that the form lying in the boat was completely still.

"*Charlie!*" Jenny climbed into the boat. The face and chest had blotches of dusky red. The eyes were unseeing. Braced against the boat, she shoved her hands beneath the back and shoulders, lifting up the huge slippery weight. The head fell back like a hinge. "*Charlie! What's your name? Who is the president?*"

Someone else leaned over, blocking the light. "Jenny. Look up here."

Jenny looked up, not like a human, more like a wild thing. Part of her was aware that Mfumo stood there, aiming her toybox. "Sorry, Jenny. Just doing my job."

There is no more difficult task for a college administrator than to inform parents of the fatal injury to their child. Of course, there is a standard protocol, which Dylan had used only once before, when a frog was overcome by alcohol overdose. Now he had three sets of parents to inform. The most difficult was Charlie—the Chase Scholar, the first-generation frog who asked the best questions. In short, the kind of student for whom a college like Frontera would always make the most difference.

To be sure, other administrators pitched in to help, Clare explaining the search effort and how the bodies were recovered, Helen extolling each student's academic accomplishments, Nora describing their vibrant contributions to the college community, and the student council president describing the deep sense of loss felt by all the fellow students upon their passing, those left behind in this mortal universe. But still, as old Witherspoon had told him back in the day, the ultimate burden, like so many others, rested upon the president.

The young families and the elderly were housed in the Mound, plus about half the students. Dylan spent the night outdoors beneath the maple tree, which was sacred to the Shawnee. He could not sleep. Above there were no human stars to count, no points of light from human habitations across the sky.

Beside him Clare rolled over and touched his arm.

Dylan asked, "Do you think we belong here?"

"You mean, the spacehab?"

"The spacehab should be independent. But we're not."

"We're interdependent," said Clare. "Like everyone else."

"We shouldn't be losing young people."

"Based on average mortality over the past decade, we'd expect to have lost four. Why should Providence favor us?"

Dylan grimaced. "The cold comfort of statistics." He added, "I hope it all proves worth it. Our little . . . exercise of frontier air."

"You're the historian. Never underestimate the march of folly."

"I detest history," Dylan exclaimed. "Despite all our folly, I believe humans were meant to reach the stars." Someday.

60

After Thanksgiving, Jenny came back to help rebuild. The hab interior was dotted with brick-shaped modulars labeled FEMA US GOVT PROPERTY. FEMA's DIRGs, generic brown-suited humanoids, swarmed everywhere. The "brownies" helped rebuild Wickett Hall and restore the flow of amyloid up to the cafeteria. All around, the mud had dried and cracked, with huge crevasses where the substratum had settled. Boardwalks and downed trees were everywhere. But help was pouring in. Jenny's HuriaNews photo was all over Toynet, the "Pietà in Space," iconic emblem of the disaster. One picture is worth a trillion in aid.

The remains of two fallen students were transported home, but Charlie's parents asked to bury him in the slope of the powwow ground. The college held a quiet memorial, no podiums or processions, just a sharing of words and flowers.

"God the Father and Mother." Father Clare spoke with the few gathered students, faculty and villagers standing amid their double shadows. He held in his hands the Anaxagoras palimpsest-Medieval prayer book, which had survived the flood. "We call upon You in your timeless realm to take up the souls of our departed companions. Their time upon Earth that revolves, with us who evolve, seemed to us all too short, but is now infinite. Your Son's time on Earth, too, was cut short; so it's left to us to continue His work."

"Amen." Leora placed a coneflower on the grave. "On behalf of Mount Gilead, we honor this volunteer's service to our emergency medical team." Leora's children looked up as a Shawnee drum sounded. An eagle feather behind his head, Bobby Foxtail Forrester tapped the drum and sang a song for fallen braves.

Dylan looked around the group, meeting the eyes of each student. "Those of you who returned to rebuild Frontera—thanks." He continued, "If we return having faced our worst fears, as indeed we have, we return in sorrow for those we miss. Their lives call on us for vigilance—the vigilance we each owe ourselves, to renew our purpose to serve our planet Earth. We rededicate our lives that Earth will endure, in its voyage amid a trillion-trillion stars."

"Oo-oo-oo *oo-aw.*" Overhead, a sleepy owl ruffled its feathers.

"And now, as the pioneer president Rosa Schwarz used to say, 'When you put your hand to the plow, you can't put it down until you get to the end of the row. No time to waste—set your sights on Jupiter.' "

As Jenny passed the grave, she left a vanilla. The flowers would fade, she thought, and who would remember? Like most ordinary Americans, there would be no toyworld about Charlie, only a balm in Gilead. But someone had to carry on his courage. People like Charlie needed her now.

Tom had spent Thanksgiving with Jenny in Somers. Now he was back in the hab, on the roof with his shirt off, nailing shingles onto the modular. Jenny swung the hammer too, getting much better at it. She took frequent rest breaks, watching Tom on the roof.

Tom stopped, extending an arm that Michelangelo could have drawn. "Come on up."

"That's okay."

"It's only a modular, not that high. Enjoy the view—you can see out to the new hospital."

"I like the view from here." Still, maybe it was worth a try. Heart pounding, she took one step up the ladder, then another. That was what college was all about: always another step up, and never dare look back.

At the roof edge, the wind lifted her hair. Tom gave her a hand. At last she sat on the shingles, with Tom's arm around her. She could see the modular rooftops, and the dorms' carboxyplast skeletons, and the academic buildings as far as Reagan. From above, the courthouse and the church spire pointed down. Little gray squares of carboxyplast appeared, as the colonists rebuilt.

"You solved today's molecule." Tom's molecule, the one he had posted.

She nodded. "It's an iridodial derivative. Another semiochemical. Where'd you find it? Pile worms?"

Tom shook his head. "It was found in shallow water off the Florida coast, above old Miami. It's a controlled substance, Semerena says."

"But . . . a human semiochemical? What's it doing there? What made it?"

"No one knows." The vast flooded coast was just the right depth for ultra. "Maybe Anouk knows."

Anouk had stayed on in the hab, still banned from Earth. "But Rafael's family got me a special dispensation for Christmas!" She beamed. "From the president of Mexico."

"Muy bien." Jenny sat with her in their modular, roommates until their deluxe housing got restored. Jenny's toybox was hopelessly full, from Tusker-12 inviting her to spend spring break at the beach, to Vice President Guzmán offering a summer internship in Havana. "We have a new semiochemical to figure out."

Anouk blinked her window several research publications. "A mind-altering agent, with distinctive properties. *Écoute,* we need a new research project."

"Preferably something legal." Jenny put her hands behind her head and leaned back in her rickety chair, back against the carboxyplast wall. "You know, you did great during the Flood," she told Anouk. "You saved my life. And the plant." Which California's governor had walked off with.

Anouk lifted her hand, her third finger gracefully curved. *"Ce n'est rien."*

The tumor mouse was back in Jenny's toybox, sniffing around the windows. "When I'm a hundred, like Rita, I'll run for president. If our husbands have passed, you can be my First Lady."

Anouk eyed her skeptically. "Aren't you forgetting something?"

"What? It's the one job where you don't have to be a citizen." They would need their own wisdom plants, though. Jenny wondered if Abaynesh had saved any. She glanced at her own temporary greenhouse, a glass box with room for half a dozen pots.

At Reagan Hall, the structure had emerged intact, maintained by the backup generator. Most of the flooded equipment was useless, but colleagues from Earth shipped up enough controllers to restore the animal colonies. And the plants; but not the lost genetic stocks.

"Your plants," Jenny asked Abaynesh. "What became of them?"

"The seeds were stored on the second floor."

"I suppose our experiment is gone."

"We can plant and start over." Abaynesh sounded as if she had other things in mind. She leaned back in her chair, her face a bit flushed, while Meg-El coiled upon her round belly.

"It will be nice for Tova," said Jenny, "having baby twins."

"One," corrected Abaynesh. "One is much healthier than twins," she added with her usual tact. "A brain needs the whole womb, to reach its potential."

Jenny thought this over. "Rita Levi-Montalcini had a twin." Her sister Paola, the Italian artist.

"That's true. Imagine if she'd been single." Abaynesh gave Jenny a sharp look. "We'll make a New Yorker of you yet."

She took the plunge. "What about the controls? Did you save any?"

The professor looked back over her shoulder, and around. She took off her diad; Jenny did the same. "I saved seeds, and the whole sequence. We're waiting to see the trial." The great presidential experiment. "The side effects, if any. I put in for a patent, just in case."

"Oh," Jenny mouthed without a sound. So far, president-elect Carrillo had promised all the right things—clean government, ban on solarplate, mission to Jupiter. But after inauguration, who could say.

"But how can I stay here, if the college won't permit my research?" The professor added, "I got a job offer from Montreal. They're about to open their first spacehab. And for Alan, their library holds the largest Judaica collection in North America."

Jenny's face fell. "I mean, how nice for you."

"And Tova would have a good school. As for me, this place was never a good fit."

"But I thought so," Jenny blurted. "I'll miss you."

"Really?" The professor looked up as if this might be a new idea. "Well, we'll see. I would hate to leave . . . her." Jenny's lost *compañera*.

"Do you ever hear from her? Text, I mean."

"She could be anywhere now."

Dylan's Senior Staff met in a sealed conference room with Glynnis Carrillo, the appointed director of Homeworld Security and Space Energy. The DIRGs' neck rings were coded blue.

Glynnis clasped her hands on the table. "We've dropped parachute teams into every agency—and at Homeworld, getting them to talk is *mano a mano*. But this much we know. Ultra mutates like a virus; we knew that ten years ago. Ever since, we've plotted their rise of complexity in evolving new forms—forms that parallel successful life on Earth. Already some grow off submerged Florida; we've had chemical problems there. Others store salt and creep over land. Salt is pretty fundamental, but at some point even that requirement may be lost."

"How far will it go?" asked Helen. "Since Earth has birds, will ultra make birds?"

"They won't be birds. But if flight works on Earth, it's a matter of time before ultra evolves something that can fly."

Ultra mosquitoes, thought Dylan gloomily.

"Primates?" ventured Quade. Around the table, hands tensed and eyes narrowed.

"You mean, creatures that swing down from the trees to solve a Phaistos disk?" Glynnis shrugged. "If you do the math . . . maybe in another ten years. It's a successful niche."

That's debatable, thought Dylan. "*Perdón,* you said ten years. So how did we get our alien student already?"

"Not alien," corrected Glynnis. "We have no aliens here. 'Undocumented.'"

"But—" He caught Nora's eye. Luis, Orin, Zari, everyone looked at one another around the table. It wasn't often they found all their human selves in one room, breathing each other's air. "There are no aliens," he said slowly, "because they are here to stay."

"*Claro.*"

"So where did this 'undocumented' come from?"

"The back-room dworks at Homeworld," said Glynnis. "The guys we don't let out in daylight. They didn't want to wait for ultra to get a brain one day and catch us unawares."

"So they made their own?"

Glynnis nodded. "They sped up the quasispecies even more, with directed evolution. The idea was to make intelligent ultra, set it loose somewhere, and see what it could do. And how to combat it."

Orin exclaimed, "They sent it here! But that's—"

"They wrote off Frontera as a loss anyhow, by the next decade. Sorry," she whispered. "Your hab is antiquated, you know. But we'll try to bring it up to code."

"But that Mary," said Nora. "She wasn't exactly a combatant."

"Of course not. Evolution is never exact." Glynnis reflected, "We think the dworks tried to model her after their boss." The toywall displayed Mary Dyer, next to the Creep. They did have about the same nose and eyes, and the way their hands moved was uncannily the same.

Nora's eyes narrowed. "Are there others?" Dylan could see her revising the student questionnaire.

"We're still digging on that. But for now," Glynnis pointed out, "your ultraphyte has reverted to single cells. The cells augment your solar power. Ultraphyte photochemistry could boost our solarrays, enough to convince Congress to build them. We'll fund a major research center here."

"Not here," exclaimed Dylan. "We can't have ultra crawling all over the hab."

"Hold on," grunted Orin. "Don't forget the indirect costs." The gravy that came with federal grants.

Glynnis turned to Quade. "To keep the ultra out in the shell, your ecoengineer has a good plan about ants. It works for some environments, especially in South America."

61

By January, the hab was drying out, and the peepers were coming back. The deer were a nuisance again, crashing through the windows of FEMA modulars. Quade appeared in the window with one of his bulletins. His gloved hand held some tiny black creatures that stood on six spindly black legs, waving their antennae and mandibles. "*Eciton burchelli* has an unfair rep," he assured the community. "Swarming in columns, they mostly consume invertebrates. They will fill an important niche in our hab." Army ants would clear ultra from the surface soil, without harming the power-enhancing "contaminant" out in the phototrophic shell.

Most important, students were repopulating their newly printed residences and filling their toyboxes with homework assignments and party invites.

"Jenny!" Dylan waved to her out on Buckeye Trail. "I'll miss you this semester."

She turned with a smile. "I'll miss Teddy." The first-semester course was done.

"The new memorial in Battery Park—it's magnificent."

Jenny took a confident step toward him; the presidential step, all the Ramos clan were taught to walk like that. "I wanted you to know," she said. "I've got beyond needing Jordi." She added reflectively, "I do wish I could have seen him again, just once. Just to say good-bye." Jordi's body was never found. "But we're all like Jordi now. Living in our moment, until the time to come."

An admirable number of fellow students agreed; enough had returned to reopen that semester. Others had transferred out, not surprising, all things considered. But more surprising, a decent number had transferred in, seeking that frontier air. The transfers, plus a hefty FEMA grant, would just about tide the college over.

"We're just one short." His travel budget pared steeply, Luis reported in from Peoria. "Just one more admit to make our quota." The admissions director added thoughtfully, "I don't suppose you might persuade those ultras in the shell to . . . um. . . ." Seeing Dylan's look, he hurriedly added, "Never mind."

Meanwhile, the hab engineering had at last got the attention it needed.

The substratum would get a permanent fix, no more pumps. President-elect Carrillo promised full protection from Kessler debris, and funded ultra studies at Reagan Hall. And alumni donors had recovered their nerve; the Campaign for Frontera was back in swing.

Gil's window blinked insistently. "Dillie, what am I to do? All these lawyers," he whined. "They want to wreck Toynet!" Like pushing over his tower of alphabet blocks.

Dylan sighed. "*Ahora*, Gil, I'm sure you can manage. Why, we all love Toynet." Aside from the growing Babynet fanatics, who Dylan did his best to contain.

"But why?" Gil rubbed his eyes. "How could anyone think I'd want to harm my very own space college?"

"Nobody thinks that," said Dylan carefully. "But Toynet got used by some . . . unscrupulous users."

"*Claro*. We'll get to the bottom of this."

Dylan hoped Gil was right, that the culprits buried in Homeworld would get found; and that finding them out would not mean worse trouble. "Gil, you might consider revisioning your image. More philanthropy, perhaps."

"Another college?"

"Something grander. Say, a global program to wipe out viruses."

"*¡Oye!* That does sound like fun."

A new project—Dylan thought wistfully how long since he'd had a chance of his own. Teddy was grand, but surely Dylan's career had room enough to pen the story of yet another great American leader? Rosa Schwartz, for instance. Rosa had banned carbon output, launched the first solarrays, reformed housing, and founded the Frontera spacehab. Tax revolt had swept her out, but she was the only president of the twenty-first century who'd done as much as Teddy the century before. It was time someone set the record straight. If only he had the time.

Resignedly Dylan checked his schedule. To his surprise, the next two weeks appeared totally blank. Impossible; what had become of his ten meetings a day? Nora's latest student disasters, Orin's investment coups, and the faculty's requests for scholarship leave?

"Fran?" His new student assistant Fran Pezarkar looked up, cheerful and well-mentaled, well-recovered from the previous semester's ordeal. "Fran, *por favor*. What's become of my schedule? Some glitch in Toynet?"

Fran's eyes defocused as she reviewed her box. "It looks right to me. What's missing?"

"Missing? Look there—a whole two weeks of my schedule, empty. Where are my appointments?"

Fran shrugged. "I guess everyone on Senior Staff thinks they can do without you just now."

With a grim frown, Dylan blinked for Orin.

"Orin's down on Wall Street," the toyroom assured him. "Enhancing liquidity in our investment portfolio." A likely story.

Nora—she couldn't possibly be out. The dean of students appeared in her window. "May I help you?" she asked, in the tone one would address a wayward student.

Dylan gritted his teeth. "What on Earth has happened to my schedule?"

She gave him a very blank look. "Don't know. What has happened?"

"Won't you need me for anything, the next two weeks? Nothing you 'thought I need to know'?"

"I guess not." She added in a stage whisper, "Ask Clare."

Dylan marched straight down to the chapel office. Leaning his arms on the desk, next to the palimpsest, he faced Clare. "What's going on?"

Clare nodded across to the puzzle.

Fuming, Dylan went to the window seat and shoved a piece somewhere into the puzzle, a new one just starting to grow. "Clare, what is it? What ghost have you put in my schedule?"

"Two weeks' vacation. The price for my silence about the 'undocumented.'"

For a moment Dylan stared. "Why didn't you just tell me?"

"I just did." A new window appeared, a beach with palm trees and a faded wooden sign.

"Lila's Beach?" Dylan sighed. "Clare, are you sure? What about those cameras?"

"True, but I keep my promises." Clare gave a half smile, the way he used to when he pulled Dylan out of an all-nighter on his Teddy honors paper.

The college president and the college chaplain, taking time out from disaster recovery at the Toynet trillionaire's private beach, with glimpses guaranteed to show up. That would do wonders for town-gown.

In the second semester, Jenny's Cuba course finally reached the point where the rebel island took in thousands of refugees from flooded Miami. Cuba's postvirtualist culture fascinated her; she looked forward to her trip down the Mariel space lift for her summer internship at the Havana Institute for Revolutionary Botany. Her Roosevelt course was done, and she finally got an art course. Life with Abaynesh, as always, went on. One day, as Jenny completed her Life exam, a new window opened. There stood Jordi, grinning like a twelve-year-old. "Hey, Jenny, it's me! How's your ultra in the cellar?"

Jenny glared. "Who are you?" What a tasteless prank. She blinked for a trace.

"I'm your brother. Come hear my speech—just for a minute, in the toyroom."

Despite herself, Jenny was curious. Besides, the trace might work better in the toyroom. She'd get Anouk to hack it.

The toyroom opened upon an ocean rolling onto a long, white beach before a dense forest. A coconut lay half buried, near a faded wooden sign, LILA'S BEACH. There stood Jordi, in his suspenders and shirt with the sleeves rolled up, performing an old speech he used to practice in middle school. "I do not believe that any of us would exchange places with any other people or any other generation. The energy, the faith, the devotion which we bring to this endeavor will light our country and all who serve it—and the glow from that fire can truly light the world."

Jordi turned to her, with a nod. "I've been watching, you know. Father Clare says I always will. You've done a mighty fine job for a frog. You earned an A-double-plus average, won the big one for Coach, and saved the breath of goodness knows how many fools, human and animal. On top of winning the prez. Not bad for a Somers Seldon."

Jenny said nothing.

"It's not been easy, has it. As Teddy used to say, 'one becomes fearless by sheer dint of practicing fearlessness.'"

She smiled despite herself. Jordi never quoted Teddy, but she knew who did.

"In fact," Jordi told her, "I couldn't have done better myself. So I think I'll leave Earth in your hands for now. You know, it's hard to believe, but there's another universe next door, even more foolish than this one. They really need my help. So that's where I'm headed. Okay?"

"Okay."

"Thanks for being the best sister ever." He stepped over and kissed her on the forehead. "Good-bye, Jenny."

"Good-bye, Jordi."

Jordi turned, and took a step up as if climbing an invisible stair. Then he faded into the sky.

Jenny watched for a long while, as the waves rolled onto the shore. Then she left the toyroom, walking slowly back to the modular. Scanning her box for messages, she froze.

"WISDOM WE ARE HERE."

Here? Frantically, her eyes scanned the four dull carboxyplast walls. Or did "HERE" just mean here in the hab?

The greenhouse box. She tore off the lid.

One of the plants was not a plant. A good approximation, but the fleshy fake leaves would need UV. And half buried in the stem was the diad. No tie-dyed shift, no more controls, no snake-like form escaping the DIRGs. Just an undocumented *compañera*. Who knows what ultra would come up with next?

"OK, MARY. YOU CAN WATCH TOO."

NOTE

When you find an elephant atop a pole, you know it didn't get there without help. I would like to thank several individuals who read part or all of the manuscript at different stages in the past ten years: Jeanne Griggs, Dave Switzer, Whitney Bratton, Sandra Lindow, Mike Levy, Ben Schumacher, Athena Andreadis, Clara Roman-Odio, Judy Kerman, and Lauren Brantley. I am also grateful for the comments of my editors, David Hartwell and Stacy Hague-Hill. While the book's faults are my own, much of what is good arose from conversations with these people.

Joan Slonczewski, September 11, 2010
http://biology.kenyon.edu/slonc/slonc.htm

Made in the USA
Middletown, DE
07 December 2015